If You Were Mine

"You only live once, but if you do it right, once is enough."
Mae West

Also by Norah Pritchard

If You Were Mine

A Northfield Novel

Norah Pritchard

WILLOWCREST LANE
Publishing

~

First edition: December 2025

Editor: Red Adept Editing

Cover design: Wildheart Graphics

Photographer: Rachel Galeazzi Photography

This one is for you, Julie Days, fellow romance author & kindred spirit. Northfield is, quite simply, better because of you.

Chapter One

Lily Hart had a bad feeling.

She tried hard to avoid bad feelings as a general rule, but the band tightening around her lungs made a mockery of that rule today. Lily took a deep, cleansing breath and repeated her mantra.

I am a still lake, not a stormy sea.

Emotions and energy were interconnected, as she taught her yoga students, and she strove to live a life with positive energy. Some people, namely the man waiting at the altar for her right now, thought she was a little woo-woo, but she didn't let it bother her.

Except that her heavy dress and the corset underneath cinched her ribs, magnifying the feeling of suffocation.

Not exactly the fairy-tale start she'd pictured.

"Of all the days for an early snowstorm," Angela Cawthorn, her future mother-in-law, muttered, turning from the window with tightly pinched lips. She cast a critical eye over Lily. "Try not to fuss with the flowers. They'll look strangled by the time Tucker sees you walking down the aisle."

The cloying fragrance of stargazer lilies filled the air of the small room to the side of the chapel, turning Lily's already twisting stomach.

She hated stargazer lilies. She hadn't picked them, or the bridesmaid colors, or the bouquet. Every choice had been Angela's because, *Lily doesn't mind, right, dear?*

Lily minded. But she hated disappointing people even more.

Once upon a time, the idea of marrying her high school sweetheart had filled her with happiness. Her sisters would groan and pretend to gag over their too-cute romance.

She'd been the bubbly cheerleader, Tucker the star quarterback. Everyone just assumed they would marry one day.

Today was the day.

She rubbed absently at her chest and forced a serene smile.

I am a still lake.

Tucker loved her, and she loved him. Of course she did. Sure, they had had bumps lately, but who wouldn't with all the extra wedding stress?

Mrs. Cawthorn could be a little much, but Tucker was her only son. This was her last hurrah, Lily fervently hoped.

So Lily had kept quiet and let everything roll off her back—she was as peaceful as a still lake, dammit.

Soon she would be happily married and, hopefully, a mother.

"God, what's that smell? Is this a wedding or a funeral?" Amber wrinkled her nose, shutting the door behind her. Her tea-length baby-blue dress caught in the doorway, and she yanked it free with a grin, tearing a neat line off the ruffled hem. "Oops."

She stuck out a long leg with a saucy smile. "Better, right?"

Even the unflattering dress couldn't make Amber look anything less than stunning, round pregnant belly and all.

Angela's lips pressed into a thin line. Lily met Amber's

laughing eyes while their mother, Annette, shot Amber a quelling look.

Safe to say there was no love lost between Angela and the Harts, but especially Amber. The two had clashed from the start, despite Lily's best attempts at smoothing things over. Lily suspected Amber delighted in pushing Angela's buttons. Those two would do well to take her Find Your Flow yoga class, although her studio might be too small for their clashing energies.

Allie, the eldest Hart sister, stepped in. "The dresses are lovely, Angela." She gave Amber a pointed look, and then turned to the two little blond flower girls climbing over the benches. "Savannah, Tessa, please sit down on your bottoms before you ruin your dresses."

Savvie jutted her lower lip but stayed put. Tessa sat and smiled angelically.

"How are you feeling?" Evie whispered. Like Savvie and Tessa, Lily and Evie were identical twins. Only Evie's ever-changing assortment of glasses set them apart.

"Never better," Lily lied. She dropped the smile under Evie's skeptical gaze. "Like I might throw up."

"Did you take your inhaler?" Evie handed Lily's purse over.

"Not yet." Lily dug inside for the inhaler never far from reach. Her phone buzzed with a new message. She opened the notification, noting the unknown number. Curiously, Lily tapped the picture to enlarge it.

Her heart stopped.

The noise in the room—the chattering, the giggles of her nieces—faded. Blood roared in her ears as she stared at the photo, her hands trembling.

"Lily." Evie's voice penetrated the buzzing in her ears, and Lily looked up at her sister in shock.

Her brain refused to process more than a few details at a time of what she was seeing.

A mirror selfie, taken in what looked like a hotel bathroom—white, sterile, with miniature toiletries neatly reflected on the sink.

Tucker—shirtless, his red underwear digging into his hips, emphasizing the extra padding there from too much beer over the years.

It was a new pair of underwear, she noticed, slightly hysterical. Bright red, silky, and expensive looking.

Her breath hitched in her chest. She knew that pair. Not because she'd seen it before—no, this wasn't one of the threadbare undies she'd washed and folded for years. They were new. A style she'd secretly wished he cared enough to wear for her.

And there, pressed to his side, her towel barely clinging to her bare skin, was Madison.

His assistant.

She slammed her eyes shut, trying to erase the image of another woman wrapped around Tucker, her lips pressed to his cheek, her hand curled possessively around his bare chest, but it was burned into her mind.

The realization hit Lily like a gut punch, knocking her breathless. Her stomach lurched violently. The future she'd imagined since she was a little girl—the white dress, the house they would build, and the family they would fill it with—shattered by a photo. Her throat tightened, and she let out a choked sound.

A firm knock on the door jolted Lily from her thoughts. Her brother-in-law, Davis, leaned in, shaking a few stray snowflakes from the shoulders of his tuxedo. "The storm slowed things down, but we're all here now. Everyone ready?"

The roomful of people turned their eyes on her, smiling expectantly.

Lily froze. For one long, horrible moment, she considered slipping the phone back into her purse, swallowing the jagged rock in her throat, and pretending as if she hadn't seen the photo.

Her body moved on its own, one shaky step forward, her vision tunneling as she wobbled on her four-inch white satin heels. Davis straightened up, his smile replaced with a frown when he caught sight of her.

"Wait." Evie's hand shot out and gripped Lily's arm like a lifeline. The familiar touch scraped against the lace of her sleeve. "What's wrong?"

Suddenly, the dress was too hot and too tight. Lily wanted to tear it off. She glanced at Evie, the one person who had always been able to read her.

Lily's lips parted, but no sound came out. The image of Tucker in his pristine new underwear, a pair she wasn't meant to see, burned in her mind.

Fire rose in her chest, her lungs twisting and expanding to get air. The serenity she had been hanging onto with her fingernails all day was replaced with something else decidedly not harmonious.

"Girls, what's going on?" Annette moved closer, her sharp eyes locking on Lily's. Lily looked down. She could never hide her emotions well. "Lily, what's wrong?"

"I—" Lily gasped, her lungs tightening painfully. "I—can't —" Her breaths came in sharp, wheezing gasps now.

"Take your inhaler," Evie said urgently, thrusting it at her. Lily fumbled for it, her sweaty palms slipping against the smooth plastic before taking a puff.

Allie and Amber surrounded her, shielding her. Her family, always watching out for her, always taking care of her.

How could she disappoint them? Embarrass them in front of their family and friends in Northfield? How could she let everyone down? Lily had spent her entire life smoothing things over, making sure that everyone was happy around her.

"You okay, honey?" Allie asked, concern etching her face.

Angela wedged herself into the circle of women and placed a firm hand on Lily's back. "Let's not keep Tucker waiting. The guests are ready."

She pressed the bouquet of lilies into Lily's hands and nudged her toward the door.

"Back off, Angela," Amber snapped, stepping in front of Lily, her belly protruding like a brick wall. "Lily goes when she's ready."

Angela bristled, but Amber ignored her. "Some people have no class," Angela said stiffly, with a militant set to her jaw. Her hair was the same expensive blond as her son's, perfectly coiffed and sprayed into an unnatural stiffness.

"And some people have giant sticks shoved so far up their ass they forgot what class looks like," Amber shot back. She turned around and patted Lily's hand. "Take your time, Lil. You don't owe anyone anything."

The door to the vestibule opened, and Lily glimpsed the crowded church—family and friends, Madison included.

Savvie and Tessa went first with their flower baskets, scattering petals down the aisle. One by one, her bridal party followed while she watched numbly.

And then it was her turn.

The first strains of the wedding march swelled through the church, and she took a step forward, her hand clenched around her bouquet.

Annette appeared at her side, her hand slipping beneath Lily's arm to guide her down the aisle. Lily didn't dare glance at her. Annette's calm, poised presence next to her was as unshakable as ever. Lily took a deep breath and tried to feel her knees.

They took a halting step forward. The crowd blurred in her

periphery, the faces of her family and friends indistinct as her vision tunneled.

And then she saw him—Tucker, rocking back and forth on his heels beside Father O'Connell, hands clasped in front of him with the same pursed-lip expression as his mother on his face.

Each step closer felt heavier than the last. The unwieldy bouquet trembled in her hand.

Madison looked away as Lily walked past her, dabbing her eyes with a tissue.

Her final step brought her up to the altar, and she paused.

Could she forget the photo? Could she pretend the last five minutes had never happened and give up her dignity, her self-respect, and live with the betrayal—just to avoid the chaos that would follow?

Bitterness filled her as she stopped in front of Tucker.

"Babe, you look so beautiful," Tucker said, reaching for her hands.

Her legs locked. Tucker's face wavered in front of her, but this time it wasn't from faintness.

It was rage.

How dare he? How dare he stand there, knowing what he'd done, and look at her as if nothing had changed?

Her voice, when it finally came, was clear and succinct in the utter silence of the chapel.

"Fuck. Off."

Shocked gasps filled the sanctuary. Savvie and Tessa looked up at her with interest, but for once, Lily didn't hang around to apologize.

She turned, her heels clicking against the tile as she headed toward the arched double doors.

"Take this!" Evie rushed forward and thrust the inhaler into her palm.

Lily stopped, her chest heaving as she looked at her sister. The fierce protectiveness in Evie's eyes nearly undid her. "I can't stay," Lily said, her voice shaking.

"We'll handle it," Evie said firmly.

Lily's eyes closed briefly, and then she turned, bursting through the stained-glass doors into the frigid November air.

The cold bit through her satin gown, sharp and bracing and somehow exhilarating at the same time.

Behind her, Savvie's mischievous little voice echoed in the stunned chapel, "Fuck. Off."

A hysterical laugh bubbled up in Lily's throat as she ran down the church steps, leaving behind everything she no longer wanted.

This was her beginning.

Chapter Two

RUSH CALLAHAN STOOD at the gas pump, pulling his cap lower as fat snowflakes drifted down. The ancient green Chevy, a gift from Pop, groaned even after he killed the engine.

Riggs sprawled in the passenger seat, his ears twitching as the pump clicked. Rush envied the dog's ability to not give a damn about anything. Lucky bastard.

Rush tugged the collar up against the cold, surveying the church lot across the street jammed with cars. There were parking violations galore, but he dismissed the thought just as quickly. He was off duty for the next week. His deputies could handle whatever happened in Northfield.

The town wasn't exactly a hotbed of crime anyway. For the most part, life here moved at a leisurely pace. Parking tickets, the occasional drunk and disorderly call from the pub, the proverbial cat stuck in a tree—those were the kinds of calls that filled his days as the sheriff. It was a far cry from the Marines, but that's exactly what had drawn him to the job.

Inside the Pump 'n Go, Norma Leggett looked up from her magazine and smiled. "Hey, Sheriff." Her short silver curls bounced as she set aside her magazine on a towering stack of well-worn *National Tattlers*. Wrapped snugly in her cardigan, Norma radiated the kind of grandmotherly concern that put Rush on high alert for what was coming.

"Been thinking about you. How are you holding up?" she asked.

Rush smiled briefly, pulling a few bills from his wallet and setting them on the counter. "I'm good, Norma. Tell Dale I said 'hi.'"

Norma's brows pinched together, concern etched across her face. *Here it comes*, Rush thought, stiffening slightly. "You know, if you ever need to talk—"

Rush flinched inwardly. "Appreciate the offer."

Without waiting for a reply, he stepped outside into the blowing snow. In a town as small as Northfield, everyone knew everyone, including all their business. It was both a blessing and a curse, especially when you were the center of the latest big news.

Outside, at least, the crisp air felt easier to breathe.

Dale Leggett, his hands stuffed deep into his down parka, hunched slightly against the biting wind, waited for him outside. "Hey, Rush. Headed up to the cabin?"

"Dale," Rush greeted, nodding at his Pop's oldest friend. For the past year, Rush had been going out of his way to get gas at the station closer to his house rather than in Northfield to avoid moments like this. Looked like his luck had finally run out. "Yep," Rush said, already edging toward the driver's-side door.

Dale's smile faded, and his tone softened. "You been over to see your Pop lately?"

"Last weekend," Rush said. He hesitated. "He was having a good day."

Which meant he remembered Rush's name, and Rachel and Sarah's, his sisters, before the confusion set in. Lately, the good days were fewer and further between, and there was only a shadow of the man who'd raised him and the girls.

Most days, Pop just stared out the window of the nursing home, his fingers still twitching like they were wrapped around a wrench.

Rush hated seeing him like that. Drifting. Silent. The man who could rebuild a carburetor in his sleep and taught Rush how to change the oil on the Chevy when he could barely see over the hood.

The truck still ran like a dream, mostly because Rush kept it alive out of pure stubbornness, and because part of him felt like if he let the truck go, he'd lose that last piece of Pop that still made sense.

Dale nodded slowly. "That's good. He always did light up when you walked in." Dale jerked his chin toward the church across the street. "Big wedding over there today. Another one of those Hart girls is getting married. Lily, I think."

Rush paused, his hand hovering over the door handle as he glanced at the church, cataloguing the information.

He knew Lily Hart and her family. Not well, but he made it a point to know everyone in town—it came with the badge.

Lily was the pretty little redheaded one who blushed whenever they ran into each other. She owned the wellness studio on Main Street across from the sheriff's department.

Even if he didn't make it a point to know the residents of Northfield, it would have been hard to miss her, since she taught a yoga class on the village green last summer. He was no more immune to long legs and big breasts begging to be freed from tight yoga outfits than the next red-blooded man.

Lily Hart had that golden-girl personality—kind, sweet, sunny, with a shy smile for everyone, which was why it was a surprise to him to hear she was marrying Tucker Cawthorn.

On paper, those two made perfect sense. The beautiful

small-town girl and the former high school football star. The problem was that Rush had had a few run-ins with Tucker over the years, usually for something minor, like getting too loud at the pub and mouthing off when he'd had a few too many beers.

Nothing serious, nothing worth arresting him over, but enough for Rush to file him under "potentially problematic."

From what he knew about the man, Tucker spent more time at the bar reminiscing about his high school football days over beers with his friends than a man should with a woman like Lily at home. A man like Tucker usually put himself first, which made him think Lily deserved better, even though he didn't know her well enough to say why.

But he wasn't in the mood for small talk about residents today. He had a tank full of gas and enough food and good whisky to last him a week up at Pop's old hunting cabin high in the Adirondack Mountains, where he could finally breathe without someone asking him how he was holding up.

Especially this week.

The one-year anniversary of the worst night of his life.

"Looks like it," Rush said, his voice carefully neutral as he tugged the door open. "Take care, Dale."

Before he could escape, Dale clapped a firm hand on his shoulder. Rush went still, bracing himself. His vision tunneled for half a second, just long enough for the world to tilt.

Cold water. A child's scream, high and piercing.

"Hey, son, I'm real sorry about what happened. I know this week is hard for you, what with the memorial coming up and all. Saving that little girl... Well, you're a hero in my book. Hell, in everyone's book." Dale hesitated, his throat working like the next words were harder to say.

"I know it don't feel like much of a victory, not when her mama didn't make it." Dale's voice trailed off, his eyes misting as he patted Rush's shoulder clumsily.

The word "hero" landed like a gut punch. Rush's jaw locked, his grip on the truck door handle turning white-knuckled.

He didn't deserve that word. He hadn't earned it. Hero implied he'd done enough. But no matter how many people insisted otherwise, he knew the truth. He'd fallen short, and nothing could change that.

And he sure as hell couldn't show up at that memorial and pretend otherwise.

Rush blinked hard and nodded at Dale. "Just doing my job," he said hoarsely, keeping his eyes on Riggs. The dog's ears tilted forward, sensing Rush's unease, and he sat up at attention.

Dale's expression softened into the kind of pity that made Rush's stomach churn. "Well, I know Pop must be proud of you too. You Callahans—always stepping up when it counts. Don't let it weigh you down, son."

Rush nodded tightly. He swung himself into the cab, the worn leather bench seat creaking under his weight. That look—the one everyone in town gave him—was suffocating. That was why he needed to get the hell out of there.

"Enjoy that cabin." Dale's face split into a grin. "Your Pop and I had a hell of a time up there back in our day on our hunting trips." He pounded the top of the truck with a hearty laugh. "You be careful up there, and keep an eye on this storm. They're saying the Adirondacks are gonna get hit hard later today."

Riggs stuffed his nose in Rush's jacket and searched for a treat as Rush pulled out of the gas station. Rush handed him one absently as he pulled up to the stoplight at the end of Main Street and checked his phone.

Three missed calls.

He didn't need to see the numbers to know those calls were from his sisters. Again. He let them go to voicemail, like he had the last time. The light was taking forever, as if the universe wanted to test his patience. He sighed, leaning back against the seat, counting down the minutes until he was on vacation.

The church doors burst open.

Rush straightened in his seat as a woman in a big puffy white dress came flying down the steps. She was all tulle and panic, her veil streaming behind her like a parachute.

Rush's instincts as a soldier jerked into place; immediately he was on high alert. *What the hell?* Northfield did not have runaway brides.

But this one was running straight for his truck in a mad dash with her skirt lifted high on her long legs. Her high heels wobbled in the snow as she raced down. Rush's eyes caught on a white band circling high on one of her slim thighs.

"Aw, hell," Rush muttered as the woman slammed both hands on the hood.

Lily Hart stared back at him, her eyes wide, her chest heaving nearly to overflowing in the tight white satin wedding gown.

Rush dragged his eyes away from that sight and swore viciously under his breath. He recognized that look. He had two sisters. Wild. Exhilarated. Trouble. He didn't want any part of this, not today, not ever. He was getting out of town, not rescuing runaway brides.

Except... she just stood there, those damn enormous eyes staring at him like he was the only thing standing between her and whatever awaited behind her at the church.

"Help." Her lips formed the words. They weren't audible, but they were enough to punch him right in the gut.

Shit. That was all it took. One word. He could never ignore that word, especially coming from a woman.

Riggs barked once, breaking the silence.

"Down," Rush said firmly to Riggs.

The dog's head tilted to the side, and Rush imagined an *"Are you shitting me?"* look on his face, but he jumped down from the passenger seat to settle on the floorboard obediently.

Rush was already halfway across the seat, shoving the passenger door open. "Get in."

Lily didn't hesitate, scrambling to yank up layers of her god-awful dress, and hopping onto the bench seat. She tried to pull the door closed, but the dress had taken over the front seat like it had a life of its own. She yanked again, falling back on the seat, her breasts threatening to spill out of the top.

The truck wasn't built for a two-hundred-twenty-pound man, a military dog, and a bride in a dress the size of Texas. She yanked hard, pulling the dress up higher, and slammed the door closed behind her. And froze.

Riggs looked between the layers of gauzy white dress that surrounded him to the woman who had stolen his spot, clearly disgruntled. Rush nearly laughed. Riggs had retired from the military with him and was already used to the creature comforts of civilian life, but he still looked like a badass.

"He doesn't bite," Rush said gruffly.

A high whistle filled the truck. Rush recognized the sound. He glanced at the woman sharply, but she was already holding a red inhaler to her lips.

"Buckle up," he growled, slamming the truck into gear. Snow sprayed as they tore away from the curb.

This was a mistake.

He knew it.

But it was one he made every time.

Chapter Three

"Can you breathe?"

Lily jumped, her heart still hammering away in her chest. Sheriff Rush Callahan already intimidated her on a good day, but scowling at her from across the bench seat, he looked downright lethal.

She'd seen her share of those cop shows, and the sheriff looked every inch the tough, hard cop, with black hair, a couple days of dark scruff on his jaw, and a tall, hard-muscled body that seemed to fill every inch of the cab. She'd sing like a bird if he ever interrogated her.

She nodded quickly, the medicine easing the tightness in her chest. *I am a still lake.*

At her feet, the massive dog tilted its head, staring at her with an expression she could interpret only as disdain and let out a low growl.

"Quiet," Rush barked. Lily flinched before she realized he was talking to the dog, not her.

Adrenaline still pumped through her veins like wildfire as she processed what had just happened. She twisted around in the seat, pushing down the layers of tulle to look out the back window. The church doors flew open, and there stood Tucker, fists planted on his hips, his face twisted with fury. His mother hovered beside him, her lips pressed into a tight line of disapproval. Tucker's eyes locked on hers as they sped away.

Holy shit. She really had done it.

A small, hysterical laugh burst out of her. It bubbled up, spilling over until she was clutching her stomach, her whole body shaking with laughter, tears streaming down her cheeks.

The sheriff shot her a sharp glance. "Put your head between your knees."

"I'm fine," she gasped, still laughing. Her chest felt looser than it had all day, her lungs working properly for once. Lord, she must look unhinged, but the absurdity was too much—it was just not how she saw this day ending.

Her fingers instinctively found the rose quartz pendant at her throat, the one thing she had insisted on wearing. She rubbed it between her fingertips, grounding herself.

She peeked at Sheriff Callahan from the corner of her eye. Not on her bingo card for her wedding day: Northfield's sheriff driving the getaway car.

Her sisters called him "Sheriff Sexy" when he first came to town, striding around in his charcoal-gray uniform and silver badge, a tan Stetson shadowing his eyes. He was always impossibly composed and untouchable in the authority of his uniform, but Lily's nervousness around him came from something else entirely. It was his rugged, unapologetically masculine presence that had always made her tongue-tied and feel slightly out of her comfort zone.

But here in the cab of his truck, he looked different. The Stetson was gone, replaced by a beat-up cap. The pressed uniform was now well-worn jeans and a shearling-lined coat pulled high against the cold, his broad frame even larger wrapped inside it. Her gaze drifted to the wheel, where his big hands gripped it tightly. His knuckles were bruised and scabbed, like he'd just been in a fight and won. A shiver of wariness curled through her at the blunt reminder of the differences between them.

Really, it was embarrassing every time they ran into each other in town. He was one of those people who made her forget how to act normal, so she just ended up smiling like a dummy while her face turned beet red. He must think her head was as fluffy as her dress.

The thought made another nervous laugh bubble up. Lily Hart, rule follower, people pleaser, had just blown up her life like a runaway bride in a rom-com.

The sheriff's jaw was set, his eyes locked on the snow-covered road ahead as if this were just another day at the office for him. Tucker always made fun of her when she talked about people's energy—he called her a hippie—but Lily was a big believer that the world could be nudged into more harmony if people just had the right vibrations. She liked to think she put out a light, peaceful energy—or she tried to, at least.

Sheriff Callahan's energy was grounded and intense, like the steady hum of a storm about to break. It wasn't loud or flashy, but it was impossible to ignore. It was calm, and controlled, and it carried a weight of authority that made people straighten up and listen. He was the kind of man who solved problems and didn't think twice about it.

The complete opposite of her.

For one sharp, breathless moment, she remembered her very first instinct—pretend she hadn't seen the photo, ignoring it the way she'd ignored so many red flags before. The late nights. The unexplained trips. The way he'd pulled further and further away while she'd clung harder, desperate to keep the picture-perfect life she'd always imagined.

For once in her life, she hadn't done the *right* thing—she'd done the *real* thing. It didn't erase the hurt, but it lit something new inside her, a fragile spark of freedom she wanted more of.

Her laugh broke into a sigh, and she slumped back. "I can't believe I just did that."

Rush frowned, looking every inch the law enforcement officer as he assessed her mental health, probably. "Do you want me to take you back?"

"No," she said quickly. The rage had burned out as quickly as it had come, leaving a wild exhilaration in its place. "I don't want to go back."

She twisted her fingers in the layers of tulle bunched around her. She didn't have anything with her. Not her keys or a change of clothes or even her purse with any money. But she had her inhaler and a bone-deep certainty that she'd just shed over two hundred pounds of deadweight in her life.

She didn't want to go back. Not to Tucker, not to their apartment, not to her family's inevitable questions, and definitely not to Northfield, where whispers would follow her everywhere.

And Angela. *Oh my God.* Angela would be furious that Lily had ruined the day and humiliated her in front of her friends. She would never understand why Lily had caused such a scene, never mind that her son was a dirty cheater. A tiny voice reminded her that she had thought for one brief moment of ignoring that fact too.

No, she couldn't go back.

"Look," Sheriff Callahan said, not unkindly. "We're running out of time. There's a storm on the way." She looked around her. For the first time, she noticed the snow swirling so thickly on the expressway that the road seemed to vanish into a white blur. Bare trees coated in ice lined the empty highway. *Perfect.* A freak blizzard on her wedding day seemed fitting.

"Where do you want me to drop you off?" Sheriff Callahan

asked, breaking the silence after a solid stretch of driving. "I can take you back to Northfield, to your family, or to a motel. Your call."

"No!" The word tore out of her, sharp and panicked. "I can't go back. They'll—Tucker—he'll..." *He'll talk me into forgiving him. His mom will guilt me into smoothing things over, and I'll cave, like I always do.*

She faltered, swallowing hard, embarrassed again at what she was about to say and what that said about her. "I don't want to go back," she said again.

Sheriff Callahan's face went stony. "Ma'am, are you in any danger?"

Lily's eyes flew open. *Oh Lord.* "No. No, nothing like that."

For all her anger with Tucker, she had never been afraid of him. If anything, he'd dismissed her in that casual way of a couple together for so long that he didn't truly see her anymore. Tucker never argued with her. He just made the decisions and assumed she'd follow. And she had, like a trusting little puppy. God, it made her sick to think about now, but she wasn't in any physical danger.

"Good." His shoulders relaxed a bit.

"I just couldn't do it," she whispered, staring out at the snow swirling across the highway. "I just need to get away for a few days before I have to go back and face... all that."

"Can you tell me what happened?" he asked in his calm sheriff's voice. She could imagine him using that tone to calm people down while still letting them know he wasn't messing around.

She shook her head. "Not yet. Please," she added quietly. "I just... need a few days before I have to face it."

"Fair enough. Where should I take you?"

Relief loosened her tense body. She shivered as her mostly bare shoulders touched the frigid leather seat while she thought.

Old Lily would've given him Evie's address, let her family sweep her up and patch her together. But, for once in her life, she didn't want to be patched. She wanted something different.

"Can you drop me at a hotel?" she asked softly.

Sheriff Callahan's eyebrows slammed down. "Do you have a plan? Any money?"

That scowl. She knew it too well. Tucker had looked at her the same way more times than she could count—as if she didn't have a lick of sense in her head when really it was that her brain worked differently than theirs. And now, the sheriff was looking at her in the same way. It shouldn't matter, not after the day she'd had, but disappointment crept in anyway. She was tired of men underestimating her.

Some people saw the world through colors and emotions and instinct. Others dealt in rules, logic, and the weight of reality. She happened to be in the first category. Rush Callahan, with his sharp eyes and hard edges, clearly was not.

"I don't have any money on me, but I can pay you back. I own Pure Bliss Wellness Studio on Main Street."

The sheriff grunted, his expression unreadable. "I know who you are."

Lily snuck a glance at him again, her curiosity piqued—he knew her?—but then ruined it when her teeth began to chatter. She bit down, trying to stop the shaking, but the cold had seeped into her bones.

He muttered something under his breath, and the truck slowed for a moment. She blinked in surprise as he shrugged off his heavy jacket, leaving him in a red-and-white flannel that clung tightly to his arms and chest. "Here," he said gruffly, tossing it over her shoulders.

The sheepskin was warm, carrying the faint scent of woodsmoke and him. She pulled it tighter and took her first deep breath of the day.

"Thank you," she murmured.

He didn't answer, just kept his eyes on the road, hands locked on the wheel. Lily closed her eyes and breathed—slow and deliberate—and found calm in the storm.

The farther they drove from Northfield, the more her lungs expanded and the steadier her breathing became.

❧

RUSH GLANCED at Lily then forced his eyes back to the road. She was too quiet. Leaning against the seat, her head tilted to one side, red curls spilled over her shoulders and caught the glow of the dashboard lights. Her lips curved faintly, her breathing even, and she looked almost serene. It was unnerving.

Growing up with two younger sisters, he was used to chatter, arguments, moods that flipped like a switch. Lily's eerie calm after the chaos of the day was something different, and he didn't trust it.

Not your problem, Callahan.

He wasn't unsympathetic. He'd help her get wherever she wanted to go, but that was it. At thirty-four, he'd had a lifetime of his younger sisters' emergencies and helping them out of various scrapes. But this particular female, with her big green eyes and distracting curves, was putting a serious cramp in his life. He just needed to figure out where to unload her.

He squinted at the heavy clouds hanging low over the sky. He'd gotten off the thruway when the roads iced over, but conditions only worsened the farther he drove into the Adirondacks. The truck crawled through steep, twisting curves where flimsy guardrails were all that stood against the cliffs they were driving on.

In the summer, the drive was picturesque; tonight it was a

snow-covered gauntlet with the wind howling through the trees and the tires fighting for grip.

Riggs looked up, alert as always to his moods. Rush quickly rubbed his head then returned his hands to the wheel.

The Adirondacks had always been his escape. Pop's hunting cabin in the woods had given him peace and solitude when nothing else did, but the beauty in these mountains came with danger, and tonight they weren't out of it yet.

This was supposed to be his reprieve. Off duty. Off-grid. No sisters checking on him, or worse, the people who slapped him on the back and wanted to buy him a beer he didn't deserve. He didn't want thanks or pity. He just wanted to forget.

The one-year mark of the accident was closing in this week, along with the memorial for Caroline Whitmore. She was blond. A single mom to a little girl with matching hair.

And now she was dead, and he was playing white knight to a runaway bride in the middle of a blizzard.

Lily Hart had no plan, no money, and no clue what she was doing.

Hell, she didn't even have a coat.

He should've turned around and driven her back to her family, but something about the look in her eyes when she said she couldn't go back had lodged under his skin.

Grimly, he turned up the radio to listen to the weather alert.

"This is the National Weather Service with an urgent winter weather advisory for the Adirondack region. Whiteout conditions and dangerously low wind chills expected. The New York State Thruway is closed due to hazardous conditions. Nonessential travel is strongly discouraged. If you must be on the roads, carry an emergency kit and be prepared for severe conditions..."

Rush's jaw clenched as the warning ended and reality set in. They weren't making it to a hotel. The only option left was the cabin.

Lily stirred beside him, pulling his jacket tighter around her small frame and looking out the icy windows. Her wide eyes stayed fixed on the snow blanketing the windshield faster than the wipers could clear it away.

"The snow's really coming down," she said nervously. "Is it safe to keep driving?"

"No," Rush said shortly. The tires skidded again, forcing him to adjust. "But stopping isn't safer."

He could feel her gaze on him. "Where were you heading?"

"My cabin." He tipped his head toward the shadowy outline of Autumn Ridge, high up in the mountains looming over them.

"What kind of cabin?"

"Hunting. There's no heat except a woodstove, no cell service. It's not exactly your kind of place." He glanced swiftly again at those long legs with the killer heels. No boots either. They were fucked if they got stuck.

He mentally ran through the emergency supplies he kept in the truck for weather like this. Blankets. Flashlight. Extra rations. First aid kit. He always planned for worst-case scenarios. It was part of his training, and second nature to him, but nothing had prepared him for being snowed in with a runaway bride.

She tilted her head as if she were considering his words. "How do you know what my kind of place is?"

He barked out a laugh, even though there was little humor in it. Everything about Lily Hart was soft and feminine, from her pretty hair to her tiny little ankle-breaker heels. She was not the "roughing it" type of gal.

Lily's chin tilted up. "I think I could handle it."

Rush shot her a look. She clutched the edges of his jacket so tight her knuckles were white. Her chest rose and fell in uneven breaths, and her eyes darted between him, Riggs, and the snow-covered road ahead of them.

Guilt tugged at him. His sisters would say he was being a grumpy asshole. He sighed, scrubbing a hand down his face.

"You don't have a choice," he said finally, resigned. "The thruway's closed. The cabin's closer than any motel. If I'm getting stuck, I'd rather it be there."

Her lips parted slightly, uncertainty flickering across her face. "We're going to your cabin?" Lily asked. "Won't we be snowed in there?"

"Better snowed in with supplies than stranded here in the middle of nowhere."

Lily nibbled her bottom lip between her teeth. "I've never been snowed in before."

Rush had spent years in the military, reading people under pressure. He knew to watch the way a soldier's hands shook before a mission, or how their breath hitched ever so slightly before they admitted they were in over their heads. As a sheriff, he was trained to pick up on people's subtle cues. Lily Hart had every red flag, from her too-tight grip, her forced calm, and the way her eyes darted just a little too much.

She was scared. Maybe not the kind of scared that made people panic, but she was in over her head, and she was trying hard not to show it.

But she was holding it together, and he had to respect that.

"It's not as fun as it sounds," he said, gripping the steering wheel as another gust of wind rocked the truck. "The cabin has wood, food, and water. It's not exactly luxury, but it beats being stranded out here." He paused for a moment. "We'll be okay."

She hesitated for half a beat before squaring her shoulders. "I'm not scared," she said, lifting her chin up higher. "This is an adventure."

Rush sent her a sidelong glance. Adventure? Sure.

"Look," he said, exhaling slowly to keep his frustration in check, "you need to call your family while we still have reception. Someone needs to know you're safe," Rush said firmly. He thought about Rachel and Sarah and how he'd feel if one of them ran away from their wedding and hopped into a stranger's truck.

Lily nodded and took the phone he handed her. As she dialed, he focused on the road, but he couldn't help but hear the conversation.

He wondered who she'd call first. He wondered about her fiancé too. He'd looked real pissed watching them drive off. Rush wasn't worried about Tucker, but he sure hoped Lily knew what she was doing. Things were about to get interesting for them.

"Evie, it's me. I'm fine," Lily said soothingly.

Not her fiancé, then. Her twin sister, Evie, the librarian in Northfield. Unlike Lily, Evie never had a problem meeting his eyes, and she'd never blushed and stammered before.

"I'm with Sheriff Callahan," Lily continued calmly. "He's taking me somewhere safe. Just tell Mom so she doesn't worry."

Evie must have said something Lily didn't like, because Lily's pink lips pressed into a thin line. "Oh my God," she gasped. She paused for a long moment, listening. "Everyone saw it?" Her head dropped, and she pinched the bridge of her nose. "Please just... let everyone know I'm safe. I need the weekend to think."

She listened for a moment longer before saying goodbye and hanging up. She handed the phone back to him silently and wiped at her cheek.

Rush froze. Tears. He hated tears.

Lily leaned back, eyes closed. He thought she muttered, "I am a still lake," but when he looked at her, she looked serene again.

Rush kept his eyes on the road. It was getting darker, and the snow was so thick the lines were gone from the road. He hadn't seen a car for miles. If they could just make it up the ridge, they could see the cabin. Easier said than done.

The truck jolted violently, a thud reverberating through the frame. Rush swore, slamming it into reverse, but the tires spun uselessly before fishtailing into a ditch.

Thank God they'd gone to the right—toward the ditch—because on the other side, the flimsy guardrail was the only thing separating the road from a sheer drop of at least fifty feet.

For a beat, stillness pressed in. His mind betrayed him, pulling him back to another road, another night. The flash of headlights in the icy water. The panicked call jolting him out of bed. The chill of the river biting into his skin as he fought the current.

Caroline's body slipping from his grasp while her daughter sobbed against his chest.

His lungs seized, suffocating on phantom water, until Lily's voice cut through.

"Hey, are you okay?" Her hand rested lightly on his sleeve, her diamond engagement ring flashing in the dim interior light.

Rush nodded tightly, forcing his fingers to unclench from the wheel. "We're fine. Just need to dig us out." His voice sounded more confident than he felt, but it would have to do.

Lily glanced toward the guardrail and the drop beyond. "Well," she said shakily, "at least we didn't go that way."

Rush grunted, already climbing out into the storm and making his way through drifts to the passenger side. The truck was going nowhere tonight. He yanked her door open.

"We're not making it farther," he said grimly. "The cabin's about one hundred yards up the slope. We'll have to walk the rest of the way."

Lily's eyes went wide. "Can we make it?"

"We don't have a choice." He reached around her for his

duffle bag. "Let's go, Riggs." The dog bounded down from the truck and took off, sniffing happily.

The wind whipped at Rush, icy flakes stinging his cheeks and soaking him through his flannel to the skin. Lily hunched deeper into his coat. Rush crouched low, using the door as protection against the wind.

"What are you doing?" Lily gasped.

"Tearing off your skirt." He didn't give her time to protest, grabbing the thick white mass of satin and tulle. He held it away from her body, the blade of his pocketknife flashing in the dim light as he sliced a clean slit up the middle of her thighs, exposing them to the frigid air when he pulled her toward him and out of the truck.

She wobbled on her flimsy heels, and Rush steadied her with a firm hand on her waist, spinning her around to attack the back of the dress. Another sharp rip and the skirt fell to a choppy hem just above her knees, leaving the garter on her white thighs exposed.

"Sheriff!" she squeaked, spinning around. Her cheeks were pink.

Rush leveled her with a stare, batting away the snow from his face impatiently. "This will give you a fair shot walking through the snow. Give me your foot."

She hesitated, but he hauled her heel into his lap, wrapping the torn skirt tight around it, then did the same with the other. His hands were already ice-cold and soaked to the bone, his flannel clinging like icy wet cement to his body.

He stood up and patted the sides of her—his—jacket, looking for his gloves and hat while she stared up at him. Her lips were parted, her breathing fast but not breathless, Rush noted. He handed her his heavy gloves and beanie. "Put these on, and make sure you have your inhaler."

"What about you?" Lily's face was pale, her green eyes huge

in her face. He wanted to reassure her, but they were going to run out of daylight soon. Shit was getting real serious, real fast.

"It's not that far. Sit tight, and I'll get the supplies. We'll walk the rest of the way."

She nodded silently, looking as grim as he felt. He had to give her credit, though. She was handling this better than he would have expected. He hoped that continued because they had a hell of a walk ahead of them.

Rush tugged the beanie over her head, grabbed her hand, and pulled her into the storm.

"Keep up," he barked over the howling wind.

Chapter Four

"Almost there! Stay with me." Sheriff Callahan's voice was barely audible over the howl of the wind. His grip tightened around her hand, and Lily stumbled after the narrow beam of his flashlight.

She had never been so cold in her life. Her eyelashes were crusted with ice, each blink a scrape of frozen needles. Her breath hitched in uneven puffs, and her legs—numb under the sheriff's huge jacket—felt like they didn't belong to her. Every step was a battle, her makeshift boots sinking into the drifts and threatening to keep her there.

She clung to her mantra, then fragments of half-remembered meditations, until finally she resorted to a simple prayer. *Please, God, let us make it to the cabin.*

Guilt twisted her stomach when she glanced at him. He was hunched over, shoulders caked in white, making a path in the snow for her to follow. Without his coat and only a baseball hat pulled low for protection, she couldn't imagine how much colder and more miserable he must be.

Everything had happened so fast. He had her out of the truck and following him blindly before she could think, and the sheriff wasn't exactly the kind of man you disagreed with. But she regretted taking his coat and hat now. They could have at least shared the gloves. She would find a way to make it up to him.

The thought pushed her forward, clinging harder to his hand when she stumbled. Her knees hit the snow with a crunch, and she stayed there, too tired to move. Truthfully, she wasn't even cold anymore. Maybe she could just take a quick rest, and he could come back for her, she thought sleepily. She sank lower in the snow.

"Goddammit, Lily, get up," the sheriff shouted.

That was rude. She frowned and listed to the left, feeling his hard hands hauling her upright. He might be insanely sexy, but he wasn't very nice. He needed an energy cleanse. The thought made her giggle. Suddenly, her feet dangled in the air and her head hung low, directly in front of the sheriff's tight ass.

She squinted through the icicles on her eyelashes. Those buns were criminal. Hard and sculpted, filling out his jeans in the best way. Bitable.

"Ow! Christ, woman," he jerked and hollered again when she giggled. She wasn't cold anymore, just sleepy. Now all the blood was rushing to her head, making her all floaty, and her laughter turned to a soft hum of contentment.

Just as a cozy darkness blurred the edges of her vision, he dumped her unceremoniously onto her feet. Sheriff Callahan propped her against something solid and dug out his keys from his pocket, his broad back shielding her from the wind.

They had made it, at last, to the cabin.

The door burst open, and they stumbled inside. He staggered forward and slammed the door closed, his breath coming in harsh, ragged gasps. The flick of a light switch, and then a savage, "Fuck!" when nothing happened.

"W-we m-made it," she chattered through half-frozen lips, sinking to the floor. *Nap time.*

"Come on." He hauled her up. "We've got to get warm."

The world tilted violently when he swept her into his arms again. Lily gasped, clutching his shoulders. The sudden motion made her head spin, though she wasn't sure if it was the cold, her adrenaline, or the man carrying her like she weighed nothing. His grip was firm under her back and knees, and protective as he carried her farther into the cabin.

Inside, the cabin was dim except for the beam of his flashlight. She caught impressions—the glint of a metal woodstove, the shadow of a small kitchen along one wall. The sheriff shouldered open a door, set her down on the closed toilet lid, then crouched to set the flashlight on the floor beside them.

"What are you doing?" she croaked.

Her lips were so frozen they barely moved, but he must have gotten the gist. "The power's out," he answered curtly. He stripped her gloves off and started chafing her hands roughly between his own. "We have to warm up before the hot-water tank gets cold."

He moved to her feet, unwinding the frozen layers of the satin dress methodically. His face was white and pinched, yet his hands were gentle while he unwrapped one and then the other foot. She nodded numbly, her teeth chattering uncontrollably.

"Get out of this dress. Do you need help?" Snow had frozen on his eyebrows and was melting into his eyes. He wiped the water off impatiently onto the shoulder of his flannel. "Lily," he said sharply. "Do you understand?"

Lily felt herself nodding automatically at the authority in his voice then frowned. *He's rude* and *bossy. His chakras are definitely off.*

Too frozen still to move, she let him shrug off his heavy coat and hat, which he tossed outside the bathroom, then he turned back to study the front of her dress with a scowl. She wanted to laugh at the look on his face, but her lips wouldn't cooperate either.

He stood up, slid the glass door of the shower stall open, and twisted to turn the shower on full spray.

The bathroom was small, with what looked like dark paneling on the walls. The only light came from the flashlight, which cast an eerie halo of light on the ceiling. He kneeled in front of her again and grasped her shoulders, frowning as he looked over the front of her torn dress.

His features in the shadows looked menacing. A twinge of nervousness pierced her stupor. Rude, bossy, but, she hoped, not a psycho. He was the upstanding sheriff of Northfield, but you never could tell who was a killer. Wasn't that how Ted Bundy tricked all those women?

"How does this thing come off?"

She blinked, pulling her thoughts back, and decided to trust him. He was friends with her brother-in-law, Theo, who was practically a saint in her eyes to put up with Amber. One time—

"Lily!" he barked again, and she jumped to attention.

"What?"

"How does your dress come off?"

"B-b-buttons," she chattered automatically. "B-b-back." She was so damn cold, sitting on the icy porcelain toilet, she didn't even care if the sheriff took her dress off. She was past the point of caring about anything besides getting warm again. Was that even a possibility at this point?

He stood up, pulling her into his body as he searched for the line of tiny buttons along her back. Lily let her head fall forward to rest on his stomach, grateful for the heat from his body.

Very solid. Warm. Nice. *Hmm.*

She rested silently, feeling the tensing and shifting of rock-hard stomach muscles as he wrestled with the dress. *Excellent core strength*, she thought dimly.

Finally, with a grunt, the dress tore, and the tiny buttons pinged in all directions, filling the bathroom. He guided her to her feet and, in one quick motion, stripped her of the wet, heavy dress. She felt almost weightless with the sudden change.

"What the fuck is this?" He froze, his gaze locking on the lacy white merry widow she wore underneath.

The corset-style lingerie hugged her curves, cinching her waist with delicate boning, the lace cups lifting her breasts almost indecently. Sheer panels skimmed over her ribs, leading down to tiny satin bows and garter straps that clipped to thigh-high stockings.

Oops. She had forgotten about the silly bit of lingerie. A hint of pink warmed her icy cheeks.

Without waiting for an answer, he lifted her again and set her in the shower under the hot spray. Tiny pinpricks of pain covered her body where the water pounded her like knives, and Lily moaned.

"Sorry," he muttered from outside the stall before she heard the click of it closing.

"S'okay," she said, leaning against the wall and closing her eyes in relief. Finally, she could relax and thaw out in peace.

The shower door clicked open, and she gasped in shock, her eyes flying open.

"What are you—?"

"Move over. I'm coming in," Rush said from outside the stall.

Chapter Five

Matter-of-factly, he stripped off his soaked flannel and the white Henley beneath, both of which he tossed on the floor with the tattered scraps of her wedding dress.

"W-what are you doing?" she stammered.

He paused, looking at her impatiently. "Getting warm."

Lily's mouth snapped shut. She couldn't help but follow his sharp movements, drawn to the hard muscles of his chest and the faint trail of dark hair disappearing beneath his jeans. When his hands went to his belt, she squeezed her eyes shut, listening to the sounds of him removing his belt, jeans, and boots.

Oh my.

She peeked. Of course she did. She was cold, not dead. His shoulders and arms were sharp lines of smooth muscle, and the way his bare abs flexed with his movements made her eyes widen. Sheriff Sexy was indeed just that.

A hand landed on her hip, and she jumped, but he only nudged her back farther under the spray. When she wavered, dizzy from the heat and the cold colliding, his big hands clamped to her hips, steadying her. "Careful," he murmured.

Oh. That felt nice.

It should've been awkward, being nearly naked with a man she barely knew, but she was too cold to care. His hands were large, palms rough against the soft flesh of her hips, dark hair dusting the backs. They were undeniably masculine hands. Something long dormant twitched to life as she stared at them against her much paler skin.

"I'm okay," she managed. Her body was thawing, but her teeth still chattered uncontrollably. A violent shiver swept through her, but at least she felt something besides frozen.

An arm slid around her waist, firmly guiding her against a chest dusted with dark hair. She sank against him, grateful again for the strength and heat. They stood under the steamy spray for a few long moments until he shifted. She made a faint sound of protest and followed his heat instinctively.

"Shh," he murmured, holding her hip to steady her while he leaned over the taps again. "Turning the heat higher. Didn't want to scald us until we could feel the temperature."

She caught a glimpse of his back flexing and tight black jockeys before he turned back. Warmth, unrelated to the hot water, curled low in her stomach, taking her by surprise. Residual adrenaline, probably. They had nearly frozen to death out there. Her body was overcompensating.

He settled her against him again, his arms loosely around her waist while the steam curled lazily around them, thickening the air.

Ah. Nice. Something like contentment filled her as she absorbed the heat from his body, and she took as deep of a breath as she could in the tight corset and burrowed closer to his heat.

Gradually, her skin stopped screaming, and new sensations crept in, sharp and impossible to ignore in the tight space of their bodies. The faint rasp of his breathing. The dusting of dark hair on his chest tickled her cheek and made her want to turn her face in. The steady thud of his heartbeat echoed through her, a solid, rhythmic pulse that seemed to anchor her in this surreal moment. His hands against her hips were firm, radiating a heat that penetrated her and slid down, low and thick, like warm honey throughout her body.

Good Lord, what was going on with her? Was she so sex-starved she was imagining things?

Cool gray eyes met hers when she looked up to find him studying her just as intently. Wet black hair curled over his brow. A high forehead and angular cheekbones looked almost sinister in the flickering shadows, making her shiver involuntarily. His square jaw was covered in dark bristles, his mouth firm and unsmiling under a dark mustache as he met her eyes with that serious gaze. She shivered, but it wasn't from the cold or adrenaline this time.

"Thank you," she whispered. She knew she must look a mess. Her hair hung half up and half down around her shoulders, and her makeup must be running. She started to pull away self-consciously and then stopped.

"I can't get this off without help," she said shyly, pointing at the merry widow. "I'm sorry to be a pain. It's one of those old-fashioned ones, and I can't reach..." She trailed off in embarrassment and looked down, aware that the corset boning was making her already large breasts push up almost indecently.

There was no help for that. The curse of being a Hart woman—every one of them endowed whether they wanted it or not. As a classically trained ballerina, she'd cursed her boobs more times than she could count. They made it hard to find costumes, and her leotards all had to have special supportive cups sewn in.

The white lace was almost transparent now that it was soaked, and her pink nipples were as plain as day, poking like diamonds against the delicate fabric. She looked up with another apology on her lips and stopped abruptly.

The sheriff's eyes roamed over her, dipping lower, and Lily was suddenly aware of her little white satin panties and bare legs. Leotards and skintight spandex were her regular uniform. Nonetheless, a flush of embarrassment swept over her body. Oh well. She needed his help. There was no way she could undo this thing by herself.

She swallowed hard and looked up. "It's cinched in the back," she said, embarrassed by the waver in her voice and the strange molten heat unfurling between her legs. Slowly. Insistently. "I can't... can you..." She turned slightly, cheeks flaming, even as her body shivered from the cold.

What was wrong with her? He was a stranger, and not all that nice of one, either. She should be frozen with fear or wrung out from shock, not humming from heat that had no business being there.

One black eyebrow arched on the sheriff's face, and she blushed even harder. He didn't say a word, just gave a curt nod. His silence unnerved her even more than anything he could've said, but she was increasingly, painstakingly, aware of every breath, every tiny shift in the air between them in the tight space.

Did he feel it too? This strange awareness between them?

She shot a quick glance up, but his expression revealed nothing. Swallowing hard, she turned around, bracing her shaking hands against the icy tile in front of her. It was just adrenaline. Cold and adrenaline. She concentrated on her breathing, which was coming in shallow pants now. It was the corset. The damn thing was like a cage around her lungs.

The first tug at the laces sent a shiver of relief down her spine that had nothing to do with the cold or the tingle of lust from his knuckles brushing against her back. Each loosened rung felt heavenly, and she took increasingly deep breaths until he pulled the sopping wet garment free and tossed it outside the stall.

"That's better." She sighed, turning automatically—then colliding with him. Her bare breasts pressed against the hard wall of his chest, and she froze, her skin electrifying where it touched his.

He was warm. Too warm for the blizzard outside. Long-legged, broad-shouldered, blocking out the flickering flashlight like a cement wall. Something primal, hot and electric, thrummed through her again, scattering the last of the cold and numbness.

What are you doing, Lily? Step back. Say something funny.

But she didn't.

She tilted her face up, tracing the droplets on his long lashes, the hard line of his jaw, the inscrutable eyes pinning her in place. They were darker gray now—watching her intently.

And then she saw it. A flicker, a change in his energy, as something hot simmered to the surface between them. She leaned forward, driven by a strange involuntary desire, swaying against him lightly.

The first brush of contact sent a bolt of something wild through her, scattering what was left of her confusion and cold. She dropped her gaze, shy and yet bolder than she had ever been before. It was exhilarating to know that he wanted her, too, that she hadn't lost that feeling of desire and being desired. *Thank God.*

She pressed even closer. Delicately. Deliberately. Letting the hard muscles of his thigh press tighter against the warm ache at the top of hers. Her breathing stuttered and came back in a quick, shallow pant. What was this? Whatever was happening, she knew she had never in her life felt this much heat for another person.

And that scared her more than anything.

The sheriff's body was long and lean—around the same height as Tucker's—but hard with the muscle of a man who didn't sit behind a desk all day. She catalogued the differences between Tucker's softer, rounder body and Sheriff Callahan's, and shivered involuntarily, rubbing against him just a little more. The dark hair on his chest teased her nipples into tight little peaks.

He pressed closer, molding his body to hers from chest to hips for a fleeting, too-brief second. An impression of a thick, hot-as-fire erection pressed into her stomach, branding her with its heat.

Oh my God.

Her breath caught, and her eyes snapped to his. He was already looking at her, and for a breathless moment, she saw her own surprise reflected in the slate gray of his eyes. But just as quickly, surprise melted into something else. A slow, pulsing current between them sparked like a live wire.

His hands slid back, big, bold, possessive, cupping her ass and pulling her flush against him. Against the undeniable, thick, rigid length of him, branding her stomach through the thin fabric of his shorts. A fleeting press of scalding heat and hardness.

Too brief. Much too brief.

Then he was gone, easing them apart carefully, and leaving every nerve ending in her body straining toward the place where he'd been. She felt the loss of his heat sharply, and she had to fight not to follow it.

"Warmer now?" he asked gruffly. His cheekbones were flushed, but his eyes were shuttered again. "Tank won't last much longer. Do you want to wash up while there's still hot water?"

Embarrassed, Lily nodded. "Yes."

He slid the glass shower door open. A long, angry scar raked his thigh, half hidden by his Jockeys. She quickly slammed her eyes shut and turned her face into the spray. What was she even doing?

She found a bar of soap and some no-frills drugstore shampoo in the shower and scrubbed briskly as she listened to the muted sounds of him drying off.

Where had that come from? She hadn't felt anything close to it in years. Maybe ever.

The thought of Tucker made anger bubble inside her, but she scrubbed harder, as if she could wash him away. She'd wasted enough years thinking about him, convincing herself that what they had was enough, that what their relationship lacked in passion, it made up for in comfort.

At twenty-seven, she wasn't sure if she'd ever felt raw, electric desire before. That truth unsettled her almost as much as who had ignited it.

She'd started dating Tucker in high school, when she barely knew her own body. Even during their "break" in college, she hadn't been with anyone else. It had always been him—or so she had believed.

Over the years, whatever spark they'd once had dulled to routine. Sex was predictable, perfunctory, and far from passionate. She'd told herself that was normal, that it was just part of being in a long-term relationship. When she worried he was losing interest, she tried lingerie, even some clumsy attempts at role-playing that had bombed dismally.

One night, inspired by an article in a magazine about spicing up your love life, she'd worked up the nerve to try out some dirty talk. It had taken all her courage, but instead of the reaction she'd hoped for, Tucker had given her a blank stare.

"Babe," he'd said with a faint look of disapproval on his face that mirrored his mother's, "that's not you."

She'd laughed it off like she'd been joking and never attempted it again.

Between teaching her dance and yoga classes and getting the studio up and running, she was too exhausted to care. She hadn't missed their intimacy—at least not consciously—and Tucker hadn't pursued her either. In fact, his attention had been increasingly absorbed by the six-packs he brought home more often than flowers.

When was the last time they had been together? A month? Longer? The question nagged at her as she rinsed the shampoo from her hair, letting the shower's heat soak in. It made her sick to think she'd gone to her annual last month, talking to her doctor about getting off birth control so she and Tucker could "start trying soon," while he'd been sneaking around behind her back.

They'd fallen into such a monotonous routine that it was hard to pinpoint the last time they'd had sex, because it certainly wasn't missed. Wasn't that just what happened when you'd been with someone for almost half your life?

Bitterness burned in her throat as the sharper truth landed. He hadn't been missing sex at all. He'd found it—just not with her.

She rinsed her hair, shut off the taps, and grabbed a towel to wrap around herself. The floor was icy cold with puddles from their clothing, but she was warm now.

Movement outside brought her back to the present. Facing Sheriff Callahan after that slip in the shower made her groan. Why did she always manage to embarrass herself around him?

A sharp knock jolted her.

"I found you something to put on." His deep voice carried through the door. "I'll leave them on the toilet."

The door cracked, and his broad shoulders filled the frame as he set down a bundle of clothes without looking her way.

"Okay," Lily said, forcing a casual note into her voice. *No big deal. She'd just molested the sheriff like a cat in heat, but it was fine. Absolutely normal behavior.* "Thanks. I'll be right out."

He closed the door. She quickly dressed, slipping into loose gray sweatpants rolled at the waist, a soft navy-and-red flannel, and thick wool socks. The clothes were warm and soft and smelled faintly of clean laundry detergent and that same masculine woodsy scent she'd noticed on his jacket.

She paused, letting the warmth and comfort of them steady her before opening the door.

Chapter Six

Lily stepped out of the bathroom, still giving herself a pep talk, and gripped the flannel shirt close to her chest. *Totally normal to be wearing Sheriff Callahan's jammies. Totally fine.*

She didn't need to look down to know the soft material molded to her without the buffer of a bra. Great. She could only imagine the show she was going to give him.

Oh well. There was nothing she could do about it now. She pasted a bright smile on her face and looked around.

A warning growl rumbled through the dark cabin, stopping her cold. Red eyes glowed from the shadows, and she caught sight of dark ears pricked forward. She swallowed hard, resisting the urge to squeak.

Of course his dog is terrifying.

"Riggs, quiet."

The command snapped through the air like a whip, making her jump to attention. Fresh embarrassment burned her cheeks. Between the two of them, the dog and his owner, these were going to be a long few days.

"I don't think your dog likes me," she said nervously, edging toward the fire where Callahan kneeled. "Which is weird. Animals usually love me."

She held her hands closer to the stove and kept a wary eye on Cujo. All that dark fur made him look as muscular and menacing as the horror-movie dog. She exhaled slowly—*still lake*—and all that.

It's fine. Just a dog. A very large, mean-looking dog. Would it kill him to wag his tail?

"My sister Allie has a golden retriever named Walter. He's a very good boy. And Amber has a rescue dog named Puddin' that loves to cuddle. They adore me." She shot Cujo a wounded look.

The dog stared her down... and won.

Dammit.

"Riggs is a retired service dog," Callahan said dryly. "Belgian Malinois. He's not exactly a cuddler."

Shocker. Neither is his owner.

"What kind of service?"

"Military. He was a working dog in my unit." Callahan glanced down at Riggs, his expression unreadable. "Explosives detection, tracking, and perimeter security. He's trained to guard and protect. Saved my ass more times than I can count."

Okay, well, that was sweet. Her heart pinched a bit thinking about the sheriff not leaving his dog behind. She looked at Riggs again, this time with fresh eyes. "And now he spends his time intimidating women in wedding dresses?"

"Sounds about right," he drawled, and Lily noticed a trace of a Southern drawl slipping into his voice, warm and smooth, making her pulse skip unexpectedly.

She ignored it and crouched to get on Riggs's level. "Listen, Cujo, I respect your service, but I'd appreciate it if you could dial down the murdery vibes. Just a little?"

Riggs didn't move, just leveled her with the same unblinking stare.

Tough crowd.

"Like I said, he's not a cuddler."

Lily shot them both a skeptical look. "What's he like with people he actually likes?"

"Tolerant."

"That's it?"

Callahan shrugged, his mouth twitching. "He doesn't let just anyone pet him. And he sure as hell doesn't cuddle."

"I'm starting to think that's a house rule," Lily muttered.

Callahan's eyes flicked to hers then back to the fire. Oops, she hadn't meant to say that out loud. But now that it was out, she found herself idly wondering if there was anyone the sheriff did cuddle with...

Shaking off the silly thought, she turned back to Riggs. "Fine. I'll win you over eventually."

Callahan laughed. The sound was rough and did something strange to her insides. "Good luck."

She watched him feed another log into the wood-burning stove. The cabin seemed to shrink when he stood. His damp hair was still pushed back from the shower. He wore another soft-looking flannel, and worn jeans clung to his long legs. The flannel pulled snug over his shoulders when he reached for the poker.

Her eyes drifted lower, catching on his hands again. Those scraped knuckles she'd noticed earlier gripping the steering wheel flexed as he used a poker to shift a log. The sight sent a little warning pulse through her. What had happened? Had he gotten into a fight? Northfield wasn't exactly crime-filled. It was the kind of town where people left their doors unlocked and the biggest scandal involved missing library books.

So who was Sheriff Callahan fighting?

She shouldn't ask. It wasn't her business. But something about his quiet, controlled energy made her feel like there was a storm brewing just under the surface. And that storm felt... intensely, powerfully male. Incredibly sexual in a way her body apparently responded to in a big way.

Nope. Not going to think about that. Not thinking about his muscular arms and shoulders and how they flexed when he ran the towel over his face.

Lily shot a quick look at him, and the sheriff's usual impassive expression made her exhale in relief. So they were going to ignore the shower interlude. Perfect. That would certainly make the next day or so less awkward, to forget that she'd practically been riding his thigh like a rodeo queen. Best to forget that little lapse in judgment.

Cheered up, she looked around the cabin.

The spark of optimism flickered.

The cabin was small—really small, as in a one-room A-frame. With the stove door open and firelight illuminating the space, the details sharpened, and she looked around with interest. *Rustic* was the kindest way to describe it.

A two-seater leather couch slumped in the center, across from the stove. Along one wall, the kitchen amounted to a sink, an avocado-green fridge and stove straight out of the seventies, and a butcher-block table with two chairs crammed into the galley-style setup. Opposite that, against the wall, was a single bed neatly made with a faded quilt and two pillows. Her pulse skipped then thudded hard in her chest.

One bed. Of course there was only one.

The entire space couldn't have been more than eight hundred feet, and not a single thing in sight suggested a woman had ever stepped foot inside. No curtains, a plain old-fashioned braided rug, no decor, just pure function and about as welcoming as the sheriff himself.

"Thanks again for letting me crash in your cabin," Lily said, flashing Rush a tiny smile. "And for..." She waved vaguely toward the bathroom, feeling her cheeks heat. "You know. Everything," she finished awkwardly.

Sheriff Callahan let out something between a laugh and a snort. He didn't sound all that amused, so Lily ignored it.

"So, home sweet home for the next couple of days, then," Lily said, injecting as much optimism into her voice as she could. She was excellent at finding silver linings. It was practically her superpower.

"Looks like it," he said, not turning around. "We'll get through it."

"I'll take the couch," she blurted, a little too quickly. "It looks... cozy," she added, taking in the two sagging cushions that suggested otherwise.

His head turned just enough for her to catch a glint of humor softening the firm line of his mouth, putting her more at ease. They'd make the best of it. What other choice did they have?

He opened the backpack he'd carried in from the truck and started unpacking with the methodical efficiency he seemed to apply to everything. Spare clothes, a battered first aid kit, another flashlight. Then a menacing black gun, followed by the glint of silver cuffs he set on the table.

Lily swallowed hard. Of course he had a gun. He was a sheriff. No reason to be silly about it. Still, the sight made her skin prickle.

She turned away, taking in the pine walls and heavy, exposed beams of the ceiling. The cabin should have felt dark, but with the fire flickering cheerfully, it was unexpectedly cozy.

"Actually, this cabin has good energy," she mused, turning in a circle to take it all in.

Callahan shot her another of those unreadable looks, but she dismissed it. Not everyone could pick up on those things.

"Good energy?" he repeated, not even trying to hide the skepticism in his voice.

"Mm-hmm." She walked toward the stove with her hands extended to soak up the warmth. "It feels settled, like there are good memories here." She glanced over her shoulder, feeling the weight of his stare. Half curiosity, half disbelief. Clearly, he fell into the Tucker camp when it came to things like this. "This was your family's cabin, right?"

"My grandfather's. I spent every summer here as a kid."

"That's nice. Was it just the two of you?" She was angling for information and hoped it wasn't too obvious. She tried to remember what else she knew about the sheriff. He wasn't from Northfield, that much she knew.

"No, it was my gran before she died, and my two sisters and me," he said, but his voice had that clipped, matter-of-fact tone that discouraged more sharing.

She ignored it. "You mentioned your grandparents," she prompted. "What about your parents?"

Callahan hesitated, his expression tightening for a moment before easing. "My mom died when I was twelve. Dad was never around. We lived in Texas, but we came up here to New York to live with Gran and Pop after Mom passed." He shot her a look, his mouth twitching slightly. "This cabin was our escape from Sarah and Rachel, my sisters. They were a pain in the ass, so Pop and I came up to hunt and fish and hide out for a couple weeks at a time from the girls."

She smiled at that. *Of course.* That explained the faint hint of a drawl in his voice. And no wonder the cabin had such a steady, grounded masculine energy. Places soaked up energy from the people who passed through them. She could almost see—

She looked up. And froze.

Staring her dead in the eye from the angled ceiling was a hulking deer's head, its enormous rack of antlers casting long, jagged shadows on the wall. Slowly, she slid her eyes to the glassy, vacant ones staring back at her in silent condemnation to the rifle hung just under it.

So much for peaceful energy.

"Is that..." she started, clearing her throat. "Is that—are those —loaded?" Her eyes wavered between the gun on the table and the rifle on the wall.

Guns had always made her uneasy. She had no experience with them—no uncles, no grandfathers, no one in her family had ever owned one. Between the police dog, the dead trophy deer, and the weapons, regret was swiftly overtaking her optimism.

The sheriff turned and followed her gaze. "Yes."

She nodded hesitantly. Okay. She could understand that. There were wild animals in these mountains, after all, and protection was necessary. It was just... "Guns make me nervous."

Slowly, the sheriff rose, the fire casting shadows across his face. All traces of heat from the shower were long gone, leaving his expression unreadable. "You know I'm a sheriff, right? It's part of my job."

"I know," Lily admitted. "I've just always been kind of a pacifist." Her eyes darted to the gun and cuffs again. "Do you really need the cuffs... on vacation?" she blurted nervously. Guns, she could see. He was a hunter, like it or not, but surely the cuffs were unnecessary.

A slow, sexy grin tugged his mouth up, and white teeth flashed against his rugged face. She blinked.

She would be lying if she didn't admit that the sight was disturbingly attractive. It was good that he kept that grin to a minimum or the ladies of Northfield would break laws all over the place.

He picked up the gun and cuffs and slid them into the back of his jeans in one smooth motion. "There's no better time to use them, darlin'."

Lily's brain short-circuited. Her mouth opened. Closed. Opened again. Nope. No witty comeback. She gave up on words and fiercely willed the telltale pink flush that she knew was creeping up her neck and cheeks to go away.

"Um." She coughed, suddenly fascinated by the interior design of the cabin. "Look at all that rustic... paneling. Really cabin-y."

The sheriff's grin widened, and she scrambled not to make any more idiotic comments. "Do you—um—chop wood?"

Oh my God. What was wrong with her? She wanted to sink into a puddle of humiliation and die, but the look of amusement on his face when he flicked a glance at her kept her rooted in a belated attempt at dignity. Clearly, she had none.

She wasn't afraid of Sheriff Callahan, exactly. Logically, she knew he was an upstanding citizen and a good man. A hero, even. The kind of man people called when they needed help.

But he was also tall and broad shouldered and oozed a masculinity that made her very jumpy. He also had another very serious, very impressive "weapon" that she'd been pressed intimately against—*naked, oh my God!*—that she had no doubt he knew how to use. And Lord help her, that image sent her already overworked nervous system into a full-blown meltdown.

"Yes," he said with extreme patience that let her know he was feeling anything but. "That's how we're going to keep warm. There's no power or cell service, but we've got plenty of canned food, water, and whiskey. It won't be fun, but we'll be fine up here for a few days until someone can plow us out." He was all calm authority again, with no trace of that wicked teasing grin, and Lily breathed a sigh of relief.

Despite herself, a tiny spark of curiosity flared. A part of her, the part that had never done anything unexpected or adventurous, perked up. "What kind of food?" she asked, realizing her stomach was growling. Aside from some toast that morning, she hadn't eaten all day, and she was starving.

"Canned soup sound good for dinner?" he asked, already turning away. "There's some in the cupboard."

"Sure, I'll look." Grateful for a task, she crossed the room to explore the kitchen. The cupboards held a mismatched set of utilitarian dishes and cups. On the counter, an electric coffee maker caught her eye. She briefly mourned the absence of coffee for the morning, but even that didn't get her down.

The alternative, she reminded herself sternly, was being on a honeymoon right now with a man who had lied to her.

She opened another cupboard and scanned the shelves. Her stomach sank. "Um... do you have anything that doesn't involve meat?"

Callahan turned, one brow raised. "You don't eat meat?"

"I'm a vegetarian," she said, a little defensively. "It's better for the planet." She shot a quick glance at the mounted deer head on the wall and winced. "And no one wants to eat Bambi," she muttered under her breath.

"Bambi tastes great in chili," he said mildly.

She turned back to the pantry with a huff, muttering to herself about Neanderthals. A moment later, she felt him behind her, close enough to raise the fine hairs on her arms. He reached past her, his solid arm brushing hers, and set a can on the counter.

"How about tomato soup and crackers?" he asked.

"Perfect. Thanks," she said.

When she turned around again, he was lighting taper

candles on the table. The warm glow cast more shadows along the walls and made the room feel even cozier.

"Mood lighting?" she teased.

He shot her another look of infinite patience. "We don't have power, Lily."

"It was a joke," she said, trying not to smile. He was so serious.

"I'm going to get more firewood," he muttered, shrugging into his coat.

~

Lily busied herself heating up two cans of soup in a small saucepan and pouring it into two bowls while Callahan and Cujo went back outside.

When the door opened, a blast of icy wind knifed through the cabin, making the fire in the stove flicker. She shivered, glancing through the window beside the door. Beyond the porch, the world was dark, the night sky swallowed by swirling snow that drifted thick and heavy, blanketing everything in white.

Outside, the dog leaped through the snow with a happiness at odds with his beastly appearance. Callahan tossed a stick and then gave him a good rubdown when he brought it back. She felt better. A man who could love a dog like that had to have a good heart buried under all that gruffness. She hoped so because they were stuck together now.

When he came back inside, stomping his boots to shake off the snow, ice clung to his dark lashes, and his cheeks were red from the wind. His energy sucked up all the air in the cabin and made her jittery again.

"I heated up dinner," she said, watching surreptitiously as he stripped the sheepskin coat off. It must have been heavy from the snow, but his movements were easy. Snow melted along the collar of his flannel as he moved toward her, and it took effort not to stare at the way it clung lovingly to his wide shoulders.

Lord, he was huge, and she was alone in a remote cabin without panties or a bra, her brain whispered helpfully.

They ate by candlelight, shoulder to shoulder on the small couch facing the stove. The cushions dipped toward the middle, forcing her thigh firmly against his. Rush's leg was hard-muscled and twice as long against her own much softer, smaller body. She held herself stiff then gave up fighting gravity and let his warmth seep into her. Awareness tingled in every nerve, making heat zing straight through her thighs to between her legs. When she glanced up, his eyes were already on her face. Then lower.

To her mouth.

Oh. She licked her lips without thinking then cleared her throat, trying to ignore the sudden flush crawling up her neck as she turned back to her soup.

The fire crackled merrily, the spoons scraping against bowls the only sounds while Lily pretended the room had not gotten a whole lot smaller.

When the last spoonful of soup was gone, Callahan took their bowls, set them on the floor, and sat back slowly, leveling her with a look. Up close, his eyes were steely gray, lit with silver flecks that caught the firelight. The weight of that cool stare made her want to squirm.

"Tell me what happened today." His voice was low and calm but laced with an unmistakable command that made her jump to attention. She frowned. She needed to get ahold of that reflex.

"I'd rather not talk about it, Sheriff." No way was she confessing Tucker's infidelity. She hadn't even told Evie yet about the photo. It was too raw and humiliating. "I just...

needed to get away." She braced herself, waiting for him to push, for the inevitable questions.

He held her gaze for a long moment while she tried not to crumble like a sandcastle at high tide.

"Fair enough." He gave her a short nod. "Call me Rush," he ordered instead.

She sighed in relief, grateful he hadn't pushed. Knowing his unfortunate effect on her, she probably would have told him everything, and she wasn't ready to face that right now, even to herself.

Silence stretched between them, but it wasn't awkward. Strangely, she felt peaceful and more than a little tired now that the adrenaline had mostly worn off.

"So, what about you?" she asked, sinking deeper into the soft couch. Their bodies touched from shoulder to hip now, but instead of pulling away, she settled into it. Maybe it shouldn't feel this easy with a man she hardly knew, but after everything they had been through today, the intimacy felt almost natural. "What brought you up here? Vacation?"

He stared at the fire. "No. It's not a vacation."

The light from the flames carved sharp shadows across his face, and something in the tightening of his jaw made her stop smiling. "Then what?" she asked gently.

No answer. He didn't move at all, still a warm, solid body pressed against her, but she sensed his withdrawal anyway. Her heart pulled tight in her chest, remembering.

She knew the story. Everyone in Northfield did. The night he pulled Chloe Whitmore from the canal was a town legend by now. The newspapers had gone crazy with the story, painting him as a local hero. "Northfield's Own Guardian Angel," one headline had read. Another had called him the "Sheriff with a Hero's Heart."

The media had eaten him up—the decorated Marine-turned-small-town-sheriff, risking his life when he wasn't even on duty to save a drowning child. The little girl's mother had slid on black ice and driven straight into the Erie Canal, and while Rush had managed to pull the five-year-old from the icy water, tragically, he hadn't been able to save the mother.

The town had celebrated him. They'd held a fundraiser for the little girl, who now lived with her grandparents in Northfield, and toasted him at the local pub. Lily and her family had all attended, but the sheriff had barely made an appearance. He'd looked visibly uncomfortable with the handshaking and people clapping him on the back, thanking him for what he'd done, and he'd left early.

Lily had been at the Northfield town meeting when he was nominated for a local award, and she'd seen his face—hard and blank—a little like it was now. His expression gave nothing away, but she could see the weight of that night in the clench of his bruised knuckles and the tic in his jaw.

"Needed to get away," he said at last, curtly.

A simple answer, but his tone made it clear he wasn't going to offer any more details. She nodded, taking the hint. She almost reached out—almost—but stopped herself. He wouldn't welcome it. Neither one of them was willing to dig too deep. Fair enough.

"I get that," she said softly. "I guess you could say the same about why I'm here."

His shoulders shifted again, and he nodded. "There's a new toothbrush in the bathroom," Rush said, getting up. "Anything else you need should be in the cabinet."

"Thanks."

Lily pushed herself off the couch. The warmth of the fire had made her limbs heavy, and exhaustion clung to her. In the bathroom, she found the toothbrush still in its packaging, along with toothpaste and a comb. As she brushed her teeth, her eyes caught on her white silk panties still in a soggy pile on the floor with her dress. She took a minute to wash them with the bar soap and hung them over the towel rack to dry before padding back out to the couch.

Rush crouched by the stove, adding another log and watching the flames catch. The warm glow flickered over the walls, making the room feel smaller and more intimate. He absently rubbed the scar she'd seen on his thigh, his frown deepening until she made a noise, and he stood up quickly.

She lay down, curled up on the couch and yawned hugely as her eyes grew heavy. Even with her eyes closed, she knew when he had stepped closer. The tiny hairs on the nape of her neck stood at attention, and she felt the heat of him as he draped a quilt over her.

"Here's another blanket." His hands hesitated for half a second at her shoulders, like he might tuck it around her. But then he pulled back.

"Thank you," she whispered.

"Get some rest, Lily."

She wanted to answer, but the pull of sleep was stronger.

Chapter Seven

LATER—WHO knew how long—Lily's own teeth chattering woke her up. The fire in the stove had burned low. Now its warmth barely reached her, and she was shivering violently on the cold leather couch.

She curled into herself, pulling the blanket closer, but it did nothing to stop the deep chill that had burrowed into her bones. Across the cabin, Rush's breathing was deep and even, completely undisturbed coming from the bed.

She was exhausted. Bone-deep tired from too many nights lying awake with a heavy sense of impending doom in her chest that she had chalked up to wedding jitters. But her body had other plans now, rattling her teeth together like a wind-up toy, making her convulse violently.

She clenched her jaw and tried to focus on her breathing. In through her nose, slow and steady, out through her mouth. Again. She visualized warmth spreading through her limbs, willing the tremors to stop, but even that didn't help.

Still, she lay there, miserable, willing herself to stay quiet. The last thing she wanted was to wake him up. He'd already given up his week of solitude at his man-cabin for her. The least she could do was suck it up for the night. She owed him that much, didn't she?

Lily hated being an inconvenience. Hated knowing she was imposing, even though he hadn't said a word about it. She wasn't going to be even more of a problem for him by complaining. She clenched her teeth and squeezed her eyes shut.

A violent shudder went through her, and her teeth clacked together so hard she wondered if she broke one.

"Jesus. You're gonna freeze on that couch, and neither one of us is gonna get any sleep," Rush said suddenly. His voice was rough, and somehow he looked even larger in the dark. "Get in. We need to sleep. It's too cold in this cabin to sleep on the couch."

"I'm f-f-fine," she whispered, clenching her teeth around the lie.

Rush sighed, deep and exasperated, and she stiffened even more. Then, he lifted the blanket and held it open. "Get in." That same bossy sheriff voice that made her a little weak in the knees.

"No, thank you," she said primly. "I'm fine over here."

"Lily," he said with a patience she could tell cost him. "It's body heat. It's called survival. It's not an invitation for anything else."

She hesitated, looking at the warm, cozy bed, almost salivating at the thought of its warmth compared to the freezing leather. "Where's your gun?"

She heard a flop back onto the bed and imagined the sound of his teeth gritting. "It's put away, and the cuffs are, too, if that's your next question."

It absolutely was.

Still, she hesitated. He didn't seem like a man plotting anything nefarious, but how would she know? She had never slept with anyone besides Tucker. Her entire experience with men was limited to one less-than-stellar example, and she knew she could be a little naïve when it came to sex.

"How do I know you're not a secret serial killer?" she managed to say, but it came out disjointed with her teeth clattering.

"Suit yourself," he said. She could just make out his broad shoulders shrugging. He dropped the blanket back in place and settled back into bed.

Something in Lily snapped. For the sake of her sanity, and the health of her teeth, she told herself, she'd sleep in the same bed.

She gripped the blanket tighter around herself and padded over to place a tentative knee on the mattress. She could make out the glint of silver handcuffs resting on the nightstand, and she shivered again, less from the chill this time and more from the sight. She hesitated, half on and half off the bed.

A low growl rumbled from the floor, and she leaped the rest of the way in. The force of her jump caused her to collide against something solid and very warm.

She gasped again when strong hands gripped her waist, lifting her like she weighed nothing. In one swift move, she was flipped onto the inside wall of the bed.

"I sleep on the outside," he said roughly.

Oh. Okay, then.

The bed dipped and let up as he got out. She listened to the sound of Rush putting another log on the fire and the jingle of Cujo's tags as he followed his master. Rush's deep voice gave a command to the dog, and then with a heavy flop and a deep, doggy sigh, the dog settled next to the bed.

The bed creaked, and she held herself stiffly until he settled behind her again. They weren't touching, but she could feel his breath on the back of her neck, warm and minty, wafting over her shoulder, like the toothpaste she'd helped herself to before bed.

At home, she'd always slept closest to the door—for safety, Tucker had said. Because she was a lighter sleeper than he was and would hear anything before he did. The thought had never sat well with her, but when she'd suggested they get a dog for extra security, Tucker had just laughed. "You sleep so lightly, Lils. You'd hear an intruder before a dog even woke up," he'd said, ruffling her hair without even looking away from the baseball game on TV. *Asshole*.

Lying stiffly, she tried to breathe as shallowly as possible and let the anger wash over her. She closed her eyes and visualized a soft, cleansing light enveloping her as she controlled her breathing. She imagined the cabin steeped in the golden light, curling into the dark corners, and felt better. The cabin had Rush's energy. Steady. Protective.

She closed her eyes and murmured sleepily, "Cujo hates me."

Silence. Then, a slight cough that sounded suspiciously like it was masking laughter. "Riggs?"

"Yeah," she said. "He hates me."

"He doesn't hate you. He just responds to authority."

Lily stiffened. Authority. Well, that explained a lot. The dog had taken one look at her and decided she was a pushover. Just like—*ugh. Don't go there.*

"So what?" she muttered. "He just instinctively knows I'm not worth listening to?"

Rush shifted behind her, and the mattress dipped, pulling her toward the center. They weren't touching, but they were close enough that the heat of his body reached her. She had to hold herself rigid to resist wrapping herself around all that delicious warmth.

"I didn't say that."

"You implied it."

"Didn't have to," he said dryly. "You just did."

She scowled at the wall, pulling the blanket higher around her shoulders. Of course he had her pegged. Not even a day and even the dog had figured it out. She was too soft. Too nice. Too easy to walk all over. "Great. So now I have to earn a dog's respect?"

"He'd probably settle for a firm command and not acting like you're scared of him."

Lily bristled. "I'm not scared of him." *Much.*

Rush didn't respond, but the silence was loud.

She turned her head slightly, just enough to make out the strong slope of his nose and the shadows of his closed eyes in the dim light. "How long have you had him?"

"Riggs?" Rush paused as if counting in his head. "About four years now. He was my partner in the Marines. We did bomb detection together."

"You adopted him when you left?"

She felt the slight rise of his shoulder in a shrug. "We finished our tours around the same time. After everything we'd been through, leaving him behind wasn't an option."

Lily absorbed that quietly. So the broody sheriff had a soft spot. Interesting. "He seems pretty happy being retired with you."

"He's mostly happy he gets to sleep in."

On cue, Riggs let out a loud, sleepy sigh from the floor as if in agreement. Lily lay there, warmth gradually returning as she listened to the pop and crackle of the fire.

"You really think I'm a pushover?" she finally asked.

"Hell no," he murmured, his voice a rough, lazy rumble. "You ran out of your own wedding. That takes some balls."

"Then what exactly are you trying to say?"

He let out a huge yawn and settled into the bed more

comfortably. "Just that whatever made you run away must have been pretty damn big. Because if I had to guess, you're not someone who walks away easily."

She swallowed hard. "Maybe you're giving me too much credit."

"I don't think so," he said quietly. "My guess is you hold on way past the point where most people would have walked."

"That sounds dangerously close to calling me a pushover."

She felt the bed shift when his massive shoulders shrugged. "I'd call it loyalty. You don't quit until there's no other choice."

She chewed on that for a while as she stared at the wall. Loyalty. It sounded nicer than "pushover" but heavier too. "Well, maybe I stayed loyal to the wrong person."

"Probably," Rush said. "But there's no shame in trying to make things work."

"Even when everyone else thinks it's not worth it?" Her thoughts drifted to Tucker, to the years she'd spent convincing herself he was what she wanted—needed—despite the concerns of her sisters and her mom. Watching Annette working herself to the bone, raising four girls on her own, had left her craving something more when she thought of her future. Stability. A love story with no missing pieces.

Now, lying in the dark, she wondered if she'd spent all those years determined to build the perfect life, clinging to Tucker despite the whispers in her heart, because admitting she was wrong felt like she was giving up that dream.

"Especially then." He shifted again, and the mattress dipped, drawing her closer to the heat of his body. "Hope isn't weak. It's brave as hell."

She let that sink in, warmth and something else making her feel softer and more vulnerable. "So, Sheriff Callahan believes in hope. Who knew?"

"Don't let it get around," he drawled.

"Are you cold?" she whispered after a moment, inching just a tiny bit closer to his side of the bed.

"No."

"Oh," she replied, easing back slightly. "Me neither."

He let out a loud snore that she was ninety-nine percent sure was fake. She rolled her eyes but got the hint and fell silent, staring at the ceiling and mulling over her life choices.

Minutes passed. Maybe longer. She lost track of how long she lay there, but gradually, inch by inch, she found herself moving closer to the furnace that was his body. His breathing slowed and deepened as she shifted again until she was almost touching him.

A faint shiver ran through her, and a steely arm shot out and wrapped around her waist, pulling her flush against a solid, overwhelmingly warm, and undeniably male body. Her eyes went wide at the feel of all that muscle and strength pressed so intimately against her body, sparking something deeper and warmer in her.

His chest rose and fell evenly against her back, his thighs solid and strong behind hers. She fit so nicely here, she thought, wiggling closer into the shape of his body.

"Lie still. Neither one of us can sleep with your teeth chattering like that," he murmured near her ear. "We need to share body heat."

She stiffened immediately, her body hyperaware of every single point where they touched. When was the last time she'd slept with someone curled around her? Years, probably. Tucker had always stayed on his side of the bed, and she wasn't a cuddler either, but right now, wrapped in warmth, she had to admit how nice it felt, even if it was just to share heat.

She shifted back slightly, testing the space between them, and his arm tightened, pulling her even closer. The heat of his body seeped into her muscles, relaxing her completely. For weeks now, she'd barely slept at all, waking up every night with an uneasy feeling in her stomach. She'd convinced herself it was nothing more than wedding jitters, but deep down, her intuition had been whispering that something was wrong. Something she had refused to see.

Now, pressed against Rush's solid warmth, those anxious thoughts finally quieted. Her lids grew heavy as a slow, sweet warmth spread through her. Maybe she was a cuddler after all, she thought drowsily.

The question had been lingering at the edge of her thoughts from earlier. Before she could stop herself, it slipped out. "Are you married? Is there someone waiting for you at home?"

He didn't answer right away. The silence stretched long enough that Lily's pulse kicked up a notch, but having been on the receiving end of a betrayal, she needed to know she wasn't doing that to someone else.

"No," he finally said. "Go to sleep."

Relief flooded her, and she relaxed fully against him. "I'm a very light sleeper," she mumbled, already starting to feel herself drifting. "And I don't need much room. You won't even notice I'm here."

Her breathing slowed, and that was the last thing she remembered.

Chapter Eight

She slept like the dead.

Not only that, she spent the entire night sleeping like the dead directly on top of him.

Rush woke up before dawn, with warm, soft, sweet weight draped over him like a blanket. Somewhere in the night, despite her reassurances, Lily had ended up on top of him, or she'd tried to anyway. He had woken up more times than he could count with her sprawled on his chest, and every time he'd gently moved her back, another body part had flung itself over him.

One of her legs over his thighs, an arm around his chest with her face buried in his neck. After an hour or so of moving her back to her own side of the bed, he'd given up and held her in place next to him just to get some sleep.

Even now, her head was on his pillow, and she was wrapped around him, soft and warm, and completely oblivious to the havoc she was wreaking on his self-control.

Rush exhaled slowly and let himself look at her as the sun rose and light filled the cabin. Her face was relaxed in sleep, and she looked younger without any makeup, fine boned and delicate. Her skin was creamy and pale against his own darker body and lightly freckled on the bridge of her nose. A stray red curl had escaped her bun.

Her lips drew his attention before he could stop himself. They were soft and full, slightly pouty and parted. He groaned silently. Those were *fuck-me* lips, and he was far from immune. Lily Hart was exactly the type of woman he went for: soft, curvy in his favorite places, with her long, smooth legs wrapped around him like an octopus.

It had been too long since he'd had a woman in bed with him.

There was no other explanation for what had happened between them in the shower the night before. She was too soft, too fucking tempting for the thought not to cross his mind. He'd tried his best to be professional and distant, but when she pressed her heat against him, *Jesus, he'd thought about it*. Of course he had.

He didn't know her. But his body didn't give a damn. He was no stranger to physical chemistry, but this was different. Sharper. Hungrier. Like his instincts had locked onto hers and weren't letting go. Even now, his hands itched to touch her and pull her into his body. She was damn inconvenient and distracting when he needed peace and calm more than anything.

She made a sleepy noise and nuzzled closer, her knee nearly leveling his morning erection. He grunted, gripping her thigh to keep her from causing permanent damage. Soft. Warm. Sleekly muscled. Wrapped around him like she wanted to climb—*nope*. He pushed it off him gently. He needed to move. Now.

Lily hummed, still half asleep, and burrowed even closer against his chest. Her nose nuzzled into his throat, and she let out a soft, contented sigh.

Rush froze, swallowing hard, and forced himself to think of anything else. Paperwork. Parking tickets. Cold showers. But his mind, traitorous bastard that it was, only fed him more images of her.

Lily standing under the hot spray in his shower, her big, gorgeous breasts all wet and gleaming, water sliding in rivulets down the slim curve of her waist and flaring over the hips he'd gripped.

He'd tried not to look. He'd tried to keep himself strictly professional by focusing on neutral spots. The old shower tile, the beam of the flashlight, literally anywhere that wasn't her body. But he wasn't a damn monk. And she'd been standing there, stripped down to nothing but a scrap of white lace panties and an unmistakable heat in her eyes.

He'd held it together until she'd pressed herself against him. Just a little nudge of her pelvis against his thigh where he could imagine the soft, slick hidden part of her riding him, and he'd lost it for a minute. He gritted his teeth, the memory washing over him like a punch to the gut.

This was a problem.

Carefully, he shifted away from her.

"Mmm." She blinked her eyes open. Rush gritted his teeth while she made cute noises, and her—his—flannel shirt rode up on her flat stomach.

She blinked up at him, sleep-heavy and disoriented, and then stretched her leg out—narrowly missing the evidence of all that morning cuddling.

"Jesus, woman. Are you trying to castrate me?" he yelped, covering himself.

Color bloomed high on her cheeks as she snapped her head away, looking at the ceiling like it was the most interesting thing she'd ever seen. He sat up, grateful for the distraction, and swung his feet to the floor, rubbing the tight muscles covered by scar tissue on his thigh. The damn thing was also always stiff in the morning.

"Oops. Sorry," she muttered, rubbing her eyes. "I can't believe how well I slept," she said through a yawn. "Did you sleep well too?"

Rush snorted. "Like a rock." *A granite one.*

Lily smiled sleepily and rolled herself onto her side, propping herself up on one elbow. "See? I told you I don't take up much space."

Rush dug his fingers into the muscles of his thigh and snorted. "I need a shower." A very cold one, which was all there was anyway.

He escaped to the bathroom and turned on the taps. The water was icy, but it was a welcome distraction. He washed up quickly and reached for a towel. Hanging from the towel bar, fluttering like a taunt, were her panties. White, lacy, delicate as hell. He held back a groan, yanked his T-shirt over his head, and dragged a hand down his face. He needed space.

The last time he'd been around a woman this intimately, it had ended with her walking away. Blake Carter had never been the settling-down type. He'd known that from the second he spotted her, and it had suited him just fine.

She'd been leaning against the bar at a club in downtown Rochester, her long legs crossed, one red-soled shoe dangling lazily from her foot. The black minidress she wore barely covered her ass, clinging to curves made for sin. She had picked up her glass, run her tongue around the rim, and tilted her head like she was already considering what it would be like to ride him.

And that was all the encouragement he needed.

The thing about Blake was she didn't pretend to be something she wasn't. She liked kinky sex, fast rides on his motorcycle, and weekend trips on a whim. She wasn't looking for forever or promises. She had enjoyed the Rush Callahan who pushed her limits and gave her a thrill. She wasn't the kind of woman who could sit through grief and dark moments.

Rush had known she would leave, and truthfully, he hadn't bothered to keep her. "You're not the same man," she'd said, foot tapping in her high-heeled sandal, standing in his kitchen like she was already out the door. "I know you're hurting, but I miss the guy who actually lived. Not... this." She'd looked at him with something close to pity. "Honey, when are you going to forgive yourself?"

She'd left him, and the quiet heaviness had taken over, pressing on him every damn day, and he didn't blame her. Hell, he respected her for it. Blake had never pretended to be something she wasn't. She didn't do grief. She didn't do broken.

And since that night a year ago, that was what he'd been.

She still periodically sent him pictures of her on the lake with friends and at concerts. "Miss you! Hope you're doing okay! See you soon!"

He usually responded with a thumbs-up or a smile and left it at that. Blake deserved that kind of life, but he no longer wanted it. He craved something he couldn't find in Northfield anymore.

He dried himself and purposefully hung his towel over Lily's panties. Lily Hart might look like an angel, but she disturbed his peace.

And when he stepped out of the bathroom, toweling his hair, the exact reason why she disturbed him was right in front of him.

Lily was on a blanket in front of the fire, her body folded in half with her head down, ass up in the air. Rush stopped in his tracks.

Jesus.

She wore his flannel, tucked in on one side into his sweatpants, but the other side had escaped to reveal just enough soft, creamy skin around the dip of her waist he had no business noticing. He leaned a shoulder against the doorframe and crossed his arms.

Lily exhaled slowly, her eyes still closed, and stretched her arms forward, the tips of her red hair touching the floor. Her back arched, and Rush felt the same bolt of pure, unadulterated lust shoot through him.

Then she hummed.

Long and deep. Like she was either orgasming or doing some seriously weird ritual. He hoped it was the second one because it would make it a hell of a lot easier to ignore the effect she had on him.

She took another deep breath and said, "I am a still lake. Not a stormy sea."

Riggs lifted his head from the floor and shot her a sideways look. *She's a nutter,* he seemed to say.

Rush's eyes narrowed. "Are you casting spells over there?"

Lily cracked an eye open and looked at him upside down. "It's called a mantra." Her cheeks were a little pink, but that could be from the blood flowing upside down. "For focus and calm."

"Never heard of talking yourself into being a pond."

"A lake," she said, sitting back on her heels. "It helps me to remember I don't have to get swept up in everything around me. I can just be still."

He almost sighed in relief. This was exactly what he needed to cool him off. Rush had never put much stock in things not footed firmly in logic and reason. He suspected she subscribed to all those alternative-healing ideas that his sisters were always talking to him about. Luckily, it further cooled his ardor.

She exhaled long and slow and rose to standing gracefully, arms high above her head, breasts thrust out against the worn fabric. "Your energy is bad."

Rush smirked. "Yeah? Tell me more." *Yes, gorgeous. Tell me all about my energy so I can forget about your body rubbing against mine all night.*

She made a noise of disapproval but didn't stop stretching, rolling her shoulders back before bending forward again, stretching her arms toward the floor.

Rush muttered, "Hell," and headed toward the kitchen. He needed coffee.

A while later, Lily wandered over, sniffing. "Please tell me that's coffee?"

Rush set two mugs down and waited for the hiss and gurgle as the water heated before pouring a dark, scalding hot stream of strong black coffee from his grandfather's old steel moka pot into the mugs. "It is."

"Oh, thank God." Lily sighed reverently and reached for the mug. "I was afraid you only had an electric coffee maker."

He tried not to watch as she inhaled the steam with her eyes closed as if she were having an orgasm. The sooner they were out of the cabin and he could drop her off in Northfield, the better. The cabin already felt too small with the two of them. This place had always been his refuge, a place to get away and find peace and quiet, but now he had a permanent, distracting image of Lily Hart bent over in front of the fireplace.

"You mentioned your sisters last night," Lily said, breaking the quiet. "Rachel and Sarah, right?"

"Yeah," Rush said, taking a sip of the scalding hot coffee. "They're younger."

"What are they like?"

He leaned against the counter and smiled reluctantly. "Good. Better than me, anyway. Sarah's finishing up her business degree in Buffalo. Rachel's a nurse at Northfield General. They're both smart as a whip and stubborn as hell."

"You sound like a proud big brother."

The familiar pull in his chest—equal parts pride and exasperation—made him grin. "They're a pain in my ass. Now that Gran is gone and Pop is in a nursing home, they've shifted their attention to mothering me. Always calling to check in on me and sending texts with all those weird emojis."

"They sound like my family," Lily said, smiling. "I love them to death, but there are very few personal boundaries."

"They call or drive to my house when I don't answer right away." He looked toward the fire. "Especially after the accident," he added gruffly.

He wasn't lying when he said the girls were a pain in his ass. He'd give his life protecting them, but they had nearly suffocated him with their worry since the accident on the canal. They meant well, but they hovered constantly. Check-ins and phone calls. Rachel had even taken to leaving dinner for him a few times, forgetting that he could fully take care of himself and had been doing so for years.

A beat of silence passed, but she didn't push. "They love you."

"Yeah, I love them too." He nodded, adding dryly, "They're big fans of therapy. And sending me Pinterest quotes."

Lily snickered. "Bet you love that."

His gaze dropped before he could catch himself, lingering on the outline of her breasts beneath the thin flannel. No bra. He'd known that the second he'd walked out of the bathroom, and now it was all he could see. Soft. Full. Fucking perfect. The kind of breasts that would fill his hands and make him forget his own name.

He shifted against the counter. *Not the time.* He needed to focus. He needed to do his damn job. He set his coffee cup down with a deliberate clink and turned to face her. "Tell me why you ran."

Lily froze mid-sip. Her gaze flickered to his before skittering away, but he didn't relent.

"I told you," she said after a beat. "I just couldn't go through with it."

Rush crossed his arms over his chest. "That's not an answer."

Her soft lips parted, and her eyes went wide and innocent, but he steeled himself against them. "Why do you need to know?" she asked, licking her lips.

She was nervous around him. Good. The more uncomfortable they both were, the less likely anything could happen.

"I need to know if I should be looking over my shoulder for some pissed-off, jilted groom," he said, his voice hard. "Or if you're in some kind of trouble."

"Trouble?" She twisted her hands in front of her. "I told you Tucker wouldn't ever hurt me."

"Legal trouble, Lily," he said quietly, watching her reaction. He needed to be sure she wasn't lying. He might have been the guy who drove her out of town, but he was also the sheriff. His job was to make sure she wasn't running from something worse than last-minute jitters.

She shook her head quickly and relaxed her shoulders. Rush relaxed too. She didn't look the type to get into any legal trouble, but he'd seen stranger things. Her reaction was reassuring to him that whatever had happened at the altar, she wasn't running from the law.

"I'm not in any legal trouble. I just couldn't marry someone I didn't love, okay?" She looked so sad for a minute that he almost relented.

He set the coffee cup down on the counter. "I had to make sure."

"I understand." She nodded, looking relieved that he didn't

press her any harder. "So," she said brightly. "What are we going to do today?"

Rush ran a hand over his jaw, looking at her.

That was the problem.

He already knew what he *wanted* to do.

He grabbed his gloves off the counter and his jacket off the hook by the door, shrugging into it. "Do whatever you want." He ignored the way her face fell. "I'm going outside to chop wood." He whistled. "Riggs, come."

Riggs leaped to attention from his spot near the fireplace and trotted after him. Rush yanked the door open, and a blast of cold slammed into him, biting at his skin and seeping into his bones.

Good.

He needed a cooldown.

Chapter Nine

Lily needed to move.

She'd been cooped up in the cabin all day. Rush had spent most of the day outside, chopping firewood, shoveling snow, and keeping himself busy with whatever mountain men did. He'd come in only to warm up with a cup of coffee, his jaw tight, his words clipped, before heading right back out again with Riggs.

Clearly his energy needed an outlet, preferably one that didn't involve being stuck inside with her. She tried not to be offended. She didn't know the man after all, but after last night, she'd thought maybe they had gotten to know each other a little bit while sharing body heat. And then there was that raging erection of his in the shower... She was certain that wasn't him ignoring her. Mentally, she shrugged. Clearly, she wasn't an expert about men.

She'd spent the morning tidying the cabin as best she could —folding blankets, straightening the bed, even wiping down the kitchen counter despite the fact that nothing was dirty. It gave her something to do besides focusing on what life would look like when she finally went back home.

She poked around the cabinets and found more cans of soup and crackers, but she wasn't hungry yet. There were a few books and a chess set, a deck of cards, and a puzzle in a cabinet. She had grabbed a thriller to read for a few hours, but it only made her more anxious, along with the soulless eyes of the deer following her around. Finally, in a burst of rebellion and maybe a little passive-aggressiveness, she'd tossed her merry widow over the buck's head.

Later in the afternoon, she caught a glimpse of Rush through the window. The snow was still coming down as the sun dipped lower in the sky. It was gentler now, soft, thick flakes settling on top of the three feet already on the ground. He was splitting logs next to a shed—she could almost see the aura of tight, controlled energy rolling off him in short, sharp waves. His broad shoulders strained the jacket he wore, his collar turned up against the wind, and his dark hair was covered in a baseball cap. Guiltily, she remembered his warm beanie was still damp from when he gave it to her to wear.

In the distance, Riggs bounded over the drifts between trees, blissfully unaware of the surrounding tension.

Lily exhaled, pressing a hand to her chest to find the warm quartz. She always reached for it when her emotions felt too big and she needed peace. The warm, homey energy from the night before was gone, replaced by something heavier that left her unsettled. When she'd woken up this morning, the first thing she'd felt, aside from Rush's solid brick of a body, was contentment.

The realization had unsettled her. She'd spent years convincing herself that she and Tucker were meant to be, that she could *make* herself happy with him, that he was the safe and logical choice. So why wasn't she shattered right now to see that dream go up in flames?

If anything, she felt relieved. Lighter. Like she'd dodged a bullet instead of taking one to the chest.

The answer hovered at the edge of her mind, but she let it float there until she was ready to face it. Right now, she needed to shake off this bad energy and step outside, breathe in the cold, and let the snow clear her head.

After helping herself to Rush's hoodie to layer over his soft flannel shirt, she dug around in a basket near the door and found an old pair of waders a few sizes too big. They'd have to do. She stepped off the porch and immediately sank up to her knees in snow.

"Oh, *fantastic*," she muttered, stumbling forward as the snow immediately packed into her boots. It was worth it, though, when she looked up.

The world outside the cabin was an untouched carpet of white. The tall pine trees stood frozen beneath the weight of heavy snow, their branches sagging under a thick layer of ice. The sky, steel gray and endless on the mountain, was thick and heavy with the promise of more snow to come. A perfect, peaceful frozen wonderland.

Lily closed her eyes, inhaling deeply. *I am a still lake.* She exhaled slowly, releasing some of the weight pressing into her chest. She could almost feel herself realigning and calming, letting the nervous energy of the last few weeks sink into the earth and dissolve away.

Behind her, an axe struck wood with a solid, rhythmic *crack* echoing through the air. She turned in the opposite direction.

She didn't want to bother him—she could take a hint—but at least out here, she could breathe. She'd just keep to the other side of the cabin and not disturb him while she centered herself.

Lily planted her boots firmly in the snow, lifted her chin, and closed her eyes, settling into the silence, inhaling again with a palm to her chest and counted. *In... one, two, three... out, one, two, three...*

There. Lily opened her eyes, calm and centered once more.

And met the sharp, assessing gaze of a big black-and-tan dog.

She shrieked, stumbling back before catching herself, then looked around, feeling silly yet again. *Get it together, Lily.* She scanned the area again, but Riggs didn't move, merely stared at her with what she imagined were faintly dismissive eyes.

A spark of stubbornness flared to life.

"So, you're ignoring me too?" she called, shaking her head in disgust. "Figures. Just like your grumpy owner."

The massive dog took a single step toward her, and she started to back up automatically, almost like muscle memory, before catching herself. No, she wasn't going to let this dog intimidate her, dammit.

A fresh wave of frustration made Lily's heart pound. It wasn't that she was afraid of dogs—she loved dogs, actually—but she didn't like being dismissed. Heat rushed to her face. The peace and stillness she'd just felt shattered, and frustration boiled over.

She spotted a fallen branch and shook the snow free, hyping herself up. *All dogs like fetch, right?* Maybe not Amber's dog, Puddin'. She wasn't much for movement, but Allie had a golden retriever who thought playing fetch was the best thing on earth.

She waved the stick a little. "Here, scary dog. Come on, big guy," she coaxed, taking a hesitant step forward. "I know you want to play." *Please don't eat me, Cujo.*

Riggs stared at her, unmoved. Unimpressed.

Lily gave the stick another enticing shake. "I know you're a big scary military dog and very dignified, but this is a very nice stick."

Nothing.

He really is Rush's dog.

She huffed out a breath. "Okay, fine. Fetch!" She tossed the stick a few feet away, hoping that might do the trick.

Riggs didn't even flick an ear. Just sat there, rock-solid and motionless, as if the stick—and she—didn't exist.

Lily's hands landed on her hips. A slow burn of irritation, years in the making, set in. It wasn't just the dog. It was Rush and his coldness this morning. It was Tucker. Angela.

It was the fact that she'd almost deluded herself one more time that she could be happy with him.

And now this damn dog was treating her like she didn't exist either?

No.

Nope.

She straightened her spine, inhaled deeply, stalked toward the stick and picked it up. Narrowing her eyes, she walked to Riggs like she meant business.

Riggs's pointed ears flicked forward just slightly, like he was finally registering her existence. But instead of waiting for her to throw the stick again, his jaws opened, and he clamped down on the stick in her hand possessively.

He growled, sounding scary and maybe a little hungry, and tugged.

Lily froze, her instincts warning her to back off slowly. *Do not challenge Cujo.*

But then Rush's voice from last night echoed in her head.

He'd probably settle for a firm command and not acting like you're scared of him.

And that pissed her off. She wasn't scared. She was cautious. Riggs just needed to see her as the boss.

Lily took a deep, cleansing breath, and lowered her voice in her best imitation of Rush's deep, no-nonsense command. "Drop it."

Riggs didn't move.

Fine.

Some instinct inside of her knew she had to win this one, come hell or high water.

She squared her feet and projected as much calm, authoritative energy as she could summon.

"Drop it."

The tension stretched, silent and heavy, as Riggs's sharp black eyes seemed to assess her and find her wanting.

Seconds passed.

Then finally he released the stick.

It worked! She whooped and jumped in the air. "Good boy. You're the goodest boy, aren't you?"

Feeling victorious, she leaned down to give him a well-deserved pat. Riggs growled, and she snapped her hand back so fast she nearly dislocated her shoulder.

Riggs gave her a long, unimpressed stare. She cleared her throat, crossed her arms, and summoned Rush's no-nonsense presence.

Riggs's tail moved the tiniest wave, and he nudged the stick toward her the tiniest bit then sat back to watch her next move.

"We'll get there," she muttered under her breath, "Eventually. Probably."

She threw the stick as far as she could into the woods, and Riggs took off like a shot out of a cannon, bounding through the snow with pure, reckless enthusiasm. Watching him, something shifted in the air. Lily's shoulders relaxed, and she smiled at the sheer enthusiasm of the dog. It was almost as if he had been dying to play the entire time; he'd just wanted to make sure she was worth the effort.

She grinned. *Hell yes.*

Riggs bounded back, stick triumphantly lopsided in his

mouth, and impulsively she scooped up a ball of snow and threw it at him.

He jumped up to catch it, jaws opened wide, showing all those pointy teeth. He landed, looking briefly offended, then pure joy lit his doggy face as he charged straight at her.

"Oh. No. No, no, no."

She shrieked just as he leaped, knocking her flat into the snow.

~

"Riggs! Off!"

Rush's voice cracked across the frozen yard, and Riggs immediately froze—but not before one bony leg caught her in the stomach. Lily yelped, twisting to escape, but the massive dog was having none of it. She let out a breathless laugh as Riggs, tail wagging wildly, his massive paws on both of her shoulders, stared down at her.

"Riggs! You big oaf—get off!" It came out more of a breathless giggle than a command.

But he wasn't listening anyway. He was too delighted. He licked the snow straight off her face, wagging his tail so hard his entire body wriggled with happiness above her. She buried her hands in the warm underbelly of the dog and pushed. He didn't budge. Instead, he lay down on her, nearly crushing her with his weight, and licked another slow, deliberate path over her face before sitting back with a pleased doggy grin.

Her lungs, already wheezy from the cold, constricted even more under his weight, but she didn't care. She stroked his soft fur and grinned back at him.

"Off!"

Rush's voice cut sharply through the air.

The dog's weight vanished instantly. Lily curled into a ball with a groan.

"Lily!" Rush's voice was tight with concern. And then he was by her side, brushing the hair off her face and turning her over.

Lily blinked up at him while she caught her breath. "I'm fine," she managed, still breathless.

His broad shoulders, encased in his sheepskin jacket, blocked out the sky, and the world narrowed to the two of them in the crystalized snow globe they were in. This close, she could see the different shades of gray in his eyes as he looked her over matter-of-factly.

Rush exhaled sharply, his frown deepening between his brows as she lay silently taking him in. She should probably reassure him, say something light. But she was distracted.

By the way the winter light caught on the perfect, individual snowflakes dotting his hat and the thick black hair that curled around the edges. She wanted to reach up, to take his hat off, and feel the silky-looking strands between her fingers. He had beautiful eyelashes, framing the most gorgeous pair of clear gray eyes she'd ever seen.

His square jawline, covered in the kind of scruff that made her want to run her fingers over it, flexed as his gloved hands skimmed lightly over her arms, waist, shoulders, searching for wounds, leaving a flutter of something wonderfully sensual low in her stomach and between her thighs. It had been a long time since someone had touched her like that, with that much focus. God, it felt so good to be touched again. Her lips curved into a smile before she could stop them.

"Does anything hurt? Did you hit your head?" he said in a low voice that caused a shiver to run through her body.

Only in a way that you're making worse.

She didn't say it. Instead, she just smiled up at him, soaking in his warmth and the careful way his fingers brushed over her skin despite the barriers of coats and gloves.

He hesitated then brushed a lock of her icy hair back from her face, his frown deepening at what he saw there.

"Are you laughing?" he asked incredulously.

She knew that look. He still thought she was a little crazy. It should have been insulting, but she'd seen that expression her whole life—from the people she loved most, who thought they understood her better than she understood herself.

Rush Callahan was no different.

"Lily, do you know where you are?" he asked, his voice cautious.

The sheer ridiculousness of the question hit her like a slap of cold air. Oh, for God's sake. Again?

Exasperation flared hot in her chest. Without thinking, she scooped up a handful of snow and smashed it into his face, grinning at the look of pure astonishment on Sheriff Rush Callahan's too-handsome, too-serious face. Snow clung to his mustache in the most distracting way, and for a second all she could think about was how much she wanted to brush it off—or maybe kiss it off, but Lily forced herself to focus. She had to kick his ass in a snowball fight.

"Oh, relax, Sheriff." Lily grinned, breath puffing in the cold air. "I haven't lost my marbles. Riggs and I were having a snowball fight. Haven't you ever done that before?"

His expression changed from concern to a slow grin that made her tremble. Lord, the man was too sexy for his own good. She reached for her only defense, a ball of snow, and leveled it at his face, before scrambling to her feet to arm herself again.

She barely had time to cover herself before a snowball hit her square in the chest. The icy shock of it took her breath away for a second before she scooped another handful of snow, whooping with delight. Riggs barked excitedly, bounding around them, his eyes pleading to join in.

So she threw a snowball right at his chest.

All hell broke loose.

She launched herself into the battle, giggling so hard her lungs ached. Rush was relentless, his aim too damn good, but she fought dirty, and years of dance and yoga had made her quick and limber. She twirled out of his aim and shot a handful of snow down his collar. Another perfectly placed shot to the back of his head when he bent down made her laugh out loud.

They were everywhere, snow flying in all directions, laughter spilling into the crisp air. Rush laughed—an actual laugh—low and unrestrained, and the sound made something flutter in her chest.

It was the most beautiful sound.

With a growl, Rush took her out by the knees, and she collapsed willingly back into the snow, happier than she could remember being in... maybe forever. Her lungs were tight, a warning she knew all too well, but the sheer joy of the moment distracted her.

Rush's hands found the back of her head as she hit the ground, his strong grip guiding her down as his body followed, solid and unyielding as he pressed her back. She barely had a second to catch her breath before he was above her, flashing strong white teeth in a wicked grin. Lily sucked in her breath, her pulse skittering as she reached for more snow, but he was faster.

His hands shot out, catching her wrists and dragging them above her head, arching her back and pinning her firmly into the cold, pillowy snow. Defeated at last, she looked up, breathless and buzzing with adrenaline from the press of his body against hers.

"Say uncle," Rush demanded, his voice huskier than before. His breath puffed against her, warm against her chilled skin.

"Never," she whispered, her grin fading as she became aware of their position. Her breasts pressed into his chest, and she wondered if he could feel the hard points of her nipples through their layers.

Lily wiggled her arms, testing the strength of his hold on her wrists, but he didn't budge. Her breath hitched. *Oh.* His thigh snugged up close between hers, and through her thin sweatpants and his jeans, she felt the solid thickness of him pressed tightly between her legs. She went still. A slow, liquid heat warmed her, pooling low and deep in a way that had nothing to do with adrenaline and everything to do with a visceral response to the man settled between her thighs.

Instinctively, her legs drew up on either side of his hips, tightening and cradling his hardness. The laughter in Rush's eyes faded, and his pupils darkened, flickering over her face lazily, down to her mouth and lingering there when her tongue darted out to lick her suddenly dry lips.

A nudge from Riggs's cold, wet muzzle in the crook of her neck broke the spell. Lily laughed at the sensation, but Rush didn't smile.

"Go play," Rush murmured, his voice lower now, more gravel than words, his gaze steady on hers. Riggs trotted off, but Lily barely registered it, so focused on the intensity of his eyes. Her smile faded slowly, replaced with something much, much heavier. Hotter.

Rush's fingers flexed around her wrists, not tight enough to hurt, but firm enough that her brain glimpsed what he was capable of. Power and submission. Control and restraint.

Strangely, the thought exhilarated her.

Her breath stuttered out unevenly while she studied his face. The sharp cut of his jaw and the storm brewing in his eyes, waiting. Testing her. He was a solid, unmovable weight on her, and it felt so good she let out a whimper and lifted her hip, pressing herself against him.

"Lily." His voice was a rough warning.

A shiver shot down her spine. She should pull away. She should say something funny, anything, to break the charged silence stretching too long between them to be anything other than what it was.

"Tell me to stop," he said.

She swallowed hard. She should. She really should.

"Don't stop," she whispered instead.

Rush let go of one wrist. His thumb came down to gently swipe away the snowflakes from her cheek. The gentle gesture made her ache. She wanted more. So much more.

So she reached up, threading her fingers through his thick black hair—his hat was long gone—to brush the snow away, her fingers lingering to caress him. The warmth of his skull, the scratch of his beard against her fingertips—just as deliciously rough as she'd imagined. He smelled like icy-cold winter and the wood he'd been chopping and the smoke of the fire in the cabin, masculine and delicious enough to make her want to twine her arms around his neck to pull him closer.

A tight, electric feeling gripped her, curling deep in her stomach, unfurling through her limbs like a slow, smoldering flame. The laughter faded, leaving behind something wicked and heavy and inevitable between them. Rush bent his head, his breath warm against her chilled lips, and she let her eyes drift closed.

And her lungs gave out.

A wheeze tore from her throat, shattering the moment. She opened her eyes, watching almost mournfully as Rush's expression shifted from molten-hot lust to a sharply clinical look.

"Where's your inhaler?" he barked, already moving, his heat vanishing as he quickly got off her and hauled her to her feet.

Just like that, the fire was gone. Lily bent forward and tried to suck in air.

Of course.

All her life, asthma had intruded at the worst possible moments.

She was seconds away from being kissed within an inch of her life...

And her lungs had decided now was the time to stop breathing.

Chapter Ten

"Take a deep breath."

Rush, his eyes sharp, pressed the inhaler to her mouth. They were on the couch in the cabin now; the fire dancing merrily in the stove, but all Lily could focus on was the tight, vise-like grip on her lungs.

She wanted to snap at him, tell him she was trying to breathe—that she always had to think about breathing, such a simple thing that most people took for granted. But her lungs stole the words from her as usual. Frustration, hot and bitter, burned through her, but she swallowed it down and focused.

One, two, three.

She inhaled another puff of the medicine, the cold mist filling her lungs, loosening the pressure that wrapped around her ribs like a clamp. The feeling of not being able to breathe never got any less terrifying, even after all these years. But what made it worse, so much worse, was that Sheriff Sexy got to see her struggle this time.

She squeezed her eyes closed in silent misery, aware that her hair was a wild mess, half of it falling from her braid, damp with melted snow. Her cheeks burned from the wind, her nose was probably pink, and she could still feel where a chunk of snow had lodged itself down the back of her shirt. She was braless, makeup-less, and feeling less than sexy.

Like a bedraggled disaster instead of the confident woman she saw reflected in Rush's eyes for that brief moment in the snow when he was on top of her.

When he was about to kiss her.

Her eyes watered, and not from lack of air this time.

Embarrassment burned hotter than the tightness in her lungs, making her feel even more exposed. She wasn't supposed to be like this. This version of her wasn't the one she wanted Rush to see. She wanted him to see her as desirable. Strong. The way she'd felt before, when he'd pinned her in the snow, when her wrists were locked in his grip and heat had curled low in her belly. Not like... this.

Rush, as stoic and unshakable as ever, was watching her like she was his problem to solve instead of kissing her senseless.

Rush's hand moved in slow, steady circles on her back, calm and methodical, like he was soothing a wounded animal. And damn it, it was working. Her body instinctively leaned into the comfort of him, chasing the heat and the solid, grounding feel of him. His hands were large and calloused from hard work, dragging against the flannel shirt of his she wore with each warm stroke. An unsteady shiver ran through her, a sharp contrast to the burning in her lungs.

"That's it. Take another one. Slow and easy," he murmured, his voice low and so damn sure of what she needed.

Lily squeezed her eyes closed, trying to will her face to stop flushing.

Rush had wanted her just as much as she wanted him. She knew it. She'd seen it in the way his cool gray-steel eyes darkened to something molten hot. In the way his gaze had lingered over her mouth, his jaw flexing when she'd licked her lips.

She'd felt it in the way his hands had gripped her, rough and firm, fingers digging into her waist like he was testing the shape of her, mapping her body. And yet, beneath his strength, there had been something precisely careful about the way he had held her down. Like he knew exactly how much force to use to make her mouth go dry and her belly flutter in anticipation.

And then her body had betrayed her.

Tucker's voice slithered in her mind. *It's always something with you, Lily,* he'd muttered under his breath more times than she could count.

She'd pretended not to hear.

She pretended now.

"I'm okay." The words scraped out of her throat. She forced herself to sit up, breaking contact with Rush's body even though she wanted—God, she wanted—to stay there. She sniffed, lifted her chin, and pushed to her feet, ignoring the wobble in her legs.

Nothing about this moment was usual. Despite her humiliation, her pulse still hummed from that almost-kiss, and the way Rush's hard body had pressed against hers in all the most sensitive places and had left her feeling quivery in a way she never had before. Lord, the man had enough sex appeal to melt all the snow on the mountain. She knew she was way out of her league with experience, but that hadn't stopped her from wanting to learn what his lips tasted like.

Rush's brows lowered. He sat back abruptly on the couch, crossing his arms over his broad chest, and looked her over with clinical precision that made her feel as womanly as a doorknob.

"Do you usually wrestle with dogs outside in the snow without your inhaler?" His bossy sheriff voice was back, and Lily stiffened. Intimidating or not, she wasn't a suspect.

"No," she said stiffly, shooting Riggs a quick glare. The dog yawned hugely and collapsed into a heap beside the stove to lick his paws, ignoring her completely as if they hadn't had a come-to-Jesus moment. *Traitor*.

She narrowed her eyes at Rush. She wasn't going to let him bulldoze her just because he was big and broody and wore a badge. "Riggs"— at his name, the dog's black ears perked up, his head tilting as if listening—"and I were coming to an understanding. He's learning to respect me," she added.

Rush exhaled sharply, looking a bit too intimidating for her comfort. "What if I wasn't here, Lily?" he asked evenly. "What then? Would Riggs have carried you inside? Found your inhaler?"

There was no accusation in the question, no lecture. Just a *what if* that landed on her like a weight. Old Lily would have apologized, rushed to smooth things over and promised to be more careful. But New Lily was done being handled, done being smothered by well-meaning people who thought they knew what was best for her.

Her chin rose a fraction higher. "I know how to take care of myself."

Rush's lips pressed together, his jaw flexing like he was holding something back. "Then act like it," he said, not unkindly, but firmly. "I've known you for a few days, and so far, I've seen you run out of church in a blaze of glory and survive a deadly snowstorm, and now you're out here wrestling with my dog." His eyes held hers steadily, something flickering behind them before his mouth curved. "Maybe just make sure your inhaler is in your pocket when you're being a badass," he added dryly.

The words knocked her off-balance more than his concern. She was used to people hovering and worrying, being handled rather than being trusted to take care of herself. But Rush wasn't looking at her like she was fragile. He was looking at her like he admired her, and it felt pretty amazing.

A slow grin spread across her lips. "For the record, I didn't get tackled. We were playing a game."

Riggs cocked his head the other way, as if contradicting her, and let out a sharp bark that made her flinch. *Dammit.* She restrained herself from sticking out her tongue at him.

Rush's eyes flicked to her mouth, just for a second, but it was enough to make her stomach swoop.

"Yeah," he said, his voice lower. "I noticed."

"I don't need a babysitter, Rush," she said quietly. Her heart thudded in her ears, but she forced herself to hold his gaze. She sensed this was too important to let go. "I don't need anyone deciding what's best for me."

His dark brows lifted, but he didn't argue. He just studied her, eyes locked on hers, holding her breath in place.

Then, to her absolute shock, the corner of his mouth curved up. "Noted."

He turned back to the fire, as if that was that, leaving her standing there, breathless and flushed with an unfamiliar thrill. New Lily *was* pretty badass.

Chapter Eleven

"You know, I have some training in massage therapy," Lily said later that evening. She tried to sound more casual than she felt. "That looks like it hurts."

She held her breath and waited for Rush to answer.

They had dinner earlier—more canned soup. Then she'd taken an unpleasantly cold shower, secretly hoping Rush would join her.

He didn't, of course.

Instead, he'd waited until she was finished then strode into the bathroom with his towel and a fresh change of clothes, depriving her of a glimpse of him in a towel. When he emerged a while later, dressed in a soft pair of gray sweatpants that hung low on his hips and a fitted cream-colored Henley that stretched across his broad chest, she felt robbed. He tugged his ever-present baseball cap low, shading his eyes from her.

They had settled into the evening like an old married couple in front of the fire, which crackled in the stove, filling the cabin with a steady, calm warmth. Outside, the wind still howled against the windows, rattling the glass like it wanted in, but the cabin felt snug and warm and very quiet.

Too quiet. Lily stretched out on the couch, her foot swinging with nervous energy over the edge, and quit pretending to read. The book couldn't hold her interest with the biggest distraction of her life—Rush Callahan—across from her in the chair by the fire, gazing into the flames. Her mind kept drifting to the storm outside, the warmth of the fire, the man across from her... and the feeling of him on top of her.

Rush's expression was unreadable while he watched the fire, but every so often, he rubbed absently at his thigh. She tried not to watch. Really tried, but her eyes had a mind of their own, and they were drawn to him like a magnet, and she had finally worked up the nerve to ask him about it.

Rush's hands tightened around his glass at her question. He had long fingers, the backs sprinkled with dark, curly hair—masculine and strong, even with the bruising and cuts. Those rough hands had slid so gently across her cheek to wipe away the snow. She dragged her eyes away to find him taking a slow sip of whiskey, and she watched his strong throat work as he swallowed.

"I'm fine," he said finally. There was a warning in his voice that she didn't acknowledge.

"You've been rubbing your thigh for the last half hour. Did you hurt it again earlier?" *Perhaps chopping wood or maybe when you guided me onto my back in the snow and came down on top of me.*

He didn't answer right away, so she pushed forward before she could overthink it. When else would she have this moment? *Brave Lily. Real Lily.*

"Here, let me." She stepped between his knees, acting on instinct, until her nerves caught up with her and she hesitated.

Riggs lifted his head when she took another step closer, and he growled a warning.

She edged back. "I thought we came to a truce," she muttered, peeved that their bonding moment hadn't lasted.

"Quiet," Rush commanded the dog. "He still thinks he's the boss of you."

"He's not the boss of me."

The corner of Rush's mouth curved crookedly. It did something to her insides. "I'd say you're wrong about that, angel."

Angel. She let the nickname slide, even though the sound of it sent a warm rush through her, and met his eyes squarely for permission.

Rush nodded slowly, and she sank to her knees between his thighs. His eyes were hidden, but she felt his reaction throughout his body. His thigh muscles bunched and flexed, and his free hand gripped the arm of the chair. She felt that deep inside.

Lily swallowed, her pulse hammering so hard she was sure he could see it, and reached for him. Her fingers brushed over the thin cotton that clung to his thighs, feeling the heat of him radiating through the material.

She pulled back and rubbed her hands together, glancing up shyly. "My hands are cold, but they'll warm up fast." She rested them lightly on top of his knees.

Rush went completely still. Then, with a slow nod, he leaned back and closed his eyes.

Her fingertips drifted higher, brushing over firm muscle. She lingered over the strong curves and ridges of his thighs, feeling the strength there. Her hand grazed higher, gliding over the ridge of scar tissue she'd glimpsed in the shower. Carefully, she traced the uneven texture, feeling the raised lines and ripples.

A sharp current of sadness filled her. She sensed that this was a piece of him he probably didn't talk about, yet he was allowing her to help ease his pain. It felt intimate in a way she wasn't used to, a peek under the armor of Sheriff Rush Callahan she wasn't entirely sure how to handle.

"From the accident?" she asked quietly, eyes lowered. She hadn't meant to bring it up, but the question slipped out as her fingers worked gently over the scarred muscle in his thigh.

Rush didn't answer. He went still in that quiet, locked-down way she was beginning to recognize, and took a long sip of whiskey. She kept her hands steady, her strokes long and firm and careful around the damaged tissue. Her training took over. *Focus on the body. Listen to what's unspoken.* She didn't need words to understand the tension locked deep inside him.

After a moment, he shifted slightly in the chair and let his legs fall open wider. His silence wasn't permission, but it wasn't refusal either.

So she kept going.

"Is that why you were heading up here?" she asked. "Because Caroline Whitmore's memorial is this week?"

The tensing of his thigh told her exactly what he thought about her questions.

Rush's eyes opened, and he looked down at her silently, his face stern. A warning, if she chose to take it.

She met his gaze steadily.

He took another slow sip of whiskey, and briefly, so briefly she would have missed it had she not been kneeling before him, his expression cracked. But Lily caught it, and her heart ached at what she saw there. Grief. Pain. The weight of that night crushing him.

"I don't want to talk about that," he said, staring into the fire.

"Because I know the Whitmores, and I know they want to thank you—"

"No." He caught her wrist in one hand, tugging her off-balance until she leaned into his body. They were so close their breaths mingled, and his eyes, dark, flinty steel, held hers.

"Don't," he said with enough finality that she found herself speechless.

Rush let go of her hand, stroking the bones along her wrist like a silent apology. He looked hard and closed off, and she got the message loud and clear: no more questions.

She pressed her fingers deeper into his muscle, smoothing her palm over the scar one last time. Rush leaned back in the chair, imposing even while relaxing—all dark stubble and broad shoulders, long legs stretched out, taking up the surrounding space. The firelight cast sharp shadows over his face, highlighting the rough edges and the quiet power he held so effortlessly.

A slow, electric shiver rolled through her, unfurling down her spine as she kneeled before his spread thighs. The heat in her chest spread lower, pooling deep and unfamiliar in its intensity. The air between them crackled with something she'd never felt so strongly. *Desire.*

She wanted him. The rough scrape of his hands, the weight of his body—she craved all of it. The kind of heat that stole reason and left only need.

Unsmiling, his hand caught hers and held it for a moment. "That feels better. Thank you."

She nodded, slipping her hand from his and rising to her feet. Her gaze locked on a deck of cards on the table from earlier. She latched onto the distraction eagerly.

"Do you know how to play poker?"

RUSH RAISED A BROW, watching Lily lean forward to expertly shuffle the deck, her delicate fingers making quick work of the cards. *Damn, she's cute when she's trying to be badass.*

"Do you?"

She raised her chin, all sexy confidence. All bravado. But he knew better now. He'd picked up on the flicker of nerves in her eyes when she thought he wasn't looking, and the way she hesitated half a second before speaking. Then there was the way she played with the pink stone around her neck, rolling it between her fingers like a habit she wasn't aware of.

But she didn't want him to know she was nervous. That was what made it cute as hell.

His gaze drifted downward, lingering over the soft curves hidden beneath the borrowed clothing. Another of his flannel shirts swallowed her slight frame, hanging almost to her knees, and his running pants rolled at her waist a few times. The soft fabrics highlighted the curves of her hips and the gentle sway of her breasts under his shirt, making him remember the lush, full shape of them in the shower. Was she wearing anything under his shirt now?

"Of course I do. Didn't they teach you that in the army?"

"Marines," he corrected.

Lily gasped, all faux innocence, then flashed him a wicked, sparkling grin that did dangerous things to his self-control. "Oorah, soldier."

She had no idea what she was doing to him. She'd rolled the sleeves up haphazardly, revealing her pale skin and delicate wrists, and the top few buttons were undone, giving him a tantalizing glimpse of deep, deep cleavage whenever she leaned over to deal him a card, answering his unspoken question. Nothing. She wasn't wearing anything under his flannel. *Ah, hell.* It was going to be a long night.

"Well, it's time for me to kick your ass, Sheriff," she said, tapping the deck confidently. "I learned from the very best."

He took the bait, shifting to relieve the growing pressure against his zipper.

"From Tucker?" he asked. That asshole. He didn't know

exactly what Lily had run from, but he had a solid enough idea, and his opinion of the guy, already low, sank even further.

"No." She laughed. "Definitely not. I kicked his ass all the time in cards. From my sister, Amber. Nobody beats her, not even her husband."

Rush nodded, filing that away. She was close to her family. He'd known that from seeing the Hart women around town, but hearing the affection in her voice made him feel better about what she would go home to.

He didn't know Lily all that well aside from a polite nod around town, and the way she blushed when she ran into him, but he knew enough. She was softer than most, but there was something about her too. A quiet kind of stubbornness under all that sweetness. He liked that. More than he should.

He looked over his cards, but any focus he had was shot to hell the second his gaze drifted back to Lily.

She was sexy in a way that turned on every one of his buttons, curvy and big-breasted, with beautiful rounded hips and strong, sleek legs he wanted wrapped around every part of his body, preferably his head first.

But the worst part—the part that was making his fingers flex around the glass of whiskey—was the way she was nibbling on that pouty bottom lip.

He nearly groaned. That mouth was driving him crazy.

He was already nearly obsessed with it. The delicate pink color that he knew matched her nipples. Oh, fuck. He needed to get his shit together. Coming so close to kissing her outside had been a mistake, but fuck if he didn't want to do it again. Over and over again until he memorized every sound she made.

And then there was the way she'd touched him earlier. Watching her kneel between his legs while she worked her hands over his thigh had been a test of pure willpower. Her hands were small but strong. Each stroke of her hands on him had sent shards of fire straight to his cock, and he'd had a hell of a time not pulling her up and onto his lap to see how she would feel against him.

Letting Lily put her hands on him wasn't his best idea. He had a feeling that she could make a man think about staying a while.

And that wasn't in the cards.

"You're close with your family," he said, forcing himself back to safer ground.

"Very," she murmured distantly, not taking her eyes off her cards. "They smother me with their concern, but I love them all the same." She paused, tucking her legs underneath her. "I have three sisters—Evie's my twin, then Amber, and Allie is the oldest. Evie and I are the youngest. And then my mom—I'm sure you've seen her around. She owns the interior design studio on Main Street."

Rush nodded, looking over his cards, suppressing a grimace. Garbage hand.

He'd met Annette Hart and most of her family in passing on his rounds through town. They were a well-known family around Northfield—wealthy and well respected.

Across from him, Lily sat cross-legged and tried to contain her glee as she looked at her hand. She was as transparent as glass. It was endearing as hell.

"How about a wager?" she asked innocently. Her color was high in her cheeks, her expression pure innocence, but she couldn't hide the mischief in her eyes. She tucked her bottom lip between her teeth again and pretended to think.

Rush sat back, watching her, and held onto his laugh.

He nodded, pretending to look over his terrible hand again, but instead let himself watch her. Hell, he enjoyed everything about her. The cabin would have been damn lonely without her. For all he teased her when she talked about her wacky energy stuff, she was a delight so far.

And he wanted to fuck her. There was that too.

"What would you like to wager?" He knew—he hoped—he knew what she would say.

Because he wanted it too. More than he could remember wanting almost anything. But he needed her to say it.

She blushed, a gorgeous rosy pink that bloomed over her cheeks, and he wondered with great interest how far down the color went.

Did it skim over her long pale throat? Spread lower past her collarbone to those beautiful, full tits? Did it touch her nipples? He knew exactly what those looked like when they were tight and flushed for him.

"Can I have a sip of that?" She nodded toward the glass in his hand.

"Have you ever had whiskey?" he asked skeptically.

"Yeah, all the time," she said archly. "While I played poker."

He didn't believe her, but it didn't matter, because she took the glass from him, inhaled deeply, and then pounded it quickly back like it was a shot instead of a sip meant to be savored.

She gasped, eyes going wide as she coughed and sputtered. Her whole body shuddered, and her eyes watered.

"All the time, huh?" he drawled, watching her try to compose herself.

Lily sucked in a breath. "All. The. Time."

He did laugh then, shaking his head at her when she grinned back at him unrepentantly. "You want to try again there, angel? See if it goes down any smoother?" He poured another shot.

"Maybe later," she said primly, making him laugh harder.

She fixed him with a look. "Let's wager a kiss," she said,

with that mix of shyness and mischief of hers that was proving to drive him wild.

Hell yes. "And if I win?" he asked, low.

Lily pulled her lip in again, her bravado flickering under the intensity of his stare. He waited, wondering if she would back out, and admiring her once again. She really was beautiful, all delicate angles and long, lovely lines. Her high cheekbones were flushed pink from the fire. Her full lips curved up and begged to be nipped and sucked, and big, expressive eyes gave her away every time.

She lifted her chin and cocked an eyebrow at him. "Anything you want."

His breath left him. *Well fucking done, Lily.*

He grinned slowly. Deliberately, letting the anticipation stretch between them. He dragged his gaze over her, taking in the way her chest rose and fell, the tight grip on her cards. "Let's see what you've got," he murmured.

Lily swallowed, a flicker of nervousness crossing her face. She put her cards down with a snap. "Full house," she declared, a challenge in her voice that made the caveman in him want to drag her to the bed and ravish her.

He showed his hand, thoroughly enjoying her little bounce when she realized she had won. His eyes dipped again. How could they not? Her breasts shifted under his flannel, soft and perfect, making his mouth go dry and his cock stiffen at a vision of Lily straddling him, those plump tits bouncing just like that while he licked and sucked them.

Fuck.

He swirled the amber liquid in his glass and watched the way it caught the light before taking a slow sip, letting the burn ground him before he did something truly reckless.

She grinned smugly and reached for his glass.

He caught her wrist, wrapping his fingers around the small bones in her wrist. "No more shots."

"No more?" she asked, raising a brow. "I think the winner deserves a drink, don't you?"

Rush shook his head slowly, still holding onto her wrist, his thumb tracing a lazy, deliberate stroke over her pulse. Fast. Fluttering wildly under her smooth skin.

"Not like that," he said quietly. Firmly. Her pupils went wide, her irises darkening to a deeper green. Dazed and wanting. "Whiskey's meant to be taken slow. Let it linger. Sink in."

She swallowed hard, her tongue darting out to wet her lips. He wanted to feel that tongue against his, slick and warm, tasting exactly how he knew she'd taste—sweet and hot. Addictive.

He exhaled slowly and sat back in the chair. "Riggs, go lie down," Rush ordered quietly. Riggs's collar jingled as he walked to the fireplace and lay down facing the fire with a huff of breath, uninterested in whatever was about to happen next.

"Come here." His voice was rough and a little bossy. He didn't miss the way her eyes dilated at his tone, as if she liked him like that, a little demanding. He filed that away for later.

She didn't hesitate, rising gracefully to lower herself onto the coffee table in front of him. For all her outward confidence, there was a note of something else in Lily that intrigued him. He could sense her hesitation. Maybe innocence. It made him want to protect her and dirty her up at the same time.

"Here?" Her voice was soft and breathy now. He felt as if she'd stroked his body with her mouth.

He nodded, never breaking eye contact. Slowly, deliberately, he took another sip of whiskey, letting the slow burn slide over his tongue, letting her watch.

Then, without hesitation, he reached out, sliding a hand through the wild red waves of her hair to curl his fingers around the nape of her neck. The strands were still damp, carrying the scent of his soap, but under it, something softer, more feminine. Lily. The mix of the two, his scent and hers, made him wild.

He felt the shiver that ran through her, a flutter of sensation against him as light as a butterfly.

And then he kissed her.

Slowly. Deeply. Decadently.

She trembled, her lips parting with a sigh. Her head tilted back, and she met his eyes while he studied her face, her full lower lip that begged to be nipped. The freckles on her nose. Her pulse fluttered wildly in her throat, and those wide green eyes stared back at him, a heady mix of bold desire and shyness.

He took his time, coaxing, brushing her mouth with his, until she melted against him with a whimper. And then he gave her what he'd been dying to give.

He parted his lips, stroking the whiskey into the sweet silkiness of her mouth, letting her taste it the way he wanted her to—from him, on him, hot and slow and intoxicating.

She whimpered, opening wider, and he groaned, taking more.

His hands slid to her face, thumbs stroking over the delicate line of her jaw as he kissed her deeper, filthier, until she had no choice but to hold on to him. She tasted like sweet, hot liquor. He worked his fingers back into the heavy fall of her hair and held her mouth still.

Teaching. Tempting. Showing her exactly how he liked to drink his whiskey best.

Chapter Twelve

RUSH CALLAHAN KISSED like a man who was used to control—firm, unyielding, daring her to stop him. She had no intention of stopping. After years without another man's mouth on hers, it felt like rain after a drought.

When he finally leaned back, licking the last taste of smoky whiskey from her lips, she opened her eyes slowly. His chest rose and fell as he flicked his eyes over her mouth hungrily. His eyes were darker than she'd seen them yet. His tongue came out, swiping a drop of whiskey from her bottom lip. The slow, hot slide of him against her mouth drove her wild.

She lunged.

The discipline she'd always clung to snapped—twisted and molded into something wild and reckless. She slid off the coffee table and landed in his lap, cupping his face, tangling her fingers in his hair as she pressed her lips to his and kissed that dirty grin right off his face.

He was ready for her.

One big hand cupped the back of her head. The other arm pulled her down, down, until she settled perfectly into the cove of his lap, her thighs spread wide on either side of his hips. His palm landed on her ass, guiding her against him while she kissed him for all she was worth.

He let her play first, tasting him in soft, delicate forays. Teasing. Caressing his jaw and feeling the scrape of his beard on her palms, using her thumbs to open his lips to her even more. He tasted like whiskey and every fantasy she'd ever had in her life, a little rough, a lot dirty, more than she could probably handle. She wanted to try.

Lord help her, she wanted everything he could give her.

She wiggled deeper into his lap, desperate to feel more of him pressed tight against where she ached. His lips were firm, his mustache silky when she traced a line with her tongue over the top of his full lip. His hands slid up her thighs, roaming over her hips, urging her on with his touch.

God, she needed this. Needed him. Needed to forget every second of doubt and loneliness that had been clawing at her. Rush burned all of it away.

He gripped her tighter, one hand gripping her ass, the other flexing around the back of her neck, keeping her core pressed tight against the thick ridge.

"Oh," she breathed, rubbing against him.

He bit her bottom lip, tugging gently, then tilted her head to take more of him, deeper, until she was trembling and needy. Everything about kissing Rush Callahan was overwhelming in the best way possible. Hot and consuming, filthy, and completely addictive.

A perfect mix of control and chaos, like they could go off the rails at any second, and that was what made her come back for more. Years of placid, routine sex had trained her to think about passion as something measured and neat, not as necessary for her as it seemed like it was for others. But Rush's kisses gave her a glimpse into what it could be like to forget decorum and let her body lead.

She melted into him, shivering, embarrassed by how close she was to coming just from a kiss. *Don't embarrass yourself, Lily.*

He nipped at her lip, teasing, before trailing lower, tasting the curve of her jaw, the delicate point of her chin. His lips slid down, capturing the tendon in her neck between his teeth, sucking just hard enough to make her gasp.

She sighed as he dragged her body along his. His cock pressed hot and hard through the thin fabric of their sweatpants, every inch outlined and throbbing against her.

It was liquid fire, the sharp currents of electricity that sparked from her neck to her pussy, making her tilt her head back for more.

"Rush," she whispered, threading her fingers through his hair, knocking his hat to the floor as she pulled him closer. Her breasts felt heavy, the ache between her legs deep and insistent, her nipples tight and pulsing with need. "More," she breathed, grinding against him—faster and harder. More pressure. More friction. More of him.

He pulled back just enough to look at her, his eyes dark and burning. His mouth hovered over hers, teasing, before he crushed another hard kiss on her lips. He groaned, low and deep, thrusting his hips up against her once, hard. But his grip was firm when he threaded his fingers through her hair and eased her back, looking her square in the face.

"Stop," he rasped. He pushed her back, shifting her away from where there had been nothing but heat and hunger. His breathing came in ragged pulls, his pupils blown as he took her in with a hot gaze.

Lily knew what he saw. She was flushed and panting; her lips felt kiss-swollen and tender. Her chest rose unevenly, the thin fabric of the flannel outlining her taut nipples straining toward him. Her thighs trembled around his body, betraying just how much need she had pent up.

"Why?" she whispered, terribly afraid that she knew what he would say.

"What's this about, Lily?" Rush asked bluntly. His tone was a low command, and she didn't think to shy away from the truth or couch her answer with coyness.

"I want you," she said, wincing at the shakiness in her voice.

Rush leaned down and delicately grazed her collarbone with his teeth, the scrape of his cheek against her tender throat making her gasp.

Then he pulled back, his hand stilling her hips, and pinned her with a hard look.

"I want to fuck you, Lily."

Her heart stuttered—*yes! God, yes!*—but before she could melt into the words, his next ones landed, sharp and measured.

"I know you can feel that," he said roughly, thrusting up, making his arousal blatant against her. "But I need to hear you say it."

Lily blinked. For her, for once, there was no confusion over what she wanted. There was only heat and need and a craving for the man whose lap she was spread out on. But as she looked at the hard set of his jaw and the heat in his eyes, she knew what he was asking, and she understood. Rush wasn't the kind of man to take something she wasn't sure about.

"I want you," she whispered. "I want this."

He grinned then, a slow, crooked tilt of his lips that made her insides do silly things. "Good, darlin'. That's real good, 'cause I'm going to give it to you."

She tilted her hips, grinding a slow, deliberate circle over his lap, her body answering for her.

A shudder rolled through her as she felt him, thick and unyielding beneath her, the friction igniting something deep and hot inside her. This. This was what had always eluded her. What she'd heard only in whispers from her sisters and friends, what she'd read about in books. Not just desire but ownership too. Of her body and her choices.

Rush wasn't stopping her. He wasn't telling her to slow down, to be careful, to think this through. He wasn't deciding anything for her. He was just here—solid, steady, sexy as sin. For once, she didn't have to think about making the right choice, weighing how her decisions would affect everyone else. She could just feel. She could want and be wanted.

Oh God, she wanted.

A wild, unashamed part of her, one she might have been ashamed of in the light of day, rose up, greedy and feral with need. She felt the shake in his big arms, the tension in his muscles, and something deep inside her reveled in the knowledge that she had done that to him. That she could unravel a man like Rush Callahan. That she, the girl who had spent her life not making waves, could make a man like him shake.

She had never been more certain of anything in her life.

She rolled her hips again for the sheer pleasure of it, chasing that delicious pressure, the exquisite press of him against her. She wasn't waiting to be told what to do or how to be in this moment. In this moment, she was nothing but sensation and want, raw and uninhibited.

She sat back, balancing her hands on either side of his knees, and arched against him, thrusting her breasts up like an offering.

His eyes flickered for an instant while she held her breath, desperately hoping he trusted her enough to know what she wanted for herself.

His eyes flared hotter than ever. His big, rough hands slid up her thighs, curved around her waist, dragging her tighter and tighter against his cock. He paused then, leaning back, looking at her hotly. A low order rumbled from him. "Show me."

With her fingers trembling, Lily unbuttoned the flannel shirt she wore, uncovering herself for him. The soft fabric slipped over her shoulders and pooled around her waist, leaving her full breasts naked in the glow of the fire. She leaned back, thrusting her chest forward proudly, watching lust spread over his face, dark and dangerous.

"Jesus," he breathed, his voice raw with desire. He cupped her breast, plumping it, watching the soft swell of it spill over his hands almost obscenely. Rush sucked in a sharp breath, looking reverent. "Never cover these up again."

His thumb brushed the pink stone nestled between her breasts. "What is this?"

"It's rose quartz," she said, smoothing the familiar, comforting shape, warm from the heat of her skin. "It's good for emotional balance."

Rush hummed, skimming the stone against the curve of her breast. "It's warm," he murmured, rolling it between his fingers before letting it slip back against her skin. "Like you."

Lily laughed breathlessly, her stomach fluttering at the look on his face. She stopped, jerking forward suddenly to wrap her arms around his head when he bent to take her nipple in his mouth. One big hand slid down her ribs, fingers tracing the sides of her breasts while he outlined her nipple lightly with his tongue.

Lily cried out. Heat shot straight to her core as his tongue flicked, slowly and deliberately, before he latched deeper and sucked harder. Rush groaned against her skin, mouthing his way to the other breast, licking and biting just enough to make her dizzy with want and keep her on the edge.

She ground down on him harder, spreading her thighs to

open herself even more as the pleasure built in her. Hotter. Sharper. More demanding.

"Oh God," she whimpered, rocking harder on him to make the ache stop. The muscles in her thighs shook, and she gripped him fiercely, pressing and rubbing in turn, anything to make that tight, unbearable ache stop.

"Yes, angel," Rush growled softly in her ear. "Just like that. Use me. Show me how you need it."

Her breath hitched. She couldn't speak. Couldn't think.

Use me.

For once, she was only feeling, not worrying about what someone else needed from her—only this sharp, wild flood of feeling. Her entire world narrowed to the ache between her thighs.

She wasn't thinking about Rush or anyone else. For the first time, it was just her desire she was chasing, and the selfishness of that lit up another part of her that reveled in taking what she wanted from the willing man under her.

She rolled her hips again, harder this time, dragging herself over the thick muscle of his thigh. A desperate, strangled sound escaped her. God, he was solid. Right there. Perfect.

"Fuck, look at you," Rush rasped against her throat. "So fuckin' wet. You're soaking me, Lily."

Her cheeks flamed, but it only made her grin harder, her clit catching at the seam of her sweatpants with every pass.

"That's it, darlin'," he groaned. His hands gripped her hips, not to take over, but to steady her. "Ride my thigh. Just like that. Get yourself off on me. Let me see how bad you need it."

She gasped, her thighs trembling. Her hips moved faster, seamlessly now. She was too far gone to care about being quiet. Too turned on to hide how close she was.

"You've been aching for this, haven't you?" he murmured against her throat, biting just enough to make her cry out.

"Knew you had it in you. All sweet and quiet with these perfect fucking tits, grinding that needy little pussy on me like you were made for it."

Her head dropped to his shoulder, clutching him as his words wound her tighter and tighter. "Oh," she gasped, her voice catching as she rocked against him, hips moving faster, more desperate. She was so close, aching for it, but the sharp edge of pleasure kept slipping just out of her reach. "I can't—" she choked out.

Rush's hands flexed, gripping her ass, slowing her frantic rhythm with firm, commanding pressure.

"Shh," he murmured roughly against her throat. "You're right there. Take it. Take what you need. Be greedy for me." He rolled his hips up into her, firm and unhurried, each stroke hitting her right where she needed. His other hand curled around her waist, anchoring her to him as he moved with slow, devastating precision.

That was all it took.

Pleasure slammed into her, a bright, hot wave that sent her spiraling, her body trembling uncontrollably. Rush held her tightly, licking and sucking her breasts while she came, head thrown back, eyes squeezed shut to wrench every drop of pleasure out of this moment.

Rush stilled as her body collapsed on his, his body rock-hard under her, their breath ragged in the silence of the cabin.

"Oh my God," she whispered, horrified as embarrassment settled in. She hid her face in his neck. "I'm so sorry. I didn't mean to—"

Rush growled low in his throat and cupped her face, making her look at him. "Don't you dare hide from me. That—" He kissed her, a slow and deep exploration of her mouth that told her without words how turned on he was.

Lily was boneless, still shaking, her body still thrumming

with her orgasm when he let her go and rested his forehead against hers.

"Was the hottest fucking thing I've ever seen," he murmured, his voice rough with satisfaction. His hands slid down her back, anchoring her against him possessively.

Lily's cheeks, already flushed, flamed hotter. "I didn't know that was going to happen. I can't believe—"

Rush traced her bottom lip with his thumb and grinned at her crookedly. "You wanted it. You took it. That's never something to be ashamed of, Lily. Ever."

Her stomach flipped. "You—"

"Loved it," he finished roughly. He pressed another kiss to her swollen lips. When he finally pulled back, his eyes were pure heat. "And I plan on making you do it again."

"Oh," she breathed, eyes wide.

Rush laughed knowingly. "Oh," he repeated. He gave her ass a firm, proprietary squeeze that made her heart race all over again. "We're just getting started, angel."

A slow smile spread over her face. She would've said yes to anything if it meant feeling like that again.

Yes to whatever this was.

Yes to the way he made her feel—untethered. Reckless. *Alive.*

But then his hands softened, and his eyes shifted as he studied her, his fingers coasting along the curve of her jaw with rough fingertips.

"I need you to know something before this goes any further," he said, his voice low.

She blinked up at him, her pulse stuttering as reality intruded. "What?"

He radiated pent-up sexual frustration, but he pulled himself tightly back under control and sat back. "I'm not staying in Northfield. I've got a job lined up in Boston in February, and I'm going to take it."

She stilled.

Oh. The words hit her harder than she expected. His eyes were still full of heat and promise, and she knew her own reflected that need back at him. But he was giving her the truth.

He held her gaze. "You deserve to know that. I don't want to give you the wrong idea."

This wasn't about forever. It wasn't even about tomorrow. They had right now, and for once in her life, she wanted to take what she needed.

Two days ago, she'd stood at the altar, about to marry a man who never really saw her. Who didn't know how to touch her or ask her what she wanted. She'd spent years burying her desires and shrinking herself to fit inside a relationship that left her hollow.

But now she was here, stripped of all expectations and standing in the middle of something she didn't quite understand but couldn't turn away from.

The snow would melt. The roads would clear. Rush would leave for Boston, while she'd return to Northfield and figure out how to rebuild her life. But tonight, in the hush of this cabin, with her hands exploring the hard planes of his body and his heat sinking into her skin, reality felt a thousand miles away.

She didn't have to be good or play it safe anymore. She could want something simply because it felt good.

Because *she* wanted it.

Don't let this chance slip through your fingers.

"Okay," she whispered. "Thank you for telling me, but I still want this... you. Please," she added politely, as if he'd asked her if she wanted cream in her coffee, then she flushed bright red. Sophisticated she was not.

Rush exhaled, smiling. "Are you this nice in bed, Lily

Hart?" He slid his hand up her neck, cupped her chin, and tilted her face to his. His thumb brushed along her jaw.

"I think so," she whispered.

"I don't have condoms here. Are you on something?" he asked quietly.

He didn't look away or fumble with words. Just met her gaze, unwaveringly, giving her the same straightforwardness he gave everything else. Rush Callahan didn't play games. Even when the answer might not be the one he wanted to hear, he asked anyway. Any lingering nerves she had settled with that knowledge.

This wasn't a promise. It wasn't a beginning. It was heat and hunger and making up for everything she'd never let herself ask for.

They had these few stolen days at the cabin, and then they would go on their separate ways. Lily would go back to North-field to face Tucker and her family, and Rush would go on running from his ghosts.

A swell of something bittersweet pressed at the edges of her heart, but she shoved it away.

They had tonight, and she meant to find out what else she'd been missing all these years.

She met his gaze. "I'm on birth control. I'm safe."

A muscle flexed in his jaw. "I'm clean," he said, his voice a rough rasp that curled around her like smoke. In one fluid motion, he pulled his flannel over her shoulders again, lifted her off his lap and into his arms, stood effortlessly with her, and strode the few steps over to the bed while she held on.

With one arm behind her head and the other around her back, Rush guided her down, her body bouncing slightly against the mattress as she hit the bed. His gaze dropped to her breasts, peeking through the unbuttoned shirt, and the heat in his eyes scorched her.

"You're sure?" he asked. One last check.

She smiled, shy but certain of this one thing, and held out her arms. "I'm sure."

SHE DID WANT THIS.

Really, really wanted it in every throbbing, aching, pulsing part of her body. Every inch of her ached for him, every nerve pulsing with need, but the second her head hit the pillow, the weight of what they were about to do hit her.

Lord help her, she was way out of her league.

Lily inhaled slowly, steadying herself and concentrating on controlled breaths the way she taught her students. *Breathe in. Breathe out. Stay present.*

But it wasn't working.

Rush Callahan was foreign to her, and she was sure to the marrow of her bones she was going to embarrass herself. She had already come from simple foreplay, for heaven's sake. What must he think of her?

And yet, she didn't want it to end.

Everything about Rush overwhelmed her. From his sheer size to the quiet authority in his voice and the way his dark eyes pinned her in place without even touching her, he was dangerous in a way that made her feel like she was strapped into the seat of a roller coaster just before the drop.

Lily hated roller coasters. Roller coasters were not still lakes. They were wild and unpredictable. Kind of like the man on top of her right now. *Oh God.*

Her whole life, she'd played it safe. Followed the rules. Chosen stability over passion and certainty over risk. She'd convinced herself that love was something you built, not something that swept you off your feet, and that what she and Tucker had was fine. It was good, even if not earth-shattering.

But now, with Rush above her, his solid weight pressing deliciously into the curves of her body, she finally understood how much she'd been missing. His hips settled into hers, his erection an insistent, steely ache against her hip.

She'd been teasing him and feeling bold in the dark, but now, with him above her, she felt that confidence fizzle out like the hiss of a balloon losing air.

Her fingers twitched. Instinctively, she reached up, searching for the comfort of the rose quartz. She looked up to find Rush watching her, studying her carefully in that unnerving way of his.

"What's wrong, Lily?" he asked in that low tone that sent a shiver down her spine.

She forced herself to meet those dark eyes. "Why do you think something's wrong?"

Rush leaned back, putting space between their bodies. "Because of this." He traced her cheekbones, where she could feel the bloom of heat giving her away.

She covered her cheeks, blushing harder. "I hate being a redhead sometimes."

Rush leaned down and nipped at her jaw. The bristles of his cheek brushed against the tender underside of her throat, and she gasped at the sensation of soft lips and rough beard. "It's one of my favorite things about you," he murmured.

"The thing is..." she said, wincing at the shakiness in her voice. *Get it together, Lily. You have a gorgeous man between your legs, and you're acting like you don't know what to do with him.*

But she kind of didn't, a small voice whispered. The memory of that disastrous attempt at seduction with Tucker flashed in her mind, reminding her of her inexperience. "I'm not very good at this," she confessed.

Rush's gaze flickered over her face. "Angel, if you were any better, I'd be dead."

Her stomach swooped hard. She looked around him at the flickering lights on the ceiling and tried not to look as naïve as she felt. Long fingers cupped her chin, gently lifting her gaze to meet his.

"Talk to me," he murmured, searching her face.

"I just…" She swallowed hard. "I don't really know what I'm doing," she admitted softly, hating the way uncertainty crept into her voice. So much for playing the temptress. "I've only ever been with…" She trailed off, not wanting to bring Tucker's name into this moment. "And I don't think I'm all that good at it."

Rush's expression softened. "You don't have to know," he murmured, sliding a hand up to cradle her jaw, his thumb brushing the sensitive skin just beneath her ear. "There are no rules here. No right or wrong."

"Ohh." She let out a sound of pure pleasure and tipped her head to give him more access. Her neck had always been sensitive. She wasn't surprised a man who paid attention to things the way Rush did would notice. Slowly, he traced a teasing line down her neck, using his lips and tongue to explore.

"Don't force it. Just feel it." He leaned in, pressing a kiss to the delicate spot where her pulse fluttered. "We go at your pace." Another kiss, lower this time. "Whatever you like."

Whatever you like…

Lily's breath hitched and came out in a rush. Maybe—just maybe—she could let herself have that.

Chapter Thirteen

SHE DIDN'T HAVE time to second-guess herself.

Rush Callahan kissed like he had all night and no intention of rushing through a single moment. His mouth moved lazily over hers, seeming to savor each slow slide of their lips. He took his time sampling the corners of her mouth, kissing her top lip, and pulling her bottom lip gently between his teeth, drawing a groan from her when it turned deep and wet.

The last of her nerves went up in smoke. His mouth was sure and gentle, his tongue stroking hers until she melted beneath him.

She wasn't nervous anymore. She was ravenous.

Her fingers curled against his skin, her body tilting into his without conscious thought. It took her a minute to gather her words, deep as she was in the sensations of pleasure and the erotic touch of his tongue and teeth on her neck. She stroked her thumbs hesitantly over his ribs and felt him shudder.

"I like everything you do to me," she breathed.

When he finally lifted his head, his thumb traced gently over her lower lip, pulling the tender skin down while he watched, his eyes heavy with desire. "God, your mouth," he murmured roughly. "I fucking love your mouth." He pulled back and looked her over hotly, and Lily knew he liked what he saw by the way he lingered on her before meeting her gaze.

He slid his hands down her waist, gripping her hips and spreading his hands wide until his thumbs met at the top of her mound and then held still.

"Tell me what you want, Lily," he murmured in that voice of his that was more of a rough command than a polite request. It slid over her skin like honey, melting away any lingering shyness and making her limbs heavy with anticipation.

She thought for a minute, knowing her face was turning bright pink—she couldn't help that—but also that she was more turned on than she'd ever been in her life.

"I want to touch you," she said shyly.

A slow, lazy smile spread across Rush's face as he leaned back, stacking the pillows behind him and folding his hands behind his head. "I'm all yours, darlin'," he drawled, the faint Southern accent sending a ripple of warmth through her body.

Excitement sparked again, hot and urgent. Lily rose up onto her knees, shifting forward to straddle his hips. She knew she wouldn't leave this cabin the same woman she'd been when she'd arrived. For once, she was going to get what she wanted, without apology.

And what she wanted was currently sprawled beneath her on the bed, looking deceptively calm. Slowly, she bent and pressed a kiss to his fascinating jaw, savoring the faint scrape of his beard. The roughness sent tiny shocks of pleasure rippling through her body. She lingered deliberately, dragging her mouth lightly along the sharp edges, dipping gently into the hollow beside his cheekbone, teasing the curve of his chin, before settling at the corner of his mouth.

The silky bristles of his mustache drew her next. She traced butterfly-soft kisses along his surprisingly full lips, tasting smoky whiskey, and beneath that, something darker and more dangerous. Something that hinted that Rush Callahan was merely allowing this moment for now.

A delicious shiver of anticipation rolled through her, tightening her nipples into aching peaks and sending heat sparking down her body to pool low in her belly. She felt wild, powerfully alive. Eagerly, she pushed Rush's Henley up and over his head, pausing to admire the view when he was bare from the waist up.

His chest was broad and beautifully sculpted, lean muscles defined beneath warm skin with dark, crisp hair that tapered down enticingly toward tight, chiseled abs. His sweatpants rode low on his hips, revealing a provocative glimpse of hair that disappeared beneath the waistband. A sexy promise of everything still hidden from view. Firelight flickered on each hard ridge and shadow of his body. She swallowed hard, curling her fingers instinctively, ready to explore every inch of him.

Sweet baby Jesus, does the man bench-press trucks in his spare time?

With a new boldness, Lily straightened and held the edges of her flannel shirt together, noticing how Rush's eyes darkened and dropped to her hands. *Her turn,* those eyes seemed to say.

His own hands, loosely crossed behind his head, came down swiftly to grip her hips in a firm hold, as if he couldn't help himself. A thrill shot through her at that small surrender. Rush Callahan wasn't the kind of man to give up control easily.

Lily drew her shoulders back, letting the soft fabric slide down her arms until it caught at her elbows. Her full, heavy breasts spilled free, her nipples tightening instantly in the cool cabin air. Before she could even register the chill, Rush moved.

He knifed upright, grabbing the flannel behind her back and trapping her arms firmly in place. Lily gasped sharply, her eyes going wide, as he openly devoured the sight of her.

Oh, he liked the sight all right.

Any hesitation Lily felt about baring herself dissolved under the pure, unfiltered desire in his eyes. Rush looked at her like a starving man, sending a thrill through her.

"Jesus, Lily. Look at you." Rush exhaled slowly as his eyes roamed hungrily over her. "You're so fucking beautiful," he murmured almost reverently.

Heat flared across her skin at his praise. She shifted restlessly, but his hands held her still while he looked his fill. He shook his head slowly, still drinking her in. "Don't even think about covering them up. These curves..." He traced the swell of her inner breast, sending a jolt of electricity through her. "You're perfect." His voice dropped lower, more intense, and he caught her gaze. "I'm going to suck these pretty nipples until they're swollen and begging for more," he said roughly. "I'm going to bite you, tease you, until you're screaming my name, begging me to fuck you." He leaned closer, his hot mouth gliding over her jaw. "And then, darlin', I'm going to give you exactly what you need."

"Oh Lord," she breathed, arching into his mouth. "If you keep talking like that, I'm not going to survive it."

She felt his smile against her throat, wicked and warm.

"I want to taste you," she whispered. "Everywhere."

Rush's mouth tilted in a slow smile. He reached out, letting go of her arms to place one rough finger at the base of her throat, and traced downward with agonizing slowness over the gentle slope of her collarbone, dragging across her skin until he reached the inner curve of her breast. She sucked in a sharp breath when his calloused fingertip teased the soft, full teardrop shape, circling beneath the heavy weight before finally settling directly on the sensitive peak.

Instantly, it tightened, partly from the chill of the cabin air, but mostly from the skillful touch. The sensation shot directly between her thighs, a hot, pulsing ache that made her lean forward instinctively with a needy whimper.

Rush pinched lightly, rolling her nipple between his thumb and forefinger, drawing another helpless moan from her throat. Her eyes fluttered closed with pleasure.

"So sensitive," he murmured, "and I haven't even begun to tease you." He gave her nipple a gentle tug, making her gasp sharply. "Tell me, Lily," he whispered, his lips sliding across her. "Will you come for me again?"

Her breath froze. His eyes were dark and knowing when they met her wide ones.

He trailed his fingers down her stomach, and paused just at the edge of her pants. Her stomach quivered at his touch. "You still wet for me, angel?" His voice was a deep growl, his fingers teasing the sensitive skin of her lower belly, threatening to dip lower where she was slick and achy.

A blush crept up Lily's chest and bloomed in her cheeks, but she met his gaze with a shy smile. "Maybe," she breathed. "Does it bother you that I... came like that? Without you."

A low laugh rumbled in his chest. "Bother me?" He echoed, his voice thick with lust. "It makes me hot as hell."

Lily grinned at the admiration in his voice, but if she had only one night, some small, selfish part of her wanted to take every advantage of the hot, hard-muscled body beneath her.

Confidence soaring through her, she splayed her fingers over his chest, the rough texture of his skin so different than hers. So different from the soft, pale skin of her former fiancé. She lowered her head and brushed her lips against his nipple.

A groan escaped him, and his body arched beneath hers. She felt the surge of his erection, hot and heavy, beneath her, pressing urgently against the curve of her ass.

She ground against his length in a slow circle. "You like that?" she asked, smiling shyly against his chest.

Rush let out a pained, appreciative laugh. "I like everything you do."

She slid lower, dragging the sensitive peaks of her breasts over his chest, feeling the erotic scrape of his hair against her skin, heightening her own arousal with every slow, deliberate movement. She continued downward, pressing small, open-mouthed kisses to the taut muscles of his abs, her tongue tracing over each defined ridge of muscle, testing the restraint of a man honed for duty and control. "You're strong," she murmured with appreciation. "So sexy."

She paused at the edge of his hip bone, resting her cheek there briefly, her eyes lifting to meet his. Rush was watching her intently, his eyes heavy lidded and his chest rising with controlled breaths.

Her breasts brushed lightly against his thighs, teasing him as her fingers slowly, carefully, danced along the waistband of his sweatpants. She pressed a kiss there, where the soft fabric met the line of dark hair.

"May I?" she asked, shy but determined.

Rush groaned deep in his chest, his muscles tensing beneath her. "All yours, darlin'."

She eased the waistband down, freeing him. He sprang forward, long, thick, and heavy, fully erect and flushed a deep, needy red. Her eyes widened in a mix of awe and trepidation. A bite of doubt worked its way up at the sight, but she released it on a slow, steady exhale. Energy was everything, and she trusted the subtle hum that flowed between them now.

A bead of clear moisture gathered at the tip, glistening and tempting. Lily leaned forward without hesitation, darting her tongue out to delicately taste him. Salty and earthy. She licked again, needing more of everything Rush Callahan had to give.

"Christ, Lily," Rush ground out.

She glanced up and found him with his head thrown back,

eyes squeezed shut, jaw clenched as if he was holding himself on a razor's edge of control, and her heart skipped a beat. The pure pleasure etched on his face sent a thrill racing through her, making her feel more feminine, more desired than she ever had before.

It was a heady feeling, and she wanted more.

She leaned forward for a longer taste, her tongue tracing the ridge before finding that small bundle of nerves on the underside, rubbing sensuously, getting him wet and slippery.

Rush's hands came to rest on her shoulders, but he didn't urge her down, didn't pull her forward. Just let them sit there, resting lightly, letting her take her time. He shifted his hips so she could tug his sweatpants the rest of the way down and helped her pull her pants off at the same time, kicking them both to the side of the bed and leaving them gloriously, deliciously bare against each other.

She smiled up at him, taking him in her mouth again, holding just the head of him and feeling him throb on her tongue. A pulse of something powerful and electric flowed through her body, and she knew how she looked—bent over him, her breasts pressed against his thighs, her mouth wrapped around him, snug and warm, just resting, not moving as he flexed in her mouth. She loved the feel of it, this big man filling her and yet utterly at her mercy.

Instinctively, she wiggled her bottom playfully in the air, feeling the slickness of herself on her thighs. She let her teeth just barely graze him before looking up, enjoying teasing him in bed. She couldn't remember ever feeling so bold and uninhibited.

She took him deeper, laving his shaft with her tongue, swirling the tip, savoring the way the muscles in his legs tensed beneath her touch. The taste of him, the heat, the way his fingers curled into the sheets—she felt drunk on watching his desire, feeling it enhance her own.

"I love this," she marveled then blushed as soon as the words left her lips.

Rush let out a ragged breath. "So do I," he gritted out. He fisted his hands in her hair, guiding her but not pushing, letting her set the pace.

She wrapped her hand around his thick base then added the other, finally reaching the dark curls framing his cock. He was big—thick and heavy and stretching her mouth in a way that made her eyes water and her thighs press together restlessly. She stroked in rhythm with her mouth, slow and steady, letting him feel just how much she enjoyed him.

His breath hitched, his stomach tensing beneath her as she hollowed her cheeks and took him deeper. She wanted him to know how much she enjoyed this. The way he filled her, the way he responded to every flick of her tongue, every squeeze of her hands.

A deep, rumbling groan escaped his chest, his control slipping as she worked him with slow, deliberate precision, and she could've howled from the thrill of it. She was the one undoing him—sweet little Lily Hart on her knees, lips stretched around his cock, taking this massive, disciplined man to the brink.

She did that. And God, it felt powerful.

"Lily," he growled. His hand smoothed over her cheek, thumb tracing her swollen lips as she pulled back just enough to look up at him, still holding him in her mouth, her tongue teasing the tip. "Look at you. Taking me so good. Fuck," he groaned, gripping her hair, holding it back from her face, and she could feel the control he was exercising not to thrust. "So goddamn pretty with your mouth on me."

Lily had never given much thought to dicks, really. She was a pleaser, and they were just appendages, a means to an end. She'd handled blow jobs with the same attitude—efficiently, sometimes even with mild enjoyment, but never like this. Never with a greedy hunger, never with this overwhelming need to have Rush heavy on her tongue, thick and pulsing, stretching her mouth and filling her throat to overflowing until her eyes watered.

She moaned softly against him, letting the sound vibrate through her throat, and felt him jerk, a deep shudder running through her body. God, she loved this. Loved the power she had in this moment, and the way she was unraveling him.

He was close. She could feel it in his ragged breathing and the way his stomach clenched. But she wasn't done with him yet. Not even close.

Slowly, deliberately, she pulled back, dragging her tongue along his length before taking him deep again, hollowing her cheeks and sucking hard, her hands stroking him in a perfect, twisting rhythm.

"Fuck, darlin'," he hissed through his teeth, his head thrown back, hips thrusting involuntarily. "You're gonna make me—"

She didn't let up. She wanted to feel him come apart. Wanted to push him past the point of control until he had no choice but to surrender.

Then he moved.

He shifted so suddenly it stole the breath from her lungs. One minute she was teasing him, taking him deeper and reveling in the power she had over him, and the next she was straddling Rush's torso. Two rough hands gripped her ass, jerking her closer to him while Lily watched wide-eyed.

Rush's eyes burned up at hers. "It's my turn," he growled, edging her closer to his mouth.

She lost her balance and tipped forward, gripping the brass rails on the headboard in shock. If Rush's energy had been blue before—cool, controlled—now it was something darker and more primal.

"What—" she whispered.

Rush's hand skimmed over her thighs firmly, then he leaned up, his mouth so close to her mound she could feel his breath on her. "Look at this," he murmured, sliding his fingers into the curls there. "All pretty and flushed for me. I wondered where else that blush went." He flicked his tongue through her folds, just once, a teasing taste that made Lily whimper. "And fuck, this red hair. You were made to be kissed here, Lily."

Her whole body clenched.

"You don't have to," he said, looking up at her with a wicked grin, "but if you let me lick this pretty pussy, I promise you'll love it."

A shiver ran down her spine, nerves at her position and hunger tangling in her making her thighs tremble around his head. He was so close and, oh my God, she was going to let him.

The scales had tipped again, she thought faintly.

"Rush," she whispered, breathless.

His hands skimmed over her hips, down her thighs, soothing and firm as he snugged her up against him. Then he leaned up, his mouth right at her pussy, his voice dark and smooth as sin. "Ride my face, darlin'."

Chapter Fourteen

LILY'S BREATH HITCHED, her fingers tightening around the brass rails of the headboard as Rush's hands guided her forward, closer and closer to that sinfully dirty mouth.

Oh God. Oh God.

She should have been embarrassed, laid bare for him like this, hovering over his face, every inch of her exposed to him. But the way he looked at her, like he needed this, like he needed her, burned through any hesitation she might have had.

Still, she hesitated, the vulnerability of it all making her breathing come shallow and fast, until Rush's hands flexed on her hips, pulling her firmly down on his mouth.

"Ooooh." Lily's head snapped back, her eyes closing. She was not going to last. Lily Hart did not do debauched things like this with sexy sheriffs. She'd been having sex with a man who marked "bone time" on their shared calendar and then barely remembered to reschedule if something came up.

The thought shattered at the first stroke of Rush's tongue, making her cry out, her hips jerking at the hot, slick stroke that sent a bolt of liquid pleasure through her. Rush groaned, deep and rough, like she was the best thing he'd ever tasted, like he needed this and couldn't get enough. His hands tightened on her hips, holding her still as he feasted, slowly and thoroughly.

He teased, circling her soft entrance, dragging his tongue through the wetness he'd drawn from her before flicking her clit with a wicked precision that made her groan.

Lily's thighs quivered as she held herself above him. "Rush—"

"That's it," he murmured against her. "Give it to me, angel."

He dragged her closer, pulling her flush against his mouth, sealing his lips over her, and sucking deeply.

The coarse brush of Rush's mustache created a deliciously foreign friction, rasping against her tender clit, making every sensation sharper and dirtier. She lost all sense of control then, grinding shamelessly down onto his face.

She couldn't help it. She rolled her hips, chasing the wicked friction of his mouth, his tongue stroking, his lips sealing over her, sucking, teasing, owning her. Pleasure built fast, sharp and unbearable, curling in her belly, crackling like a live wire through her veins.

She was close. So close she could barely think past the relentless pleasure winding tighter and tighter inside her.

"That's it, darlin'," Rush whispered against her slit, tonguing her hard and fast. "I'll give you exactly what you need." His fingers tightened their grip on her thighs. "Come for me, Lily."

"Rush—" A sharp cry tore from her throat as she shattered, pleasure wracking through her and stealing the strength from her limbs. Rush held her through it, lapping at her like he needed to feel every last tremor, like he needed to wring every ounce of pleasure from her body.

She barely had time to catch her breath before he moved, shifting them so fast her back hit the mattress in a dazed sprawl.

His mouth was on hers in an instant, kissing her filthy and deep, letting her taste herself on his tongue. The hardness of his cock pressed against her, heavy and demanding, and when she instinctively lifted her hips, he groaned into her mouth, barely holding himself back.

"Fuck, Lily. I need to be inside you."

"Yes," she whispered, urging him closer.

His breath shuddered out, and then he was there, fitting himself between her legs, pressing the broad head of his cock against her swollen, slick entrance, stretching her, filling her, stealing the breath from her lungs.

"So good, angel," he murmured against her lips. "Take me deep. Let me feel you." He wrapped his arms around her shoulders, holding her still, and kept talking while his body pressed into hers.

Lily shivered, her fingernails digging into his back as he rolled his hips, rubbing against her in a place that made her back arch. She felt his body go tight as he thrust inside her, ruthlessly stretching and filling her swollen, tender pussy. Rush groaned, burying his face in her neck and nipping at the sensitive skin there. She went suddenly still, balancing on the knife-edge of pleasure and pain.

"Fuck, that's it," he grunted. "Squeezing me so goddamn tight. So tight and wet. Are you going to come again for me?"

Again? She didn't know, truly, if she had it in her. Her body was boneless, floating in a haze of sensation, her arms and legs clutching at his shoulders and around his waist—anything to keep her anchored. But even as the aftershocks pulsed through her, the slow, rhythmic grind of his hips was already lighting her up again.

"Oh!" She gasped, arching her hips up to meet his. "Oh God!"

Rush let out a low groan and tightened his grip on her hips, his control snapping as he pulled back and thrust into her again, harder, deeper, sending pleasure sparking through every nerve in her body.

And then there was no more talking. No more thinking. Just heat and friction and desperate, aching need while Rush held her tight, dragged her hips up, and thrust into her, keeping her pinned in place for him.

She broke. A cry ripped from her as she came apart around him, pleasure rolling through her in waves so intense she couldn't breathe. Couldn't think.

Rush groaned, leaning down to take a nipple in his mouth, sucking hard as he came with a roar. He collapsed against her breasts, chest heaving while she caught her breath. He was too heavy to hold for long, but Lily didn't mind. His weight grounded her in this moment when she was fairly sure the earth had spun a little too fast. Gently, she stroked her hands down his heaving back, a delicious, satisfied smile curving her lips.

"Damn," he murmured eventually. She could feel his lips moving against her breast, kissing and mouthing it idly as his breath returned, and it gave her a deep sense of satisfaction. She closed her eyes, running her fingers through his thick hair, and floated.

"Did I hurt you?" he asked eventually. He shifted, but he didn't let go of her breasts. His thumb stroked her softly, and every once in a while, he took her nipple into his mouth, letting her feel his tongue.

"Mm, no." She sighed happily. She'd wanted something new and exciting, and she'd gotten exactly that. *And then some.*

She needed a minute to process. In a dim way, she knew her entire worldview had shifted in the last hour. It wasn't just the physical. What had happened between them was a slow, devastating unraveling of everything she knew about desire and connection.

Rush lifted his head, searching her face, but she pressed him back down again. His breath was warm against her skin. He brushed his lips over the curve of her breast, his tongue flicking lazily at her nipple before he took it into his mouth again.

She wasn't sure how long they lay like that, him still inside her, wrapped around her, but she didn't want it to end. Her body still hummed with pleasure, but something deeper was settling in her chest too. A slow smile curved her lips while she studied the shadows on the ceiling of the cabin.

Rush lifted his head again, his heavy-lidded gaze looking her over carefully. "There's red marks here," he murmured, running his fingers over her breasts, following them with his mouth, pressing soft kisses on the evidence of where his mouth had been. "Didn't realize I was marking you up."

He sounded more than satisfied with the results, Lily thought with a smile. He pressed warm, open-mouthed kisses against her throat, her collarbone, and the tender skin just under her nipple. He groaned as he kissed her there, pulling her into his mouth again.

Lily inhaled deeply, feeling the slow throb between her thighs pulse to life again.

"You're so damn pretty," he murmured against her, kissing first one breast then the other. Taking his time. Savoring. "Could spend all damn night right here." He hummed against her, sucking lightly before pulling back to admire his work.

It lit her up in a primal way, and she arched against him, shocked with the simmering awareness that he was still hard inside her. *Oh my.* Her eyes widened.

"Again?" she murmured, astonished and slightly awed.

Had she thought she was out of his league? He was playing a different sport entirely.

Rush's grin turned slow and smug. "I can go again. And again." He leaned in close, his lips teasing her ear. "And again."

The heat pooled between her thighs instantly, her body

responding eagerly despite the faint soreness lingering. Rush kissed her gently, slower this time, taking his time to savor her. He sucked her nipple deep into his mouth again, flicking his tongue in a way that sent bolts of pleasure between her legs.

He pulled back to look at her with a lazy smile. "Sensitive, hmm? Gonna have to take care of that, angel."

Lily nodded, already reaching to pull him back to her, but Rush pulled out of her and gripped her thighs, encouraging her to move.

She let him guide her up, shifting until she straddled him, her knees on either side of his waist. A tiny flutter of nerves mixed with anticipation rolled through her as she felt the heavy length of him pressing against her sensitive core—still tender and sore from minutes before.

Rush groaned beneath her, his fingers flexing on her hips as he slowly pushed just inside her slick entrance. "Take it slow," he whispered roughly.

Lily let out a little whimper at the feel of him, her body clenching, already overwhelmed at the size. Rush leaned up and caught her nipple between his teeth again, holding her gaze and sucking harder as she felt her body turn slicker, wetter, giving in to the blunt slide of his cock, inch by inch. Rush held her gaze, his mouth still on her, sucking deep before letting go with a wet, obscene *pop*.

"Oh!" she gasped, closing her eyes. The pleasure was too much. Too intense. Her senses spiraled higher, the intensity building until tears filled her eyes. "I need—" she gasped, panting, grinding, desperate, lost in the feeling inside her. "Please, Rush. Please don't stop."

One strong hand reached up to grip the back of her neck, pulling her closer to his mouth and guiding her gaze to his as he took the other nipple in his mouth and sucked. The dominance of the touch sent a quiver straight through her, and she groaned, rocking harder against the thick, rigid length beneath her.

"Tell me," he ordered, lifting his hips to meet hers, giving her more friction and driving deeper. "Tell me what you want."

"I want—" The words stuck in her throat. She couldn't think. Couldn't breathe. Wicked sensation had taken over, blotting out everything but the fire raging in her body.

"Tell me what you need." His voice was pure sin, low and rough, as he thrust into her from below. "You need this cock?"

He thrust upward, slow and deep, and the crude words, the friction right where she needed it most made her vision go white at the edges.

"Tell me how much you want it," he ordered roughly.

"Yes, Rush, yes!" The words tore from her throat. "Please, please—"

He slid one hand down her body, over her stomach, slipping through the damp red curls to find her aching clit. "Fuck, you're soaked," he growled, his thumb circling slowly at first then faster, pressing in time with her hips moving.

It was enough to break her wide open. Pleasure crashed into her, and Lily shattered, shuddering violently against him, feeling her inner muscles clenching on him in spasms. Rush groaned long and deep, rocking into her from below, grinding and pulsing while her body clenched tight as a fist around him.

"I've got you," he grunted, holding her tightly when she collapsed into his body, her face tucked into his neck as the pleasure overwhelmed her. His rhythm stuttered, his cock throbbing inside her as he held still and pulsed into her.

For a long, breathless moment, they stayed like that. Lily snuggled closer into the bristly hollow of Rush's neck, inhaling his scent—clean male sweat, sex, and whiskey—and felt the sensation of letting go sweep through her. Suddenly, her throat tightened, and a wave of emotions flooded her. A tear slipped free, then another.

Rush let out a deep exhale, his big hand smoothing lazily up and down her back. Carefully, he eased out of her.

Lily sniffed, dragging a hand over her eyes.

Rush froze immediately. She could feel him tense, his body going from post-sex bliss to full awareness in a heartbeat.

"Did I hurt you?" he asked sharply.

She blinked away the wetness and shook her head quickly. "No. God, no. It's not pain."

Rush's frown grew, along with his confusion. "Then why are you crying?"

Lily sighed, reaching up to stroke his too-serious face. "Haven't you ever cried because something felt so good? Because you felt it so deeply?"

Rush stared. "No," he finally said. A slow, deeply satisfied, very male grin spread across his face. "I usually just say 'damn, that was good' and fall asleep."

Lily let out a watery laugh and settled on his chest again. "Well, congratulations, Sheriff. You rocked my world so hard, I cried about it."

Chapter Fifteen

Lily was still catching her breath, her body a delicious pile of wreckage, when Rush eased her onto her side, giving her thigh a lazy, possessive stroke before straightening.

"Stay put," he ordered, and Lily's stomach did that somersault it always did when he ordered her in that gravelly, no-arguments tone.

He crossed the cabin to the bathroom, and she watched his broad shoulders and tight ass in the firelight. When he came back, he had a damp washcloth.

He didn't speak, just eased her thighs open with that same bossy authority that made her feel breathless. Heat rushed to her cheeks, but she watched quietly as Rush settled between her knees like it was the most natural thing in the world.

He held her legs open and looked at her with the purely male, wholly satisfied smile of a man who knew exactly what he was doing.

"Pretty," he murmured, brushing his thumb over the red curls before cleaning her with a surprising tenderness. Lily shivered, insanely shy under the weight of his stare but also more cared for than she had ever felt in her life.

Damn. It was a shame he wasn't sticking around.

When he was finished, he set the cloth aside and pulled her back onto his chest, tucking her under his arm and into the warm, solid wall of him.

"No more crying, angel. I've got you," he said quietly. His lips brushed her hair, and Lily settled bonelessly over him.

Rush's breathing had already started to even out, but Lily was getting a second wind. She stared at the ceiling for a while, trying to relax enough to fall asleep. She wiggled around to find a comfortable spot, poking surreptitiously at the steely chest under her, hoping it might prod him into a little postcoital chat.

She was determined to be the kind of woman who could have outrageously good sex and not overthink it. This was her life now. She was a woman of the world, a sexually liberated, independent goddess. She could have sex with men, lots of sex. So nonchalant! Maybe she'd lose their numbers or be too busy to pick up their calls the next day too.

Somewhere in the last few minutes, she'd decided that would be her new plan when she got back home. It was time to date and reclaim every experience she'd missed out on while wasting precious moments on Tucker.

She was mentally working through various dating scenarios when Rush shifted, skimming a hand up and down her back.

"You're thinking too loud."

Lily lifted her head to look at him. "I didn't know thinking made noise."

"It does." He looked satisfied and amused and way too sexy. "Yours is deafening."

"I'm just planning my revenge tour." She shrugged. See? She could do casual.

His fingers stilled over her ribs. "You ready to tell me what happened?" he asked more seriously.

She hesitated. Not because she didn't want Rush to know

but more because she wasn't sure if she was ready to bare her secret. Maybe she should practice being coy.

"Tucker is cheating on me," she blurted.

Dammit. She'd never been very good at subterfuge. It was Rush with his soothing hands and his solid-as-a-rock energy. There was something powerful about him that she couldn't explain, but she was more comfortable with him than she'd ever been with anyone else.

He was silent for a beat. His hands didn't stop soothing, but she could feel the tension coil in his body. "Son of a bitch."

"Wait. It gets worse," she said, trying for some levity before getting serious again. "Someone sent me a photo of him with his assistant in a hotel room right before I was supposed to walk down the aisle, and then it was air-dropped to everyone in the church after I left. My mom and my sisters, my aunts, Tucker's family. Everyone."

She was quiet for a while, letting the emotions roll over her like waves. *Still lake...*

"I should have been furious with him. I wanted a family so badly. I wanted what I thought we should have. And for a split second, I thought I could just—" she swallowed hard—"pretend I didn't see it. That I could go through with the wedding and that it wouldn't matter in the end."

He didn't say anything, but she knew. She poked him in the ribs. "I know it was dumb."

"Ow." He rubbed the spot. "I didn't say anything."

"You were thinking too loud." She smiled at him. "I knew I couldn't stay. It just took me a minute, and that scared me because if I stayed, I'd be someone I didn't want to be." *Ouch.* That one was painful to say out loud, but Lily forced herself. New Lily didn't shy away from the truth, even when it was uncomfortable. "I've pretended things were good for so long, I wasn't even sure what that person looked like... or wanted."

"Takes strength to see that," Rush said, and she smiled. He might be the only one to see it that way.

"It didn't feel like that at the time," she said wryly. "I felt like a coward."

Rush shook his head. "Running toward something better isn't cowardly. That's strength."

"I don't really know what I'm doing," she admitted, feeling shy again.

Rush's fingers found her chin and curved around it, lifting her face to meet his eyes. "No one does. But you should start with figuring out what it is you want."

Lily stared at him. The thought was too big for the tiny cabin. It stretched across years of pushing down her own wants in favor of Tucker's, years of going with the flow, making herself smaller to fit into the life she thought she was supposed to have.

Rush's eyes held too much knowing, and she felt exposed for the first time all night. She jerked her head away to escape the weight of his gaze. She knew she had work to do, but not here. That would come later. After she was done being a liberated woman.

"What about you?" she asked instead. "I was running, but isn't that what you're doing by leaving?"

Rush's brows drew down, and his expression slowly shuttered while she watched. "Maybe," he said easily enough, but Lily sensed the energy shift in him.

No excuses from Rush Callahan. She respected that, even if it made her chest squeeze uncomfortably tight. She chewed on her lip, wondering how much she could say before those beautiful storm-gray eyes went cool and distant.

"Northfield will miss you." *I will too.* She knew enough to keep that to herself. No casual hookup would ever admit she'd developed the tiniest crush in only a weekend. That would be too dumb.

But she did want to know him. Rush Callahan was a man with layers that she wanted to uncover. What they'd shared in bed was sexy—mind-blowingly sexy. She'd spend time replaying it later, but for now, she let herself have a moment of sadness that was all she'd know of this man.

Rush shrugged one well-rounded muscular shoulder, rolling onto his side and taking her with him. "You'll get a new sheriff soon enough. It's a good job."

"That's not what I meant."

Rush's gaze flickered for a moment. "I can't stay here," he finally said. "Can't keep listening to people talk about how I'm some kind of hero when I fucked up."

She inhaled sharply. "Rush, you must know it's not your fault," she said. "You did all you could do—"

"Lily," he said flatly, "I sat in a therapist's office for months, going over it over and over again. You know what I learned? Doesn't matter how many people tell you it wasn't your fault— you're the one who has to live with the truth. And I do. Every day."

Lily exhaled slowly, feeling the weight of his words settle between them. She could argue. She could tell him Northfield needed him, that he wasn't the failure he clearly believed himself to be. Her natural instinct was to comfort him, but she sensed what little intimacy they had just shared would shatter. When it came down to it, she didn't know what made Rush Callahan tick, and he didn't want her to.

His mind was made up, and she wasn't here to fix him. Just like he had respected her decisions, she would respect his. He had to walk his own path to forgiveness. She just hoped it was an easy one because if anyone deserved that, it was him. Rush Callahan was a good man, whether he saw it or not.

She settled under his arm, reached out, and let her fingers trace a slow path across the ridges of his abdomen, up across the broad expanse of his chest. She exhaled, releasing her disappointment, and let herself sink into the moment fully.

"The snow stopped, angel," Rush murmured. "Won't be long before the plows come through."

Lily swallowed down the sting of disappointment. Their time together was slipping away then. "Why do you call me that?"

"Call you what?"

"Angel."

Rush was quiet for a beat, his fingers tracing slow, absent strokes over her back. "Because you looked like one when you came flying out of the church with your big white dress and that veil streaming behind you."

Lily looked up in surprise and saw his lips curve up.

"You hopped into my truck and looked at me with those big green eyes, and I knew I was taking you with me."

Lily's stomach dipped. She hadn't expected something sweet to come out of his mouth, or to feel the warmth that spread through her, making her all soft inside.

"I didn't think you'd say yes," she said shyly.

Rush laughed, his hand smoothing up her spine, over her back to wrap around her neck. "Not a chance. You were all soft and glowy and sweet." He paused, his voice dipping lower. He brought his other hand up to cup her chin, slipping his thumb across her mouth before slipping it inside. "Except for this mouth."

Lily's breath hitched, and she instinctively closed her lips around it, tasting the salty heat of his skin. "What's wrong with my mouth?" she murmured around him.

"This?" he murmured, touching her lips, dragging his thumb back and forth slowly over them. "This mouth is too fucking sexy to belong to an angel."

Lily smiled, her eyes drifting closed as a yawn overtook her.

She nestled into the hollow between his neck and shoulder, nosing in closer. His scent was addictive, all warm and manly, making her eyes feel heavy. She thought she felt the faintest brush of lips over her hair, but she couldn't be sure. His warmth seeped into her bones, lulling her into sleepy contentment.

She didn't want to think about tomorrow or about what came next.

For now, there was only the calm energy of the cabin, the steady thrum of Rush's heartbeat, the slow stroke of his hands keeping her anchored to him just a little while longer.

Her breath evened out, her body sinking into his.

Just before sleep took her, she heard the quiet rumble of his voice.

"Sleep, angel."

And she did.

Chapter Sixteen

"CALLAHAN! YOU IN THERE?"

Lily jolted awake at the sharp crack of fists against the cabin door. Riggs let out a single, piercing bark before bounding toward it, his tail wagging like they had company he recognized. A quick glance out the window showed that the snow had stopped. It was midmorning, at least, based on the brightness.

She exhaled, relaxing just a little as she gathered her wits about her. Surely Cujo wouldn't greet a serial killer with that much enthusiasm. The dog was way too grumpy for that. Whoever was outside, Riggs knew them.

"Who's—" Her voice was husky with sleep as she sat up, yanking the quilt up when it slipped and exposed her bare breasts to the cold cabin. She peeked over the side of the bed, searching for something to wear, only to freeze when her body protested. She was deliciously, thoroughly sore, her skin still tingling from Rush's hands, his mouth, the way he'd pressed her into the mattress.

Against his mouth.

Straddling him—

Oh God.

Her brain played an explicit highlight reel she definitely hadn't asked for, flashing hot and unfiltered, as heat flooded her cheeks. She pressed her hands to her burning face.

She hadn't—

That wasn't—

The mattress shifted abruptly, and her gaze snapped to Rush. Oh, she did, and it had.

He was already up, looking enticingly rumpled and sexy with his dark hair and scruff shadowing his jaw, standing at the edge of the bed. She watched covertly as he tugged on his jeans, leaving them unbuttoned enough to see the hint of gorgeous hip bones and dark, curly hair rising from the open fly. The hard muscles in his thighs she'd rubbed all over. That seriously gorgeous butt that she had a strange desire to sink her teeth into.

He snapped his jeans closed with a sharp flick, and she flopped back on the bed with a sigh. For a split second, she thought he might turn around and give her that wicked smirk that made her toes curl, maybe even haul her back under the covers for round—what was it? Three? Four?

The first time had been wild and mind-blowingly hot, the next slower and more relaxed, and finally, the last time, Rush had reached for her in the early hours of the morning and sunk into her from behind, all sleepy and warm. They had rocked lazily like that, with her still slick and hot from him. She'd come more times in one night than she had in the last six months.

She wanted to high-five herself. She'd totally had sex with Sheriff Sexy. Wait until Evie found out. Her sister would be so proud.

"Friends of yours?" she asked lightly, wondering how he managed to look so good while she was certain her hair had crossed into Medusa territory. She offered him a smile, but when his eyes met hers, all traces of the man she had known so very intimately the night before were gone.

Rush's eyes were clear and impersonal, like last night hadn't left a single mark on him, when she could clearly see the scratches on his back from where she sat.

She let that sink in for a split second. She was the kind of woman who left scratches on a man's back after a night of crazy, no-holds-barred sex? Shocking.

But also... a little thrilling.

New Lily was definitely the kind of woman who did things like that.

Clearly, Rush was back in Sheriff Callahan mode, and she was going to put her game face on too. She straightened her shoulders and ignored the tiny bit of disappointment that snuck its way into her new, strong, confident self.

"Here, put this on." Rush tossed her something soft. His flannel and sweatpants. The same ones he'd watched her strip off the night before.

Another loud bang rattled the door. "Rush! You alive in there?" A deep, teasing voice called through the wood, followed by a round of laughter. "Wake the fuck up!"

Rush was already across the room, yanking on his sweat-shirt, scanning the room with a scowl on his face. With one hand on the door, he shot Lily a glance. "You decent?"

Okay, he was maybe a little better at being casual than she was. She was new to this.

She tried to catch his eye to offer a smile, but he turned away before she could, pulling the door open in one swift motion. A blast of icy air swept in, along with three broad-shoul-dered men who looked half-frozen. They were all dressed in some variation of the same uniform—ski parkas, snow pants, hats, gloves—coated in a dusting of snow.

One of them stepped forward and did that manly back-clap thing that men did to Rush's back. "Good to see your face, Callahan. We found your truck half-buried down the mountain.

Thought the snow took you out." He flashed an easy grin at Rush, who returned it.

So he did remember how to smile.

Lily tilted her head. She didn't know much about Rush outside of the cabin, but from what she'd seen of him around town, he wasn't big on smiling. Anytime she'd run into him, he'd had the same stoic, professional expression on his face, yet here he was, standing relaxed and looking at ease. Riggs was practically vibrating with excitement, wagging his tail at the men's feet like they were long-lost friends.

Rush ran a hand through his hair and cleared his throat. "Figured one of you would find us when the snow melted."

At the word "us," three pairs of eyes swung toward the bed.

Lily felt the blood rush to her cheeks. She already knew how she looked. Her swollen lips and tangled hair. The pink skin where Rush's beard marked her last night.

One bed. One very obvious conclusion.

Oh well. No one could really know what had happened. She could brazen this out, just as she would when she got back home and faced her family. She grinned charmingly and channeled her inner goddess. No big deal. Nothing to see here. Just two mature adults who shared a tiny cabin platonically and had absolutely not seen each other naked.

A beat of silence stretched around them until one of the men, the youngest of the three, stepped forward then stopped abruptly and lifted his eyes. "What the hell is that?"

He reached up and plucked something from the deer head mounted above the door.

Oh hell.

Lily's very risqué, very lacy merry widow dangled from his fingers. The one she'd thrown over the creepy deer's glassy eyes last night.

He held it up, frowning in confusion. Lily watched with a

sense of inevitability as the men realized what it was. The room went awkwardly silent.

So much for platonic...

Rush crossed his arms, his expression unreadable. "Got something to say, Ian?"

Ian, dark-haired and wearing a cocky-as-hell grin, obviously enjoying himself, twirled the lace between his fingers and let out a low whistle. "Not a damn thing," Ian replied, smirking. His blue eyes sparkled with mischief as he glanced at Lily, and she couldn't help but smile back.

Rush stepped forward, that no-nonsense, bossy sheriff look on his face, and plucked the lacy scrap out of Ian's hand, folded it, and slipped it into his back pocket.

Lily held her head high when she got out of bed. She had wanted new experiences, she reminded herself sternly. The metaphorical walk of shame was apparently one of them.

The three men, all dark haired and rough hewn like they'd been carved straight out of the Adirondacks, exchanged a look and seemed to reach some silent consensus. Broad chests, big frames, and those ruggedly handsome faces under their hats—Lily could practically feel the testosterone humming off them. And every one of them flicked their gaze between her and Rush with way too much knowing amusement.

Another of the men stepped forward. He had the same night-dark hair as the other two men, but his eyes were more watchful and serious. He gave her a sharp, assessing look as he took off his glove and held out his hand. "Sorry to interrupt. I'm Gage MacKenna, and these are my brothers, Ian and Connor. We live up the mountain on Autumn Ridge."

Connor clapped Rush on the shoulder, the embroidered patch that read Park Ranger on his parka catching in the sunlight. Beneath his hat, dark-blue eyes crinkled warmly at the corners as he smiled at her.

"The storm took out most of the mountain's power," Connor said. "The roads are still bad, but we brought the snowmobiles if you need a ride on the trails."

Rush didn't hesitate. "Yeah. You can give her a ride to the lodge." He shot Lily a quick, unreadable look. "You'll be able to get a ride from there."

It wasn't a question, but Lily nodded even as her stomach dropped. Just like that, it was over. Even though she knew it was coming, it still hit her like missing a step in the dark.

Rush was already moving, gathering their things with quick, effective movements. He was back to being a remote, distant sheriff. It shouldn't have been a surprise, but it was.

Lily might not have much experience, but she wasn't naïve enough to believe this could be real—at least not beyond the cozy bubble of the cabin. This had been a weekend straight out of her wildest fantasies, a chance to forget who she was and be seen as someone brave enough to chase what she wanted.

But reality was hitting hard, and the bubble had popped when Rush opened the door.

She knew from the start that what happened between them this weekend wasn't meant to last. Of course she did.

Lily stayed quiet while she picked up what was left of her dress. Her chest was strangely heavy, an ache that she hated curling behind her ribs.

The MacKenna brothers talked and laughed easily as Lily and Rush took turns washing up in the bathroom, their conversation a mix of teasing and catching up. Lily listened quietly, piecing together details about their relationship while she stuffed her ruined wedding dress in a garbage bag. The comfortable way Rush interacted with them and the funny stories they shared about Rush spending time at their lodge made her chest tighten with the realization of all the things she didn't know about him.

She had memorized the rough scrape of his beard against her skin and the deep groan he made when she took him into her mouth.

But there was so much more to Sheriff Callahan than she would ever have a chance to learn.

She felt awkward and out of place and faintly sad, but she kept her emotions locked down. There would be time later when she got home to process all that had happened. In the meantime, she tidied the cabin, erasing all traces of her stay there.

When it was time to go, Lily put on an extra coat Connor handed her and the old boots she'd found. She followed the men out on the porch, but Rush stayed back. She hesitated at the bottom of the steps, glancing back to find Rush standing at the door, his hands braced on the doorframe and his eyes unreadable. Riggs sat at attention next to him. Clearly, they were both ready to reclaim their cabin.

She offered them her sunniest smile and lifted a hand to wave. "Bye, guys. Thanks again for..." She paused, feeling warmth flooding her face. *Ride my face, darlin'.* "Well, everything," she finished lamely.

"Be safe getting home," he said quietly.

That was it. No kiss. No touch. Just a clipped nod as a goodbye. *Don't you dare cry.* Rush had made it more than clear what he could offer. She let her hand drop back to her side, swallowing against the strange lump in her throat.

Outside, the air bit sharply at Lily's cheeks, crisp and cold now that the storm had passed. Sunlight sparkled across the snow, casting the little cabin in a golden glow that felt peaceful and calm, as if it hadn't just been the scene of the most transformative weekend of her life.

Life-altering. Heart-shifting. And now over.

She kept her eyes forward as she trudged through the snow, refusing to look back.

Onward.

She concentrated on her breath. Cold air in, warm air out, and the strange, humming awareness still alive in her chest.

Gage helped her onto the snowmobile, handing her a helmet, but before she could lift it, familiar strong hands suddenly took it away. Warm fingers closed around her arms, lifting her off the machine and spinning her around until she collided with a familiar, solid chest.

And then Rush's mouth was on hers in a sweet, hot, unapologetically possessive kiss. He didn't seem to care that they had an audience. His tongue swept against hers, rough and demanding entrance even as she parted her lips eagerly, like he was trying to brand her while she clung to him. He tasted like mint toothpaste and hot, urgent male, and she clung to him, knowing that this kiss would wreck her all over again. And not caring.

Rush growled and slid a hand down to her bottom, hauling her against him while the other hand slid into her hair and tugged her head back, seeking a deeper angle. She clutched his broad shoulders and forgot about the men watching and what lay ahead for her and sank herself into the shockingly raw intensity of his kiss.

And then it was over. Lily felt herself being set back on her feet just as quickly as she'd been swept off them. Her knees were weak, her head spinning, and he was already backing away.

He hesitated, the muscle in his jaw flexing, and tilted her chin up toward him. "If you need anything," he said gruffly, "you call me at the sheriff's office. Got it?"

She nodded, her throat too tight to speak.

"'Bye, angel," he murmured. He slapped the back of the machine and turned, whistling to Riggs.

Dazed, Lily got back on the snowmobile, and Gage settled in behind her. "You okay?" he asked, handing her the helmet again.

She didn't answer right away, still breathless and feeling the imprint of Rush's mouth on hers. But as the cold air stung her cheeks, she drew in a deep breath, filling her lungs with the scent of pine and snow. And with it came something unexpected... a sense of peace.

I am a still lake.

The words settled inside her. Steady and true this time.

She turned back, meeting Gage's eyes—deep and watchful, the kind that hinted at a story of his own—and smiled. "Let's take this thing for a ride."

He revved the engine, the deep growl vibrating beneath her, and a jolt of excitement ran through her. Not just from the ride, but from the choice she was making.

She wasn't running away anymore.

Maybe whatever had ignited between her and Rush had ended before it had a chance to become something more. Maybe she'd leave the mountain with nothing more than memories that might fade with time.

But she was different.

She tightened her grip, feeling the sharp sting of the wind against her face, and inhaled deeply, feeling more alive than she ever had before.

And for the first time in a long time, she was ready to face whatever awaited her at the bottom of the mountain.

Chapter Seventeen

One Month Later...

"Bye, Miss Lily!"

A chorus of tiny voices filled the studio, all calling out their enthusiastic goodbyes as Lily zipped coats, wrapped scarves, and steered the children gently toward their waiting parents. Despite the exhaustion sinking into her bones, she smiled warmly at each child, waving as they left.

"See ya later, Aunt Lily." Savannah Henderson blew Lily an exaggerated kiss, which Lily pretended to catch and press to her chest.

"See you, Savvie girl." Lily braced a shoulder against the studio doorway, watching affectionately as her niece ran straight into her daddy's brawny arms.

"Daddy," Savvie announced breathlessly, "I'm a sheep. And Tessa's a sheep, too, but she wanted to be a unicorn. Aunt Lily said unicorns aren't in the Christmas pageant."

Davis laughed and ruffled his daughter's wild curls. "Unicorns are pretty rare, honey."

"That's what I told her," Savvie said solemnly then flashed a mischievous grin. "But she cried. So I said she can still have a horn if she uses a carrot. That's okay, right, Daddy?"

Lily bit back a laugh as Davis glanced at Savvie's twin, Tessa, who looked distinctly unamused by the idea. He cleared his throat, clearly fighting a smile.

"You know, honey, maybe check with Aunt Lily before you accessorize Tessa's costume."

"Yeah," Tessa chimed in, giving her sister a look. "No carrots."

Savvie sighed dramatically and leaned closer to whisper loudly into her daddy's ear. "She gives her carrots to Walter under the table at dinner."

Tessa gasped at the betrayal. Davis's eyes sparkled with amusement as he caught Lily's gaze, warmth and affection clear on his handsome face. "Thanks for today, Lily. Looks like we'll be having some vegetable negotiations tonight. Come on, girls, let's go home and see what Mommy thinks."

"Good luck," Lily said, laughing as they turned to go. Watching Davis carry his girls, one tucked against each hip, she felt a familiar tug deep in her chest. Allie's family was perfectly blended, warm and playful in a way that opened an ocean of yearning in her heart.

Someday. Someday that would be hers too. She sighed and rolled her shoulders, releasing the tightness in her back.

Lily loved teaching, even on days when her muscles ached and her voice was hoarse from counting over the music. The Pure Bliss Wellness Studio, tucked neatly between her mother's interior design business and a law firm on Main Street, had been her sanctuary—especially this last month.

It had been a long class. Herding dozens of tiny dancers while keeping the Christmas pageant choreography on track was no small feat, but she wouldn't trade it for anything. With the holiday season in full swing, the studio had taken on a new kind of magic... and chaos.

Lily and Evie had volunteered to direct Northfield's first Christmas pageant this year, and between rehearsals, choreography, and props, Lily's schedule was packed. She didn't mind. The kids were excited; the parents were helpful, and the extra work had kept her more than busy for the last month. Too busy to think about that weekend in a snowed-in cabin where—

Nope. Ruthlessly, Lily dragged her thoughts back to the present. She'd done that every time her mind flashed back to that wild, incredible weekend. Her future was in the here and now.

Looking around her studio, a familiar sense of calm filled her. Strings of twinkle lights glowed against the tall windows, casting soft reflections on the polished hardwood floors. The entire far wall of the studio was lined with mirrors and a ballet barre, and the rest of the studio walls showed off students' artwork. A row of yoga mats stacked neatly in one corner, next to wicker baskets filled with angel wings and the snowflake costumes the kids had stuffed haphazardly back in.

The studio had started as a dream she scribbled in her notebook years ago, and now it pulsed with the kind of energy that gave her life... especially this last month, undoubtedly one of the longest of her life.

She hung up woolly lamb costumes and carefully stored angel wings and reminded herself once again not to dwell. Her life as she had known it exploded, yes, but there was a sweetness in building her new one that she could appreciate.

And on days when it was hard to remember she was lucky she hadn't married a cheat, well, she just spent more time in her studio, where she felt happiest. And her schedule certainly kept her busy. She taught beginner ballet, jazz, slow-flow yoga and everything in between. In her studio, she got to watch the shyest of kids find their rhythm and stressed-out moms melt into Savasana.

Here, she had always remembered who she was outside of being someone's girlfriend or almost-wife. And while that wasn't always fun, to do the work of rebuilding, it was necessary.

"Bye, kids! See you on Monday for rehearsal," Lily called out to the last of the little ones leaving with their parents.

When she turned, Chloe was waiting quietly near the studio for her grandma. She was always the last to leave, always lingering just a little longer, and Lily never rushed her. Chloe was sweetly endearing, with dark curls framing her face and wide, expressive blue eyes.

She had joined Lily's studio a few months ago, and while Lily tried not to have favorites, Chloe had quickly become hers.

"Did you have fun today, Chloe?" Lily asked softly.

Chloe nodded, her tiny hands clutching the tutu she still wore, and smiled just enough to reveal a gap where her front tooth had recently gone missing.

Lily's heart melted. She reached out and gave the little girl a soft squeeze on the shoulder. "You were the most graceful snowflake tonight. Even Miss Evie said so, and she's very picky about snowflake technique."

That earned a bigger smile, still just a little curl of her mouth, but it felt like pure sunshine. Chloe hadn't spoken a word since the night of the accident that took her mother's life, but Lily understood her just fine. "Do you remember what comes next in the pageant?" she asked gently.

Chloe nodded again and shyly held up four fingers.

"Right," Lily said. "Four more weeks of rehearsals until our big show. I can't wait to see you up there with all the lights. You're going to be so brave."

Chloe glanced at the door where her grandmother had just appeared, then she turned back to Lily. Without a word, she stepped forward and wrapped her arms around Lily's neck in a quick, fierce hug.

See? How could she not have a favorite?

The hug caught Lily off guard. She dropped to her knees and hugged Chloe back, her throat tightening. Chloe was quiet and careful and pure in a way that cracked something open in Lily's chest. Brave without even knowing it. A little girl without a mom, and yet here she was, wrapped in sparkly tulle, giving away love like it cost her nothing. She rubbed her back, trying to pass some steady, healing energy between them, anything to make this easier for her.

Margaret Whitmore stepped inside the studio, the scent of winter clinging to her long wool coat. Her silver hair was swept neatly back, and she carried herself with the kind of effortless poise that came from decades of country club luncheons and charity board meetings.

Lily smiled, getting to her feet. "Hi, Mrs. Whitmore. She's just finishing up. Do you remember where to put your costume, Chloe?"

The little girl nodded shyly and headed across the room toward the baskets.

Margaret's eyes found Chloe and softened. Lily had the impression the Whitmores were trying very hard to get everything right—structure, routine, the best of everything that money could buy—but they still moved through this new chapter of their lives like people holding their breath.

They adored Chloe; that much was clear. But grief had a way of wrapping itself around love, stiffening it into something quieter and more cautious.

Margaret didn't seem cold, just careful. Like if she let herself love too loudly, it might break her wide open again. Lily could understand that. She figured Margaret was handling her daughter's death and the sudden responsibility of raising her granddaughter the best way she knew how. It wasn't easy for anyone.

"Did she talk today?" Margaret asked softly, keeping her eyes on her granddaughter. The hope laced in her voice almost made Lily wince.

"Not yet," she admitted, keeping her voice light. "But she's getting more expressive with her dancing, and she remembered the whole snowflake routine on her own."

Margaret gave a sad smile. "She's always humming it at home. You've given her something to look forward to."

Lily paused, touched. "She's a joy to have here."

Margaret nodded, her voice a little lower now. "We weren't sure how this would go, to be honest. After everything... she hasn't said a word. But with you, there's a light in her that we haven't seen in a long time."

Lily looked over at Chloe, who was twirling in front of the mirror, and felt her heart pinch.

"I think she just needed a place to be herself," Lily said gently. "We all do."

Margret watched her granddaughter for a moment longer, with her heart in her eyes, then composed her face. "We'll see you tomorrow," she said. "Come, dear. It's time for supper."

Chapter Eighteen

As THE DOOR shut behind the Whitmores, Evie popped out from the office, shrugging into her coat. Her cheeks were flushed pink with excitement, and her nose was buried in the stack of highlighted script pages.

Lily didn't have to look up to know it was her sister. They shared the same red hair and green eyes, although Evie was a librarian and very much dressed the part. Her sedate knee-length wool skirt and cream turtleneck looked out of place next to Lily's pink floaty wrap skirt and leggings, which had traces of glitter from the snowflake rehearsal. And yet, as always, they balanced each other out perfectly.

"That little girl adores you," Evie said, pushing up her glasses with her finger while juggling a mug of tea and a half-eaten apple. Her script—highlighted and color coded to hell—was jammed under her arm, the sticky notes poking out at odd angles.

Lily smiled faintly. "She's special." She held out her hand for the script and mug, very used to her sister's charming brand of distracted genius. "Here. Let me help."

Evie handed them over, taking her coat from the hook and

slipping it on while she scanned the room. "Have you seen my keys? I just had them."

Lily handed the mug back to her and tossed the apple in the garbage. "You're the only person I know who could lose her own keys while holding them."

Evie looked down, startled. "Oh. Well. I thought I put them —never mind." She flashed a sheepish grin. "Thanks."

"Did you get the lines down?"

"I was just in there rewriting the nativity scene. One of the angels had a sore throat, so I gave her lines to the donkey."

While Lily handled the choreography and wrangled the tiny ballerinas, Evie handled the acting and singing with the joy of someone who'd spent her childhood directing her twin and all their neighborhood friends in backyard musicals. Theater had always been Evie's passion, and she directed several other community shows in addition to her role at the library.

"Just a heads-up—" Evie paused, buttoning her coat with one hand. "Tucker's back in town."

Lily froze. "What?"

A month. She'd had a whole glorious month of not seeing his smug face. A blissful, Tucker-free stretch in which she could pretend she hadn't been humiliated in front of half the town by the cheating dirtbag who then took their honeymoon to Cancun with his assistant. *Their honeymoon!* The nerve of it still galled her.

Evie winced in sympathy. "I'm sorry, Lily. But honestly, everyone knows he's a walking dumpster fire now."

If it galled Lily, it was nothing compared to how the town felt about Tucker. Northfield wasn't just small; it was loyal to the bone, and when you broke that trust, everyone took it personally.

From what she'd heard, he was persona non grata around

town. And yes, the pettiest part of her—the part she tried very hard to smother—felt a tiny flicker of satisfaction hearing that.

In some ways, the aftermath of the photo was worse than the betrayal itself. Along with her privacy, she'd lost whatever thin shred of dignity she'd been clinging to. Some days she still wondered who'd actually AirDropped it. Tucker? Madison? Or someone else who couldn't mind their own business?

She was the one being whispered about in the aisles of the grocery store and dissected over coffee at Maple and Main. And the worst part was that everyone in town truly meant well. Truly. But small-town kindness came with a side of suffocation.

Somehow, she'd become Northfield's tragic sweetheart. People stopped her in the grocery store, eyeing her tub of ice cream and bag of chips with sympathy, when really it was just her usual period craving. She couldn't walk down Main Street without someone offering tearful sympathy and unsolicited advice on everything from how to get revenge to how to win him back. As if either of those was even on the table.

But then it got worse.

Once people realized she wasn't actually devastated, the matchmaking started. Suddenly, everyone had a "very sweet" nephew or brother or UPS driver who *was just the nicest guy* and so cute and could they give him her number?

It was sweet. It was exhausting. And it was impossible to say no to without disappointing someone's well-meaning grandma or aunt.

Yes, New Lily was a badass. She stood her ground, and she wasn't a pushover, dammit. But Old Lily—the people pleaser— was proving harder to shake. She still hated disappointing people, especially the grandmas. They were so cute in their determination to set her up. So earnest.

Every week before class, she told herself she'd say no. And every week, Gertie Marshall or Connie Hightower would sidle up to her with a bag of warm cinnamon buns from Morning Glory Bakery (who could say no to those?) and their grandson's business card in the other, like she was the town's pity case.

"That's almost worse," Lily muttered, rubbing her forehead. "Everyone's been treating me like I'm made of glass since I came back. I can't teach my senior yoga class without someone trying to hand me baked goods and their grandson's business card."

"They love you," Evie said. "You're like Meg Ryan in every nineties rom-com before the happy ending, and Tucker's the villain."

She wandered over to the floor-to-ceiling picture windows and looked out at the snow falling on Main Street. "I didn't want to be the sad girl when it was me who finally left, even if it was at the last possible second."

That rankled the most, that image of herself in their minds.

Poor Lily, being cheated on and lied to.

Ugh. She wanted her damn dignity back.

Evie's expression softened. "You've handled this so well," she said quietly. "Eventually, you knew you'd have to face him."

Lily stifled a sigh. On that long, snowy ride across the mountain with Gage MacKenna, she'd made herself a promise. She was going to start over. Be braver. Bolder. *What would New Lily do?* had become her mantra as much as *I am a still lake.* She was in charge of her own happy ending, dammit.

She'd been trying to move on. She'd said yes to every cinnamon bun and some of the unsolicited but well-meaning blind dates, out of sheer optimism—okay, and pressure, too— even if it all felt a little too much like dating in a fishbowl, with the entire town watching to see what she'd do next.

But three dates in, she was seriously reconsidering.

The first guy, the brother of a woman in her Mindful Yoga class, asked her if she wanted to go back to his place to see his rock collection after they had dinner. And no, it wasn't a euphemism. He was serious.

The second guy had talked about his bowel cleanse for forty-five minutes during their dinner date then taken off, leaving her with the tab because he needed to get to the bathroom.

And the third had spent two hours ranting about cryptocurrency then tried to lick her face in the parking lot of the Northfield Pub while she fended him off.

She was tired of being Northfield's tragic sweetheart. She didn't want to be whispered about or pitied. She wanted to take back her story.

"Poor Lily," my ass.

She was fun and flirty and back on the market. Okay, and maybe she wanted a little revenge on Tucker, but that was normal. She had years of fun to make up for, a whole list of fun things she'd skipped while she played the sweet, dutiful girlfriend. Things like kissing until her toes curled, and doing things that scared her, excited her, made her feel alive.

The problem was, the men she was being set up with weren't exactly inspiring any of those feelings either.

"I'm proud of you," Evie said, tying her scarf around her neck with a dramatic flourish. "You've been really putting yourself out there with all these dates since you got back."

Lily snorted. "Yeah. Putting myself out there... like bait in shark-infested water."

Okay, so New Lily was struggling a bit. But eventually, she'd meet someone without any weird obsessions or at least someone who didn't want to talk about them over dinner. Changing long-held habits took time. She just had to keep putting herself out there. Keep looking for the perfect guy. Someone tall and dark with broad shoulders and the most delicious pelt of curly hair on his chest—

Nope.

Ruthlessly, she dragged her thoughts back to the present.

Thinking about Rush wouldn't do her any good. Not when he'd made it clear that whatever had happened between them at the cabin was temporary.

"Well, tonight might be your lucky night. Bradley Benson. With a name like that, he has to be good rom-com dating material. At the very least, he must really love his mother, since he brings her to your hot yoga classes." Evie grinned mischievously.

"Gertie said he's cute in a banker kind of way, and he owns a dog, which is half the reason I said yes. That's usually a good sign," Lily said brightly. Maybe Bradley Benson had a hidden wild side, like a penchant for pinning her hands down while it snowed outside... *ugh*. She dragged her thoughts back to the present.

"That's the spirit." Evie pulled out her phone and pushed her glasses up her nose to squint at the screen. "Oh, that reminds me. I need a recipe. I have a date tonight too."

"Want to double-date?" Lily asked hopefully. "The pub does a killer Friday fish fry. And if our dates are disasters, we can hang out with each other."

"Can't," Evie said. "I'm cooking dinner for him at home."

Of course she was. Which meant Lily would have to stay out of their shared apartment for at least a few hours, since Evie had taken her in when she'd moved out of the house she and Tucker used to rent. "Who are you making dinner for?"

"Dr. Pierce," Evie said, beaming.

Lily frowned. "Evie. You have a date with your boss? The one who wears those stupid bow ties and takes credit for all your ideas?"

"Date. Meeting. Same thing," Evie mumbled, still scrolling. "I think I'll make Marry Me Chicken."

"Whoa. Let's not move too fast."

Evie looked up, arching an eyebrow. "Says the woman who ran off with the grumpy sheriff and had outrageously filthy cabin sex during a blizzard."

"Are we still talking about that?" *And thinking about it.*

"Um, yes." Evie crossed her arms, looking entirely too smug. "I'm living vicariously through you. You put the 'nailed it' in the phrase 'nailed it'. Who knew you had that in you?"

Heat soared in Lily's cheeks at the reminder. "It was a temporary lapse in judgment," she muttered.

"'*Ride my face, darlin'*,'" Evie growled in a terrible imitation of Rush's deep voice. "I haven't been able to look at Sheriff Sexy the same again."

Lily tried to look disapproving, but she grinned despite herself. "It was pretty epic."

She had zero regrets about the weekend or about telling her sister. They had a twin-level trust in which not much was off-limits. Besides, there was no hiding the beard burn on her neck and shoulders for days after. She'd practically glowed in the dark and had to wear turtlenecks for a week so her family didn't notice.

She'd told everyone else Sheriff Callahan had dropped her off at the Pine Cone Motel so she could clear her head for a few days.

Not a lie, exactly.

She just left out the part about spending those days snowed in and losing her mind—and her panties—in a small, cozy cabin with the sexiest man she'd ever laid eyes on.

Evie, of course, had seen right through her the second she came back, but her mother and sisters believed that she'd spent the weekend doing yoga, journaling, and meditating. Lily felt a teensy bit guilty about that, but the alternative—telling the truth—wasn't an option.

An involuntary shiver rolled through her at the memory of the silky scrap of mustache against her inner thighs.

She coughed to cover it and waved Evie toward the door. "Go. Make your chicken."

Evie winked. "Fine, fine. But if you need a getaway, send me a chicken emoji, and I'll come running."

The door clicked shut behind her, and suddenly the studio felt too quiet. These were the moments when it was hardest not to think about him.

She'd done an impressive job of tucking that wild, transformative weekend away into a carefully locked box, but sometimes, when she wasn't careful, memories slipped free.

They'd only spoken once since the cabin, and honestly, that was more than enough. Just that one time had left Lily flustered and scarlet cheeked for the rest of the day.

Alone in the quiet of her studio, Lily let out a long breath and reached for her coat. The floor-to-ceiling mirrors caught her reflection as she buttoned it up, and she paused. *Weeks had passed*, she told herself sternly. *You need to stop thinking about a man who'd made it abundantly clear he was leaving.*

She switched off the lights. Tonight was about moving forward. New Lily had a hot date. A fresh start.

She was definitely not hung up on a certain broody sheriff.

Maybe Bradley Benson had a mustache...

Chapter Nineteen

"D ID you guys know that the average kitchen sponge has more bacteria than a toilet seat? Like, twenty times more," Rachel announced in her most cheerful voice, the one she reserved for all things grossly scientific or medical. "And most single men don't replace theirs for—wait for it—six months." She paused for dramatic effect. "Rush, please tell me you're not using the same sponge from last summer?"

Rush leaned back in his creaky office chair, propping his phone against a stack of paperwork, and squinted at the screen. His sisters' faces split the screen, staring back at him expectantly. They ambushed him with a FaceTime call at least once a week. He loved them more than life, but damn if they didn't try his patience just as much.

At his feet, Riggs let out a loud, sleepy huff from his usual spot, curled in the corner of the office on his favorite blanket. He lifted his head to give Rush a cursory look, making sure all was well, before flopping down again with a grunt. Even in retirement, he never fully let his guard down. Riggs was loyal to the core, and he didn't take to many people other than Rush, although he tolerated Rachel and Sarah. He was protective, stubborn, and a damn good judge of character.

"See? Even Riggs is judging you," Rachel said, grinning.

He glanced at his watch. Friday night. He'd just wrapped up his shift when they'd cornered him.

Sarah wrinkled her nose, using the phone reflection to apply a thick coat of mascara. "Gross, Rach. Why do we need to know this?" She leaned in even closer until all Rush could see was her nose. Was that a—

"Sarah, is that a nose piercing?" Rush barked, narrowing his eyes.

Sarah shrugged, smiling innocently from her apartment in Buffalo, seventy-six miles safely out of his reach.

Rush braced himself. That look never meant anything good. When Sarah was a toddler, one flash of that grin, and he knew he'd find crayon scribbled on the walls, Rachel's Barbies floating face down in the toilet, or cereal trails stretching from the kitchen to the living room. Now she was twenty-two, and the chaos just came with bigger consequences.

"I think it's cute." Sarah shrugged again. "It was this or a face tattoo to impress my new friends."

Rush scowled.

"She's joking," Rachel soothed immediately. Always the mediator. "It's just a piercing. She can take it out."

Rachel had moved back to Northfield after finishing nursing school to help with Pop and start her new job at Northfield General. She was always the steadier and more responsible of the two girls, but right now, Rush knew she was gearing up for another ambush.

"And by the way, it matters because we're worried about you."

Rush rubbed the bridge of his nose, already regretting where this was heading. "My kitchen sponge is new, Rach."

"You've been through a lot this year. It's okay to admit it," Rachel said gently.

Rachel might have caused him fewer headaches over the years than Sarah, but she was harder to fool. Still, he'd never burden them with what lived in his head.

Sirens. Limp bodies. Blue lips.

His mind blocked the images quickly, same as usual.

The three of them had always been close, even with the ten-year age gap between him and Rachel. After the accident, his little sisters had clung to him like a lifeline. Rush had stepped into the role of protector without hesitation, guiding them through the move from Texas to New York, helping them settle in with Gran and Pop, doing his best to keep their world from falling apart. He took care of them in the best way he knew how, by protecting them.

But the accident on the canal had changed their dynamic, much as he hated to admit it. Lately, their roles had flipped. It was his sisters who hovered, calling and showing up at his house to check on him.

They were still young. They should be out living their lives. Falling in love. Traveling. Laughing. Not worrying if their big brother was unraveling one sleepless night at a time.

Icy-cold water. Blue, blue lips.

Jesus. Cold sweat broke out on his forehead. His skin went clammy.

A child whimpering. A blond head slipping beneath the black water.

He pressed the heels of his hands to his eyes as the gray specks flickered in his vision.

"I think you just need to get laid," Sarah said, smearing on red gloss. "I have some girlfriends who think you're hot. Something about the uniform and cuffs." She made a gagging sound. "Gross. But I could give them your number if you want?"

"Yeah," Rush muttered automatically.

"What? For real?" Sarah's face lit up. "I'm texting Monica now. She texts me every time you come into Maple and Main for coffee."

Rush snapped back into the conversation, scowling. "What? Hell no."

Lately, his mind had been doing that—drifting back to that night without warning. One second he was present; the next he was back in the water, the cold sinking into his bones and the sirens blaring in his ears. He shook it off. Now wasn't the time.

"But you just said—"

"Sarah," he barked, "don't you dare set me up with your friends again. They're babies."

"We're not babies. We're twenty-two," she said indignantly. "And they date guys way older than you. You're not still mad about what Monica did, are you? She said she was sorry."

"Don't say another word," he growled, pointing at the screen. Good Lord. He wasn't desperate, and even if he was, he still would never even consider dating one of Sarah's friends.

Especially not after Monica. Monica, who'd snuck into his truck during the Fourth of July fireworks, wearing a tiny red bikini and smelling like spiked lemonade. By the time he'd found her, she'd taken her top off and was sprawled across the seat, snapping selfies like she was doing a damn photo shoot.

He'd marched her straight back to Sarah while Monica pouted and tried to climb him like a tree. Then he'd put the fear of God into the whole giggling group, found them rides, and went home, wishing he could scrub the whole night from his memory.

Never again.

What he actually needed was to get the hell out of North-field and away from the well-meaning people who kept thanking him, shaking his hand, calling him a hero like he hadn't failed. Like he hadn't stood in ice-cold water and watched a mother slip below the surface while he cradled her daughter in his arms.

Every time he saw the Whitmores around town, it twisted the knife.

He needed space.

Quiet.

Somewhere he could go without being reminded of everything he couldn't save.

"Fine," Sarah huffed. "Rachel's friends are older. What if she sets you up with that one girl who calls you Sheriff Sugar Buns?"

"That's not a bad idea," Rachel said. "Lyssa and Kaylin have both asked about you since you helped me move."

"Oh yeah." Sarah nodded. "Bold move, leaving their panties in your coat pocket. Did you ever give those back?"

Rush groaned, heat crawling up his neck as his sisters cackled. This was what he'd been dealing with for months, and it was getting worse. The girls had it in their heads that all he needed was a girlfriend or a hookup.

What he really needed was distance—to get away from the guilt, the praise, the pity, and the memories that hit like a sledgehammer when he wasn't expecting them.

Besides, he'd already had a hookup. If you could call a weekend snowed in with Lily Hart a hookup. Which, technically, you could.

But he hadn't exactly walked away from it feeling lighter. Yet another avenue he didn't let his mind wander down, at least at the office.

But in the middle of the night, her breathy little moans haunted him.

Definitely not appropriate thoughts at work.

He dragged his mind back to the present. The girls didn't

know yet, but he'd flown to Boston for the interview with the security firm he'd be contracting with. They'd offered him the job, and he'd accepted it. The words had come out easily enough, but ever since, he'd been talking himself into it like a man trying to believe he wanted what he didn't

The girls didn't need him around anymore. They were grown and living on their own, building lives that didn't revolve around him. Still, the guilt gnawed at him. The idea of leaving town, leaving Pop in the nursing home, leaving the girls, sat heavy on his chest. He told himself they'd be fine. That he'd come back often to visit and that they didn't need him like they used to. Rachel was a nurse, and she'd moved back home to help take care of Pop. Sarah had her own apartment, and she was a semester away from graduating. They were okay. They would be okay.

He didn't want to abandon them.

But living and working in Northfield was starting to bleed into him in ways he couldn't shake, even a year later. Every siren brought him back to the water. Every time he drove the long, winding road next to the canal. The ice. The little girl's soaked hair tangled in his arms. The mother he couldn't reach in time.

He was slowly unraveling.

Grant Clairmont had seen it in him when they met for a drink over the summer. Grant was Mayor Theo Clairmont's older brother, a Boston detective, and one of the few men Rush still trusted from his days in the Marines. They'd been through fire together overseas, and it was Grant who'd quietly pulled strings to get Rush an interview at the private security firm in Boston.

If not for that, Rush might've talked himself out of leaving. But Grant had given him an out—a chance to disappear into a city where no one knew his name, where no one called him a hero, and no one looked at him with pity for not saving her mother.

Rachel snorted. "Sex releases endorphins. It also boosts your immune system and burns about one hundred calories per session."

"I'm dropping Riggs at home and getting some dinner," he muttered, grabbing his keys and shoving them into his pocket. He hadn't had much of an appetite lately, but he wasn't ready to go home to half-packed boxes and an empty fridge. "And we're never talking about this again."

"Oh, please," Sarah said, rolling her eyes. "You're even grumpier than Riggs, and you know it."

"Bye," he said pointedly.

"Fine. We love you," Rachel said softly, her voice sobering. "You're always worrying about everyone else. Maybe let someone worry about you for once?"

"I'll tell Monica to call—" Sarah said just as he clicked End.

Rush locked his office, said good night to the two deputies who were just starting their shift, and stepped out into the icy evening.

Twinkle lights framed every shop up and down Main Street, casting a warm, welcoming glow on the snow-covered sidewalk. With a month until Christmas, Northfield looked like something from a vintage postcard—charming and peaceful, with garlands wrapped around everything and wreaths on every door. Somewhere down the block, the scent of woodsmoke and kettle corn drifted from the Christmas tree lot.

His Chevy was dusted with snow, and his boots made a crunching sound as he walked across the parking lot, yanking up the collar of his sheepskin jacket against the cold.

The engine groaned before turning over, and he settled in behind the wheel, exhaling a long, frosty breath while he waited for the truck to warm up.

He didn't turn on the radio. Just sat there, hands resting on the frozen leather steering wheel, watching his breath fog the windshield while the heater slowly came to life.

And of course, because his brain was an asshole, his eyes flicked toward Lily's studio, like they did every night when he got off shift. The lights were off tonight. He bit down on the disappointment.

Sometimes when he left work, he'd catch a glimpse of her in the big windows, her curly hair tamed and sleek in the bun, wearing one of those tight things that didn't leave much to the imagination. Jesus, he loved when she wore that thing.

She'd moved into her sister's apartment over Morning Glory Bakery. More than once, when he was burning the midnight oil at the station, he'd caught a glimpse of her from his office window, her curls bouncing, always in motion as she closed up the studio and walked home.

And more than once, he'd seen her out on dates. Blind dates, if the stiff smiles and awkward body language were any indication. He told himself he was glad she was moving on and rebuilding her life. That was what she deserved.

Still. It ate at him that she was looking for someone else to give her what she wanted. He told himself it was none of his business, that she deserved the whole damn world after wasting years on a man who never took care of her. Rush knew that beneath all her sweetness and shy glances, Lily was a woman who could burn hot and wild if she let herself.

He'd been the one to feel it—her nails raking down his back in the cabin, her soft, dazed sighs as she came apart around him, trembling and fierce and so gorgeous. He could still taste her on his tongue, still feel the way she gave herself over without hesitation. Most people held something back, blunted the edges of their desire to protect themselves. Not Lily. She was all heart, all heat, and he'd fucking drunk it in like a starving man.

The thought of her giving that to someone else made his hands curl into fists.

So he did the only thing he could: nodded politely when he saw her and kept his distance. He was a gentleman; he didn't make it a habit to sleep with a woman and then ignore her. He wasn't sticking around Northfield, but if he was... there was something about Lily he wanted more of. Sex, yeah. Of course. That had been the single hottest night of his life, but there was something else about Lily he couldn't get out of his thoughts.

He'd planned to stop by and check in with her at the studio, to make sure she was okay, but she'd surprised him by coming to the sheriff's department about a week after they got back home from the cabin.

He'd stepped out of his office because he'd heard her laugh —that soft, musical sound that had been haunting him ever since the weekend at the cabin. For a second, he thought he was imagining it—maybe he'd finally cracked after all—but then he saw her.

Standing in the lobby of the Northfield Sheriff's Department, cheeks pink from the cold, laughing at something Ben Tanner said like she belonged there. Her hair was pulled back in a loose braid, wisps curling around her face, and she looked so goddamn sweet it knocked the air from his lungs. Her laugh hit him right in the chest. Warm. Familiar. Dangerous.

"Miss Hart," he'd greeted her, aiming for professional.

But then she'd looked up at him, with that familiar mix of shyness and humor he remembered so well, and his chest went tight. Her lush pink lips curved up in a warm smile, her eyes dancing with amusement. And damned if he didn't find himself smiling for the first time in a week.

Then Ben had leaned against the front counter, trying surreptitiously to sneak a peek in the grocery bag Lily clutched to her chest.

"Are those cookies?" Ben asked, eyeing Lily with the same smooth grin he used on half the female population in Northfield.

Rush knew that look. Hell, every woman within a ten-mile radius knew that look. Ben Tanner was charming, cocky, and shameless. He was a decent deputy. Loyal. Sharp.

But the way he was looking at Lily—like he wanted to lick her up and down—made Rush's jaw tighten.

"No, just Sheriff Callahan's clothes," Lily had blurted, and then she'd frozen as the implication sank in like a brick.

Ben's eyebrows shot up, and he grinned, clearly enjoying himself. "Well," he drawled, his gaze dipping to the bag in Lily's arms. "That explains absolutely nothing." Then he winked, full of cocky smolder that made Rush want to jerk him up by the collar. "Like I said, if you ever need a ride, Miss Hart, you just let me know. I've got lights, sirens... the whole nine yards."

"Deputy Tanner," Rush had barked, making both Lily and Ben jump. "You on break or just forgetting what your job is?"

Ben straightened immediately and cleared his throat. "No, sir. Just keeping Miss Hart company, Sheriff."

Rush's eyes never left Lily's. "She's not your company."

A tense silence stretched between them until Ben finally mumbled, "Roger that, sir," and slipped out of the room, leaving them staring at each other.

Rush folded his arms across his chest. "You okay?"

Lily's pink cheeks bloomed with heat. Rush's eyes dipped to her lips before he could stop himself.

"I'm great," she'd said brightly. "Totally great. Everything's... great." She'd trailed off, looking shy and delicious.

Rush cleared his throat. He glanced toward the doorway Ben had just gone through and scowled. "If he—if anyone— bothers you, let me know."

He knew he sounded possessive. It wasn't like him, but the

truth was, he didn't want anyone looking at Lily Hart like that. Not when he could still feel her smooth legs wrapped around his waist while he slid into her heat.

"He's harmless," she'd assured him. "Anyway, thanks again. For... everything." She thrust the bag into his hands. Their fingers had touched, and she'd jumped back like an electric current had shocked her.

"You need anything, Lily, I'm around," he'd finally said gruffly.

"Great, thanks." She'd nodded quickly and hightailed it out of there before he could think of a reason to have her stay.

Now, weeks later, he was still thinking about the way her hands had trembled and her cheeks had burned, giving her away.

He couldn't be missing her. Not when they'd shared only one weekend of the hottest sex he'd ever had in his life.

And yet here he was, alone in his truck, half frozen, and fully miserable, replaying the way she'd smiled at him in the lobby, like some teenager.

He shifted on the bench seat, loosening his limbs as the heat finally pushed through the vents.

One weekend. That was all it was supposed to be. But Lily Hart had a way of getting under his skin.

He hadn't figured out how to get her out.

Chapter Twenty

"IT'S DAIRY. It's definitely dairy, but..." Bradley Benson closed his eyes, savoring another gigantic bite of the bacon-and-cheese-loaded potato skin, and moaned orgasmically. "Oh my gosh. It's so worth it. I haven't been able to eat cheese in years. It gives me liquid diarrhea." He stuffed the last bite in and closed his eyes, nodding happily with a long string of melted cheddar hanging from his mouth.

"So sorry to hear," Lily murmured, glancing surreptitiously at her watch.

Alas, Bradley Benson did not have a mustache.

He did, however, have a fascination with his food allergies, and after an hour and a half of being regaled with the intimate details of his gastrointestinal distress, Lily was ready to fake an asthma attack just to get out of there.

The date had crashed and burned somewhere around the phrase *noxious gas*, and now she was just focused on holding the flaming wreckage together until she could escape back to Evie's apartment.

Lily let her gaze wander around the crowded Northfield Pub, packed as always on a Friday night with locals enjoying one of Killian Kennedy's famous dinner specials and the wide selection of local Finger Lakes wine and beer. Lily's stomach rumbled pitifully—no maple bourbon-glazed pork chops with crispy brussels sprouts for her, thanks to Bradley Benson's confessions.

She *had* to stop agreeing to these blind dates.

Amber sat at the bar, chatting with Killian and Ford Clairmont, Theo's youngest brother, while Theo stood behind her, sipping a beer. Amber caught Lily's eye and gave her a knowing wink and an eyebrow waggle, silently asking what everyone else in the bar was wondering.

Good date?

Lily smiled brightly and gave her a subtle thumbs-up. *The best! So fun!*

Then she looked away before her sister could read the truth on her face.

Amber looked radiant as usual, heavily pregnant and glowing, wearing a cream-colored sweater that would've made anyone else resemble a hay bale. But not Amber. Of course not. Her sister glowed, like one of those women in maternity shoots who somehow managed to look ethereal while preparing to launch a human.

Theo reached over mid-conversation to rub his wife's shoulders and press a kiss to her temple.

Lily swallowed, blinking fast.

It must be nice to be loved that way. She had certainly pictured that in her future. The happy home, the adorable kids. The husband who chose her without question. She was happy for her sisters, of course. Allie had Davis. Amber had Theo. And Lily... she had Bradley Benson and his cheddar string.

Lily glanced toward the dartboard, where a few of the guys from the Northfield Fire Department were playing darts.

There was Johnny Rossi with his fiancée, Grace Kelly lookalike Charlotte Thornton—they were getting married this summer—plus that handsome firefighter Jake Kinsey, Ethan Doyle, a whole table of rookies, and the fire chief, Peter Buttaglia. Cap, as he was known around town, was dating her aunt Sophia. He caught her eye and lifted a bushy white brow. *You good?*

She gave him a reassuring smile.

Across the room, the fire department heckled the sheriff deputies from the dartboard corner. The rivalry between the sheriff's department and the firehouse was as old as Northfield itself. Mostly it played out over pool, darts, and the summer baseball league, where things got heated enough that Lily had once seen Cap throw his glove.

She knew many of the people here tonight. She'd grown up with some of the younger guys, gone to school with their sisters, danced at a few of their weddings with Tucker. They were good guys, and they were not subtle about watching out for her like their own kid sister.

Most of the friends she and Tucker had once shared had reached out over the last month to let her know they supported her, and what they thought of Tucker and the version of the story that he was trying to sell. At first, he'd tried telling people she'd gotten cold feet and left him at the altar, humiliated and heartbroken. That Lily was the flaky, sensitive one. Too dramatic to commit, instead leaving him behind to face everyone.

In Tucker's version, he was the victim and Lily was a liar who'd just lit her life on fire on a crazy whim.

It wasn't until the photo had leaked that the cracks in his story began to show, because it was hard to play the victim when the whole town had seen him with her best friend, virtually naked in a hotel room. There was no coming back from that.

But the flip side of the coin was that now everyone was watching out for her.

Small towns were fun.

Lily pasted a smile on her face and turned back to Bradley, ignoring the looks and the way her stomach growled. If she was lucky, Evie would save some leftovers of the Marry Me chicken. Strangely, she wasn't hungry right at the moment.

Bradley wiped his mouth on a napkin, grinning across the table at her. He wasn't a bad-looking guy. His mother had told Lily privately that he just hadn't found anyone meaningful who he clicked with yet, but Lily suspected there might be a few other reasons Bradley had trouble getting a date.

"Speaking of risks, did I tell you about that time I thought I could handle pepper jack? Disaster." He leaned forward excitedly, and Lily let herself tune out.

She felt him before she saw him.

A flicker of sharp, bright energy that made the tiny hairs on the back of her neck tingle and tiny pricks of awareness skim down her spine.

Her gaze drifted back toward the entrance and the man standing there, shaking the snow off his big sheepskin jacket and ever-present baseball hat.

Oh God. He was here.

It shouldn't have been a surprise. This was Northfield—everyone ran into everyone, eventually. They'd crossed paths here and there since the cabin. And yet, like always, the second she spotted him, her cheeks went hot. Damn her fair, redheaded complexion, giving her away like a human mood ring.

Rush Callahan filled the doorway, pausing to survey the room with that quiet, alert energy that made people shift out of his way without realizing they'd done it. A mix between awareness and protective watchfulness that her body automatically responded to.

A cheer went up almost instantly, rowdy applause and whistles from the deputies and firefighters clustered around the bar, and Rush's expression went carefully blank.

"There he is! Hometown hero!" someone shouted enthusiastically, followed by whistles and claps on his broad shoulders, along with several calls to buy him a drink. Ever since the accident, Rush had been elevated to hero status in the eyes of Northfield, even though Lily knew he didn't see it that way. He'd saved Chloe Whitmore, after all, swimming out into the canal that cold November night and pulling her from the wreckage when no one else could have. The fact that he hadn't been able to save Caroline didn't diminish their admiration. If anything, it deepened their respect for the mysterious, humble sheriff who hated the spotlight.

Rush ducked his head slightly, politely, and if she wasn't watching him carefully, she would have missed the way his jaw tightened and how his smile was fixed on his face. Her gaze trailed after him as he moved through the room, nodding to old friends and stopping to say a few words here and there, but even surrounded by the noise and welcoming in the bar, there was something about him that seemed... lonely.

The sight tugged at her heart.

He stopped to greet Amber and Theo, who also happened to be the mayor of Northfield. Rush wasn't in uniform tonight. When he shrugged off his jacket, the dark Henley underneath clung to the heavy muscles in his shoulders and chest. His jeans rode low on his hips, worn and soft and faded in all the right places, and when he leaned a forearm on the bar to order, muscles flexing under his swarthy skin, it was honestly just unfair.

He looked rugged and sexy and, unlike her date, not afflicted with a single dietary issue.

She let her eyes linger a few seconds longer, wondering idly if anyone else in this town fully understood that the sheriff of Northfield was, in fact, a walking sex fantasy. Then she raised her eyes—to find him looking straight at her. His lips curved just slightly, and he stared back. Dark. Steady. Knowing.

Busted.

A rush of heat flooded her cheeks so fast she was almost dizzy with it. She whipped her head back around like she'd just been caught staring at the sun.

"So," Bradley was saying, gleefully dragging his potato skin through the sour cream, "you ever try oat cheese? It's surprisingly moist."

Kill me now.

She could still feel it. The weight of Rush's gaze and the hum of chemistry that had about taken her out at the cabin.

"Are you gonna eat that last one?" Bradley asked, pointing at the plate between them.

Lily blinked. "You can have it."

She reached for her drink, taking a slow sip, trying to cool the flush in her cheeks. She was *not* still thinking about the way Rush's warm body had felt moving over hers, the way his thigh had slid between hers. The silky feel of his hair on her fingers as she held him to her breasts while he sucked and licked.

She pressed the glass to her cheeks as casually as she could manage.

And then the door opened again.

The cozy hum of the pub didn't quite stop, but a subtle hush rippled through the room and the energy shifted, like someone had opened the door to let in a gust of something cold and unwanted.

Tucker. Oh, lovely. And he'd brought Madison.

She sensed his presence like a change in barometric pressure. Loud, smug, and utterly oblivious to the fact that he and Madison were not welcome faces. He strutted in, puffed up with his usual self-importance, and stomped the snow off his boots, one hand curled around Madison's elbow.

Lily took them in at a glance; both looked tanned and well rested from what should've been her honeymoon.

How lovely for them. A complicated mix of emotions swirled through her. Grief and anger. Sadness and embarrassment. Hurt.

She focused on her breathing, slowly inhaling calm and exhaling tension—*I am a still lake*—and kept her expression composed, uncomfortably aware that every eye in the pub was watching her, Tucker, and Madison.

They stood there at the entrance just a little too long. No one greeted them. No one waved. Tucker, still wearing that cocky smile and Madison, less smiley and more subdued. She actually looked a little miserable, Lily couldn't help but notice, being dragged along on Tucker's arm. Her smile was brittle, and she wouldn't meet anyone's eyes. Guilt, or nerves. Maybe both.

Tucker searched the pub, and when he spotted her, his smile widened.

That smile—wide and polished and sharp around the edges —sent a warning straight to her gut. She knew that smile. Tucker could be charming when he wanted to be, but when he was feeling petty or mean, that smile was the opening shot. He always did have a massive ego.

Lily sat up straighter, lifted her spine, and straightened her shoulders. *New Lily*, she reminded herself sternly.

Tucker leaned down and murmured something to Madison, who crossed her arms and started biting her thumbnail, looking anywhere but at Lily. Then he steered them both toward the table.

Shit. She closed her eyes for half a second, searching for that inner strength she kept promising herself she had, but it felt slippery now and just out of her reach. When she opened them, her gaze went unerringly to the man across the bar, watching her intently with cool gray eyes.

She reached for the rose quartz around her throat and drew in a shaky breath.

I am a still lake.

"Lily," Tucker said smoothly, arms crossing over his chest like he was settling in for a show. His gaze bounced between her and Bradley with mock curiosity. "This your new boyfriend?"

Bradley let out a loud burp.

Lily blinked slowly. The universe, it seemed, had a real sense of humor.

"Oh no," Bradley muttered. He fished a folded white handkerchief out of his pocket like he was ninety and dabbed the sweat glistening on his forehead. "Thought I took enough anti-gas meds, but it's hard to tell sometimes." He looked at Lily apologetically. "IBS can be so inconvenient." He scooted out of the booth with a groan. "Excuse me. I might be a while."

Lily stared at the table, her fingers wrapped tight around her glass, her knuckles white. She could feel the weight of a dozen eyes on her—some curious, some protective, all watching, and she wanted to slide under the table and out the front door and vanish.

From the corner of her eye, she saw Amber and Theo making their way over to her from across the bar. Amber's eyes were fiery, despite her awkward, belly-first waddle. She looked ready to brawl. Theo looked grim, already loosening his tie like he might need to drag his wife off someone.

Cap was heading over, too, weaving around tables with a thunderous look on his leathery face. Killian stepped out from behind the bar, drying his hands on a dish towel, his jaw tight as he eyed Tucker.

The cavalry was coming.

Which somehow made the entire situation even worse.

She could not handle her family coming to her rescue right now.

Tucker was practically cackling. "Didn't think you'd have the guts to show your face," he said, dragging Madison against his side like a trophy he'd won at the carnival.

"I mean, it's not like we planned this little reunion." Tucker's grin turned smug, and his eyes glittered with something mean. "You're the one who decided to make a public spectacle of yourself. But then, you always did love attention, didn't you, Lils?"

Lily refused to rise to the bait. Not here. Not like this. But the words she wanted to scream trembled on her lips, and she pressed them firmly together, staring straight ahead as her hands curled into fists beneath the table.

But, of course, Tucker wasn't finished.

"Guess I should thank you," he said, louder now, like he thought this was some kind of comedy roast. "If you hadn't run off, I wouldn't have ended up with Madison." His laughter sliced through the crowded bar loudly. "Worked out pretty great for me. Not so much for you, huh?" *Har har har*. Tucker grinned slyly, looking around the bar for someone to join in on the joke. The bar stayed uncomfortably quiet.

Tucker either didn't notice or didn't care.

Her throat tightened painfully. Her eyes burned. Damn her emotions. *Don't cry. Not here. Not for him.*

He looked around like he was working the crowd. "Hey, all I'm saying is that trade-ups happen for some of us, right? So that's the new guy, huh?" Tucker jerked his chin toward the bathroom. "Looks like a real downgrade."

That was when she felt it.

A heavy, familiar arm slid over her shoulders, pulling her back against a solid wall of warmth and strength. A hard thigh pressed along hers as he slid into the booth beside her, anchoring her in place.

Rush.

His name moved through her like a sigh. She tilted her head slightly, catching the strong line of his jaw and the dark scruff darkening his face. He didn't look at her. He looked straight at Tucker, with that calm, unreadable expression that somehow said everything.

"No," Rush drawled, in a voice she felt more than heard in the rumble where she rested against his side. "That would be me. Right, darlin'?"

He looked down at her and raised one dark brow in question.

This okay?

"I... um...." Lily tried to form words, but instead, a huge grin spread slowly over her face.

Yes.

Rush returned it with one of his own, a lazy, lethal grin that tugged up the corner of his mustache and made her stomach flutter with memories.

Then, just as quickly, the smile vanished, and before her eyes, he changed as he turned to Tucker, the authority of a sheriff settling into his bones like a second skin.

"Is there a problem?"

Tucker's mouth, which had dropped open enough to see the gold fillings in his back molars, snapped shut. Lily bit the inside of her cheek to fight the hysterical urge to laugh.

"No problem," Tucker said, all false, chummy charm now. "Just catching up with my ex."

Rush didn't break eye contact. Instead, he reached down, took Lily's hand, and threaded his fingers through hers like it was the most natural thing in the world. His palm was warm and calloused against hers.

Tucker let out a bark of laughter, shaking his head like he finally caught the joke. "You had me going for a second there, Rush."

Rush didn't blink. "It's Sheriff Callahan."

Tucker's smirk faltered then slid off his face. "Look, I get it. You're playing the hero, but Lily and I have a history."

Madison tugged on Tucker's arm. "Let's just go," she said, looking uncomfortable.

Rush tilted his head slightly and fixed Tucker with a level stare. "You had history. Now you don't. I suggest you leave Lily alone now." Rush's words weren't a suggestion, and Tucker knew it.

Tucker hesitated, but he wasn't stupid, not when the sheriff of Northfield was looking at him like that.

Rush leaned in, his breath warm against the shell of her ear. "You ready to call it a night, sweetheart?"

Lily swallowed hard. "Y-yes." It came out as more of a squeak than a statement, but no one seemed to notice.

Tucker choked on his drink and stepped back as Rush stood to his full height, towering over Tucker and forcing him to move aside as he stared at them with his mouth open again.

Rush slid out of the booth and turned, offering his hand.

For a heartbeat, she didn't move. She just stared at the broad, calloused hand in front of her—followed it up with his thick wrist dusted with a few dark wisps of hair, along the hard slope of his forearm where he'd shoved up his sleeves, over the curve of his biceps and up, up, up until she met those amused steel-gray eyes that seemed to see straight into her thoughts.

Her mind flashed to all the deliciously naughty ways those powerful hands had felt against her much softer body, and heat surged through her in a dizzying wave.

Rush's mouth curved into a knowing grin, sealing her fate.

She didn't even hesitate.

"I'm ready," she said, her voice stronger now. She grabbed her jacket, slipped her hand into his, and stood.

The entire bar seemed to let out a collective exhale.

"Have fun with Sheriff Sexy!" Amber shouted from across the pub.

Laughter and raucous cheers erupted, replacing the tension with good-natured teasing. Someone whistled. Cap tipped his head toward them in approval, and the rookies raised their beers, not entirely sure of the occasion but happy to be a part of it anyway.

Rush stopped abruptly.

"Oof." Lily grunted as she walked into what felt like a brick wall.

He turned around, and for a moment, she wasn't sure how he would react, knowing how much he disliked public attention.

Instead, a slow, wicked grin crept across his face, and he lifted his chin toward Amber.

"We intend to, ma'am."

A fresh wave of laughter broke out behind them as he slung his arm around Lily's shoulders, tugging her close to the heat of his body.

And just like that, they walked out into the snow like a couple.

Chapter Twenty-One

"OH MY GOD. Did that really just happen?"

Lily closed her eyes and leaned back against the brick wall just outside the entrance of the pub, her breath puffing into the cold night air. Snow drifted down in lazy spirals, dusting her red curls and catching in her lashes like glitter. Her sexy mouth curved in a grin, and for the first time since he'd walked into the pub and seen her, the tension was gone from her face, replaced by laughter.

Fierce satisfaction settled in his chest at that look. The tight, pinched expression she'd worn while staring down that smug asshole ex of hers was gone, replaced by the smile he hadn't stopped thinking about in a month. Rush leaned a shoulder against the wall and didn't even try to hide the way he stared.

Her cheeks were flushed a deep, rosy pink. Her hair was down tonight, those soft wild curls spilling over the shoulders of her coat, a far cry from the tight, efficient little bun she'd worn the last time he saw her. The wool hugged her close, but he'd caught sight of the dark-green dress underneath from inside the pub. Sleek, clinging to her curves, and skimming over her waist and thighs in a way that made it hard to tear his eyes away.

A snowflake landed on her bottom lip, the pillowy, perfect pink mouth he'd kissed. Tasted. Bitten. He couldn't look away. Her tongue peeked out and swept across it absently. Lust slammed into him, brutal and sharp, making every muscle in his body tense.

She looked relaxed. Radiant. Beautiful.

And he wanted her so badly it physically hurt.

"You okay?" he asked, his voice rougher than he intended.

She opened her eyes and smiled. "Yeah. I mean—no. But I will be. That was humiliating."

"You didn't look humiliated. You were holding your own."

"Until you rescued me? Again?" Lily added ruefully.

Rush studied her, trying to pull himself back in. Her breath was coming in shallow little puffs, and he knew her well enough now to recognize the signs. "Shit. I shouldn't have brought you out here in the cold. Do you have your inhaler?"

"Yes," she gasped, already searching her purse. "I'm fine."

"You say that every time you can't breathe," he said dryly.

She took out the inhaler and puffed on it twice, pausing between inhales to hold the medicine in her lungs before replying. "You really can't help yourself, can you?"

He raised an eyebrow, not sure he wanted to know what she meant. "Meaning?"

"You have white-knight syndrome. Always there when the ladies need you." She tried to laugh, but it came out tight as she struggled to breathe in the cold air.

He rolled a shoulder and looked out over Main Street instead of at her, uncomfortably aware of the accuracy of that statement. "I'm sorry if I overstepped," he said.

She stared back at him, her eyes suddenly serious and more direct than he'd ever seen her look. "I know what it looked like in there." She winced. "But I don't need any more people treating me like I'm fragile."

"Hell, I know that," he said gruffly, his voice low and rough. "That's not why I did it."

Unable to resist, he reached up and gently tucked a wild curl behind her ear, letting his fingers linger just a moment on the smooth warmth of her skin. He didn't miss the way her breath hitched and her pupils widened slightly in the dim light, or how her lips parted just a little.

"You really sold it in there," she said huskily. They were just a step apart now. Their breaths puffed out icy-cold puffs that mingled together. "That boyfriend act. All growly and possessive."

Rush stared down at her and let his gaze drop to her mouth lazily. Tension coiled inside him. "Wasn't much of an act," he murmured. "If you were mine, I'd spend every damn day making sure you knew it."

Lily's playful smile faltered, and they stood that way, eyes locked on each other, for a beat. The silence between them was heavy with something else. Something unsettled and unfinished. The connection between them hit him like a gut check again. The first woman he'd even looked twice at in the last year, and she was staring at him like she could see directly into his soul.

"So why did you do it?" she asked, too gently.

There it was, glaring at him. He knew Lily Hart didn't need saving. She was strong. Smart. Capable as hell, even with the air of vulnerability he knew she tried to hide. But when he'd seen Tucker Cawthorn tower over her, smug and condescending like he hadn't been caught fucking another woman, something in him had snapped.

He hated drama. Avoided it like the plague. But when she reached for the little pink stone around her neck, he was crossing the room before he even knew what he was doing. He'd acted on instinct, like he always did when someone needed help. She was right about that.

He'd spent his life protecting people, especially women.

What the Callahan family didn't talk about was the night their mother died. Christina Callahan had packed up Rush, Rachel, and Sarah in the middle of the night, still in their pajamas, and bundled them into the back seat. The little girls were half asleep, clutching their stuffed animals, and hastily thrown together overnight bags.

Rush remembered the curve of the dry Texas highway, the black stretch of road ahead. His mom's white knuckles on the steering wheel, the sudden glare of headlights from a truck taking the bend too fast. The screech of tires. The sickening crunch of metal.

Mostly, he remembered her voice, calm even after their car slammed into the guardrail and twisted to a stop. "Rush, are you okay? Okay, be careful now. Get the girls out."

He'd shoved the panic down and done what she'd asked, unbuckling his sisters from their car seats, dragging them clear of the wrecked car. A bystander stayed with them while Rush went back for his mom. He'd tried so hard, but the front end had crumpled inward, pinning her in place.

Her face was bloody, and her voice was shaky, but she kept talking to him even as the firefighters arrived with the Jaws of Life.

"You're okay, baby. Take care of the girls. You're going to be okay. I love you."

He'd always loved his mother's voice. She used to sing to him and the girls at night, and he'd pretend not to listen because he was a boy and older and not a baby like his sisters, but he'd always secretly listened. Christina Callahan had already started fading away on the side of the road on that hot, sticky night, but she spent her last moments comforting her three kids.

He remembered the smell of motor oil and felt the heat of twisted metal. He'd held Rachel's hand and pressed Sarah's head down into his shoulder so she wouldn't see their mother's broken body being cut from the wreck.

He hadn't saved her.

But he'd spent the rest of his life trying to save everyone else.

Their father had been gone long before that night. He'd dragged them from state to state, chasing jobs that never lasted, until one day he just didn't come back. After that, their mother had done it all—worked shifts at a diner, paid the bills, and kept the three of them fed and clothed. She was strong, but she was tired, and somewhere along the way, she let someone into her life who made things harder instead of easier.

After the night of the accident, it was decided that the kids would move to New York to live with Gram and Pop. They loved them fiercely and gave them a safe home, but Rush had made a promise. No one had asked him to step in, but he did— taking care of Rachel and Sarah the way his mom had told him to.

When he left home at eighteen, it wasn't to escape; it was to serve. First in the Marines and then in the sheriff's department. He traded one uniform for another, but he never stopped protecting. It was the one thing he knew how to do.

Service was the only space he knew how to put all the things he didn't have words for—guilt, grief, loyalty, love. He never unpacked those feelings, but they were always there.

He couldn't save his mother, but damned if he wouldn't spend the rest of his life trying to make up for it.

Except the one time he hadn't been able to.

The dark little reminder twisted his gut.

Lily shivered beside him, pulling her thin coat tighter around her and stamping her feet in her flimsy leather boots. He frowned. She was a native upstate New Yorker. She should know better. That coat and those boots wouldn't hold off a stiff breeze, much less a Northfield winter.

"Come on," he said abruptly, jerking his head toward his Chevy parked under the streetlight on Main. "Let's get you warm. I'll take you home."

Lily nodded, falling into step beside him. The snow crunching under their boots was unnaturally loud in the silence. When they reached the truck, Rush opened the passenger door for her, and she climbed in with a murmured "Nice truck" while running her hand along the worn brown leather seat.

"Thanks. Pop handed it down." He closed the door and rounded the hood. He exhaled hard, watching his breath curl in the cold air. Gut check time.

What the hell are you doing, Callahan?

He was leaving in a month. No strings. No complications. He'd told her that, made sure she knew it before he let her take it a step further at the cabin, and now he'd just done exactly that. He knew better.

But as he slid into the driver's seat and shot a glance over at her—huddled in her puffy jacket, pink cheeks glowing, snowflakes caught in her hair—he couldn't bring himself to regret it. She was still breathing a little too fast, and an edge of worry slid under his ribs.

"You're wheezing," he said quietly.

"I'm fine," Lily said.

He leaned over and turned the heat to full blast. Her scent—warm and sweet—filled the small cabin of the truck, curling under his skin. He shifted back, resting one wrist on the leather steering wheel, the other draped across the back of the bench seat.

"I can't go home yet," Lily said, almost apologetically. "Evie's got a dinner date, and I don't want to crash."

"Then come to my place."

Her eyes flicked to his, and just like that, the electric current between them roared back to life. He forced himself to take a steadying breath and tried to ignore the way his body went haywire when she was this close.

"I did just stick my nose in your business," he added with a shrug. "Least I can do is let you yell at me in private."

His phone lit up with an incoming FaceTime call just as hers buzzed from somewhere in the folds of her coat.

Buzz. Buzz. Buzz.

He checked the screen. Sarah. Decline. Almost immediately, a message lit the screen. Rachel this time.

You have a GIRLFRIEND and you didn't tell us?? Kaylin saw you at the pub!!! You were SMILING with your FACE. Explain or we're coming over!

Lily pulled her phone from her pocket. "Three texts from Amber, one from Allie, and Evie just sent me a teacup emoji." She groaned. "I can't believe how fast this is spreading."

She checked her phone again and winced. "And now my mom wants to know when you're coming to Sunday dinner."

"It's Northfield," Rush said dryly. "By now, my sisters have probably already stalked your socials and planned our wedding."

"Oh my God," Lily said, leaning against the headrest. "We need damage control. How are we going to get out of this?"

Rush glanced over at her again, his eyes catching on the way she pulled her lip into her mouth and bit it. The surge of heat in his spine doubled. She really needed to stop doing that.

"I'll think of something," he said evenly. The wheels were already turning. If there was one thing he was good at, it was getting out of tight situations.

"Okay."

He put the Chevy in gear and glanced at her again. She was

watching him with those wide green eyes, calm and trusting. More trusting than she should be.

A snapshot of the last time she was in his truck flickered through his mind. Lily in her wedding dress, snow melting in her curls, looking at him with those calm, trusting green eyes.

He hadn't hesitated then.

And he didn't want to now.

"We can talk at my house."

Chapter Twenty-Two

SNOW SWIRLED STEADILY in the beam of the headlights, the kind that muffled the world, turning everything still and calm, like a perfect scene from a snow globe someone had just shaken. Lily had always enjoyed winter, especially in Northfield, where the town transformed into something straight out of a Charles Dickens novel.

Honestly, it was kind of magical. People came from all over to experience Christmastime in Northfield, and the town never disappointed. An army of volunteers decked every lamppost on Main Street with pine garlands and big red bows, stringing twinkle lights on everything that didn't move. The shops went all in, hanging festive colored lights and menorahs in their windows. The annual Christmas tree lighting on the village green kicked off the season, and it was happening this week.

It was impossible to be tense around all that cheer.

And yet, the man next to her was just that. Rush had grown rigid and quiet the moment they turned off Main Street onto the long, winding road that ran alongside the Erie Canal. She glanced over at him. His shoulders were stiff, jaw tight, and—

she noticed—his knuckles, still bruised and scabbed over, were wrapped so tightly around the wheel they were white.

The dark water of the canal was hidden beneath a fresh blanket of snow and ice.

For most people, the canal was a landmark of beauty that the town centered around. Serene and slow-moving, with a trail that drew joggers and bikers in warmer months. In winter, it turned magical. The water was drained just enough to freeze solid, and on the weekends, the banks came alive with skaters and sledders and vendors offering hot chocolate and steaming mugs of cider. Some of Lily's happiest memories had been made there—wrapped in scarves and mittens, pink-nosed, laughing with her family and friends.

Even after the accident, Northfield had gathered there. A town full of aching hearts brought flowers and candles to honor Caroline Whitmore's life.

She couldn't see the memorial now in the dark, but she knew the spot by heart—the bend in the road where her car had veered off, now marked by a wrought iron bench bearing her name and a bed of seasonal flowers the family lovingly tended. Two of Lily's aunts owned the florist shop in town, and she knew there was a standing order for a lavish bouquet every week.

She snuck a glance at the man beside her.

Rush stared straight ahead, his shoulders rigid, as they passed the memorial. Tension rolled off him in waves. The truck's heater hummed steadily, and the radio played a faint, cheerful Christmas tune, at odds with the somber heaviness that had settled inside the cab.

Her memories of this stretch of road were laced with twinkle lights and the scent of cinnamon, while his were carved in loss. It made her heart ache, seeing the way he kept himself from looking across at the canal.

"You okay?" she asked softly.

Rush didn't look at her. "Fine."

The word sounded like it had been dragged out of him with barbed wire. The man who had stared her up and down with heavy-lidded eyes outside the pub was gone, but she didn't push. Every line of his body read *Keep out*, and Lily got the message loud and clear.

After a while, he pulled onto a long country road not far from the Northfield town limits, and Lily's breath caught, this time, thankfully, not from asthma.

"*This* is your house?" Lily leaned closer to the windshield.

She'd driven by the old white farmhouse a hundred times on her way in and out of Northfield, always wondering who was lucky enough to live there. It was *the* house—her dream house. Big and charming, with a lovely wraparound porch and a big oak tree in the front yard just begging for a tire swing with a gaggle of kids taking turns on it. She freaking loved this house.

There were apple trees behind it, and a big frozen pond shimmered from the road. There wasn't a more perfect home to raise a family. She'd daydreamed about it often: kids running barefoot through the grass in the summer, and at Christmastime, a cheerful glowing tree in the front window.

And a hunky husband who loved her beyond measure.

Tucker had never seen the appeal. "It's not even in Northfield, babe," he'd complained. "Why would you want to live in an old house when we could build new?"

She'd just tuned him out and pressed her face against the window as they drove by, busy imagining all her cute babies being raised in a house that held generations of stories.

When they pulled into his driveway, the headlights glanced across the driveway, shining for a moment on the white-and-blue For Sale sign in a planter, half buried by the snow.

A strange ache bloomed—fast and sharp. Silly, really. It

wasn't her home, and it probably never would be, but it had looked like everything she wanted in tangible form.

"For another month," Rush said flatly, cutting the engine and with it, her strange nostalgia.

She turned to him slowly. "You took the job in Boston, then?"

"Yeah." He didn't look at her. "Figured it was time to move on."

She'd known he wasn't planning on staying, so the sharp ache in her chest shouldn't have been there. But seeing the sign, staked into the frozen planter, made it real in a way words hadn't before.

"I wonder who'll be lucky enough to end up here?" she wondered out loud.

Rush finally looked at her, gray eyes as cool as stone. "It's just a house, Lily."

But she knew better.

Chapter Twenty-Three

A sharp, piercing bark rang out as they climbed the porch steps. Rush pushed the door open, and a blur of brown-and-black fur barreled out to greet him.

"Hey, boy." Rush gave him a firm ear rub and solid pats as Riggs wriggled and shivered in doggy ecstasy, until his sharp black eyes locked on Lily.

She froze in the doorway as Riggs trotted over, nose twitching.

Good dog. Remember me? I'm the nice lady from the cabin.

Riggs's pointy ears tilted forward, and his long, regal head cocked. Lily tensed, too, half expecting him to growl or lunge for her throat. Both were terrifying, but she schooled her expression and tried to project cool, confident energy as he made his way over to her.

He nosed her directly right in the crotch.

"Oh!" she squeaked, confidence be damned.

"I think he missed you," Rush murmured, amusement etched all over his unfairly handsome face. He'd taken off his coat, leaving his broad shoulders perfectly framed against the doorframe he leaned against with his arms crossed. The casual, unapologetically masculine energy he emanated made her belly flutter. Lily frowned, hoping it hid the color she knew was creeping up her cheeks. Rush's grin deepened.

"I think he's looking for dinner," she grumbled, stepping back gingerly. Riggs followed, ears perking up with an interest that was equal parts intimidating and strangely appealing. He really was a majestic-looking dog, with his regal head and powerful body, and if she squinted just right, he seemed less scary and more badass.

Kind of like his owner, now that she thought about it.

Riggs sniffed again. *Good, Cujo. Nice boy. Remember me? We had a moment at the cabin? You like me, remember?*

She caught a glimpse of pointy white teeth. Her hands went clammy.

"Riggs," Rush barked. "Manners."

Riggs pulled back and seemed to judge her yet again and find her lacking before trotting back to his owner. She tried not to be offended. Instead, her attention drifted back to Rush's hands as he gave Riggs another rubdown while the dog closed his eyes and leaned into his touch blissfully.

That makes two of us, bud.

Inside, the house was even better than she'd imagined. Warm, extra-wide hardwood, a huge stone fireplace in the living room, and the kind of cozy charm she loved. The furniture was oversized and simple, covered in country florals and meant to last generations. None of that big-box store furniture for this gorgeous, character-filled home.

But the house felt hollow too.

And then she spotted why. Boxes lined the walls, some packed, some full and taped neatly up. There was no Christmas tree in the corner. No pine wreath on the door, no stocking hung from the fireplace. Just a stack of firewood neatly stacked by the hearth and a flannel she recognized tossed over the couch.

"It's a beautiful home," she finally said, strangely sad again and trying to hide it.

"It was Gram and Pop's." He shrugged out of his sheepskin coat and turned to hang it in the closet. "After Gram died and Pop went into the nursing home, he left it to me." He bent to pet Riggs. "Time for the next thing," he finally said, straightening. "The girls don't want it. It's too much house for them."

She nodded, her chest weirdly heavy again. For him, this house was an end, but for her it had always looked like her beginning. Ah. Well. She shook off the strange ache and smiled instead.

Rush held out his hands for her coat, and she stepped out of her boots. "Come back to the kitchen."

She tried not to watch his butt as he led them into the spacious, open kitchen, but she was only human, and Rush Callahan had the world's sexiest ass. She vaguely remembered sinking her teeth into those tight cheeks as he carried her over his shoulder to the cabin, and she grinned at the image.

God, he really was ridiculously gorgeous. The kind of gorgeous that made rational thought optional. Strong enough to scoop her up and carry her through a snowstorm, straight into the hottest weekend of her life. Yes, maybe that was dramatic, but he'd saved her in more ways than one. Who knew what would have happened to her if she had been alone in that storm?

Rush Callahan was dark and sexy and just dangerous enough to make her knees weak and her stomach flip like she was a teenager again. Too much to handle—and she wanted it all anyway.

Get it together, Lily.

The kitchen opened wide and bright—with a deep farmhouse sink under an oversized window. Instinctively, Lily glanced through it, searching for a glimpse of the apple orchard. Even in the winter dark, she could almost see the faint outline of rows of trees. For as long as she could remember, she'd imagined herself there, a basket in her arms, a family to pick apples with.

He glanced back from the open fridge, lifting one eyebrow at her. "Okay?"

"Of course," she said, aware of the blush rising hotly in her cheeks, but she smiled anyway. If she was going to spend any more time around Sheriff Callahan, she might as well get used to being permanently flushed.

She perched on a stool at the butcher-block island, forcing herself to focus on the kitchen instead of the way his back flexed with muscle as he worked. His hair was longer now than at the cabin, still just as silky looking, and suddenly she wanted to run her fingers through it. She'd kiss him right where it ended, just above the collar of his shirt, and taste all that warm, musky male skin.

Lord. One weekend of the greatest sex of her life and she was suddenly a hormonal teenager again.

She looked around to distract herself. The kitchen was safe territory, at least. It was straight out of her dreams. Open shelves, plenty of counter space, and a large window above the sink that probably framed a perfect view of the apple trees in bloom in the orchard out back.

"Did you eat?" Rush asked over his shoulder.

She winced, remembering her unfortunate date. "Does pretending to eat the breadbasket count?"

Rush glanced over. A swirl of dark, silky-looking hair fell over his forehead, giving him a rakish look. His mouth twitched in amusement. "That bad, huh?"

Guilt pricked at her. "I'm sure Bradley's a very nice man." She hesitated then added wickedly, "When he's not ingesting cheese. But alas, I don't think he's the one for me," she said lightly. "I just hate disappointing all the well-meaning grandmas who keep setting me up with these wholesome, sensible men who talk about their digestion on the first date."

He gave her a look that pinned her in place. "You could just say no."

Heat crept up her throat, and she tugged at her sleeve. "I don't like letting people down," she admitted a trifle defensively. "I'm working on it."

He didn't press, just held her gaze with a steady look that made her want to squirm, and went back to rummaging in the fridge. "I'll make you something to eat."

"Okay," she said, eyeing the contents of the fridge skeptically. The shelves were exactly what she expected: a few take-out cartons of Chinese food, a gallon of milk, a package of deli meat and... wine coolers? "Interesting choice of drink you have there," she teased, nodding toward the fridge. "I would've pegged you for a beer guy."

Rush glanced at the pink bottles, a smile tugging the corner of his mouth up and making her insides do a little dance again. *Down, girl.*

"Rachel and Sarah," he said with a wry grin. "They drop by way too often to check on me. Rachel's convinced I'll become a hermit out here, and Sarah's convinced my soulmate is one of her sorority sisters." He shuddered and shook his head. "Drives me nuts. You want one? Or there's beer, coffee—"

"A beer sounds perfect," she said impulsively, surprising herself.

His smile widened as he handed her a bottle, and his fingers brushed against hers, sending another warm jolt straight through her body and all the way up to her nipples, making them tighten in response.

Still crazy amounts of chemistry there.

"How are your sisters?" she asked, trying desperately to look worldly and sophisticated, like standing in a man's kitchen after she'd had life-altering sex with him and making small talk was a normal occurrence for her.

Rush turned back to the fridge, shifting and gathering things. Clearly, he was not a stranger to this kind of situation. "They're good, mostly grown up now. Rachel lives in Northfield now to be closer to Pop, and Sarah's in Buffalo, finishing up her senior year." He pulled out a sad-looking onion and a bell pepper that had seen better days.

"And your grandpa? How's he doing?" she asked.

Rush bent again to get the eggs and add them to the ingredients on the counter. "Pop's good. He doesn't complain. He's eighty-eight. Alzheimer's is tough, and his heart's not great, but he's hanging in there. This house got to be too much for him to keep up with a few years ago. I see him once a week at least. The girls visit whenever they can."

"I'm sorry," she murmured soberly. "That must be hard."

"Some days are good, some bad."

She shifted the mood back toward easier territory. "You know that thing's supposed to be red, right?" she teased, nodding at the pepper when he finally turned around.

Rush grinned. "Color's optional. Texture's what matters."

"Words to live by," she said, watching as he pushed up the sleeves of his Henley, exposing strong, corded forearms, and started chopping. He was more efficient than graceful, but he clearly knew his way around a kitchen.

She tried not to stare. Really. But there was something about the way he moved that made it impossible not to. He was confident and efficient with his motions, and the dancer in her admired the strong lines of his body as he sliced and chopped.

His strong shoulders shifted beneath the fitted fabric of his shirt with each slice of the knife, and her mind, horny and traitorous, flicked back to the cabin for the millionth time. To his long, strong body above hers. To the way he'd kissed her. Tasted her. Spread her open and grinned up at her, his white teeth flashing against the dark silk of his mustache, just before he—

She fanned herself discreetly and forced herself to look somewhere, anywhere other than at pure temptation.

"Was tonight the first time you've seen Tucker?" he asked without looking up.

The heat flash abruptly cooled. "Yes. The first time I've seen him in person." She wrapped her hands around the beer bottle and peeled the damp wrapper. "I called him when I got back from the cabin."

The chopping continued, slow and steady. "How did that go?"

"I told him I saw the photo of him and Madison." She cleared her throat. "He didn't deny it. He said that it 'wasn't planned,' like that somehow makes it better."

Rush scraped the vegetables into a pan and reached for the carton of eggs. "What did you say?"

"I told him I hope they're happy. And I told him I never wanted to hear from him again."

"Good." Rush nodded, stirred the eggs in the pan, and fixed her with one of his direct looks. Man, he had the cop thing down pat. She tried not to squirm under all that intensity. "Have you been okay since the cabin?"

"Okay? Oh, you mean—" *Not pregnant. Not thinking about the best weekend of my life. Not hoping you might stick around.* "Yes, I'm fine," she said.

"Good," he said simply. He cut the omelet in half and slid the pieces neatly onto two plates, popped up the toast and buttered it generously. Settling onto the stool next to her, he slid one plate her way.

She smiled her gratitude and dug in enthusiastically.

"So," she said between bites, "tell me about the new job."

"It starts in February. I'll be working at a private security firm. Grant Clairmont set it up for me. Theo's brother—your brother-in-law, right? Grant and I served in the Marines together."

"Oh, that's right. We met at the wedding. Grant, Ford, and Lieren, and their grandma Georgie, right?"

"That's them."

"That's a big change—sheriff to working security," she observed.

For the first time, his gaze slipped. "It's work," he said dismissively.

"Well," she said, setting down her fork, "thanks again for stepping in tonight. I knew I'd run into them eventually." A sigh slipped out before she could stop it. "Now we have to explain it was all a misunderstanding—that we're not actually together."

Rush finished the last bite on his plate, stood, and collected their dishes. He rinsed the plates, wiped down the counter with his usual efficiency, then dried his hands and turned back to her.

He didn't speak right away. Just watched her. His gaze dipped to her mouth, lingering there before meeting her eyes again. The frank interest in his expression hit her, hot and dark, pulsing low in her stomach until her breath stuttered.

Rush's energy, when he let her see it, took her breath away.

"We don't have to do that," he said.

SURELY HER EARS HAD GLITCHED. "What did you just say?"

"We could make it true," he said.

That smile. Those damn crinkles at the corners of his eyes that softened the whole stoic-sheriff thing and made him look so unfairly handsome her heart actually throbbed. For one unguarded second, elation shot through her. More of Sheriff

Sexy? Her body did a little shimmy of delight before his next words landed like a stone.

"A temporary arrangement." His voice dipped lower and a little rougher. "No more god-awful blind dates. My sisters stop hounding me, and in the meantime..." His eyes dragged over her again, slowly moving from the soft rise of her breasts to the curve of her waist, and then lower. She hadn't realized how much she missed that look—how much she'd missed feeling like a woman someone couldn't take his eyes off.

Rush's unapologetic appreciation sparked something wild in her, something reckless and overdue. She was tired of playing it safe. Tired of being pitied. She wanted to want things, and take them, just because she could.

"We both get exactly what we want until I leave for Boston," he finished.

"Temporary..." she said thoughtfully, testing the word. It didn't scare her. If anything, it felt... perfect. No promises. Not forever. No more shrinking herself to fit someone else's life. Just fun, freedom, and maybe a few firsts she'd been too busy being the good girl to even imagine. "Temporary I can do. But what exactly do you think I want?"

He cocked his head, studying her. "I think you should be the one to answer that question."

"I've spent a long time doing what I was supposed to want," she said slowly. "I think I'm ready to figure out what I really like."

"Yeah," he said, his eyes warmer now. "I can handle that."

She hesitated. "And it's not—there aren't other women, are there? I don't want to be one of many."

"No." He looked at her unflinchingly. "There's no one else, Lily. Just you and me."

Something inside her softened. Relief, yes, that there was no one else, but also something deeper that she didn't want to examine just yet.

He leaned in, his broad frame blocking out the kitchen light. So close she could smell the cold winter air and lingering woodsmoke clinging to him, and a flash of heat surged through her, making her knees wobbly. "If our chemistry's any indication," he said, his voice a husky murmur near her ear, "we're going to have a real good time together."

Her breath hitched. The weekend at the cabin flashed hot and fast through her mind. The idea of more of that was so far out of her neat and tidy norm... and yet, maybe that was the point.

She wanted to be that free-spirited, braver version of herself. The one who chose bigger, bolder moves instead of swallowing herself whole to keep everyone else comfortable.

He raised a hand to her cheek and brushed his fingers along her jaw. "I've missed kissing you, Lily."

Her mouth opened then closed again, along with her eyes. Kissing Rush had been almost obsessively on her mind the last month. The way he was so sure in touching her, knowing her body in a way that she was just beginning to understand. The idea of exploring that was seductive. Liberating. Dangerous. Thrilling. *Fun.* Very un-Lily-like. And maybe that was exactly the point.

It didn't get more real than spending a few months with Rush Callahan—taking what she wanted instead of what was expected. Heat flushed through her, and her mind crowded with X-rated images of his mouth on hers, the slow grind of his hips, the rough drag of his hands down her spine. God, she still wanted him.

She licked her lips without thinking. His eyes tracked the motion like a hawk.

Her brain short-circuited, melting straight into a puddle at her feet. Just like that, the memories of tasting whiskey on his lips and the scrape of his mustache over her skin flooded her.

And he knew exactly what he was doing.

He lifted his gaze slowly, a crooked, slow-burn smile tugging at the corner of his mouth.

"I'm not usually like that," she blurted before she could stop the confession. Heat climbed her throat. "That weekend... the cabin. It was..." She swallowed. "I don't just... I don't usually..."

Rush's eyes went a deep, smoky gray. "Maybe it was more you than you think," he said softly. "Either way, I'll count myself lucky it was me you let loose with."

He draped his arm along the back of her stool, shirt stretching over muscle, crowding her with heat and intent. She was way out of her league again.

Her fingers curled against the countertop. *Neat* had been her safe zone for years. The polite smile when she wanted to scream. The yes when she meant no, years of swallowing her needs to keep everyone else comfortable. Always doing the "right" thing.

But the cabin had cracked something open in her. For one wild, breathless weekend, she'd wanted without apology, and on the way back down the mountain, she'd promised herself she wouldn't go back.

Do the real thing, not the right thing. Even if it scared her.

And nothing felt more real than Rush Callahan.

"Okay," she heard herself say unsteadily. "We'll just... enjoy this. Until Boston?"

He dipped his head, his lips brushing dangerously close to hers, close enough to make her sway. "Until Boston," he murmured, then his hand slid to the back of her neck, drawing her inexorably toward him, and then he kissed her.

Not tentatively or carefully. His mouth claimed hers in a way that made her think of all the other places she'd like to feel that kiss again. Sparks that had teased for weeks went up like dry tinder catching fire. It was slick heat and teeth and tongue, his mouth devouring her while she pressed against him until she was more in his lap than on her own stool. The counter pressed against her hip as she leaned into him, hard muscles against soft curves. His other hand settled low on her hip, urging her closer, closer to all that fire.

He slid off the stool and dragged her off with two firm hands on her hips, settling her against him as he leaned back and kissed her deeply. He tasted like sweet, hot trouble—bold and dangerous, and oh so tempting.

She moaned into his mouth, her hips moving restlessly against his to chase more friction. She wanted him deeper, harder, her hips making tiny, pulsing moves, anything to ease the ache he'd left her with since that last kiss on the mountain. When his tongue swept deeper, she met him with a sharp, needy suck that had him groaning deep in his chest.

His hands skimmed up and cupped her breasts through her dress while she arched into his palms. She tugged at his shirt, frantic for skin, for more, for all of him. Suddenly, the last month melted away, and she was right back to those long, uninhibited hours they had spent exploring each other in bed.

She rose on her toes, threading her fingers through the crisp hair at the back of his neck, leaning her breasts fully against his hard-muscled chest. Her nipples tightened at the delicious contact and budded, a tiny sting of want, and she rubbed herself against him again, yearning for more.

He dropped his hands to her ass, pulling her into him until she felt his steel length imprinted against her, and she whimpered, rubbing herself against him shamelessly.

Her bottom and hips felt the draft of cool air before her mind realized what was happening. She looked down to find her dress pulled up to the tops of her thighs, leaving her black tights-covered legs exposed in the bright kitchen light. She looked up, suddenly shy again, only to stop, mesmerized by the look on Rush's face as he took in her body.

"I have to touch you, angel," he said huskily, sliding the fabric up higher, past the waistband of the stockings, exposing her hips and pale, bare stomach. "God, I've got to touch you," he groaned. "Put your arms up," he ordered, pushing the dress up and over her arms.

The innate command had her obeying before she thought twice, and suddenly she was nearly naked, standing before him in her delicate cream lace bra and tights while he was fully dressed. Instinctively, she crossed her arms over her chest, but he held her wrists and pinned them to the counter on either side of her. The sight of her arms pinned in his strong grip sent a delicious shock through her, and she shivered, making her breasts tremble and her nipples tighten.

"Fuck," he groaned, taking in her body with a hot, deeply appreciative gaze. "I can't stop thinking about your gorgeous fucking tits. Licking them and biting them until you—"

Lily whimpered. She couldn't help it.

"Yes," he muttered, nuzzling between the deep cleavage in her bra. She was suddenly very, very grateful she'd taken the time to put on pretty underthings. Not with any thought of her date—but for herself and now for the molten-hot look of the man in front of her. "That sound. I fucking love it when you make that sound."

The flick of his tongue down into the cups of her bra nearly undid her, and she tugged at her hands, her fingers flexing with the need to touch him.

"Not yet, angel," he murmured into her. "Let me touch you first. These nipples are begging to be sucked."

He dragged the lacy cups down with his teeth, and her nipples—dark pink and flushed already—popped up and over, and he latched onto one eagerly. "Jesus fuck, you're gorgeous," he groaned around the bud, and the enthusiasm in his voice made Lily melt. "Look how tight they are." His tongue swept across the ridged bud, and Lily heard her own soft groan at the erotic sight of his dark head at her chest, worshipping her with words and lips and tongue. "I want to bite them until they're red and swollen and then suck them until you come."

Her eyes rolled back at his words, and, hands still pinned, she arched her back, offering herself unabashedly to his mouth. He took deep mouthfuls of her, alternating between sucking hard and sweeping kisses across her collarbone and neck as if he couldn't get enough of her. "Rush..." she moaned, shifting her thighs together, already feeling the flutters down her spine.

"So needy," he muttered between deep sucks. "I'm going to make you feel all better." He let go of her hands abruptly, grasping her waist to turn and lift her onto the counter with an ease that took her breath away. Lily held onto his broad shoulders as he settled her where he wanted then tugged the waistband of her tights, along with her panties, down, down, first off one hip as she shifted, then the other, and finally off her legs completely.

Lily gazed down at the red line her tights had made around her waist, self-conscious once again, but Rush settled his mouth there, tenderly soothing the marks with his tongue, and she didn't think anymore.

"Oh, God," she moaned, trying to keep her eyes open. She didn't want to miss the sight of him, but his tongue gliding slowly down her body was enough to push her over the dark edge of reason.

"You need this, don't you?" he murmured, nuzzling her pussy. "Are you wet here for me, darlin'?"

Lily looked down, one arm supporting herself behind her on the counter and one thrust tightly into his hair, holding his mouth to hers, and she whimpered, unable to stop herself from trying to rub against his hot, eager mouth.

"Put your foot on the counter," he ordered, helping her when she just stared dazedly at him.

The position exposed her to him fully, in minute detail, and the same threat of shyness pulled at her, but Rush didn't hesitate. He pushed her thighs even farther apart, groaning at the sight of her pink, slick flesh, her clit a throbbing little bundle of nerves just begging for attention.

He slid his lips down over her belly and, nuzzling the damp red curls between her legs, murmured dark, erotic things that made Lily want to push his head down and her pussy straight into his dirty mouth because, holy hell, she wanted to come. All thoughts of shyness evaporated, and she threaded her hand through his hair, pulling him closer even as he willingly pressed his mouth to her slit.

"Goddamn," he groaned, one hand spreading her wide as he settled his mouth directly over her clit.

Lily let out a scream of pleasure.

"You taste so good," he groaned into her, taking a tiny nip at her clit and making her gasp before soothing it with a kiss. "Gonna make you come so hard. You deserve that, don't you, angel?"

His mouth was raw and rough, gentle and tender, and he was absolutely relentless as he ate at her. The dark riptide of pleasure threatened to carry her away, and she panicked once again, trying to edge away and see to his pleasure. She should— he didn't have to—"Rush, let me—"

"Don't fucking move," he murmured, shifting hard against her. The jangle of a belt buckle registered, along with the rhythmic movement of his arm, but all she could see was the back of his head, and all she heard was the slick sounds of his mouth working between her legs like he couldn't get enough.

Her eyes slid closed, and her head tilted back, her attention narrowed to one throbbing, aching need that only he could take care of.

"Christ, Lily," he growled against her wet flesh, the words making her vibrate. "You've been torturing me, walking around town in those tight little outfits, with these perfect fucking tits bouncing." His hand shot up, squeezing her breast hard, almost desperately.

In the space between their bodies, she caught sight of the muscles in his abdomen, tight and flexing, and below, his dick, a long, thick shaft, gleaming wet at the tip from his hand. Her mouth went dry.

"I've been picturing you in front of that mirror in your studio, nipples all tight and begging for my mouth."

He groaned again, sucking harder at her clit, and slid two fingers into her, gliding knowingly over the sensitive spot inside her that made her clench and flutter on his fingers. Lily's eyesight went blurry, and she tensed against the onslaught of desire threatening to take her under. "Oh, I'm—"

She gripped his shoulders and held on, a high-pitched whimper echoing in the kitchen as the wave took her over, again and again, making her body stiffen and shake while he stayed with her, absorbing the ripples with his mouth.

"Fuck, that was beautiful," Rush muttered when she finally stopped shaking. He rose, kissing her quickly on the mouth, where she tasted herself, musk and salt and pleasure, before he gripped her hand and brought it to his cock, fisting himself in both of their hands. His cock was flushed a deep, angry red, almost throbbing with need, and Lily stroked gently, afraid of hurting him.

Rush gripped her hand tighter, jerking their hands harder and firmer than she would have alone—several short, sharp pulls —until his cock, impossibly, swelled even more, and he pushed her back, coming on her pale belly with his jaw tight and his eyes fierce as they watched together.

Rush's breath came out rough against her ear. He leaned his head into her neck, panting in time with her own gasps.

Buzz. Buzz.

Rush's forehead lifted as he looked behind her to the phone vibrating insistently on the counter.

"Check it," he said gruffly. "Could be your family."

She fumbled for it, without looking away from his lips, still wet, still parted.

Lord have mercy, the man was pure sin.

She looked down and frowned. "It's Evie." She cleared her throat. "She said if I don't call her right now, she's calling the sheriff's office."

Chapter Twenty-Four

THE LAST STEP at the top of the wooden stairs squeaked loudly, and Lily winced. So much for slipping into Evie's apartment unnoticed. She touched her lips, knowing she also looked like a woman who'd just had a screaming orgasm ripped from her. There was no hiding that either.

Rush's hand was steady at her back as he guided her down the hallway, the warmth of his touch burning through her coat, or maybe that was just leftover heat. And now here they were. The respectable sheriff of Northfield had insisted on escorting her to her door as if they hadn't just ravaged each other in his kitchen.

Hard launch, apparently.

At Evie's apartment door, Rush's hand dropped, and they both stared at the big red velvet bow taped there.

"You okay?" Rush asked, eyeing her when she hesitated.

"Yep," Lily said, staring at the door. "Just realizing you'll probably have to meet my family at some point." She made a face. "They can be... a lot. Sweet, but a lot."

Rush grinned. "I've met them, remember?"

"Oh, I bet," Lily muttered, just imagining the inappropriate things the aunts had probably said to Rush. "Evie knows... by the way. About the cabin." She shot him a glance. "We don't keep secrets from each other. It's a twin thing, but everyone else thinks you dropped me off at a motel for the weekend."

He raised an eyebrow. "She knows how we spent the weekend?"

"She knows I wasn't up there crocheting an afghan, if that's what you're asking," Lily said dryly, while Rush let out a laugh. "But no, not everything." Evie's teasing imitation of Rush's *ride my face, sweetheart* echoed in her ears, and she felt a guilty flush staining her cheeks. "Some things are better left private," she said primly.

Rush laughed knowingly, but she took a deep breath, gathering herself to open the door just as another door across the hall opened. Evie's new neighbor stepped out with a tall, leggy blonde in a tiny red dress and heels behind him.

The woman melted bonelessly against the man's tall frame with a satisfied little hum. "You know where to find me, Lukey," she purred, her finger trailing down his chest to the dark ink peeking just above the waistband of his low-slung jeans.

Her blond hair was tousled, and the strap of her dress slipped down over her shoulder, revealing a lacy black bra and a deep swell of cleavage.

Lily tried to keep her eyes down politely, but it didn't matter. She had eyes only for one person, and it wasn't her.

Luke Holloway's jeans rode low enough to flash the cut lines of his pelvis. His arms bracketed the woman easily, all the muscles flexing as the woman draped herself over him. From what she'd picked up in the month since he'd moved into Evie's building, Luke was all rough edges and undeniable charm, if the ladies coming out of his apartment over the last few weeks were anything to go by.

He dipped his head and nuzzled the woman's neck, pulling

a breathless giggle from the blonde that echoed down the hall before he let her go. "I sure do. Night, Darcy," Luke said, leaning against the doorframe with his arms crossed, barefoot despite the chilly hallway, with a smear of red lipstick on the corner of his mouth. Utterly shameless.

The blonde giggled and swayed off toward the stairs. Lily straightened up and gave her a smile, but the woman seemed to be in some sort of sex haze and didn't spare her a glance. Luke didn't watch her go.

Instead, he aimed those charming blues straight at Lily.

"Evening, Miss Hart," he drawled shamelessly, like he hadn't just sent home a satisfied, glowing woman. He tipped his head at Rush. "Sheriff Callahan."

Evie's door swung open, and her sister appeared, her eyes immediately narrowing on Luke's bare chest.

"Do you ever close that revolving door?" she snapped.

Lily glanced at her sister, a tad taken aback at the venom in her voice. Evie's nose crinkled, and her lips pressed together into a thin white line. Lily did a double take, looking between the two of them. It wasn't like her sister to be such a prude.

Luke's grin only widened. "Hello, Lady Librarian. Didn't know you kept such close tabs on my comings and goings." He scratched his unfair abs lazily.

Color rose in Evie's cheeks, though her glare stayed firmly in place. "The entire building can hear your *comings* and *goings*," Evie snapped back. She spotted Rush, and her eyes widened. "Oh. Hello, Sheriff," she greeted in a much different voice. "Lily." There was a world of meaning in that *Lily*.

"Rush, this is my sister Evelyn, or Evie for short," Lily said. "Evie, you know Sheriff Callahan. Rush," she added shyly. Another world of meaning in that word that Evie no doubt picked up on. *Rush.*

An image of the back of Rush's dark hair bent between her spread thighs made her fan herself weakly.

Evie's eyebrows skyrocketed. "Of course. Would you like to come in?" she asked politely enough, although Lily knew her sister's thoughts almost as well as her own.

Promise I'll explain it all later.

"Thank you, but I'd better get home." He bent down and pressed a hard kiss to her lips. "Make sure you lock up." His gaze lingered on Lily for a beat before he nodded at Luke, who was watching them all with lazy amusement. "Night."

"Night, Sheriff, Lily. Evelyn," Luke added mockingly.

Evie grabbed Lily's wrist and pulled her inside to the sound of very masculine laughter in the hallway.

"Comings," Lily said, half in awe, as she leaned against the door and eyed her sister's pink cheeks. "That was a good one."

"I hate him," Evie said flatly, taking Lily's coat and hanging it on the peg by the door with more force than necessary. "That man is a human peacock. All swagger and no substance. The kind who thinks smirking and abs are a personality."

Lily tilted her head, studying her sister. "Funny. For someone you find so disgusting, you sure seemed... invested."

Evie froze for half a second before shooting her a deadly glare. "Don't even go there. Luke Holloway is irresponsible, reckless..." she sputtered, and Lily's suspicions grew even more. "He's absolutely the *worst man.*"

Lily watched her sister with open fascination. "Right, which explains why your face turned the color of the bow on your front door the second he saw you."

Evie spun on her heel and stalked toward the kitchen. Lily trailed after, braced for a lecture, and stopped short. Flour dusted every counter, cookie cutters littered the table, and a bowl of red and green sprinkles had tipped onto its side, scattering across the floor like confetti. Trays of crooked stars and lopsided trees cooled by the oven while Bing Crosby crooned "It's Beginning to Look a Lot Like Christmas." The air smelled like butter and sugar—pure holiday comfort—but Evie's scowl was anything but merry.

"Stress-baking?" Lily asked carefully.

Evie muttered something about *peacocks* and yanked open the oven to slide in another tray. A wave of vanilla sweetness rolled out with the heat. "Yes. Sugar cookies. Rolling the dough is therapeutic."

Lily plucked a still-warm star from the cooling rack and bit into it. "Mmm. Delicious."

"Some people do yoga," Evie said, shooting Lily a look, "and some of us bake." She reached for a bowl of rainbow sprinkles and shook them over a tray of frosted snowmen a little too aggressively.

"Same thing," Lily teased, licking the sugar off her thumb. "Inner peace, but yours is tastier."

She eyed the dining table, noticing the unlit candles on the table and the pair of untouched wineglasses. Oof. Maybe that explained why her sister was breathing fire.

"How was your dinner with Dr. Pierce?" she asked, tugging her sleeves up and grabbing an apron from the peg on the wall to slip over her head. She washed her hands and turned around, ready for some therapy of her own.

Evie handed her the rolling pin. "Canceled."

"Canceled?" Lily echoed, raising her brows. She spread more flour on the counter and plopped the dough onto it to roll. "On a Friday night?"

Evie picked up a heap of buttercream frosting on a knife, muttering, "Emergency board meeting that Dr. Pierce forgot to add to his calendar."

"And you didn't go with him?"

"He said he'd present my notes," Evie said, frosting the snowmen.

"Oh, Evie," Lily said, all teasing aside. "Why do you let him do that? You spent hours on those renovation notes, and now he gets to stand there and take credit... again."

"It's fine." Evie sighed, moving on to sprinkling the bells with red-colored sugar. "He's the library director. I work for him. That's how it goes. I'm just... disappointed, that's all."

Again, Lily added silently, biting back the words she'd said a dozen times. Dr. Adrian Pierce—rumpled hair, smug bow tie, and all—knew exactly how to charm a room. He made any woman feel brilliant while pocketing the credit for her ideas. And Evie *was* the brilliant one. He kept using that.

He's using you, Evie. You know he is.

"At least this means I get to eat with you instead." Evie set the cookie down and leveled Lily with a look. "Speaking of dates, explain how you're suddenly kissing Sheriff Sexy good night. I've had no fewer than ten texts swearing you two were cozied up at the pub and then were seen leaving together." She eyed Lily's lips and hair. "Explain."

"It's a long story," Lily mumbled. She looked through the old metal cutters until she found the gingerbread man and started rolling and cutting each cookie from the dough.

Evie adjusted her glasses on her nose and arched her brow, the same one she arched when people were talking too loudly at her library. It had a similar effect on Lily. "My night is wide open," she said dryly.

"It's complicated. This recipe is amazing." Lily bit into one of the thickly frosted snowmen and let it keep her mouth too busy to explain. She wasn't exactly hungry after Rush's omelet earlier, but chewing was easier than admitting to her twin that she was in an *arrangement* with the sheriff.

"Mmm." She reached for another cookie, a green-frosted wreath this time, but Evie's hand landed on hers.

"I had to hear this from someone else?"

The hurt in her voice made Lily wince. They didn't keep secrets. Not the big ones.

"We're not exactly dating," Lily said carefully. "He's moving to Boston at the beginning of February, so this is more of a..." She paused, aware of how ridiculous it sounded. "... a temporary arrangement."

Evie's eyes widened. "A temporary arrangement?" Her voice dropped to a scandalized whisper, even though it was just the two of them. "So... friends with benefits?" She gave Lily a knowing once-over. "That explains the sex hair and the swollen lips. He must be a god in bed," she added half enviously.

Lily groaned, touching her tender mouth. Already, she wanted more of those kisses. "Not quite," she muttered. *Yes, exactly.* "We're just having fun with each other... temporarily. No strings attached."

"Uh-huh." Evie nodded, as solemn as a judge. She got up to remove the trays and put in two more. "Because that always works so well." She turned with the kettle in her hand. "Hot chocolate?"

"Definitely." Lily sighed, glad that Evie's back was turned. She had her fair share of concerns, but she was all in now, no matter the outcome. After a month of thinking about the man, she knew there was something between them that deserved to be explored. "This wasn't planned. Tucker showed up at the pub with Madison, my date imploded over a cheese plate"—she waved off Evie's choked laughter—"and Rush just stepped in. Next thing I know, Tucker thinks we're together."

"How does this help you?" Evie asked mildly, pouring the hot water into two mugs. "You've always said you wanted a house and a family, the whole package. Marriage, kids, house with the front porch. You're not exactly built for temporary."

"It helps me stop being everyone's pity project," Lily said firmly. "No more awful blind dates, no more grandmas whispering about 'poor Lily.' Just me taking control for once with a clear end date."

She set aside the rolling pin. "I want firsts, Evie. I've spent more than half my life muting my feelings and settling even when I knew it wasn't what I wanted." She shuddered. "I don't want polite anymore. I want real, even if it scares me."

Evie leaned against the counter, studying her. "Just be careful, okay, Lil? Rush seems like a good man, but good men can break hearts without meaning to."

Lily forced a smile, even though the warning made her stomach twist. "We're just having fun. I'll be fine."

Evie pushed her glasses up with one delicate finger, giving her a look that saw right through her big words. Twins. Couldn't have any secrets. "Good luck explaining your temporary boyfriend at Sunday dinner. Mom already texted me—Rush is on the guest list."

"I know." Lily rubbed her forehead. "She texted me too. I'm not sure if family introductions are on the agenda for a 'temporary arrangement.'" Not that she had the faintest idea what *was* on their agenda. Sex, probably. Lots of hot, dirty sex with the Sheriff Sexy. Her heart thudded wildly in her chest even thinking about that.

"Oh, this is going to be fun," Evie said, rubbing her hands together. "One of us needs an exciting love life."

"It will be fun." Lily grinned reluctantly. "No more Bradleys or Coopers, and most of all..." Her smile turned wicked. "I can't wait to see Tucker's face when he realizes we weren't pretending."

Evie tilted her head. "Weren't you?"

Lily swallowed, her grin faltering for half a beat. "Oh yeah. We were. Totally pretending."

Chapter Twenty-Five

"There's an ice dam on Mr. Kang's roof. I sent Murphy over to check it before it brought down half his gutters. Mrs. Wasinski swore someone was rattling her back door last night—Wendell made a report. Looked like maybe a stray cat looking to get warm."

Deputy Ben Tanner leaned against Rush's office door, grinning and flexing his biceps. "Oh, and the bunco club called again to ask if you'd reconsider being their 'special guest.' They said all you have to do is take your shirt off. Pants optional."

Rush scrubbed a hand over his face. "Christ, not again."

At his feet, Riggs cracked open one eye, as if to check if he needed backup. Rush gave the dog's head a quick stroke, earning a grumbly sigh before Riggs settled back down. He had a perfectly good bed in the corner, but when Rush was in the office, Riggs always planted himself next to him like a shadow.

"They claim it's perfectly legal. Gets real warm in Mrs. Solano's living room."

Laughter drifted in from the squad room. Rush grimaced. Judy Solano and her blue-haired crew had been asking him to come to their Bunco night for weeks. If she didn't remind him so much of his Gram, he would've shut it down harder, but that mischievous twinkle in her eyes made it impossible to be more than mildly irritated that she wanted to see him naked in her living room.

"Don't worry. I told them I'd step in." Ben spread his arms, puffed his chest, and gave his badge an exaggerated shimmy.

Riggs lifted his head again, a low rumble building in his throat when Ben stepped closer. Ben froze, his hands half raised. "Whoa, Riggs. I thought we were friends."

Rush didn't glance up from the paperwork. How it kept piling up when he took time every morning to work through it was a mystery. "He's protective," he said flatly. "You should take the hint."

Ben just grinned, unabashed. "Times are tough. I'd even give them a discount."

"There's a reason they don't want you," Rush muttered back, neatly stacking the reports on his desk. His deputies ribbed him often enough, but only Ben was brave—or stupid—enough to keep pushing this particular joke.

"Pretty sure Judy Solano would tip extra if you flexed those sheriff muscles. I heard bunco ladies go wild for authority."

Rush leveled him a glare. "Shift's over, Tanner. Get the hell out," he barked.

Ben just grinned, tapping the doorframe before sauntering off to clock out. Cocky little bastard, but the kid had a good heart.

With his office quiet again, Rush stared down at the pile of paperwork. He loved his job—most of it, anyway. Enough patrol work to keep him moving, enough people problems to keep him useful, and the community, while sometimes testing the limits of his patience, consisted of the kind of people who looked out for one another.

He liked everything except the damn reports.

Boston wouldn't be better. Grant had been up-front about that when Rush had first asked about the job. Working in private security sounded active only on the TV shows. In reality, it was long hours standing outside penthouses and venues, checking badges, and waiting for people.

His phone buzzed on the corner of his desk, Grant's name lighting up the screen. Rush let it ring until it went dark. He wasn't in the mood to talk about Boston.

But at least he'd never have to hear the word *canal* come over the radio again.

Rush dropped the pen, automatically looking at the clock. Eleven forty-five. Almost lunch.

The squad room carried the scent of burnt coffee and stale doughnuts, which he never touched. He leaned back in his chair and glanced out the window. From where he sat, he had a clear view of Lily's studio, Pure Bliss Wellness.

The picture windows across Main Street glowed with Christmas lights, and Lily had hung festive garlands over the blue door like all the other shops and buildings in the village. Rush told himself he was just surveying the town, keeping an eye on things, but the truth was he'd glanced in that direction too many times to count already this morning, knowing he was looking for a glimpse of red hair twisted into the bun she wore when she was teaching.

Last night, she'd worn her hair down. The copper shimmer of it in his kitchen played in his mind, along with her shy agreement to explore the arrangement he'd half talked himself out of before it even left his mouth. He hadn't expected her to say yes, but as soon as the words were out, he'd found himself praying she would.

Lily Hart hadn't been far from his mind since the night she'd jumped into his truck, leaving behind a man who didn't have the first clue how to take care of a woman. Rush meant to make damn sure she felt every bit of his attention. She deserved that and more.

He forced his eyes back to the reports, but his focus was a lost cause. She was the most dangerous mix of woman he'd ever known—soft innocence wrapped around a sensuality that got under his skin faster than any bottle of whiskey he'd ever seen the bottom of.

Then there was the way she flushed whenever she had a naughty thought. Christ. She didn't even realize he could read her thoughts in the rosy pink blooming up her throat. His body reacted instantly at just the thought of his mouth following that trail of all the heat under her pale skin, tracing the path to her breasts and burying his face in all that lushness.

That was the problem. She made him want.

While he watched like some lovesick teen with his first crush, a scraggly group of kids in what looked like angel wings and maybe a sheep costume tumbled out the studio door. Lily's Christmas rehearsal must have finished.

Fuck it. He pushed to his feet, grabbed his jacket, and jammed his tan Stetson low on his forehead. Maybe he'd see if she wanted to grab lunch. Did she even have a lunch break? Hell, she needed to eat. He would just check on her. Make sure she had an inhaler with her and offer to grab a sandwich at the diner.

Make sure she didn't have any regrets about last night in his kitchen. He sure as hell didn't.

"Going out," he said to Myrna Bryne, at the front desk.

She looked up from her crossword, wearing the same long-suffering expression she gave anyone trying to sweet-talk their way out of a ticket. Myrna had been holding down the front desk longer than half his deputies had been wearing a badge, and she didn't take shit from anyone. He liked her no-nonsense approach, and he made it a point to grab her favorite cinnamon-sugar doughnuts from Morning Glory whenever he stopped in for the crew.

"Should've just moved your desk across the street," she said, eyeing him knowingly. "Save yourself the neck strain."

Rush grunted, shoving into his jacket.

Myrna smirked and went back to the crossword.

Never mind doughnuts. Next time, she was getting a bagel.

Outside, the sidewalks were shoveled, but an inch of fresh powder cushioned his footsteps as he walked, and deep slush piles lined the road when he crossed. The newscasters were crowing about this being the snowiest winter on record in the last twenty years.

He didn't mind the snow itself. It was peaceful, even pretty, especially on the early-morning drive into work when it was still fresh and made the world look quiet. What he hated was the jolt of dread every time the radio crackled with another accident. Fender benders were fine. He could handle those, but the calls that came for anything near the Canal made cold sweat break out on his forehead. Those were rare, and so far minor enough he'd been able to send Tanner or Wendell to the scene.

He tugged the collar of his sheepskin jacket higher and nodded to the people he passed. They smiled and waved. The best thing about Northfield was also the worst thing: There was no chance of anonymity here. Everyone knew one another and looked out for one another, for the most part.

He was the only person who hadn't done that, and walking up and down the streets day in and day out, he knew they all deserved a better sheriff. Someone who didn't break out in a cold sweat when he went near water. Someone who wasn't still carrying ghosts he couldn't manage to put down.

Movement caught his eye—an older woman stepping onto the curb in front of the studio from a sleek black Mercedes. A second later, her feet slipped, and she went down hard on her knees.

Rush's adrenaline spiked as it always did in that split second, and his boots were moving before he had time to think.

"Ouch," the woman said, bundled up in a scarf and some sort of fur-lined hat against the cold.

"Are you okay, ma'am?" he asked, dropping to his knees.

"Oh yes," she said, laughing.

Automatically, Rush clocked the details—expensive hat, soft brown leather gloves, pearl earrings. "I think so."

Rush's next words froze, unspoken, as he stared into the woman's eyes—Caroline Whitmore's cool blue eyes stared back at him from her mother's face.

Then she looked at him fully. "Sheriff Callahan," she said, uncertainty flickering across her face. She hesitated then extended her gloved hand. "If you'd be so kind as to give me your arm."

His arm moved automatically, steadying her as she rose and brushed the snow off her fine wool coat.

"Are you injured anywhere?" he asked briskly, schooling his features into the impassive mask he wore on duty. He scanned her, running through an assessment of potential injuries. "Anything hurt? Did you hit your head?"

"No, I don't think so. Except maybe my pride." She smiled ruefully. "Thank you, Sheriff."

"No thanks needed, ma'am. Just doing my job," he said formally, everything within him completely shut down and locked away behind a mask of professionalism.

"I've been meaning to talk to you," Mrs. Whitmore said gently, her hand still on his arm when he tried to pull away.

Panic clawed up his throat. For twelve months, he'd

managed to avoid this. He'd gone to Caroline's funeral, stood in the back with the rest of the deputies and first responders, and watched her family mourn their only daughter. Watched as Caroline's daughter, Chloe Whitmore, placed a single red rose on her mother's casket.

That image drove him to the punching bag night after night until his fists bled and exhaustion finally forced him to sleep.

"I wanted to thank you," Mrs. Whitmore went on, her voice catching, "for everything you did for Caroline and Chloe."

"I appreciate that," he said through the hard knot in his throat. "But that's not necessary."

"I think it is. And… we noticed you didn't make it to the memorial." Her eyes were too soft, too knowing, and Rush took a step back, forcing her to let his hand go.

"No, ma'am, I was out of town." He fixed his gaze on Lily's soft blue studio door at the top of the steps, clinging to it like a lifeline.

"We'd like you to come to dinner," Mrs. Whitmore said quietly. "Mr. Whitmore and I would like the chance to thank you."

Every muscle in his body screamed to retreat. "My schedule's tight," he began. "Trying to pack and move—"

"Yes, I heard," she said calmly. "Still, I'd like you to consider it."

"If you're all right," he repeated, taking another half step back. He just needed to escape those eyes, that feeling, that small face before the panic swallowed him whole.

"Sheriff Callahan," Mrs. Whitmore said firmly.

Her voice blurred into static, replaced by another, softer and slightly breathless.

"Hi there. Sorry we're running a little later than usual this morning."

His head snapped up. One pair of grief-hallowed eyes

vanished, replaced by another—Lily's. Gentle, steady green, smiling down at him from the top of the stairs. She held the mittened hand of a little girl bundled in pink, her dark curls tucked under a knit hat.

Chloe Whitmore.

His lungs cinched tight. Of all the places—of all the people —of course Caroline's little girl would end up here, in Lily's studio.

Mrs. Whitmore's face softened as she spotted them. "Hello, Lily. Chloe, darling, do you remember Sheriff Callahan?"

Chloe peeked at him and nodded silently.

Rush's grip on the railing turned punishing as the iron bit into his palms. The world narrowed to a tunnel, the edges blurring until it felt like he was back on the iced-over canal bank. His chest froze, and his breathing turned shallow and sharp. He could almost feel the water numbing his legs and torso, turning him into a deadweight as he sliced through the water to haul the little girl to the shore—alive but motherless. His stomach churned, and cold sweat broke out on his forehead, chilling him despite his warm sheepskin coat.

The rush of icy cold sharpened to a hard, electrical buzz, and for a horrifying second, Rush thought he might pass out right there on the steps. Instinct kicked in—the training drilled into him in places where panicking meant death. Anchor to the present. Catalogue. Control. Breathe.

The bite of iron under his palm, grounding him. The scent of pine resin drifting from the garlands strung along Main Street, clean and fresh. Down the street, a car door slammed, and children's laughter from inside the studio spilled out, high and bright. He locked onto the details, forcing his mind to track them like coordinates, anything to keep from sliding back into the soundless black water.

Mrs. Whitmore led Chloe down the steps to the sidewalk

until they were directly in front of him. She was a tiny thing, properly bundled up for the Northeast winter with a hat, a scarf tied neatly under her chin, and warm boots. All the winter gear couldn't hide those solemn blue eyes.

It took every shred of will not to see Caroline's eyes wide in the dark water.

"Do you remember Sheriff Callahan, darling? He was the brave man who helped you and your mommy." Mrs. Whitmore bent over to smooth a curl back under the little girl's hat.

The word made him stiffen before he could stop it. He cleared his throat and reached a place inside him that only years of military training and boots-on-the-ground experience could have prepared him for. What did you say to a little girl with sad blue eyes and no mother?

He focused somewhere above the little girl's shoulder before swallowing hard and forcing himself to meet her solemn eyes. "It's good to meet you."

There was an awkward pause as they waited for Chloe to respond. Rush glanced at Margaret Whitmore, then Lily, finding them both focused on the little girl as if waiting for something.

There was only silence. Chloe looked down, fiddling with her scarf.

Finally, Margaret explained. "Chloe's not quite ready to talk yet, but I know she thinks highly of you and how heroically you acted that night. Come along, darling. Grandpa is waiting with lunch." She looked at Rush directly. "I hope to hear from you soon, Sheriff Callahan."

Chloe glanced up at him then, and Rush caught sight of wide blue eyes and round cheeks as Mrs. Whitmore buckled her in and shut the door with a wave. The car pulled away, leaving the echo of the word *hero* ringing in his ears.

His vision narrowed again, and he looked up—Lily.

She stood a few feet up, green eyes steady on him, soft and unflinching at what she must have seen. The ice inside him creaked, a hairline crack reminding him he was still on solid ground, not sliding back under black water.

Chapter Twenty-Six

INSTINCT TOOK OVER. He took the stairs two at a time and reached for Lily.

He didn't think—he never did when it came to Lily. He bent to kiss her because words had never been his strong suit, and because maybe if he kissed her, he wouldn't see Caroline's eyes begging him.

Her lips parted under his like they'd been waiting, warm and yielding, unraveling the last shred of control he had. A hard, claiming kiss, meant to make him forget and to stake his place at the same time.

"Hi," she whispered when he finally lifted his head, slightly breathless, her arms looped around his neck.

He kissed her again, quick and hungry, until the sound of giggles cut through. Lily broke away, her cheeks blooming as pink as her lips. That shy, gorgeous smile knocked the air out of him.

"Is that your boyfriend, Miss Lily?" a little boy demanded, stuffing his arms into a puffy orange coat with a disgruntled look.

Rush gave him an unrepentant grin. *Sorry, boss.*

"We're good friends," Lily said evasively, shooting him a glance. "Bash, you know Sheriff Callahan."

"I should hope that's your girlfriend after that kiss," Mrs. Solano huffed, rounding the corner. "Now I know why you won't come to bunco, Sheriff. I wouldn't let him out of my sight, either, Lily." She winked at Lily, tugging the boy along. "Come on, Bash. Grandma's got to make a new plan."

Bash side-eyed him, skirting around his body like he had cooties, before throwing his arms around Lily's waist to hug her tightly.

Rush's smile threatened, but he kept his expression solemn. Hell. He planned to do the same thing the second they were alone.

"See you next rehearsal, buddy," Lily called after him. "Don't forget to bring the frankincense."

When the door shut, silence filled the studio. Rush's gaze lingered on Lily's flushed cheeks then dragged lower. The skintight black thing she wore hugged her breasts tight, lifting them high, the creamy swells begging for his mouth. His eyes tracked down to the sheer black skirt and pink tights outlining her hips and long legs—legs he suddenly needed wrapped around him again.

He swallowed a groan as she moved across the room. The back of her outfit dipped low in the back, leaving a smooth expanse of porcelain skin. Graceful, feminine, and so goddamn sexy he couldn't think straight. All curves and soft lines wrapped up and begging for him to tear her clothing off her body and get his hands on her bare skin.

Last night's kitchen scene slammed into him—Lily sprawled out on his counter, her thighs spread wide. He hadn't been able to think straight then either. Clearly, nothing had changed.

"Hey," she murmured, resting against the door. "That must

have been hard," she said, her eyes too soft and too knowing. "Was that the first time you've seen—"

The air in his chest turned thick and suffocating, threatening to choke him. He cut her off fast. "Have you had lunch?" He needed to replace the look in her eyes. Needed to erase it with something else. Something that wouldn't make him sweat and panic. Something he could control.

"Not yet." She tipped her head, studying him and apparently choosing to let it go. "I was going to eat now. I don't have any classes until the afternoon."

"Good," he said curtly.

"I'll just grab my purse." She flipped the sign in the window to Be Back Soon and brushed past him.

Rush moved to the door, locked it with a decisive *click*, and hung his coat on the rack.

He followed her down the short hall, his eyes on her round ass. His gaze snagged on another door before they reached her office. It was a small, windowless studio with a barre running the length of the mirrored wall. His pulse kicked hard.

"That's my private studio," Lily said, coming up behind him. She flicked the lights on. "I use it for one-on-one lessons or when I want to dance by myself."

Rush flicked the lights back off. Lily's eyes lifted to his, widening when she saw his jacket gone.

"Come here," he ordered, reaching for her hand, his cock already thickening at the thought of drowning out everything else but her.

She flushed prettily, hesitated, then stepped forward into the room. A slow smile tugged at his mouth. Lily liked when he took control. Perfect. He liked giving orders.

"Closer," he said, firmer, using his body to crowd her toward the barre.

She took another step, then another, until she stood in front of him, tilting her face up, trust he hadn't earned shining in her eyes.

Two strides and he had her against the mirrored wall with the barre at her back. He breathed her in like oxygen after drowning—her warmth, her calm. She was all soft, sweet woman, so open and pure in her want.

"Give me your wrists, Lily."

"But—"

"Let go," he said roughly. "That's what you said you wanted, isn't it? To stop being so damn scared."

Her lips parted, cheeks tinged a deep pink, but she held his eyes steadily. "Yes."

He curled his hand around her slim, pale neck, his thumb pressing just enough to feel the frantic flutter of her pulse. A few red curls had escaped from her bun, teasing his knuckles as he tilted her head back.

"You've played it safe your whole life. Missionary sex on Saturdays. Birthday blow jobs like a good little girlfriend. Never let yourself want more. Never let yourself lose control." He traced his fingertip along her neckline, dipping into the shadowy valley between her breasts, feeling her body tremble at his touch. "But you want more than that, don't you, darlin'?"

Her chest rose faster, her eyes huge in her face. Finally, she nodded.

"Say it." He leaned into her, letting her feel his hardness.

"I want more," she whispered.

He pressed his body flush against hers, letting her feel exactly what more meant.

"You ever been kissed in cuffs?"

Her eyes went huge. "N—no."

"I think you'd love that," he growled, turning her until she faced the mirror. He pushed her slightly forward, guiding her hands to the barre. He caught her wrists and pressed them there, holding her there easily with one hand. "You know I could put you in cuffs for real," he murmured against her ear. "You ever been fucked in cuffs, Lily?" He scraped her ear lightly with his teeth.

"No," she whispered, her breathing picking up. She didn't pull away. If anything, her body arched closer.

Her reflection stared back at them, face sex-flushed, lips parted, eyes wide with something between nerves and excitement. Behind her, he towered over her, a sharp contrast between his dark sheriff uniform and her delicate dancer's body. A rush of pure, primal lust seared through him.

He bent close to her ear. "I want to protect you and fucking tear you apart at the same time."

Her breath caught while she stared at him in the mirror.

Rush pressed his palm to her chest. "You have to breathe, Lily," he ordered.

He tilted her head back to rest against his chest and kissed her. He tasted her slowly at first, coaxing, savoring the sweetness of her response. Her full lower lip trembled before he caught it between his teeth and sucked until she whimpered, melting against him.

"Open that pretty mouth, Lily." His thumb swept over her lip, and she shivered, parting for him until he saw the flash of her pink tongue and her small white teeth. It made him crazy, remembering the sounds she'd made last night with his mouth between her thighs—how she'd writhed, begging, until he'd coaxed that sweet release from her right there on his kitchen counter.

He angled her chin up higher and kissed her, deeper, with nothing gentle about it now. He claimed her, demanding she meet him the way he wanted—lips and teeth and tongue, until they were both panting.

His hands skimmed down to her hips, catching the restless

grind of her body back against his aching cock. He stilled her with a low growl then rolled forward, pressing the hard length of himself into the curve of her ass.

She gasped, her body jerking against the barre.

Any other man might have backed off or treated her like a lady. He was sure that fucking ex of hers hadn't pushed Lily's boundaries the way he did, but Lily didn't need polite. She needed fucking. She was soaking wet for him, grinding back against him like she couldn't get enough of the way he tested her limits. That's what she wanted, and that's what he could give her.

"Feel that," he murmured against her ear, tightening his grip to grind against her harder. "That's what you do to me."

She whimpered, her hands fluttering at the barre, her body hot and desperate against him. Every shift dragged her damp heat against him, burning him even through his trousers. The thin barrier of tights and bodysuit was no match for how wet she was. He felt her slick warmth, and the knowledge that she was soaking wet made him throb painfully.

One of his hands slid up from her hip to yank her neckline down, freeing both perfect, flushed breasts into his palms. Her nipples were gorgeous, tight in the cool air, begging for his mouth. "Fucking perfect," he murmured reverently, pinching the taut, straining peak while he watched in the mirror.

His other hand shoved her top down, dragging her tights and skirt down just far enough to cinch around her thighs, far enough until he could slip his fingers down to her mound and into her soaked cleft. He circled her clit with the heel of his hand. "Dripping for me, just from playing with your tits," he groaned.

Her cry echoed in the studio, and her hips writhed back against him uncontrollably.

He withdrew his hand and stepped up behind her, jerking

open his belt and freeing his cock. "You want more?" he rasped, staring at her in the mirror.

Lily bucked backward, her naked breasts bouncing and sending him over the edge. "Yes."

"Then keep those pretty eyes open," he growled, lining his cock up with her entrance and pushing into her from behind. The tights bound her legs together, making her squeeze him even tighter. He gritted his teeth, his throbbing cock inside her, and held still, letting her adjust to him. "And watch."

He gave her slow, lazy thrusts, dragging his cock through her slick heat, pulling out almost all the way before sinking back in again. The friction made them both shudder.

The mirror gave him everything—her breasts bouncing with each thrust, her wrists held in his hands at the barre. Her eyes closed, lips parted on a silent moan.

"Eyes open," he ordered, snapping his hips forward. One hand found her clit, the other her breast, and he thrust harder. Her body rocked between his hand and his cock, seesawing until she was on her tiptoes, thrusting back against him hard, taking him deeper, wetter, faster. The sound of their bodies filled the studio, filthy and hot.

Her reflection was wrecked now. No, not wrecked. Gorgeous—red swollen lips, wild hair tumbling around her shoulders, eyes wide as she met her own gaze. "Watch yourself come."

Dimly, he wondered if she saw herself the way he did. Strong, stunning. Every inch the woman who took him apart without trying.

"Oh," she gasped, eyes squeezed closed. "I can't—I'm going to—"

Her release ripped through her with a shuddering sob, her body clenching so tight he swore. Rush held her steady, playing with her breasts gently until she sagged back against him, spent and trembling.

He kissed her bare shoulder then chased his own release with several deep thrusts before spilling deep inside her with a groan. For a long moment, he stayed curved over her, trying to catch his breath, their sated reflections still staring back.

She sank to the floor, the tights bunched around her knees.

"Oops." She looked up at him with a shaky smile, eyes glassy with unshed tears. "My legs aren't working."

"Fuck, Lily." His gut twisted. "Are you okay?"

She nodded, laughing as she wiped her cheeks. "Better than okay. I just... need a minute."

Rush tucked himself back in his pants, guilt roaring in his head. Christ, what the hell had he just done? He'd had plenty of rough sex before but not with someone like Lily. She was too sweet for that depravity. He was horrified at himself.

"Wait here," he said. He ducked into her office and came back with a water bottle, a towel, and a long cardigan he'd found draped over her chair. She was still sitting against the mirror with her knees against her chest.

He dropped down beside her and tugged her gently into his lap. Carefully, he untangled her tights, pulled them off, then held up the towel with a silent question.

She let her legs fall open, and he used the towel on her tenderly before wrapping her in the sweater and pressing the bottle in her hands. "I'm sorry—" He started to apologize for whatever the fuck that was. "That was—fuck, Lily. I shouldn't have—"

"That was a first," she cut him off with a shaky laugh.

His brow furrowed. "First?"

She smiled shyly. "I've never had sex at work before."

He searched her face. "You liked it, then?"

"Loved it." Her smile widened. "I told you I wanted new.

Real. That was both." She laid her head against his chest and sighed, a happy sound that made his arms tighten around her. He buried his face in her hair and inhaled deeply.

"Still up for lunch?" he asked after a beat.

"Starved. You have to feed me after that," she said, her lips swollen and as flushed as her nipples, both still damp from his mouth.

He grinned, unable to resist dipping his head to press a quick, hard kiss there. "Let's go eat," he said, his equilibrium back in place—for now, anyway.

Chapter Twenty-Seven

"Great. Just what this place needed—more romance."

Eden didn't bother hiding the disgust in her voice as she appeared at their booth with her notepad. Her sleek raven-black ponytail showed off the elegant line of her jaw, and the tiny silver stud in her nose glinted under the lights.

The Maple and Main uniform was supposed to be kitschy—white blouse, a little red apron over a black skirt and stockings, but Eden had somehow stamped it with her own brand of attitude. The blouse was tight, the skirt short enough to earn a second look, but the Doc Martens on her feet screamed *don't even fucking think about it.*

Lily had always thought Eden's vibe was far too cool for the old-fashioned diner. Today, Lily was especially grateful for Eden's blunt indifference.

If only everyone felt that way.

She risked a glance around. Three of her yoga grannies were parked in a booth across from them, pretending to look over their menus but peeking like they were at a show. At the counter, a cluster of off-duty firefighters and deputies nursing coffees, not even trying to hide their stares. Rush had nodded at their greetings when they came in, but the fishbowl effect of a small town was real.

Lily lowered her gaze to her menu. The words blurred. No one here had a clue she'd just let Sheriff Callahan pin her hands to a barre and fuck her against a mirror until she cried. Her lips still tingled. Her thighs pressed together beneath the table, every shift reminding her how hard he'd taken her... and how desperately she needed it. Outwardly, she was just a shy redhead blushing at a diner, when in truth, she'd never felt more undone in her life.

Another woman—a girl, really—a lovely brunette, stood at the hostess desk, shooting Rush soulful looks.

Lily recognized her vaguely. "Is that a friend of yours?" she asked, tilting her head discreetly.

"Sarah's friend," he said somewhat darkly. "That's Monica."

The girl sighed deeply, twirling her long hair around a pencil. Lily caught herself wondering about Rush's love life, and a sharp prickle she didn't want to name surfaced. "Did you break her heart or something?" Lily murmured.

"Doubtful." His lip curved. "More like her ego."

Before she could dig a little deeper, Gertie Marshall stage whispered loud enough to carry, "Such a shame she and my grandson didn't work out. He's a dentist, you know. Good with his hands."

Connie Hightower snorted. "My Jeffery's a CPA. He's got a steady job and good benefits. Lily would have been set for life."

"Who wants to kiss a CPA?" Gertie swatted her with a menu. "Dentists have better oral skills."

Lily forced her eyes back to the specials list, but the words "set for life" dug sharply. That was exactly what she'd almost chosen—a safe, steady life where passion wasn't required, where she could ignore the gnawing ache that she was settling. But sitting across from Rush Callahan, with her body still shaking from what he'd just done to her, she finally understood the difference. Security was numb. Passion was heat.

One of the deputies swiveled his stool. "Looks to me like she's already traded up. Isn't that right, Sheriff Callahan?"

Heat shot up Lily's neck, but Rush merely nodded at the teasing. Clearly, he was used to ribbing, but Lily wasn't.

Eden rolled her eyes. "This is all riveting. Are you two ready to order?"

"Hi, Eden," Lily said brightly, pasting on a smile. "I'll have a maple cinnamon latte and the soup-and-salad special. Tomato basil and Chicken Apple Harvest—no chicken, please."

"Vegetarian. Shocker." Eden's brows arched, highlighting her spectacularly drawn cat-eye. "And the usual for you, Sheriff?"

Rush didn't even glance at his menu. "Chicken pot pie and coffee, please."

When Eden stalked away, Lily let out a shaky breath. Lunch with Sheriff Callahan in uniform would've been surreal on its own, but after he'd had her spread out and coming apart an hour ago, she could barely make eye contact with anyone.

Eden dropped off their drinks, and Lily snuck a peek at him as he sipped the coffee, watching his strong, square jaw move. The black stubble on his face gave him a swarthy, sexy look, and his mustache only added to the appeal. His gray uniform stretched across broad shoulders, the badge pinned high on his chest. His Stetson rested on the seat beside him. The duty belt at his hips—gun, cuffs, authority—wasn't abstract anymore. She knew exactly what it felt like to be at its mercy.

And yet, sitting here, she realized how little she truly knew about him. She knew the groan he made when he came, the exact shade of smoke his eyes turned when he wanted her. But everything else about Rush was a mystery.

Last night in his kitchen and even during the weekend at his cabin, they had both been so far from their jobs and their identities that the situation had stripped away the reservations and awkwardness. Just two people, suspended from titles and baggage and other people's opinions.

But here, in the light of day in the middle of a lunch rush at Maple and Main, everything felt more complicated.

Her stomach growled, reminding her that she hadn't eaten anything since a rushed bowl of oatmeal early that morning before teaching two yoga classes and directing pageant rehearsal.

Rush's brow arched. "Hungry?"

"Starving." She took a sip, more to keep her hands busy than anything else. "So. We did this kind of backward."

"How so?" Rush caught her with that direct look of his.

"I don't know much about you other than you drink your coffee black, you always have a plan, and you..." Her voice trailed off, picturing him behind her in the mirror. "And..." She cleared her throat. "You don't exactly hesitate when you want something."

"Other things," he repeated thoughtfully, amusement flickering in his eyes. His shoulders relaxed against the booth, settling in comfortably, and she did the same, crossing her legs under the table. She'd thrown on an oversized soft cream sweater and leg warmers over her leotard and tights before they left the studio. The sweater slipped down one shoulder as she shifted, exposing the V of her leotard.

Rush's eyes flicked lower, lingered for a moment, before he dragged them back up to hers. A muscle in his jaw tightened, and her pulse jumped as a sweet, reckless thrill sparked in her belly.

"What do you want to know?"

She thought for a minute before starting with a softball question. "What's it like being a sheriff here?"

The diner door jingled, and Rush glanced over her shoulder. She realized he'd deliberately taken the seat with his back to the wall. Another stark difference between the two of them. She would rather slink down in the booth and hide, while he was built to protect and serve.

He shrugged. "Some days it's shaking hands and letting people see you around town. That does more to keep the peace than anything else. Other days it's paperwork, and sometimes there are emergencies."

His gaze drifted to the window, his smile fading as he watched the snow dust Main Street. For a second, she caught the shadow of the weight he carried. Her fingers itched to reach out and cover his hand with hers, just a small human connection at the sadness on his face, but just as quickly, it cleared and he looked back at her, the emotionless stone wall back in place.

"Was that the first time you'd seen Chloe?" The question slipped out before she could stop it.

His eyes went from warm teasing to gunmetal cold, answering her even before he spoke.

"No." The single word was final—a "push and we're done."

Lily blinked against the unexpected sting of it. What was she doing? This was supposed to be fun, a temporary escape where they could both take what they needed without dredging up all the dark, tangled emotions that made things messy.

And yet, her chest pinched, knowing he hurt. Her instinct, for better or worse, was to comfort, even when he refused to let her in.

"Tell me about your studio," he said instead, pulling them both back and into safer waters. "What made you decide to open a place like that?"

She thought for a moment, ready to give her canned answer about wellness, the one she'd repeated to the bankers and nosy neighbors a hundred times. But something about Rush's steady gaze made her tell the truth instead.

"Since I was little, dance has always been my dream. My mom encouraged it to help strengthen my lungs, and it worked. I got stronger. Happier too. Teaching yoga and wellness classes just felt like a natural extension—and a smart business move when I finally sat down to write a business plan." She gave a self-conscious shrug as old instincts to downplay herself kicked in.

Tucker had never liked when she talked about the studio. Her business plans and marketing ideas bored him, or so he said, although she'd always suspected it had more to do with him not being at the center of her world. One of the proudest moments of her life had been the day she'd picked up the keys to the studio—just her and Evie, buzzing with excitement. They'd scrubbed the place clean, painted it with the help of Allie and Amber and the rest of her family, while Tucker slipped away with some flimsy excuse. She should have seen it then, she thought absently, how little space he made for her dreams. How quick he was to prove that his came first.

"Smart move," Rush said quietly.

"I really am proud of it," she admitted. "My mom drilled it into all of us that college was nonnegotiable. I always knew I wanted to dance, but she pushed me to add a business minor. It panned out, I guess."

"No guessing about it. I see the traffic coming in and out of your studio. You built something solid." The admiration in his voice filled her with unexpected pleasure.

"She didn't want us to end up like she did when my dad left," Lily went on, getting more comfortable. "She went back to work with four kids, worked nights, weekends, whatever it took, until she built the success she has now." Pride laced her voice.

"She made sure we'd never have to rely on anyone else to survive."

Rush's gaze sharpened, and he nodded. "That's exactly what I tell Rachel and Sarah. Your mom sounds tough but fair."

"She is." Lily smiled, thinking about Annette. "She's tough and amazing and a little intimidating. Everything I am is because of her. I admire her more than anyone," she said simply.

Eden dropped off their lunches, and they dug in, chatting about lighter topics. Rush was wry and self-deprecating, and she laughed, enjoying herself as they ate. She asked him about his favorite color—black, which she teased him about. His favorite food—burgers. Deep sigh. She asked about his plans for Christmas—a quiet lunch with Pop and his sisters on Christmas Day but otherwise no plans.

"That sounds wonderful," she said, smiling. "Theo and Amber are hosting their annual Christmas Eve party, and my family always has dinner on Christmas Day." Gathering a little courage, she added shyly, "Maybe you could come."

"We'll see," he said easily. "What are you doing later this week?" he asked.

There it was again—the pivot. Clearly, meeting each other's families wasn't part of their arrangement. She'd asked about his family, about growing up in Texas, but every time she asked him a personal question, he only gave a brief answer before directing the conversation back to her.

Unless it was sex or teasing her, Rush kept his feelings close to his chest.

Except when he'd seen Chloe at the studio.

She couldn't forget the way his body had gone rigid or the panic flashing in his eyes when he'd looked up and seen her on the steps. Or the way he'd kissed her after the Whitmores left— hard, almost desperately, as if he needed her to burn something out of him... or maybe into him. That kiss had stayed with her, gnawing at the edges of her thoughts as they ate, but she couldn't put her finger on why.

"Was that the first time you've seen Chloe?" she asked, wondering if he'd answer this time.

He stilled, the easy smile fading from his face, and his eyes went cool and remote. The change was enough to make her blink. All that warmth and teasing and then nothing. "Are you done?" He nodded at her empty plate and glanced around as if looking for the check, avoiding her eyes.

Impulsively, she reached out her hand and touched the bruised skin of his knuckles. "What are these from?" she asked instead of answering him.

Rush turned his palm up, still holding her much more delicate hand but taking control.

Heat filled her at the contact. "Boxing. I've got a bag at the house. What are you doing this weekend?" He stroked the faint indent on her left finger where her engagement ring had been before tracing the sensitive skin of her palm.

"I teach on Saturday mornings and have Sunday dinner with my family, but otherwise I'm free," she said, aware that he'd pivoted once again and distracted her with his touch.

"Listen, you two." Gertie paused by their table, shrugging her puffy coat on. "Don't mean to interrupt this eyeballing thing you have going on right now, but I just want to say, good on ya, Lily." She stuffed her bright-pink beanie on her head, leaving iron-gray curls smashed around her head. "Those other dates were wasting your time when you've got a man like Sheriff Callahan." She eyed Rush with blatant appreciation.

"Gertie," Lily began, shooting Rush a look of mortification.

She tried discreetly to tug her hand back, but he only tightened his grip.

"Appreciate the vote of confidence, ma'am," he said with a small, amused smile.

"Don't 'ma'am' me." Gertie snorted. "That one's the real deal, sweetheart." She jerked her chin toward Rush and winked at Lily. "Don't let him get away."

Lily wanted the floor to open up beneath her.

"We'll keep that in mind," he said smoothly. His thumb brushed slow and steady over her palm, anchoring her with a weight and intensity that made her both calm and dizzy, as if she were about to step off a cliff and change everything.

Temporary, her mind whispered. *This is temporary*.

Chapter Twenty-Eight

THE STUDIO WAS QUIET AGAIN, the kind of quiet Lily loved best—when her students had gone home tired and smiling, and it was just her at the barre, finally free to move for no one but herself.

She flexed her toes in the soft silk of her ballet shoes, stretched her leg along the barre, and folded forward until she draped nose to knee, enjoying the pull along her hamstring and calves. Each breath she took lengthening and loosening her body as it softened.

The wall of mirrors reflected the clean lines she'd practiced until they were second nature—the deep arch of her back, the point of her toes, the sweep of her arm—rather than the restless flutter she'd been carrying inside all week.

Since Saturday, when Rush had walked her back to the studio after lunch, she'd only caught him in glimpses—his sheriff's truck cruising down Main Street, parked outside the hardware store, idling at the light in front of Maple and Main. She'd forced her mind to focus on her classes and the pageant rehearsal, well aware of the dangers of daydreaming about

Sheriff Callahan. He was wrestling with things he didn't—or couldn't—share.

But when she closed her eyes at night, or now, alone in her studio, it wasn't long before the memory of his mouth on hers distracted her. Her body flushed scarlet hot just thinking about it.

Before he'd walked back to his office on Saturday, he'd keyed his number into her phone. Rush Callahan, as Lily suspected, wasn't one to chat over text. For her part, she'd sent him only one message, a picture of her midweek pick-me-up latte from the diner. Someone had drawn what looked suspiciously like a broken heart in the foam on top.

LILY

Is Monica trying to send me a message?

His reply had been immediate, and she'd grinned at the screen like a schoolgirl with a crush for an embarrassingly long time when it came through.

RUSH

Monica who?

Was that how dating worked now? She was so long out of practice; she wasn't sure if she was even doing it right—if that was what they were even doing. Were insanely mind-blowing sex and clipped text messages how dating worked? If so, it was definitely more fun than any of the excruciating blind dates she'd suffered through. She wasn't even sure she'd ever really dated Tucker. They had been too young for that.

The contradiction gnawed at her. With Rush, intimacy had come almost frighteningly easily. At the cabin, they'd both been pushed to the edge, and in that pressure cooker, pretenses had burned away. Yet when it came to sharing anything but the heat of their bodies, Rush pulled the walls right back up.

Evie was no help. When they talked, she just warned Lily not to get hurt and to set clear boundaries.

That was the problem. Evie didn't have the faintest idea how messy and exhilarating it felt to push on those boundaries until she wasn't certain what "too much" or "not enough" looked like anymore.

After everyone left that night, Lily had slipped into her smaller private studio to dance and burn off some of the anticipation and confusion. Dancing had always calmed her, a way to strengthen her lungs and body and still her mind, but somewhere between opening the studio, teaching classes, and planning a wedding, she'd lost the part where she danced for herself. In the weeks since she'd bolted from the church, she'd been gathering those pieces back, one by one. Tonight, she was here again, breathing and reclaiming.

The faint scent of lavender drifted from the dried bundles she'd tucked around the studio, filling her with calm as she sank deeper into the stretch. *Inhale. Exhale.*

I am a still lake, not a stormy sea.

Movement at the doorway caught her eye.

Her head snapped up. Rush leaned one shoulder against the doorframe, watching her. Snow dusted the brim of his Stetson and the shoulders of his sheepskin coat. A to-go cup steamed in his hand, mixing cinnamon with the scent of lavender.

Something in the set of his shoulders looked heavy.

"What's wrong?" she asked, straightening from the barre.

"Nothing," he said, not moving from the doorway. His weight rested easily against the frame, just watching her with those quiet, steady eyes hidden under the brim of his Stetson. She wished she could see the color. His face may not have given away any hints of emotion, but his eyes told another story. Were they storm-dark with passion, like the ominous thunderclouds that rolled through Northfield in summer, or that pale, steel gray she'd seen before, cold and remote as a winter sky?

He shifted the cup, and the light caught on his knuckles—split and bruised, fresh marks layered over old. The punching bag again. She wanted to ask—would have asked if it was anyone else, but that's not what he wanted from her. Rush didn't want her poking at his bruises, not the ones on his hands and definitely not the ones under his skin, the bruises no one could see.

And that's not what you want, either, a voice inside mocked her.

"Keep going," he murmured. "I want to see you."

A delicate shiver coursed through her. The thin black leotard clung to her curves, the black tights leaving her hips bare without the buffer of a skirt, and she'd never been more aware of her body. She was used to being watched for form and rhythm, but under Rush's gaze, every nerve sharpened, tuned into the roiling energy he controlled so well.

The playlist shifted, the opening notes of a sultry track filling the studio—one she reserved for nights when she danced only for herself. Lily closed her eyes, surrendering to the music, letting her body move. She told herself it was muscle memory, but the truth was, she was dancing for him.

Her body found the rhythm easily. The familiar graceful glide of arms and legs, arching and bending her spine in the mirror's reflection, didn't feel like practice anymore. Every movement hummed with the raw, electric awareness of the man watching her bare herself in a way she'd never done before.

Her pulse fluttered wildly. Rush wasn't a student or a safe audience. This was the man who'd stripped her down past skin and bones, to the part of her she was still learning to claim. And yet she continued to dance, the music pulling her into a place where she felt most comfortable. Brave.

Even for Tucker, she'd never exposed so much of herself.

Her chest was heaving now, not from the exertion but from the sharp, aching awareness of him. The music throbbed low and steady, pulling her toward him on a current she didn't bother to fight.

On the last notes, she spun slowly and stopped a foot away, facing him fully. Rush hadn't moved, but the energy crackled across the space between them, alive and dangerous.

"I've never done that before either," she admitted, her voice slightly unsteady.

His eyes flickered over her, lingering on her breasts and hips, before finally meeting hers.

Storm-gray. She had her answer.

For a long moment, he said nothing. Then his hand rose, the rough pads of his fingers skimming up along her jaw, featherlight, to tuck a wayward curl behind her ear. Just two fingers. That was all it took for her body to go loose and warm and wet with need. She leaned into him, letting herself sink into the pleasure of being touched.

"You do this every day," he murmured, his thumb brushing her cheekbone.

"Not like that," she whispered. "Not for anyone else."

The words felt daring and foreign coming from her, and she wondered if she'd said too much, revealed too much for what they were. The truth was, she'd been collecting *firsts* with him since the moment she'd hopped into his truck, and she wanted as many as she could get before he left.

Emotions were messy and real, and she was done hiding hers.

"Good," he said. His hand slid lower, paused at the column of her throat, and stopped just above the rapid beat of her pulse.

She swallowed hard, pushing back against his hold slightly. "I didn't know you were coming."

His mouth curved wryly. "I didn't either."

"So why are you here?"

He didn't answer. Instead, he tugged her against him, one broad hand skimming the bare skin of her back, the other still holding the to-go cup. His grip shifted lower, cupping her bottom in that proprietary way that drove her wild, fitting her into the hard lines of his body. Her own much softer form gave no resistance as she rested against him.

"What is it about you, Lily Hart," he murmured, studying her face, "that I can't get enough of?"

Elation soared through her, which she quickly tamped down. For all her inexperience, she wasn't naïve. Rush had made it clear he wanted her, yes, but just as clear that was where he drew the line. She didn't let the thought sully the night ahead. He needed her physically, and she needed him too. It was more than enough.

She rose on tiptoe to press a soft kiss to the side of his mouth, smiling when his mustache tickled her. "I have some ideas," she said. Her eyes dropped to the cup with a Maple and Main stamp on the side. "What's this?"

"For you." He held it out to her. "Maple cinnamon latte."

Steam curled up, sweet and spiced, and she inhaled appreciatively, letting it steady her racing pulse. "Mmm. You remembered. Thank you."

Of course, he had. She shouldn't be surprised—Rush noticed everything. He was the kind of man who paid attention to the details no one else did. It was what made him excel as the sheriff... and devastate her in bed, reading the tiny sighs and gasps she made when he found the most sensitive places on her body.

Lucky, lucky her.

The radio at his shoulder crackled with Ben's voice. Rush's

hand disappeared under his coat to turn it down without looking away from her.

"Do you have plans tonight?"

She let a slow grin spread across her face. "Actually, yes. I have a hot date."

The effect was instant. Rush stiffened, pulling away. "You do?"

"Oh yes," she breathed, raising herself on tiptoe to brush her lips against the corners of his firm mouth. It still shocked her that she could do that. "Big plans. Huge."

Finally, the tiny lines at the corners of his eyes crinkled, softening the hard line of his jaw when he caught her teasing. His gaze dropped to her mouth before snapping back up, and her body thrummed in response. Her nipples tightened painfully under the thin Lycra, puckering for his mouth to abuse and then soothe. She pressed them delicately to his chest, feeling him stiffen in response.

She kept her free hand low and to her side, aware of the heavy weight of his duty belt—gun, cuffs, and any number of other mysterious things—and pressed her hips against his, rubbing back and forth delicately. The tips of her breasts pressed flush against the hard wall of his chest, and her achy, damp mound molded to the stiff length in his uniform trousers. Her eyes fluttered closed, and she lifted her mouth for a kiss.

Rush gripped her hips, pulling her flush against him, and dipped his head to kiss her. The kiss was deliciously rough and hungry. He parted her lips and flicked his tongue against hers, tasting her deeply. Shyly, she met his tongue with hers, caught the hint of cinnamon and maple, maybe from his own latte, and grew bolder when he groaned.

"Let's get out of here," he said roughly against her neck, his hot breath coming unevenly while he nuzzled her there.

"Okay," she gasped, almost dizzy with anticipation. "I'll get my stuff."

When she reappeared, she'd pulled on a long rose-colored wrap dress over her leotard and tights. Knit leg warmers and boots, along with her long camel cashmere coat—a gift from Amber from her secondhand boutique—belted at her waist, would keep her warm enough for where they were going. In front of the mirror, she tugged the pins from her bun and let her hair tumble in loose curls over her shoulders. A quick swipe of lip gloss for shine finished her look.

Rush's unblinking, hungry expression as he watched her let her know he liked what he saw.

"I'm ready. Oh, wait. We need this." She turned back around, balancing her latte in one hand while she picked up a neatly taped cardboard box near the front door. Rush took it from her.

He hefted the slight weight. "What's this?"

"It's for your tree," she said, distracted as she bent down to dig one-handed through her big purse for her keys. She never remembered where they were, and truthfully, she rarely locked the door. Northfield was incredibly safe, and her studio was across from the sheriff's station. She shrugged and gave up. "Let's go."

Rush put his hands on his hips. "Lily. Lock your damn door."

She glanced up at him, startled. "It's Northfield. Nothing happens here."

"Doesn't matter." He was back in his bossy sheriff mode again. "You lock up. Every time. You hear me?"

"Yes, Sheriff," she muttered, half exasperated, half turned on. It was annoying how much Rush Callahan's bossy tone really did it for her.

"I'm not kidding," he warned, narrowing his eyes. Only

when she turned the lock did his shoulders ease. "And I don't have a Christmas tree."

"You do now." She tossed the keys back into her purse and linked her arm with his. It was a perfect night for what she had planned. Cold but not unbearable, with big, fat flakes of snow swirling. Happiness bubbled in her, and she tugged him down the stairs.

"Come on," she said. "We're going to the tree lot."

"I don't need a tree."

"Spoken like the Grinch himself."

His eyes narrowed in warning, but she only grinned and stepped closer, tilting her face up to him in the glow of the streetlamp. Up and down the street, shop windows twinkled light and garlands. The sugary-sweet scent of kettle corn from the vendor set up in the Christmas tree lot drifted through the cold night air.

"It's not about what you need," she said softly. "It's about letting yourself enjoy something." Her gaze held his. "Like me."

Rush stared at her a beat too long. For one long, charged moment, she thought he might refuse. Then he exhaled, the frosty puff of his breath curling between them, and let her tug him toward the lot ahead.

"Fine," he said gruffly. "But I'm not stringing popcorn garland."

Chapter Twenty-Nine

"You're scowling," Lily murmured, tucking her arm through Rush's as they stepped between rows of trees. "It's ruining the vibe."

Rush looked wildly out of place in his uniform, the tense set of his mouth at odds with the strings of white lights zigzagging overhead. At her glance, he made an effort, lifting the corner of his firm mouth into something like a smile. "Sorry. Habit."

Except it wasn't just habit. Whatever had followed him from work still clung to him, even if he tried to disguise it.

"It's part of your charm." She handed him a tiny paper cup of warm cider, one of the free samples set out for shoppers. "Here. Drink and be merry."

He grunted, scanning the crowded parking lot beside the Northfield Dairy. Every year, it transformed into a Christmas tree lot, complete with carols crackling faintly from an old speaker and blending into the happy shrieks of kids darting in and out of the rows. The sweet scent of pine sap and kettle corn hung in the cold air, and Lily inhaled deeply, happiness curling through her. For her, the scene was pure comfort. For Rush, she suspected, the scene felt like chaos.

She and Evie had already been to the lot to pick out Evie's tree, a slim one that fit perfectly in the apartment. Still, it felt strange not to choose one for her own home. For years, she'd gone with her family to pick out a tree for the apartment she shared with Tucker. He'd stopped coming years ago, and she stopped asking, secretly glad not to have to watch him fidget and check his watch like he had someplace better to be.

Another first, she thought, smiling to herself as she leaned closer into Rush's warmth. At this rate, this was going to be a very exciting year.

At Rush's house, one of the first things she'd noticed was the lack of a tree. Moving or not, it was too bleak for December. A house needed at least a little light and cheer.

"Admit it," she said, looking up at him under the glow of the strung lights. "This is cozy."

"It's crowded."

"Hey," she said softly, squeezing his arm. "If this isn't your thing, we don't have to stay." A snowflake drifted down, catching on her eyelashes and refusing to melt.

He exhaled hard. "I'm not the best company tonight."

"Let's go then," she said immediately, her old reflexes kicking in despite her disappointment. "We can grab dinner instead, or call it a night—"

"No," he said firmly. "I want to be here, Lily. I'm just keyed up over work. It's hard to turn it off sometimes."

"What happened?" She held her breath, wondering if he'd answer.

"Nothing worth talking about." Before she could push, he lifted a hand to her chin and tilted her face up. He studied her for a moment, something unreadable flickering in his eyes before his shoulders eased. "Show me the perfect tree you've been talking about."

She tugged him down the nearest row to inspect the trees

until her eyes lit up in front of the giant fir. The branches were full and wild, and the top tapered to a precise point, just waiting for the star she'd put in the box she'd packed for him. Alongside it, she'd packed an assortment of ornaments scavenged from her mom and aunts, and an old metal tree stand she'd dug out of Annette's attic. Nothing matched, but they would add some cheer to his bare house. She couldn't stand to think of him going home to such bleakness.

"This one," she said with certainty. "I love it."

Rush eyed it, skepticism written on his face. "That thing's enormous. No way it's fitting in my living room. How about this one?" he asked, pointing at a much smaller, more typically proportioned tree.

"That one's boring," she said absently, circling the tree to see the back. "If I wanted perfect, I'd get a fake tree. This one has character. It will fit. I know it. I'm an expert at this."

"If you say so." His brow rose, but he didn't argue.

They brought the slip to the makeshift wooden hut, where a bundled-up teenager in a puffy coat checked them out. When Lily pulled out her wallet, Rush was faster, sliding a card across the counter.

"That was supposed to be my treat," she said as they wandered over to the tables set up with holiday crafts and gifts while the tree was bound and loaded onto Rush's truck.

"That's not how this works," he said simply, and she let it lie, understanding that Rush was old-fashioned enough to think going dutch was a terrible idea, and that, with him, there wasn't much room for debate.

"This will be fun," she said, warming her hands with a new cup of cider. The latte had done its job, giving her a boost of energy, and she fairly sparkled with excitement.

"What's the plan now?"

"The plan is to decorate," she said. "Technically, you're

supposed to wait a day for the branches to fall, but we can at least water it tonight and put up the lights. The lights are my favorite part of Christmas."

She paused to admire a table of handmade jewelry and bowls of polished stones. "Christmas has always been huge in my family. My mom bakes for days—cookies and pies, and cinnamon rolls the size of your head. Evie and I still watch Christmas movies in our jammies, and make hot chocolate when we decorate the tree. And of course, Theo and Amber are hosting their Christmas Eve party again."

She glanced up at him and kept her voice light. "Are you going?"

Theo usually invited half the town, although Rush hadn't ever come before. She held her breath, aware that she was asking more than he probably wanted, but she wanted him to meet her family. They were always so worried about her asthma and how she was handling the breakup. She wanted them to see the man in front of her and know that she was handling everything fine. Just fine.

But it was a lot to ask, and she knew it. Her family was loud and nosy and impossible to ignore. She loved them all dearly, but Tucker had never taken to them, and it had hurt her. She was afraid Rush would feel the same, and she knew it was unreasonable, but that would hurt even more.

What was happening to her?

"I hadn't planned on it," he said, not meeting her eyes.

The brush-off didn't surprise her, but it still left a pinch in her chest. She chose a delicate necklace with a heart-shaped rose quartz and held it up to her neck to look in the mirror. "What about you? Any Christmas traditions in your family?"

Rush shrugged. "Sarah and Rachel and Gram always took care of that. Pop and I usually went hunting at the cabin."

"Typical boys," she teased.

"I was almost a teenager by the time we moved here." He flashed a crooked smile. "Hunting deer had a lot more appeal. And it was a helluva lot quieter at the cabin."

She laughed, delighted at the thought of a teenage broody Rush Callahan escaping from a houseful of girls.

Then his hand covered hers, large and warm, folding her fingers around the quartz. He lifted it in the glow of the lights, turning it so the facets shimmered. "What's this?"

"Rose quartz," she said. "It's for healing and"—she flushed slightly, aware that she was treading into woo-woo territory—"love." She picked up the smaller, well-worn stone she always wore around her neck, holding it up for him to see. "My mom gave this to me when I was little to remind me to breathe. Some people think it's silly, but I swear it helps."

"It's not silly," he said, setting the necklace carefully back on the tray. "Tree's ready. Time to get our Christmas jammies on and decorate," he said with a wicked grin.

She bumped his arm with her shoulder. "I knew you were too good to be true."

"Careful—don't break it," Lily called, stepping back as Rush wrestled the enormous fir through the front door. Pine needles rained down on his Stetson, catching on his coat while he cursed under his breath and muscled the tree through the house.

She'd offered to help, but in true Sheriff Callahan form, he'd just given her a look and kept going.

Men. Lily leaned back against the wall, biting back a smile as she admired the view. Broad shoulders, made even broader by his sheepskin coat, narrowed to a trim waist and powerful legs in his dark-gray uniform trousers.

Riggs wanted no part of their nonsense. He'd taken one look at the tree, sighed in his deeply unimpressed manner, and retreated to his bed in the kitchen. He wasn't as menacing as usual with her, so she counted it as a win.

"Christ," Rush grunted, giving the tree one last heave into the corner of the living room next to the hearth—exactly where she'd pictured it the moment she first saw his house. "This thing belongs on the village green."

"Shush," she said, just as the top of the tree scraped the ceiling beam with a loud *shhhkkkk* that made him wince. "Wait until the lights are on. You'll see."

The house was quiet when they walked in, the kind of quiet that echoed off bare hardwood floors and half-packed boxes. Lily glanced around and felt a pang—she'd always pictured the farmhouse as warm and full of life, but in reality, it felt stripped of life.

She set her bag near the door, scanning the empty living room. "Do you actually live here or just squat between shifts?"

Rush gave her one of those unreadable looks. "No sense waiting."

She nodded toward the box she'd packed for him, keeping her voice light. "Well, we're going to unpack Christmas tonight."

He dropped to a crouch and wrestled the trunk into the tree stand. It groaned in protest as he tightened the bolts before stepping back to test its balance. Apparently satisfied, he took a utility knife from his duty belt and sliced through the plastic netting holding it together. The tree exploded comically outward in every direction. Rush threw up an arm to protect his face as the thing wobbled precariously, knocking into the mantel before finally settling upright.

"So pretty," Lily said happily.

"Pretty's one word for it." He tugged his Stetson off and tossed it onto the coffee table, followed by his coat, which he hung on a hook by the door. He ran a hand through his hair, scattering a few stray needles and stretching the uniform shirt tight across his shoulders.

When she turned, Rush was leaning in the doorway, one shoulder braced against the frame, a booted foot crossed in front of the other. He looked tired and tense, worn down in a way that made her chest ache, made her want to ease the weight he carried. There was nothing fragile about him. The broad set of his shoulders and the badge on his chest revealed him as every inch the tough, invincible sheriff, and yet the look in his eyes told a different, more vulnerable story.

"You're safe from the Christmas jammies. They didn't have your size," she teased.

He nodded, a faint smile on his lips. "What's next in this Christmas fantasy of yours?"

"Not exactly the wildest fantasy, but I planned for hot chocolate and popcorn." She took the ingredients for both out of the box she'd brought and headed toward the kitchen. "Why don't you make a fire, and I'll get these started?"

She headed to the kitchen and busied herself with making cocoa and popping the corn in an old-fashioned stovetop popcorn maker she'd found stashed in the cupboard. She added cinnamon and sugar to the melted coconut oil, turning the crank slowly as the popcorn snapped and popped. As far back as she could remember, Annette and the aunts had made popcorn like this. No microwave popcorn for the Harts.

When the last kernel had exploded, she poured it all into a bowl and carried it, along with two steaming mugs of hot chocolate, back to the living room, only to stop short.

The tree glowed now. Strands of mismatched colorful lights wound around the branches, casting the room in a twinkly, jewel-toned hue. Like the tree, the lights weren't perfect. Some were bunched in places, stretched too thin in others, but they were on, transforming Rush's living room with the homey, glowing warmth she'd pictured.

Rush sat sprawled on the couch, eyes heavy lidded as he watched the flames lick up the kindling. Riggs had planted himself at his boots. Master and his most loyal companion.

He'd taken his boots off, leaving him in his uniform, minus his radio, which he'd set on the end table next to him. Weariness carved deeper lines along his face, and scruff shadowed his jaw, but it only made him look rougher, powerfully male, and heart-breakingly human all at once. Her heart squeezed.

"You know," she said, setting the cocoa and popcorn down and curling onto the couch next to him, "I've always loved this house. Even before I knew you lived here."

Rush rolled his head toward her and waited, his eyes solemn with exhaustion.

"I used to drive by and imagine the family inside," she said after a moment. "A mom baking, kids in the yard, a dad coming home tired but happy. The orchard out back turning gold in September. I always wanted to know what that felt like." She let out a quick, self-conscious laugh. "My mom and aunts did everything for me and my sisters when my dad left, but it wasn't the same. I wanted a normal family." She paused then added quietly. "I still do." She took a sip of cocoa, letting the sweetness settle the lump in her throat.

She could have mentioned that her earliest memories were of living in the concrete complex of government-subsidized housing on the outskirts of Northfield while her mom worked as a waitress and went to school at night, but that would have shifted them from easy small talk into real feelings—and from the brooding set of Rush's mouth, she knew he wasn't willing to go there.

"How about you? You must not have stuck around for long after high school?"

"I couldn't wait to leave," he said bluntly. "I wanted to pull my own weight. Didn't want my grandparents carrying me when they already had their hands full with my sisters. Figured the best way to make myself useful was to join up. The Marines took me, gave me structure and a way to take care of myself. That's all I wanted back then. That and to see the world."

Lily took a deep breath, concentrating on energy. His. Hers. Theirs. Rush was charged with it, either awaiting more unwanted questions or hearing about her own upbringing. *That isn't what this is, Lily,* she chided herself. *That's not what you need from him.* At least not now. Not yet.

"You must have stuck out like a sore thumb with that Texas drawl," she teased, wanting to lighten the mood.

It worked. Rush's shoulders loosened the slightest bit. "We did. None of us really lost it."

"Thank God for that," she murmured before she could stop herself.

He grinned suddenly, showing a flash of white in the dim light. "You like that, do you?"

Her cheeks warmed, but she nodded anyway. "It's not bad," she murmured. "What made you come back home?" she asked after a comfortable silence.

He looked into the fire broodingly. "I came back because this is home."

She leaned in a little, searching his face. "And now you're leaving again?"

For a long moment, he didn't answer. Then his gaze cut to hers, his eyes a cool flat gray. "I guess I'm not meant to stay in one place."

Lily leaned back, the quiet settling heavily between them.

Her gaze drifted to the crooked tree in the corner, its top bent where it hit the ceiling. A smile curved her lips, more from habit than happiness. "Maybe that's for the best," she said softly. "This place deserves someone who'll put down roots."

Chapter Thirty

"You look tired," she murmured a moment later, setting her mug down. "We can always do this another night."

"I'm fine," he said, sinking deeper into the couch until his head tipped back against the cushion. Firelight caught the gleam of his silver badge and the faint shadow of a bruise along his jaw. "Fuck. Long day."

"Want to tell me about it?" she asked lightly.

His eyes went distant, his beautifully sensual mouth flattened under the sweep of his mustache. Silence stretched between them while she forced herself to meet his eyes calmly as a storm gathered in his. She'd never regret asking, but damn, it hurt to be shut out.

She untucked her legs and stood to leave. "You know, let's call it a night. I should—"

His hand shot out, catching her thigh above her leg warmers.

"Stay," he said. Half command, half request.

She hesitated, torn between what she wanted to do and what was good for her, before nodding. His big hands wrapped around both thighs, just under her sweater, and kneaded. She watched his face as he touched her, noticing as exhaustion melted into something darker. Hungrier. His touch was firm, strong hands working the tired muscles until her breathing deepened. He worked his way down, pushing the warmers out of the way and up her calves again, working her tired legs until warm, liquid relaxation flowed through her.

She wasn't blind to it—how he'd pivoted again from sharing any emotions—this time with his body instead of words. *That's what we agreed to*, she reminded herself. *A distraction for him and an experience for me. Nothing more.*

"Rush," she whispered, torn. He looked tired and worn, exuding a broody remoteness that screamed, *keep out...* and yet he caught her waist, tugging her closer.

"Come here."

"You're tired and—"

"I'm not tired," he cut in, his head shaking slowly, his gaze locked on hers. There was no softness in his expression, only the magnetic pull of a man who needed something she could give him.

He drew her in until her knees touched the couch. There was nowhere left to go but into him, and Lord help her, that was exactly where she wanted to be.

A low huff drew her attention downward. Riggs had shifted on the rug at Rush's boots. His big head rested on his paws, his amber eyes alert and following her every move. Lily stiffened automatically.

Rush must have felt her tense because he glanced down. "Riggs," he said quietly, "guard the door."

The dog heaved a put-upon sigh but got to his feet and padded out of the room, nails clicking on the hardwood before disappearing somewhere down the hall.

"Good boy," Rush said, then his attention was back on her. His hands slid up her thighs, pulling her closer, guiding her legs open and around his hips until she settled astride the hard length of him.

The weight of his duty belt pressed into her thighs, the cold, foreign outline of his weapon digging into her knee. A sharp, undeniable reminder in the warm, fire-lit room of who he was outside of it. She didn't know if the sight would ever become normal. It still filled her with dread, but like the man who wore it, she was learning to be more comfortable. Stretching her limits.

And when his hands flexed at her waist, she knew comfort wasn't the only thing she was learning.

She traced the metal buckle with tentative fingers. "What's this called?"

"Duty belt," he said shortly.

She trailed her hand away from the gun, brushing more metal she didn't recognize. "And this?"

"Taser. Flashlight. Baton." He listed them succinctly, watching her closely.

She stopped, looking at him. "Have you ever used the Taser?"

"Yeah. It drops a man to the ground in seconds." He hesitated then added matter-of-factly, "Had it used on me too."

She flinched, imagining it, but she only nodded. "It's in my way," she said, softer this time, with meaning he picked up immediately. The energy in the room sharpened, condensed into something tangible, quivering between them. Lily felt the slow, liquid pulse in her pussy.

His eyes went smoke-dark. He undid the buckle, lifted his hips, and placed it on the table next to the radio. "My turn," he said, rougher this time. He wrapped his hands around her calves, folded under her and covered in the leg warmers. "What about these?"

"Leg warmers," she said. "To keep dancers' legs limber between classes... or in Christmas tree lots."

"Cute," he murmured. He peeled the knit down each of her legs and tossed them aside before leaning back to drag his eyes over her, left in tights, leotard, and the loose wrap of her sweater.

Lily's pulse skittered at the contrast of it all—her softness against his hardness, the whisper-thin feel of her tights against the coarser material of his work trousers. She leaned forward, flattening her hands on his chest and feeling the hard expanse beneath—until the feel of something hard and unyielding under it stopped her short.

"What's this?" she asked, frowning.

His eyes flicked down then back up. "Vest," he said simply. "Part of the job."

Her fingers lingered, tracing the edge beneath the fabric of his shirt. It was heavy and warm from his skin. Another barrier between them and another reminder that while she spent her days using her body for healing and creativity, Rush spent his in a much darker world.

Emotion tightened her throat. She leaned down and kissed him, a gentle, appreciative kiss on his lips.

She ran her hands over his chest as she worked each button open, feeling the tight muscles in his abdomen clench and release when she tugged his shirt free from his trousers. He shrugged it off, and then it was Lily's turn to sit back and admire.

"Better," she murmured appreciatively. Broad shoulders tapered to a hard, sculpted chest, every muscle defined beneath a swirl of dark hair trailing down the ridges in his abdomen. His skin was warm, almost hot to the touch, and turned bronze from the firelight. Gently, she traced her fingers over a few old scars, wondering how he'd come by them, knowing his deepest scars were invisible.

She lifted herself off his thighs, suddenly remembering. "Oh, your scar—I didn't mean to hurt you."

"The only thing that hurts is here," he growled, catching her hand and pressing it against the thick, straining ridge of his cock.

Heat flared in her cheeks at his bluntness—shock, desire, both tangled until she couldn't tell them apart. She held his gaze then nodded, accepting the challenge there. This was sex. Raw, consuming sex. A way to keep it simple. No catching feelings. Just warm bodies on a cold winter night in a living room she'd once pictured so differently.

That dream had been softer, domestic, filled with laughter and love, but Lily let the thought go, surrendering to the fire in his eyes. She wanted this—raw, intense, maybe even out of her comfort zone, where she could explore her body, her desire, her power.

"Take this off," he ordered. His hands went to her sweater, tugging the bow around her waist until it came loose. The edges fell open, baring the deep scoop of her leotard. His eyes went molten hot and hungry. Possessive.

Then he dipped his head. His stubble rasped deliciously against her neck when he nuzzled, inhaling deeply before sucking the skin until she whimpered. His mustache scraped over the swell of her breasts through the thin fabric, the rough drag making her arch helplessly against him.

"Oh," she gasped, clutching at his head. His hair was thick, just starting to curl at the ends, and she threaded her fingers through it, holding him to her.

"Fuck, yes. Harder," he groaned, gripped her ass, and rocking her against him. Lily's pulse skittered, her breath catching at the rough insistence, teetering on that edge where fear bled into anticipation until she couldn't tell the difference anymore, and she let herself feel.

She tipped her head back, allowing him to devour her with his mouth. His tongue traced the delicate line of her collarbone, making her shiver.

When he pulled back, his gaze dropped to her breasts rising and falling erratically with every shallow breath. He brushed his knuckles over one tight peak straining beneath the thin fabric then caught it between his thumb and forefinger.

Lily cried out, her whole body jolting at the sharp, electric pleasure. "Fuck," he grunted, rolling her nipple harder. "These perfect tits, stuffed into that damn—" He glanced down at the clinging fabric. "What the fuck do you call this thing?"

Her laugh broke into a gasp. "It's a leotard."

"Leotard," he gritted out, grinding her down on his cock as if punishing her for distracting him. "Drives me out of my goddamn mind."

He pinched again, harder this time, making her whimper and jerk her hips against him at the shot of pain and pleasure. "No bra. Nothing between me and these perfect nipples but a scrap of fabric." He groaned. "Jesus, do you know what that does to me?"

His mouth was hot and rough against hers before she could come up with an answer. One big hand pushed the shoulders of the leotard down both arms to her elbows, trapping her arms to her sides and her breasts thrust upward.

"There is," she gasped, her hands tightening in his hair, but he wasn't stopping. "It's built in."

His breath hissed through his teeth as he yanked the tight fabric lower, exposing more of her with every rough pull until the peaks he'd teased were bare and tight under his fingers.

"Up," he ordered with the unmistakable sheriff's authority

that made her obey before her mind caught up, pushing her off his lap and onto unsteady legs in front of him.

A small part of her wanted to object, to test the power and strength he held so firmly in his hands, but another, more elemental part of her—the part she'd never admit to in the light of day—reveled in the knowledge of how he saw her. Not fragile. Not delicate. Strong enough to meet him where he was without flinching.

Rush hooked his fingers into the waistband of her tights, jerking the stretchy fabric down her thighs and off in one impatient tug. She shivered when the air hit her, her every nerve heightened, the rawness of it making her whimper.

He leaned back, his gaze sweeping her with an intensity that made her knees shake even as she saw herself through his eyes. Her body was a tool of her trade, lithe and strong from years at the barre, soft in places where his eyes lingered the longest. Her hair teased her back, tumbling around her flushed face, leaving her looking wanton. Undone.

She didn't recognize herself, and yet she did. She felt the siren song of lust and desire coursing through her, leaving her face flushed and her body achy, trembling... and wet. So very wet.

"Perfect," he murmured, pulling her closer to suck one rosy nipple in his mouth while the other hand pressed into her taut stomach. His fingers spread until his thumb rested at the top of the dark-red curls of her mound, a stark sight resting boldly on her most secret, sensitive place. He stroked her then, a light glide of his thumb into the slick folds, his fingers sliding easily into her heat.

She jolted, her head snapping back as a sob caught in her throat.

"So wet for me, angel," he rasped, watching her hungrily. His mouth closed over her nipple, working her with a slow, merciless precision that pushed her higher, balancing her on the knife-edge of reason.

When his thumb slipped away and two long fingers pressed inside her, there was no hesitation and no resistance from her body. He grazed over a hot spot that made her come up on her toes.

He grinned around her breasts, dark satisfaction in his eyes. "Liked that, did you?"

She bent to kiss him, rubbing her tongue softly against his, tasting dark chocolate and even darker lust. The contrast was tantalizing.

Her thighs trembled, heat flooding her veins as she watched his hand move between them, so much darker against her pale skin. The scrape of his stubble against her breast, the blunt strength of his fingers working her—it was too much and not nearly enough. She clung to his shoulders, fighting the dizzy climb he was ruthlessly pushing her toward, knowing he was showing her exactly how much she could take.

"No." The word tore out of her on a gasp, her body jerking back from his tempting hands.

Rush stilled instantly, sitting back with his chest heaving and his eyes gone storm dark. Wary. "No?"

She shook her head and forced herself to hold his gaze. "I want to feel you—" Her throat tightened, but she pushed the words out anyway. "I want to feel you inside me when I come."

Rush's eyes went even darker at her words. He seemed to see right through her before leaning back against the couch, his eyes watchful. "You want this?" He took her hand and pressed it tightly against his cock, straining against the zipper of his trousers. "Then take it."

Heat licked down her spine, and she wondered why she hadn't just let him take over. She would have come in another second, had been so close. But some part of her, a tiny piece she'd ignored for too long, had wanted to take control the way he did so easily.

And once again, she'd bitten off more than she could chew.

She concentrated on her breathing, thighs shaking as she bent her knees and settled astride him, snugging herself tight against the thick bulge straining the zipper of his trousers. He didn't soothe or coax her; he stretched his arms along the back of the couch and gazed at her with heavy-lidded eyes as she considered him.

She rolled her hips slowly, dragging herself along his cock, and glanced at him to see his reaction. His nostrils flared, but he stayed still, only his eyes betraying his tension.

Good. She wanted him to feel it.

She pressed down harder on the next pass; the zipper scraped a whisper of friction against her clit, sending sparks through her nipples and tightening them to aching points. His jaw ticked, and his fingers flexed against the couch, but he resisted the urge to grab hold of her and take over.

She rewarded him with a light kiss, teasing his mouth open with her tongue and pulling back when he did. She ignored the growl and smiled inwardly.

"Rush," she murmured. "Look at me."

His gaze snapped up, and she held it, refusing to look away. She shifted again, slower this time, letting him feel the slick heat of her through the fabric of his trousers. Her hands drifted lower, brushing over the tight ridges of his stomach, and she smiled faintly when he inhaled sharply—an inhale that never quite made its way back out—as she traced the outline of his cock through his trousers.

She didn't rush. She took her time unbuttoning him, savoring the way anticipation sharpened the tension in his body. The button came loose under her fingers, then the zipper, shockingly loud in the quiet room. She pushed the fabric aside and slipped her hand inside, her fingertips brushing warm skin and coarse hair before curling around him.

She freed him slowly. He was beautifully erect, thick and heavy, jutting up proudly through a thick nest of dark hair, and she shivered at the knowledge of what he could do to her.

The pleasure he could bring her. She wanted it all.

She stroked him, marveling at the contrast—the hot, silken skin stretched over steel. He twitched in her hand, the muscles in his chest and stomach hardening, but he stayed utterly still, letting her explore. His restraint made her bolder. She shifted to guide him lower, teasing the thick head through her slick folds, coating him but keeping him just outside her entrance. Just enough to make them both groan.

His eyes caught on her hand between them, watching as she slicked him up and down her wetness before circling her clit for the sheer pleasure of it. Again. Again. Again, until she shuddered.

"Now. I want to fuck you now," she gasped.

His composure snapped. His big hands clamped down hard on her waist, hauling her over him. Thighs trembling, she lowered herself slowly onto him, inch by inch. The stretch was exquisite, stealing her breath, pulling a sound from her throat she couldn't have smothered if she'd tried.

She sank down until he was buried fully inside her. A low sound dragged out of him, rougher than a groan, and she paused. The fullness made her dizzy, the pulse of him throbbing deep where she was stretched tightly around him. Her fingers dug into his shoulders, clinging to the solid wall of muscle beneath.

The world narrowed to the hot slide of her body over his, the unbearable heat of him inside her. She rolled her hips to feel every ridge, every deep drag of him, forcing him to take all of her, forcing him to feel.

His hands twitched at her waist while they stayed like that, eyes locked on each other. His next breath caught and held, their breathing mingling. The rawness of it all made her dizzy. For the first time, something flared in his eyes, something vulnerable and raw she'd never seen before. She smiled in return, content to give now instead of take.

Then the connection snapped. His breath hitched—not with lust, but something sharper. He masked it fast, but she caught it anyway. Whatever softness she'd almost coaxed out of him vanished, sealed under steel.

His grip clamped down hard when he surged up, dislodging and then disconnecting them. "On your knees," he ordered. He set his jaw, changing before her eyes. Walling himself off.

Dazed at the suddenness, the change, she hesitated. "What—"

"Do you want this, darlin'?" he said, all liquid-honey Texas drawl and carefully blank eyes. He gripped his cock and stroked once, a rough pull that made her insides quiver with longing.

"Yes." The whisper tore from her. Lord, at this moment, she did. She wanted him—wanted this—but God, she wished he'd stayed with her in that moment. Tender. Open.

The corner of his mouth curved, but whatever vulnerability she'd glimpsed in him moments before was gone.

"How?" she asked somewhat uncertainly. Her repertoire of sex positions was lacking.

"Knees here," he grunted, guiding her hands and knees across the couch cushions. Her face turned toward the Christmas tree, a happy twinkle in an otherwise somber room. A large, rough hand pressed between her shoulders, bending her forward until her hair spilled over her face, covering her eyes and blocking out the lights.

The first heavy thrust stole her breath.

The careful, tender rhythm she'd built was gone; a new one

took its place. Every stroke was relentless, and her body was ready to take it. His cock stretched her, dragging over sensitive nerve endings until her toes curled against the cushions and she bit down on a cry. Her body met his instinctively, caught on the tenterhooks of pleasure and pain, even as her head still reeled.

"Oh," she breathed into her arms, unable to stop herself from pushing back into each heavy thrust. Her frantic motions put them out of sync, and he gripped her hips harder to keep her still. It was hard and rough enough to drown out any other physical sensation.

"Take it," he growled.

Pleasure tore through her, jagged enough to leave invisible cuts. She let it build because her body demanded release, even as her heart reeled at what had just happened.

He pounded into her, driving her into the couch until her muscles collapsed under his weight and she let go, spiraling higher, tighter, until it all snapped.

Her orgasm ripped through her in a violent surge, shattering her. She cried out, her body clenching around him, even as he yanked her hips back to him, chasing his own release with a single-minded determination. With one last deep thrust, he buried himself deep, his entire body shuddering.

Lily's muscles gave out under her weight, and she sank deep into the cushions, trying to catch her breath and understand what had just happened.

Before the thoughts could settle, he was moving—pulling out of her body, turning and gathering her up carefully. He dropped back onto the couch, cradling her across his lap. His chest was slick with sweat under her cheek, and his heartbeat thudded steadily beneath her ear.

His arms tightened around her, smoothing down her spine in long, steady strokes.

"Jesus. I'm sorry, Lily," he said eventually when their breathing had returned to normal.

"WHAT WAS THAT?" Lily asked quietly, her cheek still pressed to Rush's chest.

Rush closed his eyes and sighed, bone-tired and more sorry than he could find words for. His hand kept moving, slow strokes down her back. Her hair brushed his chin, and he breathed her in— light and clean, lavender and soap, along with the raw edge of warm female skin and hot sex. Comfort wrapped in sin. Just like Lily.

"We had a domestic violence call out at Cedarwood early this morning," he said finally. His voice sounded strange to his own ears, scraped raw. "Came in around seven, just after my shift started. Guy had just finished an overnight at the factory. His girlfriend said he came in swinging even before he took his boots off." He rubbed the bruise on his jaw absently.

"When Ben and I got there, he was piss drunk and tearing the place up. The kids were upstairs, crying so hard you could hear them from the street." His jaw locked, the muscle twitching under the bruise. "It took both of us to pull him off her."

Lily reached up, brushing her fingertips lightly against his jaw. "Is that where this is from?"

He caught her hand and pulled it away, knowing what she was offering, just as certain he couldn't accept it. "He caught me with an elbow, but she took the worst of it," he said matter-of-factly.

"After we cuffed him and had him in the car, she refused to

press charges or go to the hospital—kept saying she was fine." He laughed, a harsh, humorless sound. "Two black eyes, a dislocated shoulder, and she was still trying to protect him." His mouth twisted bitterly. "Finally convinced her to take the kids and go stay with her sister."

"Rush..." she whispered.

"Don't." He shook his head, eyes closed. "It's part of the job." The words were supposed to sound steady. They weren't. "Calls like that... they stick, because I've lived it."

She went very still against him.

"My mom was with someone like that after my dad died." Rush kept his gaze on the fire. "She was with a guy who drank too much and hit her. One night, she packed us up, me and Sarah and Rachel, and tried to get us out." His throat worked. "A tractor missed a turn and hit us. Crushed my mom inside the car. I helped get the girls out then watched while they cut her free."

Lily didn't say anything, and he was grateful. He didn't want pity. Didn't want comfort. He didn't want to feel anything at all except the clean hit of a punching bag or the numbing distraction of sex. Both were simple—heat and friction—a way to bleed out what was coiled too tight in him.

She just looked at him, green eyes gentle, softer than he could stand, and he had to look away. Didn't she know what happened to people who cared that way? Didn't she understand you couldn't go around loving people, not when love didn't stop fists, didn't stop trucks from crossing yellow lines, didn't stop death? There was no armor for that kind of pain.

"I know what you mean," she said softly after a moment. "I grew up in Cedarwood."

That made him raise his eyebrows. Annette Hart's home was known in Northfield for its charm, its comfort, and its money. Not the kind of wealth that started out in seedy apartment complexes.

"Yeah, it's wild, considering what she's built." Lily nodded, accurately guessing his thoughts as usual. "But that's where she started. Where we all did. For years, when we were younger, after my dad left. It wasn't the same as what you went through, but I remember Evie and me hiding in the closet in our room just to get away from the neighbors screaming at each other. I remember my mom working herself raw just to keep us fed and safe."

Her hand tightened on his. "I respect her so much for that. She kept going when it would've been easier to give up. Just like your mom, she wanted a better life for her kids." She swallowed hard, her eyes shining. "I think your mom would be proud of you, Rush. To know you grew up to be the man who protects people. To know you kept your promise to her."

Something deep in his chest threatened to split wide open. He wanted to tell her not to give him pieces of herself he couldn't be trusted with, but the words stuck. He wanted to tell her to guard that soft heart of hers, to protect herself. But still, the words stuck, cemented behind a wall he wasn't even sure he could scale anymore. Or if he wanted to.

What he could do was this: he could apologize when he fucked up. He looked her in the eye unflinchingly. "I'm sorry for being an asshole."

She sighed, too and reached up to press a kiss to his throat. "You're not an asshole, Rush. You're just a man."

He wrapped his arms around her, as if that could erase what he'd done. Lily deserved better. Better than him. But he didn't want to let her go. Not yet.

He was an asshole for that, too—too selfish to let her go and too fucked up to stop holding on.

Chapter Thirty-One

"Ms. Lily," Bash said, tugging on her arm at the end of the pageant rehearsal, the red-and-blue-Spider-Man mask he refused to take off, sliding down to cover one eye. "Watch this!" He twisted his wrists and crouched, pretending to shoot webs across the studio floor.

"Nice, Bash," Lily said, suitably impressed. "Although the three wise men traditionally bring gold, frankincense, and myrrh, not Spider-Man webs."

Bash puffed up proudly. "Yeah, but if Baby Jesus needed saving from bad guys, I'd totally handle it."

"I'd smash a bad guy with my Hulk fists—" another boy started, pounding his fist into his palm for good measure.

"Hold on," Lily cut in quickly, well aware of how fast her trio of wise men could descend into imaginary bloodshed. She crouched to their level and smiled. "This is a Christmas pageant, not a superhero smackdown. How about this—if anyone needs saving on stage, we call in the angels to carry them off. Much less mess to clean up. Agreed?"

The boys looked at the little angels in the corner, who were taking off their wings. Bash frowned. "But they don't even have swords."

"Maybe they can use their halos as a secret weapon?" Zeke offered.

"Okay, superheroes," Lily said, laughing, "Off you go. Don't forget to practice your lines."

The boys scattered toward their waiting parents, still arguing about which Avenger would win in Bethlehem. Savvie and Tessa were fighting about who got to hold baby Jesus, but Allie had just arrived to pick them up. Lily waved as they left, still bickering, then caught sight of one little angel struggling with her wings in the corner.

"Need some help, Chloe?" she asked, kneeling down. Chloe nodded, and Lily began untangling the straps, chatting quietly with her. "You were amazing today, sweetheart. You knew all your cues, and did I hear you humming?"

Chloe looked up, her eyes sparkling, and nodded shyly.

Lily's heart nearly burst. "I'm so proud of you."

Chloe raised two fingers to mimic counting steps. Lily mirrored her slowly and clearly. "Exactly. Just like that. Show me the spin you did when we practiced."

Chloe twirled, a small, tentative spin. At Lily's encouraging nod, she spun again—this time smiling from ear to ear.

"Beautiful!" Lily clapped, delighted by her progress. This wasn't the same silent, somber little girl from months ago. Chloe was starting to bloom, and Lily felt her own heart swell with every step.

Her skirt settled around her knees as she stopped spinning, breathless with the effort. She looked up at Lily for approval, cheeks pink and curls damp with sweat.

Lily smoothed a flyaway strand back gently. "You've worked so hard, sweetheart. You know what I see when you dance now?"

Chloe blinked at her.

"Confidence." Lily nodded. "You're a very brave girl, Chloe Whitmore."

Chloe's lips parted like she might say something, but only a tiny, soundless breath came out. Then she ducked her head, smiling.

Lily swallowed around the lump in her throat. Some days her job wasn't just about teaching steps and keeping the pageant on track—it was about this. Watching students bloom. Chloe was proof that healing was possible, that even from the most painful experiences, light could find its way into the smallest cracks of darkness.

Of course, Lily's thoughts turned to the one person she'd been trying not to think about all week.

Rush.

The last time she'd seen him—on his couch a week ago when they played the dirtiest game of show-and-tell of her life— she'd felt him teeter on the edge of opening up, his tension vibrating palpably from his body, and then, like always, she'd watched him slam that door closed. What came after had been sex, raw and consuming, the kind that left her reeling with satisfaction, yet somehow emptier as the week went on too.

Since that night, he'd texted her a few times. Brief check-ins in his signature blunt style that kept him in her orbit without letting her closer.

Not that she was chasing more. At least, she reassured herself, she wasn't. Although if she was honest, Rush was the kind of man a woman could lose her heart to without meaning to. He was honorable and good, whether he saw it in himself or not.

Still, she couldn't ignore the pattern. He kept her at arm's length with his body, using pleasure like a wall between them. Only when that wall cracked did she glimpse the pain he carried. And oh, how it ached—knowing he was punishing himself for something out of his control.

But standing there with Chloe, Lily knew the truth: Connection didn't break you. It saved you.

"Ready for the big night?" she asked, helping Chloe into her coat and hat.

Chloe nodded, giving Lily's hand a squeeze.

This was what she wanted: family, belonging, love. The ache of it hadn't left after Tucker, although it had subsided for now. What she was doing with Rush wasn't that, but it was a chance to experience something new. Maybe learn something about herself she'd missed out on all the years she'd been stalled with Tucker.

A movement near the door caught her eye. It was Rush, fresh from the cold. He was in street clothes today—worn jeans and a gray Henley peeking from the collar of his sheepskin coat. Instead of his Stetson, he wore a ball cap pulled low over his eyes.

"Brought this for you." He held out the to-go cup steaming in his hand.

The sound of his voice—that deep, rich baritone— reminded her far too vividly of the last time they were together.

The last of her pageant parents were bundling their kids into coats and sneaking curious looks at the sheriff of Northfield, so out of place in her dainty studio filled with tutus and halos. Rush gave them his polite nod, but his attention stayed pinned on her.

Which was unfair because she was still in her leotard— black again, this time with pale-pink tights—and her curls had escaped her bun. She felt rumpled and tired after their late night together. Hardly glamorous. Meanwhile, he strode in looking like sin, the kind of hot that made women trip over themselves in the grocery aisle when they saw him—and he was staring at her.

She resisted the urge to fan herself as he made his way over, her pulse at hot-yoga level, dragging her right back to their slow, wicked strip-show game on his couch last week.

"Thank you," she murmured quickly, taking the cup he offered to cover the flutter in her chest. "You're spoiling me."

"Figured you'd need it after pageant rehearsal," he said, his gaze taking in the leftover tinsel and crooked angel wings still scattered across the room. "I heard your wise men are blood-thirsty."

"You figured right." The warmth seeped into her palm and, traitorously, deeper than that.

A tug at her skirt pulled her back to earth. Lily glanced down. "Hi, sweetheart."

Chloe stood there, curls neatly tucked under her hat, staring up with solemn blue eyes.

"What's wrong?" Lily scanned the nearly empty room for the Whitmores. "Your grandma should be here any minute. Want to wait with me?"

Chloe shook her head, tugging again.

Lily bent to eye level. "Bathroom? Snack?"

Another shake. Chloe darted to the cubbies and returned clutching a folded sheet of paper to her chest.

"Oh, you made something." Lily reached for it, but Chloe shook her head firmly. Then she turned, those big blue eyes locking straight onto Rush.

Lily's breath caught. "It's... for the sheriff?"

Beside her, Rush went rigid, his shoulders locking tight as if bracing for a fight. His face, partially hidden beneath the brim of his hat, gave nothing away. But Lily felt the tension radiating off him, raw and jagged, like he was holding back a tide that threatened to break loose. It was the same look he'd worn that day outside her studio when he'd seen Chloe for the first time—frozen. Stricken.

For a long moment, he didn't move.

Chloe nodded and held the paper out toward him with both hands.

Please, Lily begged silently. *Please don't shut her down.*

At last, he reached for the picture as if Chloe had handed him a live grenade. His big hand dwarfed the rumpled paper as he unfolded it as carefully as if it were made of glass.

A crooked sun smiled from the corner. Two stick figures stood beneath—one tall with a wide circle of a hat, the other small with a halo of squiggle curls.

Tears threatened to choke Lily. Chloe had drawn them together.

Rush's face turned to stone. Lily could almost feel the storm gathering inside him, chaos roiling just beneath his skin, threatening to tear through the seams of his composure. He didn't speak, and she didn't push. This was between Rush and Chloe.

He cleared his throat; the muscles working were visible to everyone. "Thank you."

Chloe's face lit up. She rocked back on her heels and let out a huff of delight, and Lily's chest nearly exploded with emotion.

"She worked on that all week, hoping to see you," Margaret Whitmore said quietly from the doorway. Her eyes glistened, and Lily knew she saw what Chloe and the entire town did: a man who carried the weight of the life he couldn't save instead of the one he did.

Mrs. Whitmore guided Chloe to the door. The little girl looked back once, her eyes solemn, and she lifted her hand in a shy wave.

Rush lifted his hand—too late. He didn't move until the door clicked shut.

Then he turned away sharply. He tore off his hat and shoved a hand through his hair.

She didn't press. She didn't even move, sensing he needed a moment to wrestle his emotions back under lock and key.

He put his hands on his hips, tipping his head back with a heavy sigh. "Christ. Wasn't expecting that."

"What were you expecting?" Lily asked softly.

"That she'd be scared of me," he admitted with a humorless laugh.

"She's not," Lily said. "She remembers you helping."

He rubbed the back of his neck and stared at the drawing. "I didn't know what to say to her."

"You said exactly the right thing."

For a beat, she thought he might say more, but then his gaze caught hers, and the air between them shifted again.

She went to him, rising on her toes to press a soft kiss to his jaw, right where the muscles still clenched beneath the stubble. He didn't move, so she tried again, brushing her parted lips along the strong column of his throat.

Gentle. Healing.

He exhaled raggedly. Then his hand came up, sliding to the nape of her neck, tilting her face to his. His thumb swept across her cheek, and only then did she realize there were tears.

"You are so goddamn *good*, Lily," he said roughly.

She curled her fingers around his wrists, holding on. "So are you," she whispered, wishing he believed it.

But instead of kissing her, he let her go and stepped back, breaking their connection. "I should go. Rachel and Sarah are meeting me at the nursing home to see Pop."

She nodded, forcing a smile as he tugged up the collar of his coat and left, closing the door behind him with a soft thud.

When are you going to stop running, Rush?

Chapter Thirty-Two

THE CELL PHONE buzzed against the hood of the Chevy, but Rush ignored it. One glance at the screen told him enough.

Grant. Again.

Shit. He wiped his hands on a rag and fitted the oil cap back into place with more care than necessary. He didn't know how many years this truck had in it, but he wasn't about to rush the end. The old Chevy had history—she'd chauffeured his mom when she was a teenager, taught him how to drive, carried him around in between deployments when the world still felt sharp around the edges. Pop had handed him the keys when he came home from overseas, gruff as usual but with pride shining in his eyes, and Rush had promised he'd take care of her.

It wasn't a hard promise to keep. The truck was the one thing that didn't ask more from him than he could give. He loved the routine—changing her oil in the garage, washing her down in the summer heat, listening to the low, steady rumble that said she wasn't done yet. The green-and-white paint had faded to an ancient patina, but she still purred to life better than any other truck he'd driven.

Boston didn't have anything like this. Boston was anonymity, another body in a suit collecting a paycheck. Here he was somebody's grandson, a brother, a sheriff, a lover.

His phone buzzed again, and this time he picked it up. He had to. Whenever he didn't, his sisters showed up on his doorstep.

With a resigned sigh, he answered.

Two grainy faces filled the screen.

"There he is!" Sarah sang, jabbing a finger at the camera. "I bet five bucks you'd hit the asshole button."

"You look tired," Rachel said, frowning. "Are you still not sleeping?"

"I bet I know why you're tired," Sarah said, a smirk in her voice. "A certain jilted hostess at Maple and Main told me you've got a new lady."

"Did you get that paper written yet?" Rush asked pointedly. The last time they'd talked, he'd driven out to Buffalo to bring her groceries because she'd claimed she was too busy studying for finals to eat. He hadn't bought it then, but he hadn't minded either. He missed the girls.

"Yep," she said breezily. "Now quit dodging. Who's Lily, and when do we get to meet her?"

She was relentless.

"Nobody," he said, guilt pricking him as soon as the words left his mouth.

"Liar," Sarah shot back. "You haven't dated anyone seriously since that chick who worked in Rochester—the one with the killer shoes. Blake?"

"Oh," Rachel said, frowning. "I remember her. You two were a disaster."

"Drop it," he muttered. He lowered the Chevy's hood gently and whistled for Riggs. The dog bounded up from the snow, tennis ball clamped in his jaw, tail wagging like he was ready for another hour of fetch. Rush gave him a good, solid pat. "Not now, boy. We already played."

Besides, he had plans tonight.

"Look, girls, I've got to go—"

"It's Saturday night. Why do you have to get off the phone so quick?" Sarah pushed her face close to the screen and then squealed. "You're going out with her tonight! Oh my God, you *so* like her!"

"He totally does," Rachel chimed in. "When can we meet her?"

"Did you two forget I'm moving to Boston in less than two months?" His voice came out sharper than he had intended. "No, you can't meet her. And no, it's not serious."

"Fine." Sarah looked disappointed. "We were just excited, that's all. You never let us be excited for you."

"Love you, Rush," Rachel said, more gently. "We'll see you Sunday at Pop's, right?"

"Love you both. See you Sunday," Rush said.

Rush ended the call before they could push further. He shoved the phone in his pocket and headed inside to get ready because, yeah, he did have a date with Lily tonight, not that he'd admit that to his sisters. He didn't need them involved, and he didn't need Lily dragged into their lives either. Not when he was already halfway out the door.

He gave the Chevy one last pat and headed inside with Riggs on his heels. The house felt more bare than it had last week. He'd hauled another load of stuff to the donation center, but the Christmas tree was still in the corner. For reasons he didn't care to explain, he turned the damn thing on every night when he came home. Tonight was no different.

He tugged off his sweatshirt and tossed it over a chair then stepped into the bathroom and cranked the shower on full blast.

He scrubbed his body, then shaved and messed around with his hair until he caught himself and barked out a laugh. Since when did he care? He shoved on a thick winter hat and called it good enough.

They were going to Candlelight Night, Northfield's annual winter festival on Main Street. Crowds, carolers, the whole town out. The kind of thing that made his skin itch. Normally, he'd steer clear unless he was on patrol, but Lily wanted to go, and he was growing very invested in making Lily happy.

Hell, he didn't think about much else lately.

Every time he closed his eyes, he saw her on his lap on the couch, curls spilling around her shoulders, playing peekaboo with those gorgeous breasts like she didn't know she was driving him out of his mind. She'd been a trembling mix of nerves and mischief, and he hadn't been able to get enough. The way she looked at him—wide-eyed when he said something filthy, or dazed and then sleepy when he made her come hard enough to shake.

Christ, she was addictive.

So damn responsive it floored him. Every gasp, every needy little sound she couldn't hold back made him want to push further, to show her something new. She'd been shy at first, and tentative, but the second he pressed, she'd leaned in and wanted more. Even when things got rougher than she was used to, she still wanted more.

It shook him, that kind of trust.

He had no business taking it. Not when he had less than two months before Boston pulled him out of here for good. When he left, she'd be alone again, chasing those farmhouse-and-babies-on-the-porch dreams with someone else.

A flood of something he hadn't felt in years surged through him—ugly, hot, and impossible to ignore. Jealousy.

Rush swore under his breath and shoved the thought down

hard. He didn't have the right to be jealous. That wasn't part of this deal with Lily.

But what if it could be?

He shoved that thought away even faster.

By the time he pulled the Chevy onto a side street near Main, he had himself fully locked down again.

Chapter Thirty-Three

Lily was already waiting out front of her studio, nearly skipping in her excitement. She spotted him and waved, a smile that stopped him in his tracks spreading across her face. The front windows were fogged from the crush of people inside for her holiday open house, and music drifted out every time the door opened and closed.

Like the rest of Main Street, the studio was part of the Candlelight Night celebration. She had canceled evening classes, and she and Evie were splitting hostess duties, giving the visitors who stopped by a sneak peek of the pageant performance.

He walked through the streams of people on the sidewalk, meaning to give her a quick hug, but instead he found himself stopping dead in front of her.

"Sheriff Callahan," someone called, and half a dozen heads turned his way.

Rush lifted a hand, forcing a nod as kids darted past and someone clapped him on the shoulder. One elderly man in a beaver hat stopped long enough to thank him for checking on his wife after her fall last week. A boy in a red puffer coat asked him where Riggs was. Down the street, a group of teenage girls yelled something that sounded suspiciously like "Sheriff Sexy," as they ran off, giggling maniacally.

Rush never took his eyes off Lily.

Her cheeks were rosy pink, first from the cold, no doubt, but the longer he stared at her, the deeper the flush grew. Her curls escaped from under her hat, and a scarf looped around her neck, hiding where else the blush covered. She looked like every one of his fantasies, and she was waiting for him.

He reached out and took her mittened hands and pulled her into his chest just to breathe her in for a moment. She smelled like lavender, and she was warm against his chest. He meant to let go, but she tilted her head back to look at him, and he couldn't move.

"Hi," she said. There was glitter on her cheek, probably from the halos, and the sight did something to him. He wanted to devour her right here, drag her back home, strip her clothes off, and bury himself in all that sweetness. When he'd turned into a caveman, he didn't know, but Lily had always brought out his basest instincts.

See her. Want her. Keep her.

He shook his head at his ridiculous thoughts.

"Hey," he replied. It came out rougher than he had intended. He cleared his throat and tried again. "You look beautiful."

Color bloomed in her cheeks. "So do you. I mean—you look handsome." She laughed self-consciously, and he forgot to breathe.

Out of the corner of his eye, he spotted Ben, in full uniform and on patrol. He gave Rush a quick two-finger salute, smirking when he caught sight of where his attention was focused.

A painfully sharp note from a caroler inside sliced through

his haze, and he eased back another inch, pulse still hammering away, to find her green eyes dancing.

"Those are my students," she said, nodding toward the studio's door. "I'd know Bash's pitch anywhere."

Right on cue, another off-key blast from "Rudolph the Red-Nosed Reindeer" made them both wince.

"Aren't you their director?"

"Evie's in charge of the vocals and acting. I can only take credit for the choreography. I did my part earlier, so I could walk with you now. Let's go," she said, tugging his hand. "You can see the whole thing come together next week, if you want," she added almost shyly. "I know you might have plans with your family, but..."

Rush shook his head. "Only plans I have are with Riggs."

The sidewalks were jammed full of people bundled up to visit Northfield for the annual Candlelight Night. The village went all out with decorations, and all the shops and businesses on Main Street handed out hot chocolate and cookies. Horse-drawn carriage rides, a visit from Santa, and ice-skating on the canal, which had been drained to create a skating rink surrounded by string lights.

It wasn't really his thing to wander in crowds, but Lily stopped by each shop, waving and hugging everyone, and he was content to simply be in her orbit. She was clearly known and loved by many. It wasn't hard to see why. With Lily, her sweetness wasn't an act. It was bone-deep, and she poured it out on everyone she touched. He couldn't help wondering what it would be like if she ever gave it all to him.

They wove their way toward the gazebo, where more carolers, older and more talented, from the sound of it, sang.

"Hmm," Lily said, sipping her cider. "They're pretty good. We should try recruiting them."

"Not a terrible idea," he said dryly.

She tipped her head up to look at him, her eyes sparkling with humor.

He couldn't wait a second longer. He bent and kissed her, right there on Main Street.

Warm, sweet cinnamon and cider lingered on her pretty lips. When she parted for him, he caught her bottom lip gently between his teeth, savoring the little gasp of surprise she gave him.

People streamed past them on the sidewalk, but he didn't care. Not when she was pressed against him, her mittened hands fisting his coat to pull him closer. He kissed her deeper, angling his mouth over hers, taking every bit she gave and giving it back.

He dimly registered the buzz of voices and boots crunching on the snowy sidewalks around them. Someone cleared their throat pointedly. It probably wasn't a good look for the sheriff to maul the pretty ballerina in the middle of a winter festival, but he didn't give a fuck. *Caveman.*

She made a tiny sound in the back of her throat—half sigh, half whimper—that nearly undid him.

It was too much, too public, too close to the edge. He dragged his mouth away from hers, breathing hard. Her eyes fluttered open, lips swollen and parted like she wanted more. She flicked her tongue across them as if she could still taste him.

A sharp shriek pulled his gaze toward the canal. The makeshift rink stretched wide under the lights, full of skaters looping the ice while little kids weaved around them, holding plastic chairs to keep them upright. His stomach turned over. He'd been avoiding looking that way since he'd arrived there.

"Look," Lily said, pointing at a bobbing pink cap moving across the rink. Mrs. Whitmore held onto one side of the plastic chair, and Chloe held onto the other. Chloe was smiling, and then she laughed, high and bright.

"She's started talking again," Lily murmured, watching along with him. "Just a few words but more each time I see her."

He couldn't answer. His throat was closing. The lights, the shrieks, the scrape of skates—they all pressed in until he wasn't sure where he was anymore. He knew logically, but his heart hammered in that wild, punishing way that told him he was losing the fight.

Breathe. Goddammit, breathe.

"Rush," Lily said, but he could barely hear her over the whooshing in his ears. "Let's sit down. Come on."

He grabbed her wrist and let her pull him into the empty gazebo, sitting where she guided him until they were side by side.

"Hey," she was saying. "You're okay. Breathe with me. In..." She did it with him, long steady breaths. "... and out."

He concentrated on her voice and her touch, the way she rubbed his hand, bringing it to her lips to kiss the back. He clung to that and breathed through the chaos until the noise dulled and air finally eased into his lungs again.

He yanked his hat off and shoved his hand through his hair as shame crawled hot under his skin. *Fuck.* He was supposed to be protecting her. Not falling apart like a train wreck.

Her green eyes, wide and worried now, searched his face. "How long have you had panic attacks?"

He jerked his hand back from hers and shoved it into his coat pocket to hide the shaking. "I'm fine."

"What just happened is normal after what you've been through, Rush," she said, too gentle. "It's your body remembering. Have you ever thought about therapy—"

"Don't," he said brusquely. "I've been. Sat in the chair, said the words, checked the boxes. It didn't fix a damn thing." Then, because he wanted to change the pity in her eyes to something—anything else—he lashed out. "No amount of chanting or mantras will bring back Caroline Whitmore, Lily."

Her lips parted, and hurt flashed across her face, but she didn't lash back. That gutted him worse than the panic had. He fucking loved Lily's approach to the world. What was wrong with him?

She blinked at him, still calm, which only made the shame burn hotter. Christ. He was the sheriff. People were supposed to look to him in a crisis, not watch him fall apart on a damn park bench while the whole town skated circles around him.

"I know it won't, but—" she started.

He pushed to his feet and grabbed his hat. "Come on. I'll walk you back to the studio."

She didn't say anything on the walk back up Main Street. When they reached her door, the studio windows glowed, full of parents and kids laughing and dancing to music. It was her world—warm, bright, alive. Everything he wasn't.

"Want to come inside?" she asked quietly, still looking at him with those soft green eyes that saw too much.

He looked away. "Not tonight. Good night, Lily," he said instead, stepping back off the curb.

She hesitated at the bottom of the steps while he waited, in pure agony, for the words he deserved.

You're a mess.

A failure.

Not enough.

But she said nothing. She slipped inside, and he was left in the cold with the burn of self-disgust tightening his throat.

~

~

Lily closed the studio door behind her and sagged against it, surveying the carnage of open house. The studio looked like a glitter bomb had gone off—streamers tangled in the barre, sequins ground into the floor, and half the pageant costumes stuffed haphazardly into their plastic tubs.

"Looks like the open house was a hit," she said brightly, though her voice wobbled on the last word.

"We came to help clean up," Allie called from the cider-and-donuts corner, where she was stuffing a line of empty cups into a trash bag. Her honey-blond hair was twisted up in its usual, no-fuss knot, and her green sweater was flecked with glitter, probably from wrangling the twins. Practical as ever, her older sister already had the chaos mostly under control. She shot Lily a quick smile. "Evie said reinforcements were necessary."

"I can't bend over, or I'll tip, so I'm here for moral support only," Amber announced from one of the folding chairs against the wall. Savvie had curled up in what little lap space her aunt had left, thumb tucked firmly in her mouth as she slept.

"Baby Jesus has been recovered," Davis added dryly. He had Tessa draped, half asleep over one arm and a raggedy baby doll clutched in the other. "Found him in the costume bin with a tutu over his head."

Theo walked in behind Davis, still in his suit and tie from his own open house down the street in the mayor's office. "Don't let her fool you," he warned, balancing a tray of empty plates and cups. "Amber was bossing us all around like a drill sergeant five minutes ago."

Amber stroked her enormous belly, covered in a vintage navy satin dress, contentedly. "If I'm going to be miserable, everyone else might as well be useful."

Amber didn't look almost nine months pregnant with twins, that was for sure. A cropped cardigan covered her shoulders, along with a vintage silk scarf around her neck for flair. The effect was gorgeous and glamorous, as usual for her sister.

Evie slipped out from behind the reception desk, her arms full of props. She met Lily's gaze across the messy studio, and her eyes widened at what she must have seen reflected there.

Lily's throat closed. She looked at all of them—her sisters with their wildly different energies, her nieces precious and sleeping like angels, Davis and Theo pitching in without question—and the warmth of it hit her square in the chest. Her eyes stung, and before she could stop herself, she burst into noisy tears.

Ah, hell. She was overdue for a good cry anyway.

"What is it, honey?" Allie dropped the trash bag and rushed over. "Are you sick? Do you need your inhaler?"

"Lil," Evie said softly from across the room, the one word laced with understanding.

Amber leaned her head back against the wall, one hand absently stroking Savvie's hair. "If this is about a man, he better be worth crying over."

Allie frowned and tipped her face toward Lily. "That's not why you're crying, right? These tears aren't for the sheriff?"

Lily tried to buck up and put a smile on her face. She did. But the effort crumbled as fast as it came. She couldn't stop seeing Rush on the edge of the canal—that stricken look had gutted her.

She'd wanted to comfort him, to tell him it was okay—that he could forgive himself, that diving into icy black water to save someone was the bravest thing anyone could have done. That he was a hero, whether he believed it or not. All of Northfield saw it. She wished he could see it too. Instead, he carried the weight like a punishment, grinding him down and shutting out someone who was coming to care about him deeply.

She couldn't say any of that because he'd lashed out at her and pushed her away. Again.

So yes, she was crying, and it felt good. For weeks she'd carried a brick in her chest, an intuition she hadn't wanted to name. Tonight had made it impossible to ignore. Rush didn't want her comfort. He didn't want her help. He wanted only the pieces of her he could take without opening himself up in return.

And if that was all he had to give... she'd have to decide if it was enough.

"I'm just saying, men should make you laugh, not cry, and if they can't keep up with you, you leave them behind."

Lily swiped at her eyes, managing a shaky laugh, but she didn't argue with Amber because deep down she knew her sister was right. The words lodged somewhere deep, clinging like burrs she couldn't quite brush off.

Theo crossed the room, setting a steaming cup of cider in front of her, before brushing a kiss against Amber's temple. "Ignore her," he said mildly. "Pregnancy makes her mean."

Amber snorted, but just then her face pinched, and she let out a groan, one hand flying to her stomach. "Lord, these babies are doing somersaults," she muttered.

Theo's whole expression softened. He crouched in front of her, rubbing her lower back with one hand while the other covered hers on her belly. "They're strong, just like their mom."

Amber grabbed Lily's hand suddenly and pressed it against the taut curve of her stomach. "Feel that?"

The sharp kick beneath Lily's palm stole her breath away. A ripple of movement rolled under her hand, so real and alive, and something inside of her split open.

Her chest ached with longing. This—this was what she wanted more than anything. A life growing inside her, a family of her own to take care of. She pictured tiny arms reaching for her, a warm weight curled against her chest at night. She'd wanted this since she was little, so clearly it felt stitched into her bones as early as she could remember.

She pulled her hand back gently, smiling at Amber, but inside she was unraveling. Across the room, Davis gave Allie a look, something warm and unspoken passing between them, before he shifted Tessa in his arms more comfortably. "What your sisters mean, Lily," he said quietly, "is you don't have to settle."

Lily's chest ached at the sight of them—her sisters so loved, so steady in ways she'd always dreamed about. Theo's hand on Amber's stomach, Davis's patient calm with Allie. That kind of devotion seemed so easy for them. She wanted that. God, she wanted that.

When she finally looked away, Evie was already watching her. That twin thing. It astounded people how they could finish each other's sentences or, like now, know exactly what the other was feeling. A surge of fierce love for Evie—for her whole family —rose in her, and she sniffed again.

The real thing, she promised herself. *Don't settle for less.*

Amber shifted Savvie and let out a dramatic groan, rubbing her belly. "I swear these twins are trying to kill me. If they don't come soon, I'm going to lose my mind."

"You're not due for another month," Theo reminded her, rubbing her back soothingly. "Come on. Let's go home and get you in the bath."

Savvie opened one eye, blinking sleepily at her favorite uncle. "I'm a sugarplum," she mumbled before snuggling deeper into Amber's lap and drifting off again.

The little group began gathering coats and hats, and Allie and Davis roused the girls to get them bundled up for the cold. All the normal family sounds that Lily never thought twice about, the soundtrack of her family as it grew, but tonight, after she closed the door behind them, she was aware of the silence left behind.

Was this what waited for her? A quiet studio when everyone else had someone to go home to?

Evie came out of the office with her coat and purse. "Walk home together?"

Lily glanced around the studio. Part of her wanted to stay, to hide in the silence and think, but then she looked at Evie—her twin, her anchor—and the choice was easy.

"Yeah," she said. "I'll come."

Evie waited while she gathered her things then looped her arm through Lily's as they locked up and headed home together.

Lily had her sister. She had her family. It wasn't the same as having someone who was hers, but for tonight, it was enough.

Still, as their boots crunched over the snow, she couldn't help but wonder who Rush had to hold on to.

Chapter Thirty-Four

On Sunday, Rush, with Riggs on a leash next to him, walked into the Canalside Nursing Home and straight into a standoff.

Joanne, usually Pop's favorite nurse, stood in the middle of the room with her hands on her hips and a frown on her face. Two other nurses lined up behind her, looking equally unimpressed with their patient.

Pop sat in his recliner in his room, arms folded across his chest, lips pursed in that same stubborn line that Rush remembered from his boyhood, the one Gram never could budge when he decided something wasn't worth doing.

"I'm not taking another damn pill," Pop barked, glowering. "You people are trying to kill me."

At his side, Riggs stiffened, sensing the tension, but Rush gave him a quiet *hush*.

Marley, a pretty brunette he vaguely remembered from Rachel's grade, shot Rush a look of pure exasperation. "He needs his heart meds."

"Poison," Pop said flatly. He leaned around the nurses and grinned slyly. "And here's my lawyer. Tell 'em I don't need any more of their snake oil."

Rush's heart sank, although he kept his expression neutral. On his bad days, Pop didn't recognize him at all or thought he was someone from the past. Guess today was a bad day.

Riggs padded forward and set his chin on Pop's knee. Pop's hand dropped automatically to scratch behind his ears even while his eyes stayed locked on Rush.

"If you don't take these, Riggs will," Rush said, crouching down to scoop up the paper cup and pills on the floor.

Pop narrowed his eyes. "You wouldn't let him."

"No," Rush said easily. "But if you keep throwing them around, he might find one by accident."

Riggs sighed long and loud, as if in agreement.

"Fine." Pop heaved a sigh, making a big show of downing a fresh set of pills with a swig of apple juice. The nurses left, but not before Marley tossed a grateful wink his way. When the door shut, Rush caught the gleam in Pop's eye. The old man looked too pleased with himself to be having a bad day.

Relief washed through him. That was the thing about Alzheimer's—you never knew what you were walking into. Some days, Pop was lost in the past and had no recollection of him or the girls, but on others, he was as sharp and clear as the man who'd raised them. It was impossible to anticipate, and Rush never realized how much he braced himself until moments like this one, when the tension broke and left him grateful for something as simple as recognition. Even if Pop was a pain in the ass to his nurses.

Riggs's ears pricked up, and a second later, Rachel breezed into the room with Sarah behind her. Rachel still wore her blue scrubs from her early shift at Northfield General, carrying two grocery bags, while Sarah held a tray of fancy coffees.

"We brought lunch," Rachel said, bending to kiss Pop on the cheek and plant one on Riggs's snout too.

"Thanks," Rush said automatically, already reaching for his wallet. "Pops and I are starving. How much do I owe you?"

"Nothing," Rachel cut in, giving him the same no-nonsense look Pop used to shoot across the dinner table. "My treat. I'm working now, remember?"

Rush frowned. "Rachel, how much? I've got it."

Rachel straightened and put her hands on her hips. "I realize this is hard for you to accept, but we're not kids anymore. Thanks to you, we both have degrees—or almost do. We can buy lunch for you and Pop if we want to." Her expression softened. "Let us take care of you for once."

"Hold on. Let's not be hasty." Sarah popped the lid off her coffee and licked the whipped cream. "If Rush wants to keep funding us after graduation, who am I to argue?"

"Sarah," Rachel barked, in full big-sister mode, and Rush nearly laughed. Even he recognized himself in that tone. "He's paid every dime of our college education so we could get good jobs and pay for ourselves."

"Kidding, kidding," Sarah said, rolling her eyes. She sipped her coffee then grinned. "But for the record, I don't graduate until the spring. And you know we love you, Rush."

He didn't doubt it. Taking care of the girls had never felt like a burden. He didn't mind—he liked knowing they were safe and happy. He'd kept that promise, at least.

Pop poked through the grocery bags, muttering with approval as he pulled out an assortment of cured deli meats and cheeses, antipasto, and a loaf of Italian bread. "He's right, girls," he said gruffly. "He's looked after you all this time."

Rush's throat tightened, and he cleared it quickly. Okay. Enough of that. "What's new with you two?"

Sarah tore off the end of the crusty loaf of bread and slathered it with butter. "Let's talk about you instead. How was your date with Lily?"

Pop's head lifted sharply. "Lily who?"

"Lily Hart," Rachel said. "One of the Hart girls from the village. She owns that yoga-and-dance studio, right?"

Here we go. Rush concentrated on making his sandwich. "We're friends." *And maybe not even that anymore,* the helpful voice in his head reminded him.

Not after Friday night when he'd messed things up by having a panic attack and practically drop-kicking Lily at her door.

Sarah arched a brow. "Funny, Monica saw you two walking around Candlelight Night together, looking real cozy."

Of course Monica did. He should've arrested her last summer for indecent exposure when she climbed half naked into his truck.

"I'm not dating Lily," Rush said flatly. He tossed Riggs the last bite of his sandwich and folded up his paper plate, already planning his exit. It was his day off. There were a hundred things on his to-do list before his move next month.

Rachel only smiled faintly. "You shaved your scruff. Even trimmed that mustache. Men only bother with grooming when they want to impress someone."

Pop gave a wheezy chuckle. "She's got you there."

Rush scowled. "I shave."

"Barely," Rachel countered, looking amused. "Rush, we're not meddling. We just want you to be happy."

"Yeah," Sarah added quickly. "And maybe not spend Christmas alone again. You and Riggs can't just hole up in the house."

Rush leaned back in his chair, crossing his arms. "Where are you two headed?"

"Ski trip with friends," Rachel said.

"Perfect," Rush said. "I'll pick up some overtime."

"Or," Rachel said softly, "you could spend Christmas with

someone who actually makes you smile." She hesitated, searching his face. "Boston's not the only future you could have, you know."

Rush kept his face unreadable, even if that one stung. "Boston's the future I want."

Sarah exchanged a look with Rachel. "Fine. You and Pop can spend the holiday together."

"Leave me out of it," Pop said. "Joanne promised me a rematch of our game."

Rush pushed back his chair and stood. "Don't worry about me. I'm fine."

The girls exchanged another look, but they didn't press, and he was thankful.

They finished lunch and a few hands of poker, during which Pops cheated outrageously and still managed to win every hand. Eventually, he began to fade, the sharp glint in his eyes softening to a hazy tiredness. He got turned around looking for the bathroom down the hall, muttering to himself, so the girls gathered their bags and kissed him goodbye, promising to be back next Sunday.

Rush stayed behind, helping Pop into his flannel pajama top and guiding him into bed. Pop's hands shook as he climbed under the covers, and his eyes went glassy and unfocused.

"You're all right, Pop. Just rest," Rush murmured.

Pop blinked up at him, confusion flickering in and out. He reached out and caught Rush's wrist with a surprisingly forceful grip.

"I'm proud of you, my boy," Pop said.

Rush froze. He looked up, searching Pop's face for signs of confusion, expecting to see the distant haze that came more and more often. Instead, he found sharp recognition staring back at him.

"Thanks, Pop," he managed, forcing his voice to stay even. "I'm proud of you too."

Pop shook his head faintly. "No. I mean it. You've been a good grandson. Better than good. You took care of your sisters. Now you're taking care of me. You've carried us all when you didn't have to."

The words landed like a punch, straight to the center of his chest. Rush looked down at the remote, concentrating on the numbers instead of the emotions swelling inside.

"Loving people means forgiving yourself too," Pop said quietly. "You can't keep punishing yourself forever."

The bottom dropped out of Rush's stomach. He stiffened, pulse spiking as icy-cold water threatened to drown him again. Forgive himself? Christ. He didn't even know what that would look like. How could he, when a little girl lived without her mom because of him? Because he didn't do enough.

Lily's soft green eyes flashed in his mind, and Rush knew she'd say the same thing. He shoved the thought away hard, fumbled for the remote, and clicked through the channels. "What channel do you want to watch? The Bills play tonight. It's their year, ya know?" He kept his voice calm even as his heart surged in his chest, thumping madly.

Pop sighed and leaned back, and just as quickly, the clarity dimmed. He closed his eyes, already drifting in a world that didn't include Rush.

Rush sank back in the chair with the remote loose in his hand now. Riggs pressed warm and solid against his leg, sensing that Rush was in another world too.

Love. Forgiveness. He wasn't sure either belonged to him.

Chapter Thirty-Five

THE BAD NEWS was that Baby Jesus had gone missing. Again.

The good news was that no one in the audience had a clue.

By the time the curtain rose in the community center auditorium for the last part of the pageant, Lily had located the baby, replaced two bent halos, and bribed a shepherd with a cookie to stop picking his nose. From the seats, it probably looked charming. From backstage, it was utter chaos.

To Lily, it was perfection.

The music for the last carol began, and Savvie and Tessa were front and center. After waving at Allie and Davis, Savvie loudly and proudly sang off-key and two beats behind everyone while Tessa elbowed her and tried to steal the show. By the time the final song notes played from the speaker, the audience was holding their sides from laughing. Lily and Evie laughed too. Those girls were a delightful menace, God bless them, but they added so much joy to their family too.

Finally, the beginning notes to the last song, "Silent Night," began, and the packed auditorium quieted. Some of Lily's older students handed out candles, and row by row, they flickered to life, warm light spilling out over their faces. It was Lily's favorite part of the pageant—the whole town joined in to sing the final song of the evening.

Her gaze stayed locked on Chloe. For weeks in rehearsal, they'd only mouthed the words together, with no sound at first. Then, gradually, Chloe began humming, and lately, Lily had thought maybe she'd been ready to really sing. She never pushed, of course. She firmly believed Chloe would talk when she was ready. It was enough that she was here, smiling and twirling in her angel costume and part of the magic of Christmas after her little life had been devastated.

The music swelled, and Lily joined in with Evie next to her.

Chloe opened her mouth, and her voice rang out in the hushed auditorium, clear and certain, along with the others.

"Silent night, holy night, all is calm, all is bright."

It wasn't louder or sweeter than any of the other children's voices, but Lily heard it. She knew it because she'd been waiting for it for months. That small, brave voice weaving into the chorus like it had always belonged.

Her heart nearly burst. Tears stung her eyes as she reached for Evie's hand, and her twin squeezed back.

In the first row, Lily caught sight of the Whitmores. Chloe's grandparents were on their feet, candles trembling in their hands, tears streaming openly down their faces. They clung to each other, pride in their granddaughter etched alongside the grief for their daughter.

Lily's own eyes blurred. All she could think, through the lump in her throat, was how much it would mean if Rush were here to see this. If he could see what she saw—that Chloe wasn't broken. That she was healing.

Chloe was finding her voice again.

The final verse rose, the children's voices sweet and soft, the audience's deeper ones layering beneath them until the sound filled the room. It was magical. Lily swiped at her cheeks, trying to compose herself before the curtain fell.

The door at the back of the auditorium opened, letting in a sliver of light.

Her head turned instinctively, and she knew who it was even before the tall figure slipped inside. Her body always knew. The air seemed to shift when he was near, prickling over her skin, and sending a shiver of tingles up the back of her neck.

She let herself look toward the one place she'd avoided all night.

Dark uniform. Silver badge catching the light. The Stetson's unmistakable shape as he crossed his arms over his broad chest and leaned against the back wall.

Rush.

Her breath caught. Across the sea of flickering candles, their eyes met, and something unspoken stretched between them—warm and achingly sharp all at once.

She forced herself to look forward again and focus on the last notes, the bows and applause, and the final curtain call. To finish the show with her full attention where it should be, on the kids. This night had been weeks of hard work, and she let them shine in the wild applause, even if she suddenly felt... well... unsettled.

When the crowd began thinning, Lily slipped away to check the wings one last time. Sure enough, Rush was there, leaning against the wall, hat in his hands, looking broody and manly and good enough to eat.

"Good show," he said. His eyes softened when they met hers. "Sorry I missed most of it."

"You caught the best part," she said, forcing her voice light. "You saw Chloe sing."

His mouth curved in that half smile that she loved. "Yeah, I did."

They stood there in the hallway just a beat too long.

"Well—" she said, just as Rush spoke.

"I should've—" He stopped, and they both smiled, for real this time.

"Go ahead," she said.

"I should've said this before," he went on, shifting his hat in his hands, "but I'm sorry, Lily. For dropping off the map after Candlelight Night. That wasn't fair to you."

Something inside Lily relaxed. This was Rush: handsome, stoic, impossibly noble. A wash of affection swept through her, but she kept her tone casual. "You did what you needed to do. And I've been busy too. Wrangling angels, obviously. I didn't exactly have time to miss you, Sheriff."

One dark brow arched, and he shifted more comfortably against the wall. "You sure about that?"

"Well," she added, smiling, "maybe I missed parts of you."

His eyes dipped down to her mouth before he glanced up. "Good."

The heat in her belly flared. Flirting with Rush Callahan had become her new favorite pastime, and now that she knew he wasn't ghosting her, she could lean into it. This—this delicious teasing and stealing a few moments in a dark hallway— was fun. Light. Safer than what simmered beneath it. She could stay here forever, soaking up the push and pull of the man in front of her, the warmth he kept buried under that gruff exterior.

That was the whole point of their arrangement, wasn't it? Temporary and fun.

Rush wasn't sticking around, and she wasn't asking him to. She'd already learned the cost of giving her heart to a man who couldn't give her the future she wanted. She wasn't falling in love with Rush... but she could if she wasn't very careful.

Lucky for her, he made it easy to draw a line. He simply walked away when they got too close to crossing it.

His radio crackled with static, then Myrna Bryne's voice came through, and the moment ended.

"Copy that," he said into the radio. "I have to go," he said, looking very much like he wouldn't mind staying.

She smiled. "Merry Christmas, Rush."

"Merry Christmas, Lily." He brushed her lips with his, probably meaning it as a quick holiday kiss. But the second his mouth touched hers, she closed her eyes and let herself savor it. By the time she opened them, he was striding away, shoving his hat down low over his ears, heading out to serve and protect the snowy streets of Northfield. Much like a hero, although she knew how he felt about that word.

Later, back with her family, Evie slipped her arm through hers as they walked home. Lily tucked her sister close, smiling at her excited chatter, even as something hollow settled in her chest. By the time she washed up and sank into Evie's guest bed, the ache was still there.

And maybe that was exactly why she was thankful for the reminder that this was all temporary. Because if she wasn't careful, there was a very good possibility she'd fall for him completely.

It was better this way. Better to live in the now. Better to enjoy him while she had him and keep her heart out of it.

Chapter Thirty-Six

THE CLAIRMONT HOUSE had never looked so festive. As Northfield's most popular mayor, Theo's Christmas Eve party was always the highlight of the season, but since marrying Amber, the festivities had gone up several hundred notches under her guidance.

The huge old Victorian was lit up from the roofline to the ground, garlands draped every surface, and the tree in the front parlor window was even bigger than Rush's.

Knowing her sister's tendency for being over-the-top, Lily had gone all out for the night, too—hair curled, lips glossed, and a silky cranberry-red dress that Evie swore made her look like a Christmas ornament come to life. The neckline dipped low enough to feel daring but not embarrassed by her aunts, and the skirt had a long slit on one side to show off a little thigh.

Evie, unfortunately, hadn't made it. Dr. Pierce had asked her to spend the evening helping him "prepare" for a conference he was presenting at next week. From the outfit Evie had chosen, Lily had a feeling she had other plans. Her twin didn't break out the silk blouse and pencil skirt combo just to alphabetize research articles.

So Lily was on her own tonight, determined to shake off the melancholy of the last week and enjoy the night, surrounded by family and more than a hundred of Northfield's residents.

So she smiled. She mingled. She took the wine Theo offered and even let that cute Deputy Ben Tanner make a joke about saving him a dance. At least, she thought he was joking.

Everyone was in high spirits—Annette and the aunts, including Cap, looking dashing in his fire chief uniform, the firefighters and their wives, a scattering of deputies and their families. Lily chatted and laughed, aided by a little alcohol, yes, but she was enjoying herself.

A week since the pageant, longer since Candlelight Night, and Lily hadn't seen Rush once. A week of silence, but not by accident. She'd made sure of it. She kept herself busy: wrapping presents with Allie for her nieces and nephews, baking cookies with Evie—being careful to steer clear of the sheriff's office across the street, even walking the long way around the block when she needed to.

It wasn't that she didn't want to see him. She wanted to—Lord, did she. She'd wanted real and raw and something that felt alive, and that was exactly what he'd given her. A handful of weeks she could tuck away, a secret stash of heat and memories to pull out years from now when she wanted to remember what it felt like to be consumed.

Rush didn't owe her anything more. He'd made it clear he wasn't interested in forever, or even talking, just what they could steal together in the bedroom. Or the couch. Or her studio.

She missed that too.

But tonight, at Theo and Amber's Christmas Eve party, she was determined to smile, to drink good wine, flirt if she felt like it, and lean on her family. She had her flaws, but self-destruction wasn't one of them.

Then the tingle started—that telltale prickle she always felt right before she saw him. The roar of the party dulled to a buzz, and she went still.

And then she saw him.

His uniform was gone tonight. He wore a dark suit jacket open over a white button-down. Even out of uniform, Rush's presence held the same gravity. He didn't bother with polite sheriff smiles tonight—he moved like a man on a mission, searching the room with his eyes. People stepped aside without realizing they'd done it, carving him a path straight to her.

Ben said something at her side, but she didn't catch it. Rush was walking through the room, right toward her.

"Excuse me," he rumbled when he reached her, his hand cupping her bare elbow. The heat of it made her shiver.

"Looking for someone?" Ben taunted with an easy grin, but Rush didn't even glance his way.

He simply steered her away from the crush of people, into a quieter room off the living room.

Her pulse hammered so loudly she wondered if he could hear it. She swallowed, trying to summon her cool. "Didn't expect to see you here, Sheriff."

His eyes dragged over her, from the cranberry silk skimming her curves to the gloss on her lips before locking on her eyes. "Yeah," he said gruffly. "Figured that out."

"I've been busy," she said, only half lying.

"Busy avoiding me." He didn't soften the accusation, but his thumb skimmed the tender skin of her inner arm, almost as if he had to touch her. "You think I haven't noticed?"

Lily lifted her chin. His eyes were silver-gray and clear with purpose. "Have you?"

"Drove me out of my fucking mind all week."

The words landed hot in her belly. She wanted to be cautious, to protect the rather small part of her heart left that he hadn't already touched, but that wasn't her nature. "Well, I'm here now," she said softly, smiling up at him.

"I can't stay away from you." He brushed his fingers against her cheek. "Every damn day I walk into work and have to force myself not to walk across the street. But every damn day, it feels like I can't breathe without you."

The honesty in his voice melted through her, even as her heart thudded so hard it hurt. "Then stop trying," she whispered.

He leaned closer and rested his forehead on hers. "You look beautiful," he said roughly.

"Thank you. So do you. Look handsome, I mean," she added with the start of a flush because the way he was looking at her—like he wanted to devour her—made heat slide low and slow in her veins.

Up close, she could see the shadows under his eyes, the faint strain of tiredness, but he was still Rush. All hard lines and quiet strength, coiled tight with the kind of pent-up energy that made her pulse trip. Just being near him lit her up in places she'd been trying to ignore all week.

"I'm glad you came," she murmured.

"Only to see you." His voice dropped, low enough that it teased over her skin and left goose bumps in its wake. "I hate these things."

The faint curve of his mouth wasn't much, but it was solely for her. It was enough to make her feel like liquid honey was in her veins. Her lips curved too.

Then his eyes flicked to her mouth.

Everything inside her went still. His eyes darkened, turning darker, like he was remembering how good they were together.

"Aunt Lily, who's that man?"

Lily blinked, snapping back to reality.

Savvie stood at her side, staring up at them curiously. Her

blond curls, once tamed neatly into a braid, had come loose and were tangled wildly around her face. She wore her purple princess dress with a straggly piece of lace trailing after her, and her tiara was crooked.

"I'm Savvie," she announced, popping two fingers out of her mouth.

Rush took a subtle step back and held out a hand to shake. "Nice to meet you, Savvie. I'm Rush Callahan."

They eyed each other for a long minute, seeming to size each other up.

Then Savvie grabbed Rush's hand and held on.

"I'm gonna need that back," Rush said solemnly.

She tilted her head the same way Bash had weeks earlier. "Are you Aunt Lily's boyfriend?"

Heat flared across Lily's cheeks. "Savvie..." *What's with kids asking that question?*

Rush's eyes locked with Lily's. "Yes, ma'am," he said firmly. "I am."

Oh my.

"You like her."

"Yes, I do. A lot."

Before Lily could form a reply, Savvie pointed upward, smiling slyly. "You're under the mistletoe."

Rush followed her finger, and sure enough, a ball of fresh mistletoe hung above them. "Looks like it."

The flash of amusement in his expression didn't soften the intent in his eyes. He bent down, put a hand on her waist, and brushed his mouth slowly against hers. He squeezed her waist gently before letting her go.

When he drew back, Lily was still reeling from the feel of him. Her chest cinched tight.

"What's in your hair, Savvie?" Lily asked to break the tension.

Savvie pulled a sticky curl over her hair and looked at it distastefully. "Peanut butter," she said, sticking her bottom lip out. "Mama washed it out, but I was saving it."

Lily stifled a laugh. *Oh, Savvie.*

"Peanut butter's better on a sandwich than in your hair," Lily murmured, catching sight of Rush's smile.

Savvie huffed, unimpressed, and tugged Rush's hand. "Wanna play Barbies?" she asked. "You can be Ken," she added generously, tugging Rush toward Theo's expensive ottoman, where a Barbie house currently sat.

And just like that, the sheriff of Northfield planted himself on the rug with a plastic Ken doll in his big hand and impressed them both with his Ken voice.

His sisters had taught him well.

Lily stood rooted to the spot, watching them. He wasn't hers. She couldn't fix him. But she couldn't seem to stop the hope blooming almost painfully in her chest because there, sitting on the rug next to her niece, he was exactly what she wanted.

Annette appeared by her side and followed her gaze. "Well," she said, "would you look at that?"

A rustle in the doorway—the aunts had arrived. Giulia, Sophia, and Rosa, all looking festive, and all holding wineglasses, eyes fixed on Rush.

"So," Giulia said thoughtfully, "explain something to us. When you left the church that day with Sheriff Callahan, you said he dropped you off at the Pine Cone Lodge to wait out the storm."

Oh, hell. She knew that little detail would come up again.

"Well, it wasn't exactly like that," Lily mumbled.

"I knew it." Aunt Sophia snorted. "No woman climbs into the truck of a man who looks like that and gets out at a motel alone."

"Unless it's the honeymoon suite," Amber said, rounding the corner, rubbing her belly with a wicked grin.

The aunts cackled, but Lily mentally shrugged. She was an adult woman, and it had all turned out for the best.

"So what did happen, Lily?" Annette asked.

Fine, she'd come clean. Lying, even a small white lie, wasn't in her nature anyway. She'd been shocked her family had believed her at all. "It wasn't a motel. We spent the weekend at his cabin in Autumn Ridge and then reconnected back at home."

Heat rushed to Lily's cheeks as the room erupted in talk. Rush caught her gaze, and Lily smiled shyly.

Then Aunt Sophia gasped, her eyes going to Lily's flat stomach. "I knew it! Lily, you're pregnant?"

"What—?" Lily choked. "No—"

But like her whole life, everyone talked and fussed over her.

Rush looked up at her then, and she knew he'd heard by his wolfish grin. The aunts zeroed in on it, of course.

"I had a feeling he was the one," Aunt Rosa said, serenely sipping her wine.

Allie and Amber both gasped, staring at her red-silk-covered stomach. "You didn't tell us?"

"I'm not pregnant!" Lily protested, but Aunt Giulia was already beaming as she swept the wineglass out of Lily's hand.

"Lily, darling, why didn't you just say so? A bun in the oven explains everything."

"Lillian," Annette said quietly, "is this true?"

Before she could answer, Sophia dinged a fork against her glass. "A toast! To the happy couple—and their little blessing on the way!"

A glass shattered, and everyone's heads whipped around to find Tucker swaying near the bar cart, a broken glass at his feet, and red wine dripping down his knuckles. His eyes were blood-shot and furious and locked on Lily.

"You've got to be kidding me," he slurred. "You're pregnant?" His gaze shot toward Rush on the floor next to Savvie. "Christ, Lil. Playing house already?"

Rush's eyes went gray and flat, and he rose to his feet instantly, setting the toy down carefully on the ottoman before standing to his full height.

The sheriff of Northfield once again.

"You need to leave, Tucker," Lily said quickly. "You've had too much to drink."

Tucker's lip curled as he looked back and forth between them. "How long has this been going on?"

"Excuse me?" Lily's mouth dropped. The nerve shocked her.

"My mother was right about you," he spat. "Was this going on the whole time? While we were engaged? While my mother was planning our damn wedding?"

Amber's heels clicked forward, her eyes glacial. "You're not on the guest list, Tucker. Leave. Now. Before you make an even bigger fool of yourself."

"You bitch," he said, turning back to Lily. Bitterness twisted his mouth. "You made me look like a fool."

Before she could react, Rush stepped between them. "That's enough," he said sharply.

The room went dead silent.

"So what? You're her bodyguard now? Be careful, Lil. Everyone knows his track record with saving women."

The room went dead silent.

Rage and heartbreak tore through Lily's chest, making it hard to catch her breath. How dare he. How dare Tucker take Rush's rawest, deepest wound and fling it at him like it was a weapon.

Rush didn't physically react. If anything, his face went even stonier.

Tears sprang to her eyes, and she wiped them away, impatient with herself. "Don't you say another word," she said fiercely. "Don't you dare."

Her voice cracked, but it didn't matter—she put every bit of her disgust into it, and it hit Tucker right where she wanted it to as shame flickered for the briefest moment on his face.

"You're done here," Rush said calmly enough, but the muscle was ticking in his jaw again, and Lily saw the lethal fury in his eyes. "Leave. Now. Or I'll help you."

Tucker sneered, "You don't get to tell me—"

Rush cut him off. "Good choice."

Rush moved too fast for Tucker to see him coming until Rush's hand clamped around his wrist and the broken glass was gone. With his other hand, Rush pressed a firm palm to Tucker's shoulders and steered him backward, making it look easy.

Theo, Davis, and Ben appeared, looking ready to drag Tucker out themselves if Rush hadn't already handled it. The crowd parted silently as Rush guided him toward the front door without breaking stride. He opened it, and they disappeared.

Amber was the first to reach her. She pulled her into a hug around the curve of her belly. "He's the worst. I'm so sorry you had to deal with that, honey."

Allie hugged her from the other side. "You okay?"

Then the aunts descended, and all hell broke loose.

Chapter Thirty-Seven

THE COLD AIR felt like a sucker punch to her lungs, making them instantly wheezy, when Lily followed Rush outside, but she ignored it. She'd slipped past her family, grabbed her coat from the rack, and flown down the steps after Rush, her pulse drumming as hard as her heels against the pavement.

Rush stood at the end of the driveway with Theo and Davis. Even in the soft glow of the Christmas lights, Rush's face was set in harsh, no-nonsense lines. Tucker was nowhere in sight, but Rush was clearly still in sheriff mode.

It was hot. Very, very hot.

Theo, looking very debonair in his dark suit, spotted her first and stepped forward. "I'm sorry, Lily. I don't know how he got in. He wasn't on the guest list." Theo glanced at Rush. "Grant always said you were solid under pressure. He was right."

Lily blinked. "Grant..."

Theo's brows rose. "My brother. You met him at the wedding, remember?"

Her stomach swooped. Grant Clairmont. Rush's buddy in the Marines—the one who'd pulled him to Northfield in the first place. She'd met him at Amber and Theo's wedding, of course, but somehow she hadn't connected the dots when Rush mentioned him.

She shook her head quickly. "Right. Your brother. I did meet him." She managed a quick smile. "But this wasn't your fault. You couldn't have known."

Beside him, Davis—quiet and steady as ever—put a hand on her shoulder and gave it a reassuring squeeze. "You okay?"

Her chest still felt tight, but she nodded. She really did love those brothers-in-law of hers, handsome and protective in their own right. "I will be. Thank you. Both of you."

Rush stepped forward then, pissed and protective at once, and her stomach swooped because that look really, really did it for her.

Theo and Davis exchanged one of those silent glances that spoke volumes before backing away toward the house, wisely leaving the two of them staring at each other.

And then it was just Lily and Rush, with music and light drifting from the house.

The set of his shoulders should have been a warning, but that slow, liquid honey slid through her body again, absorbing his energy and giving it back.

She walked straight to him and laid her palms flat on his chest, feeling the tense muscles and the thud of his heart under her hands. Just that. Just lightly rested her palms against his hard body and let him feel her calm.

And desire.

He looked at her, his gaze sharp. "Come home with me, Lily."

"Yes." No hesitation.

They walked in silence to his truck, the tension between them an electric charge ready to go off. Rush opened the door, and her satin dress caught at the knees, forcing her to hike it high before getting in. When she turned, he was in the driver's seat, his stare fixed on her bare, smooth thighs, hunger carved into every hard line of his face.

"Rush," she whispered, pouring every bit of longing into that one word.

That was all it took.

He was on her instantly, cradling her jaw and kissing her hard, pinning her back against the leather seat with the solid weight of his body. His mouth was rough and consuming, his tongue hot and insistent until she was arching beneath him, almost lying down, trying to drag him even closer.

The taste of him—whiskey, heat, and relief—made her dizzy.

It wasn't enough. It never was with him.

His hands slid down, rough palms cupping her ass and hauling her into his lap. She straddled him, the satin of her dress riding higher until it barely covered her hips. The thick press of him strained against her core, and Lily rocked greedily, a moan tearing from her throat.

"Please," she gasped, grinding down against him. Her thong slid into her folds, giving her even more of the delicious pressure. She shuddered, heat shooting through her as she moved restlessly.

"Goddamn, Lily," he gritted out, shoving her dress higher and finding the thin scrap of her thong. One sweep of his fingers through her slick heat, and he groaned. "Fucking soaked for me."

"Yes," she panted, shuddering. She was drenched, aching, and she wanted this man branded into her bones. She whimpered when he pushed two fingers inside, her body clenching greedily around him. His thumb pressed down on her clit as he pushed deeper, the slick sounds almost obscene and unbearably erotic in the small cab.

He leaned back far enough to dip into the low scoop of her

dress, pushing the satin aside to bare more of her breasts. His head dropped to scrape his teeth on the inside curve.

"What the fuck is this?" he grunted against her skin, licking and nipping.

Startled, Lily looked down—and let out a shaky laugh. The damn nipple covers were still stuck in place, stark against her rosy-pink skin while Rush bit and sucked around them.

"Nipple covers," she gasped, trying to pull them off.

He batted her hands away with a grunt. "Let me," he muttered, tugging each one off. Then he was back, hot and relentless, latching onto her now bare nipple while she melted against the steering wheel, content to let him take his fill. "I love your tits," he groaned.

His hair slid silkily through her fingers when she tugged him closer, offering more. Rush groaned, shoving her down harder on his cock and latching deeply onto the opposite breast, sucking hard enough that Lily felt the corresponding pull between her legs. She held him to her and ground down, chasing friction until the truck rocked faintly under their rhythm.

"Rush," she gasped.

His hands spread her thighs wider, dragging her closer. Then he was there, bold and proprietary, touching her in a way that made her knees weak, pushing straight into her dripping wet pussy.

"Oh, God," she moaned as he withdrew, stroking over her clit next, firm and agonizingly slowly.

"Look at me, angel," he demanded.

She forced her eyes open, meeting his while his hand worked her—one finger, then two, stretching her, thrusting slowly and deliberately while his thumb stroked mercilessly on her clit.

Then he eased away, and she nearly moaned at the loss.

Rush held his fingers up, glistening in the dim light, his gaze never leaving hers, and painted her wetness across her nipples before dipping his head again. His groan vibrated through her chest as he sucked one nipple deep into his mouth, his tongue swirling over her hungrily.

The filthy sound of it had her clawing at his shoulders, rocking against him helplessly. "Please," she whispered, digging her nails into his shoulders while she rode him harder.

"You want it here, Lily?" he growled against her breast. "Right fucking here in my truck where anyone could walk past and see you getting fucked?"

Her breath hitched. "Yes," she gasped, beyond caring. "God, yes, right here. Now."

He jerked his belt buckle open, the clang loud in the stillness of the night, and yanked down his zipper.

Her heart pounded as she shifted higher on his lap, satin riding to her waist, her thong shoved aside, bare and wet, and ready. She felt the thick, blunt head press against her entrance, and a shudder rippled through her.

Her body clenched in anticipation, every nerve stretched so tight, waiting for him to push inside her and make the ache go away.

But before she could beg again—before he could drive home —her lungs betrayed her.

The gasp that should have broken into a moan caught in her chest, seizing viciously and stealing the moment.

Her chest locked tight, and panic flared in her. She jerked, clutching at her chest, and curled into him, trying to force air into her lungs.

"Lily." Rush froze. He pushed her back, searching her face. "Fuck," he swore viciously.

She gasped, clawing around the seat for her bag. Her

inhaler. Inside. She didn't take her purse when she left the party.

"I've got you," he said firmly, already shifting her off his lap. "Don't waste the air you've got."

Panic was setting in. Black dots danced at the corner of her vision. She closed her eyes, unable to look at Rush when he realized she didn't have her inhaler with her.

"Breathe," he said roughly, pushing something between her lips. "Hold it."

She puffed again, holding it until her lungs felt like they would burst, either from lack of oxygen or the medicine seeping into her, and stared at him.

He held her gaze unflinchingly. "That's it, angel. One more."

She wheezed in a breath and coughed. Rush rubbed her back in soothing circles while she repeated her mantra until her chest loosened.

I am a still lake, not a stormy sea.

"That's it," he murmured, pulling her into his chest. "I've got you."

Gradually, the tightness eased, and Lily sagged against him, trembling. "Where—?" She gestured toward the inhaler.

"I picked one up after the cabin," Rush said, holding her gaze steadily. "For you. In case this happened and you didn't have yours."

A few tears spilled down her cheeks. He brushed them away with his thumb before leaning back with a heavy sigh. His belt was still undone, his skin still flushed and hot to the touch from everything they had done.

"I'm so sorry," Lily said, shame burning her throat. Tucker's voice filled her head. *Too much work. Too fragile.* "I left my purse inside—I should've been more careful."

"Hey." Rush tipped her chin up, brushing her tears away with his thumb. "Don't apologize."

Her eyes filled again, tears spilling hot down her cheeks. "I feel so stupid. I've had asthma my whole life. How could I forget I need my inhaler?" She tried to duck her head, but Rush held her steady.

"Because you're human," he said simply. "It happens. That's why I picked up another one, just in case. You're not a burden, Lily."

Something in her chest wrenched. "But don't you see? I feel the same way about you." She let that sit with him the same way his words had landed with her.

Rush's hand dropped. He stared out the windshield, his jaw clenching. "Forgetting an inhaler and letting a woman drown are not the same thing," he said flatly.

"They're not. Not even close. But they are both survivable. Both are forgivable." She reached for his hand. "If you can't forgive yourself yet... at least let me."

Silence filled the cabin, but he didn't push her away. Not this time.

"Let's go home," he said finally.

She nodded, swallowing past the ache in her throat. "Okay."

THE SECOND they stepped through his door, he had her.

Rush shoved it shut with his boot and backed her against the wall, his mouth unerringly finding hers. She opened for him instantly, sweet and eager, and the second her lips parted under his, he lost whatever grip on control he had left.

Her coat hit the floor, and then his hands were under her dress, dragging it up, baring smooth skin he couldn't get enough of. Lily gasped when the cold air hit her legs, but he was there to cover her, his palms possessive and greedy for her narrow waist, her ribs, and finally the soft weight of her breasts under the thin dress.

No bra. No nipple covers, thank God. Her nipples were already hard, pressing against his palms through the fabric. He wanted them in his mouth.

"Rush—" Her whimper only made him hungrier.

Behind him, a sharp bark broke through the fog of his desire, followed by the click of nails on wood. Riggs nosed them curiously, and Rush dropped his head to the crook of Lily's shoulder with a grumbled *fuck.*

Christ. He needed to get himself under control.

He couldn't help it. Lily, with her sweet eyes and her body made for sin, made him lose his damn mind every time he touched her.

"Hi, Riggs," Lily said cheerfully, reaching to scratch his head. The nosy dog leaned into her touch and sat at her feet like he'd been waiting his whole life for her attention. "I think he likes me now."

Rush's mouth trailed down her neck—how the fuck did she always smell so good?—biting and sucking at the graceful column. "I like you now," he said gruffly. "Go lie down, Riggs. This is mine." He was only half joking.

Riggs gave a sharp bark of protest then nudged Lily's hand for more pets. She laughed, delighted, and obliged him while Rush glared at his dog.

"Who's a handsome boy? I knew you'd come around," she baby-talked him while Rush's cock throbbed painfully, begging for her attention. Figured Riggs would turn into a lapdog at the worst possible moment. He'd never liked any of the women Rush had brought home over the years, but now, apparently, he couldn't get enough of Lily. Damn dog.

"Go," he said more sternly. "She'll pet you later."

Riggs gave an annoyed huff but padded back to the kitchen with a long-suffering sigh.

Rush turned back to Lily and lightly scraped his teeth on her neck.

"Mmm," she sighed, tilting her head for more. "Where were we?"

She wrapped her arms around his neck, kissing him like she couldn't get close enough. He pressed her into the wall, eating up every sound she made, every arch of her body against his... until she froze.

Her arm brushed against the cold weight at his side. His gun.

Shit. He shrugged out of his suit coat and tossed it over the banister.

"What's that?" She leaned back, her eyes widening at the sight of his shoulder holster.

"My gun," he said shortly. He drew it, checked the safety, and set it on the table by the door. Out of habit, he pulled the cuffs from his pocket to set down, but he paused.

He turned back to Lily. Lips swollen the same deep red as her dress. Breathing fast and watching him with those same wide, curious eyes she'd had at his cabin.

Something darker unfurled inside him.

He caught her hand and tugged her closer to the stairs. She followed, her eyes flickering nervously to the table, to the gun, then back to the cuffs still in his hand. Jesus. That shouldn't have been as fucking hot as it was.

"Cuffs? At a Christmas party?" she whispered.

The tiny shiver gave her away. She knew exactly what he was going to do, and she wanted it, even if it made her nervous.

"Everywhere," he said roughly, backing her against the banister. He stepped close enough to feel the heat of her body, nudging her legs apart with his thigh, and taking her hands firmly in his.

The *snick* of steel closing around her wrists echoed in the house.

Her lips parted on a gasp, her breasts rising sharply, and fuck if that didn't go straight to his cock. His mouth curved slowly. His good girl was turned on.

He tested the hold—firm, secure, but not tight enough to hurt her. Just enough to keep her where he wanted her after a week of ducking his calls, dodging him, and making him crazy.

He lifted her arms above her head and hooked them over the banister. The position arched her back, thrusting her breasts out. He shoved down the neckline of her dress with his hand and caught her tight nipple lightly in his teeth. She tipped her head back against the wall and closed her eyes with a groan.

Pinned like this, she couldn't cling to him, couldn't grab hold. She had no choice but to let him touch her. Let him kiss her. And Jesus, she looked gorgeous restrained like this, trembling and open to him. Molten-hot desire clenched his belly, surging through his body.

"Perfect," he growled, crowding her closer, his mouth already searching for hers again.

"Rush," she whispered, flexing her arms and testing the hold.

"Yeah, angel," he muttered against her throat, biting and sucking the sensitive skin there. "You're not going anywhere."

He slid a hand down, fisting her dress and dragging it high over her thighs. Satin bunched at her waist, baring smooth, pale skin and the thin strip of lace barely covering her. He lifted her leg over his hip. The wet heat of her pussy pressed right against the ache straining his zipper, and he nearly came in his pants. Thank fuck she was ready.

"Fucking soaked." He pushed two fingers into her, using his

thumb to circle her clit until her head dropped back and her hips bucked against his hand. He kept the pressure on her hard little clit just relentless enough to make her gasp again. Groaning, she closed her eyes and tipped her head back. "You like being tied up, don't you? Say it," he said roughly.

Her eyes flew open, green fire burning into his. "Yes," she gasped. Her voice broke as he thrust into her again, curling his fingers against the sensitive places inside until she cried out, "God, yes. I love it."

The admission snapped what little restraint he had left.

"Fuck, Lily," he groaned. "I can't wait, darlin'. I need to be inside your tight little pussy."

"Yes, now, please," she begged. With her arms cuffed above her head, she had no choice but to let him take control.

"Lock your legs around me," he grunted. Using his body to pin her in place, he shoved her thong aside, yanked at his belt with one hand, unzipped just far enough to free his cock, notched the blunt head to her cleft, and pushed inside her in one bold thrust.

"Oh God, oh God, oh God," she chanted in that breathy way of hers that made him want to lick her up.

"Look at me, Lily." He braced one hand on the rail above her head, the other gripping her ass, using her bound body to take him as deep as he needed.

"Do you know what you've been doing to me?" he growled, thrusting up and grinding against her clit before pulling back. "Ducking me." Another thrust. She moaned. "Running every time I get close." Thrust. Thrust. Grind. "I've been losing my goddamn mind wanting you." He gripped her, keeping her exactly where he wanted her, using his hips to keep her slick and swollen pussy spread open for him, as he ground against her.

"Ohh," she whimpered. Her pussy fluttered, her tell. She

tried to push down on him, chasing her orgasm, but he tightened his grip on her ass, using his body to control hers.

"No," he said, low and rough near her ear. "Don't you dare come yet. I'm not done fucking you."

"Oh," she cried out, squeezing her strong dancer's legs around him, bouncing herself harder on his cock.

He felt her inner muscles clench around him, grasping at him, and nearly lost it right then. She was hot, slick, tight as sin, gripping him like she was made for him. He set a steady pace, driving into her deeper, harder, faster while she arched in the cuffs. Sweat gathered near her hairline, and he licked it, tasting salty, sweet, perfect woman.

Fucking Lily—her soft, pleading cries in his ear—was the only thing anchoring him. Every moan she gave him cut through the roar in his head like a lifeline. When she gasped louder, a high-pitched, shuddering sound that punched straight into his gut, he shifted his angle, chasing the needy little noise he craved.

For a few blessed moments, he escaped. There was no canal, no failure, no guilt when he was inside Lily. It was just the two of them. There was no finesse, but they had gone past that point in his truck. She was slippery wet, pulling him into her so tight he couldn't be anywhere but this moment, right now.

His Lily, gasping his name with that faint, breathy sound that he knew meant she was close to coming.

Fuck, he wanted to make her come. He needed it.

"Christ, Lily—you have the greediest pussy. My sweet girl's cunt was made just for me." He didn't know what the fuck he was saying, but he couldn't seem to stop talking.

His breath came raggedly. He didn't just want her—he needed her, needed to bury himself so deep he'd forget every dark thought that had haunted him for the last year. It was hot and fast, consuming them both because if he stopped, she would see who he really was.

He thought he might die if she ever stopped looking at him like she did now.

"Please, Rush," she groaned as if in pain. Her lips were swollen and puffy from his kisses. He dipped his knees, holding her ass pinned to the wall still, and kissed her hard again.

"Ohh," she gasped, her eyes squeezing shut as the flutters turned to a tight grip, and her legs locked around him so hard they shook. "I'm—I'm—oh, God!" She shrieked the last word and quivered, forcing him to hold still while she trembled on him, braced between his body and the banister.

It was the hottest goddamn moment of his life watching Lily come harder than a freight train. It sparked something primitive, something darkly possessive, in him.

He braced her tighter, holding her gaze hard. "Mine. You hear me, Lily? You're mine—" he groaned, his own control shredding. He thrust up hard, once, twice, and came with a guttural sound while she still fluttered around him, milking every last drop from him.

She buried her head in the crook of his shoulder, taking deep breaths while they recovered. He kissed her hair, her cheek, anywhere he could reach, while her body trembled from the aftershock and his words echoed in the house.

You're mine.

He hadn't meant to say it out loud. Christ, he hadn't even meant to think it.

But the words were still hanging in the air like smoke, thick and impossible to take back.

"Let me down," she whispered eventually. She tightened her fingers around his shoulders.

Every muscle in his body went taut. Shit. Had he hurt her?

He eased out of her slowly, found the key in his pocket, and unlocked the cuffs with shaking hands. The steel clicked open, and her arms dropped down. Faint red marks ringed the delicate skin.

"Christ." He rubbed the tender spots with his thumbs, guilt choking over him. "You—" His voice cracked. He cleared it roughly. "Okay?"

He leaned back to look at her face carefully. She was breathing shakily, but he didn't hear the telltale wheeze in her lungs.

"God, no," she breathed, nuzzling his jaw. She looped her freed arms around his neck. "I don't think I can stand."

"Stay the night," he heard himself say. "Please." The words seemed to shock her as much as they shocked him. They hadn't spent the night together since the cabin, and suddenly he knew he didn't want her to go. He wanted to sit on the couch with her under a blanket and stare at the Christmas lights she'd made him string up, and wake up with her next to him in bed on Christmas morning.

Who the fuck was he?

She blinked up at him. "Sleepover? But... it's Christmas. Don't you have plans with your family?"

He brushed a curl behind her ear, grazing the scattering of freckles on her cheek. "The girls are away with friends. I'm going to visit Pop in the afternoon." His throat felt tight, but he forced it out casually. "You could come with me."

Lily went very still, searching his face. He didn't know what she'd find there because he wasn't sure himself, but he sure as hell knew he didn't want her to leave him again. He'd had a week of that fucking misery, and it was enough to let him know he wanted her with him.

"Are you sure?"

He nodded. "Yeah, I'm sure."

She grinned then, and he remembered to breathe. He kissed

her soft pink lips and patted her bottom. "Come on. Let's go sit down."

Chapter Thirty-Eight

Rush jerked awake, his chest heaving, fighting for air that felt like icy black water. For a second, he couldn't draw himself free—Chloe's screams in his ear as he carried her back, Caroline's blue eyes locked on him as he swam away. The weight pulling him under. The choke of failure.

He forced himself to sit on the side of the bed until he stopped shaking, consciously listing his surroundings. The sheets were tangled at his waist. He was in bed. He was naked. He wasn't in the canal. He repeated it until the tremors eased.

Beside him, Lily slept peacefully, her red hair spilling across his pillows, her freckled shoulders soft in the faint wash of moonlight. She looked like an angel, peaceful and untouched from the nightmares in him.

For a second, he let himself breathe her in. Remembered her soft sighs on the couch in the glow of the Christmas lights when he'd made her come again, the hot shower they'd taken after, the way she'd curled up next to him and fallen asleep almost immediately. He wanted to sink into her calm and let it take away the chaos.

But he wouldn't put that on anyone. No one else deserved that weight.

Soundlessly, he slipped from the bed, pulled on a pair of gym shorts, and padded down the hall to the spare room where the heavy bag in the corner waited for him. It called to him, the only place he could pound away his rage with his fists. His failure.

He didn't bother taping his hands. He rarely did when he woke up from the nightmare. The raw burn of his knuckles was the point. Punishment. Pain that made sense. If he was lucky, he'd hit hard enough that he'd feel empty instead of everything all at once.

Steadily, methodically, he drove his fists into the bag, trying to beat the nightmare out of himself. Reducing emotion to muscle and blocking out the screams. The bag took it, and he lost himself in the rhythm of punishment.

"Rush?"

Her voice cut through the steady drumming. He froze in mid-swing, his chest heaving.

She was in the doorway, barefoot, drowning in one of his T-shirts. Her hair was mussed, her eyes wide and somehow sad as she saw him in a place he hadn't wanted her to see.

"Go back to bed," he rasped, turning back to the bag, praying she'd turn around.

But she crossed the room, slid her arms around his waist from behind, and laid her cheek between his shoulder blades.

Rush went rigid, breathing shallowly, cautiously, for a different reason now. "You should go back to bed."

"No," she murmured gently. "I want to be with you."

He exhaled and dropped his head, squeezing his eyes closed. He was so goddamn tired of fighting.

She turned him toward her until she was facing him. He let her.

"Lily, I can't—" he choked out. "I'm not—"

"Shh," she said so gently. Her eyes were tender, too tender. He couldn't look at them, not like this. He looked down instead —pink toenails, slender feet on the hardwood. Graceful like her.

"You don't have to," she said.

She stepped closer. He wanted to tell her to stop. To move away. Didn't she know he didn't deserve this? But he closed his eyes instead and buried his face in her hair, breathing her in.

"Come here," she whispered. She ran her hands over his back, up and down, soothing him, calming him. "Let me make you feel good. You deserve to feel good."

He let her lead him over to the weight bench across from a dresser and mirror.

"Sit here," she said. "Please," she added, with a hint of shyness in her voice for the first time that night. "I want to take care of you now."

When he was close enough, she pressed lightly at his chest until he dropped back onto the seat, legs spread. He wasn't hard yet—he was still strung tight, knuckles throbbing, adrenaline racing in his blood—but watching her, hearing her, something hot and electric stirred. His cock thickened, heavy on his thigh, coming alive under the heat of her eyes. He clenched his jaw and waited to see what she'd do next, already fighting the urge to take control.

In all their sexual encounters, he'd led. He'd always enjoyed taking control in bed, even before he'd needed it—before it became the only way he knew how to quiet his head. Control meant focus. Direction. Something to hold on to when everything else spun out.

But now, watching Lily stand over him with that intriguing mix of nerves and determination in her eyes, something inside him shifted. The fight bled out of him, leaving only her—soft and steady in the dim light.

Then she did something that broke him open.

She stepped between his knees, close enough that her scent surrounded him, and drew him closer until his forehead dropped against her chest. His cheek brushed the curve of her breast, the warmth of her skin seeping into him as her heartbeat thudded steadily under his ear. She held him there, one hand cradling his head, the other tracing over his back in slow, soothing circles.

He sank into her without meaning to, breathing her in, letting her heartbeat sync with his until he stopped shaking. The panic loosened its grip, replaced by something that pulsed slower, hotter. *Her.*

When she finally stepped back, his hands slid to her hips, not ready to let go.

She reached for the hem of the T-shirt and lifted it slowly, deliberately dragging the material up over her thighs, her hips, and then her head. She tossed it aside and stood proudly in front of him, letting him look his fill. The one table lamp turned on in the corner illuminated her lush body, turning it into a work of art.

Rush's throat went dry. He loved the way she was built— soft curves over sleek strength, graceful lines and full hips that begged for his hands. His Lily—grace wrapped in fire. Gentle and unflinching, and so damn brave it made his chest ache.

"Do you like what you see?" she asked, her voice husky.

She cupped her breasts. The full teardrop shape framed by her delicate hands made his breath come faster. For a second, he thought she meant to hide herself, his shy, sweet Lily. But then she pinched her nipples, tugging and rolling them between her fingers, getting them ready for his mouth. She tilted her head back in a blend of innocence and daring he wanted to drink in.

He'd been with enough women to know a performance, but Lily wasn't putting on a show for him. He sensed she was finding her footing, testing the edges of her desire and what she could do. It was the sexiest thing he'd ever seen in his life.

He leaned back, more comfortable with this game now that he knew the rules.

"You know I do," he murmured.

"Let me make you feel good," she whispered, gracefully sinking to her knees in front of him. She held his gaze and pressed a kiss to the scar on his thigh. Then she reached for the waistband of his shorts.

Rush swallowed hard.

She tugged his shorts down, her knuckles brushing his belly. Her breasts were level with his thighs, the soft weight of them brushing against him, taunting him, every time she leaned closer to tug them off.

Rush gripped the arms of the chair, fighting the urge to take back control, to pick her up and bend her over the dresser and fuck her hard, the way he knew they both liked. He concentrated on his breathing instead.

What the fuck did she say when she wanted to focus? *I am a still lake?*

It didn't work.

She moved closer then closer still, her lips curved as if she liked what she saw on his face. Her lips grazed his collarbone, pressing soft kisses there and then slowly, so damn slowly, down his chest, teasing his nipples with gentle strokes. "You deserve that," she said huskily, "to feel good."

Her red hair trailed over his thighs, her mouth skimmed his stomach, and his whole body went taut. He was hard as a steel pike now, aching, every nerve stretched thin. Gently, she fondled his balls, tracing the seam there, and rolling them lightly between her long fingers before leaning down to nuzzle them. He spread his legs farther apart and gripped the sides of the bench, fighting the instinct to drag her up on his lap and take back control.

She didn't give him a chance. In one fluid motion, she rose, stepping between his thighs, and his cock jerked painfully at the sight of her naked body, her pussy flushed and glistening with arousal. Her clit was a hard nub, peeking out and begging for him to touch, to taste and lose himself in her sweetness. He leaned forward, intent on doing just that.

"No," she said, backing away. Her fingers trailed down, circling her clit in slow, lazy strokes as his breath caught and held. "You took care of me so well," she whispered. "Now it's my turn."

"Lily," he ground out. "Come here and let me lick that pretty pussy."

Her face went slack with desire, but then she doubled down, shaking her head. "Later," she promised. "Now I want to ride you. Make you feel so good."

His cock jerked hard, leaking and desperate for relief. She took mercy on him and climbed onto his lap, but when he took her hips in hand, ready to drive her down, she caught his wrists and pinned them to the edge of the bench.

"Let me," she whispered, and fuck if he could deny her anything when she looked at him like that.

She gripped his cock and guided him to her slick entrance. Then, with a slow, deliberate roll of her hips, she sank down onto him, inch by inch, until he was buried to the hilt. Her body stretched to take him, their gazes locked. The sight of her red curls against the stark black of his pubic hair was so erotic his vision went white around the edges. Every muscle strained, trembling from the effort of holding still, of not ripping his wrists free of her grip and driving into her like his body screamed for.

She seemed to sense that he was at his limit and set a pace

that was firm and maddening in its control. Slow. Deep. Relentless. He tried to thrust up into her, to set the rhythm faster, but she shook her head and pressed his wrists down tighter.

"Oh, fuck," he choked, his voice coming embarrassingly close to breaking. "Fuck me harder, Lily." He squeezed his eyes shut, trying to find some shred of control.

"Look at me," she whispered again, letting go of his wrist to cup his jaw, tilting his face until his gaze locked with hers. "I've got you."

He did... and it was too much. Every roll of her hips stripped him bare, leaving him helpless under her as she rode him, forcing him to feel every second of it.

Her green eyes were soft, unflinching. There was no hiding here, even if he tried. She saw him—all of him—and she didn't flinch.

Rush's chest ached, his control splintering with every slow roll of her hips. "Lily... what are you doing to me?" His voice cracked, a rasp dragged from deep in his chest.

She leaned down, her forehead brushing his, her lips grazing his ear as she whispered, fierce and gentle all at once, "I want you exactly the way you are."

God. She undid him. He came with a guttural groan, shuddering hard, spilling into her slick heat as she held him, her eyes never leaving his as she ground herself against him.

She followed seconds later, clinging to him, trembling around him as she came apart in his arms.

Rush closed his eyes and tried to catch his breath. He wrapped his arms tight around Lily as she curled against his chest and buried his face in her hair, inhaling her clean, sweet scent.

His hand wandered, slower now, reverent instead of greedy. He traced the outline of her ribs, felt the fragile rise and fall of her breathing, automatically checking for wheezing. Down, over the soft skin of her stomach. Flat now, but his palm lingered there, and an image of Lily, round and full with his baby, took shape.

The vision gutted him. Primitive desire roared through him, so strong his arms tightened around her. His woman. His baby. A family he could almost see if he let himself.

Fear chased the thought almost immediately. He wasn't built for that. Not after what he'd failed to save. The hunger twisted into terror until his hands shook, and he moved them back to her ribs.

Control had always been his anchor. In boot camp, he'd learned early that discomfort—physical or mental—wasn't something you felt; it was something you shut down. Pain, fear, exhaustion—none of it mattered if you could lock it in a box. He took orders, held the line, and ruthlessly blocked out anything that got in the way.

Eventually, he'd been the one giving orders, and the need to stay shut down was even greater. When lives depended on clear eyes and steady hands, emotion was a liability. There was no room for panic or softness. He'd gotten so good at it he barely remembered how to feel at all.

After the night of Caroline Whitmore's accident, he'd clung to that control like a lifeline. The therapist the department had made him see had told him what he already knew: He was damn good at compartmentalizing, at putting his feelings in a locked box and walking away. Except lately, the box didn't always hold. The panic came anyway, in a sick rush of failure, and every time it did, it cut straight through the walls he'd spent a lifetime building, reminding him of the one truth he couldn't outrun—when it mattered the most, he hadn't been enough.

Lily scared him in some ways more than panic did. Panic he could ride out, breathe through. It had an end, if he could just force his mind to push past the feelings. But Lily stripped him of that ability with nothing more than a look. She didn't see a Marine barking orders or a sheriff holding the line. She saw the man underneath, the one who wanted her more than he wanted to keep his walls intact.

It fucking terrified him. Because if she was wrong about him —if she looked too closely and saw the failure he really was—he didn't know if he was strong enough to survive that.

"You okay?" she asked, tilting her face to look at him with drowsy, sated eyes.

"Yeah," he said roughly, softening his words by pressing a kiss to her pretty, freckled cheek.

He couldn't give her what she wanted most—not the family or the babies she deserved—and she deserved it all. But as she settled back into his arms, trusting him to keep her safe, he knew he was too damn selfish to let her go. For tonight anyway, he'd hold on, even if he had no right to.

Chapter Thirty-Nine

The kitchen smelled like Christmas.

Barefoot at the stove, Lily hummed along with the radio while the griddle hissed and popped. She poured another circle of batter, waited for the bubbles to rise, then piped a spiral of cinnamon brown sugar across the top.

The swirl melted into the pancake, caramelizing and making the kitchen smell divine, despite Rush's sparse pantry. A box of cereal, protein bars, and one lonely pancake mix, which she was using now. She'd scavenged cinnamon, sugar, eggs, and butter, and then hit the jackpot when she found cream cheese in the fridge.

Riggs hovered close, eyes locked on her, ever hopeful for another taste of pancake. She slipped him another piece as both a peace offering and a *good doggy, don't bite me* incentive. Honestly, she probably didn't need to worry anymore. Somewhere between last night and this morning, she and Riggs had come to an understanding: She pretended he wasn't a big scary police dog, and he pretended she was in charge so long as she kept the treats coming. So far, it was working beautifully.

After Rush had taken her back to his bed last night—well,

early this morning—Lily had slept like the dead until Riggs woke her with a long, cold nose in her neck. Apparently, she was in his spot, but when she'd put on another one of Rush's oversized T-shirts and padded downstairs, the dog had followed her.

She let him out into the frosty air, and when he was done with his business, he'd herded her over to the container of dog food in the mudroom, nudging her insistently until she'd fed him. Then he'd sighed deeply and stationed himself near her as she moved through slow sun salutations in the sunlight pouring in through the picture window.

Breath by breath, she'd eased herself into calm. Back to her center. Because last night had been... intense. It always was with Rush, but something had shifted. For the first time, she'd felt him cracking open and letting her in.

When she'd woken up to find his side of the bed empty, she'd followed the steady thump of fists down the hall and found him in front of a punching bag. The look in his eyes when he'd turned—God. It had nearly put her on her knees.

She'd once thought he was stoic. Guarded. Removed from the tsunami of emotions she felt so deeply sometimes it hurt, but she was wrong. Every emotion lived on his face last night—every punishing thought, every memory, every shard of guilt bleeding through his eyes.

Her own throat had burned. She'd wanted to weep for him, to scream at the injustice of it all—that a man who gave everything to protect would torture himself for the one life he couldn't save.

But she didn't because if she cried, he would've comforted her instead, and that wasn't what he needed.

It was her turn to take care of him.

So she had, the only way he'd let her. She'd slid her hands over sweat-slicked muscles and kissed the salt from his skin.

She'd used her body, slowly, gently, until his body stopped shaking with anger and started trembling with want.

The sex hadn't been frantic or rough this time. She'd held his gaze while she'd rolled her hips, smoothing her hands over his chest and taking him deeper and holding his gaze when he'd tried to look away. She'd wanted him to see her, to feel her, to know he wasn't alone in that darkness.

Now, the first wistful notes of "Have Yourself a Merry Little Christmas" played over the radio. She'd always thought it was one of the sadder Christmas songs. Ah, well. Mixed emotions all around today, apparently.

She whisked the batter briskly and poured big circles onto the buttered griddle.

A sound behind her made her glance up. Rush leaned in the doorway, hair mussed from sleep, wearing sweatpants slung low on his hips. His arms were folded across his bare chest as he watched her. She smiled, thinking once again that he and Riggs shared many similarities.

He glanced at the messy counter—powdered sugar, butter, and cream cheese ready for the icing—and raised a brow. "What's that?" he asked, looking with interest at the bowl she was mixing.

"Cream cheese icing," she said. "For cinnamon roll pancakes. Merry Christmas," she added, smiling when he came closer, backing her against the counter and nuzzling her neck. "I hope you don't mind." She sighed, closing her eyes. Rush woke up hungry and horny, if the tent in his pants was any indication. She relaxed and let his hands wander under the hem of the T-shirt. Looked like last night hadn't ruined things between them.

"I'm starving," he murmured, cupping her ass and kneading. He bent to kiss her, all minty and addictive, and she settled into his chest as he took the kiss deeper.

"Mmm," she sighed happily when he pulled away and smiled at her, scruffy and barely awake.

Rumpled morning-after Rush was the only Christmas present she needed.

"What can I do to help?" he asked, his voice still rough from sleep.

"Set the table?" Deftly, she slid another pancake onto a plate and drizzled the glaze in looping ribbons, dusting it with more cinnamon for good measure.

He moved around the kitchen, setting out cups and silverware and topping off her coffee. When she turned with two short stacks, he was waiting with her chair pulled out.

The gentlemanly gesture made her smile. "Let's eat."

For a while, the only sounds were forks scraping plates and Riggs's sighing, ever hopeful for scraps but not daring to nose his master, Lily noted. She tucked her bare legs beneath her chair and picked at her own plate, suddenly aware of the quiet stretching between them. She looked up to find him watching her with that unreadable expression that made her want to squirm.

Rush broke it first. "Haven't had pancakes on Christmas morning since..." He trailed off, shaking his head. "A long time."

She tilted her head. "Did you have another tradition?"

"Girls would tear into their presents. Pop would make coffee. Sometimes I'd fry eggs." He cut into his stack with the edge of his fork. "Nothing like this." He gestured at his plate.

Warmth unfurled in her chest at that news. She liked thinking she'd made something new with him.

"Well," she said lightly, "they're not gourmet, but a box mix and"— she lifted her fork, miming a flourish—"cinnamon swirl glaze turned out pretty good."

"Pretty damn good." His mouth tipped in the faintest smile. The sunlight streaming into the kitchen caught on the cuts on his hand as he lifted another bite, and before she could stop herself, the words spilled out.

"How are your hands?"

His fork froze in midair. For a heartbeat, he didn't answer, just flexed his fingers. "They're fine."

"Rush..." Impulsively, she reached across the table and brushed her fingers lightly over his knuckles.

His jaw flexed. He stared down at the cinnamon swirl on his plate. "I'm sorry about last night. You shouldn't have had to see that."

"I'm glad I did." She smoothed her thumb over his skin, feeling the roughness there. "You don't have to hide the hard parts from me."

His eyes rose then, storm dark, meeting hers, and for a moment, her breath caught. There it was again—that rawness he tried so hard to lock away.

Then it was gone, shuttered again. He cleared his throat, nodding at her unfinished plate. "You gonna finish those?"

She pushed the plate over wordlessly and let him retreat. Baby steps.

Except that he got up and left the table. Searing disappointment filled her. The walls had gone up again. She sipped her coffee and concentrated on her breathing, only to look up a moment later when he set a small, plainly wrapped box in front of her.

"Merry Christmas, Lily."

Her eyes widened in dismay. "I don't have your present with me."

"I don't need anything." He nodded at the box, smiling. "Open it."

Carefully, she unwrapped the paper and opened the lid, gasping when she saw the rose quartz from the Christmas market nestled inside. "You remembered." Her throat got tight, and her eyes filled.

"Don't cry, angel." He got up and took the necklace from her. "Lift your hair." He buckled the clasp and left a lingering kiss on her shoulder before returning to his seat. "Figured it belonged on you."

She sniffed, truly touched. "I can't help it. You're very thoughtful."

She got up, slid onto his lap, and kissed him. "Thank you," she whispered against his lips, resting her forehead against his.

Rush's arms locked around her lightly. After a beat, he cleared his throat. "You still want to go with me today to visit Pop?"

"Yes," she said quickly, sitting up. "I'd like that."

"He's... Pop's not always himself. Some days he doesn't know me." He hesitated. "I just want you to be prepared."

"Rush, you know what my family's like. We're chaotic and nosy. I can handle anything."

A faint smile tugged at his mouth. "What about your family? The Harts must have Christmas plans?"

"We have dinner tonight with the whole family." She hesitated, wanting to invite him, to bring him into the center of all that chaos and warmth, but she sensed a wary edge still clinging to him. He'd opened up so much last night—she almost let the words die there, afraid of a brush-off, but she made herself say, "I'd like you to come."

Instead, he nodded. "All right."

She smiled. "We'll have to stop by Evie's apartment. I can't exactly show up to meet Pop in a red satin dress."

That earned her a grin. His gaze dipped to her bare legs under the hem of his T-shirt. "He wouldn't mind if you did."

She tossed a napkin at him, laughing.

While Rush cleaned the kitchen, Lily took a quick shower

and tried very hard not to snoop in his room. It wasn't difficult—most of his life was packed in boxes along the wall. Still, a few things caught her eye.

On the dresser, leaning against a lamp, was a photo in a simple black frame. Rush couldn't have been more than twenty, all sharp shoulders and buzz-cut hair, with two younger girls by his side, looking up at him like he hung the moon. Rachel and Sarah. He had an arm hooked around each of them, protective even back then.

Next to it, tucked beneath a stack of mail, was the picture Chloe had drawn him. She smoothed a curled edge, her eyes prickling. He'd never mentioned it, but it had meant something. For all his gruffness, Rush carried the weight of these people who loved him, and he took it seriously. She touched his face in the photo, wondering what else he carried silently... and if he'd ever let her in.

Sleepovers, breakfast, and now—meeting Pop.

For something she kept reminding herself was temporary, it felt dangerously close to everything she wanted.

Chapter Forty

THE SMELL of antiseptic and bleach hit Lily the moment she and Rush stepped into Canalside. Sharp and sterile and fighting to cover the lingering trace of last night's dinner. Instinctively, she tucked herself closer to Rush's side, but the brush of her shoulder against his made him even stiffer.

The ride into town had been strangely tense too. The closer they got to the nursing home, the more Rush seemed to withdraw. Lily had asked if he still wanted her to meet Pop, thinking he'd changed his mind, but Rush had just looked at her, unsmiling. "Of course," he'd said, but the morning's intimacy had faded the closer they got to town.

Riggs trotted ahead, his nails clicking on the linoleum as they followed him into the nursing home's lobby, which was lit with a little Christmas tree in the corner, its twinkle lights doing double time to make the space cheerful.

They passed a cluster of residents chatting near the nurses' station. A woman rocked a swaddled baby doll as tenderly as if it were real. A man dozed in a chair in front of a gas fireplace. The place was trying for holiday cheer—there were garlands strung over the doorframes and paper snowflakes taped to the walls, but the sadness of the place was unmistakable. No amount of tinsel could disguise the fact that these people were waiting. Lily absorbed it all quietly, tucking the feeling somewhere she wouldn't forget.

Riggs padded straight into a large dayroom with a sitting area in the center and tables surrounding it and wove his way to a man in a wheelchair by the window. A plaid blanket was tucked over his knees, and his eyes were closed; his chin dipped to his chest.

Riggs put his long nose in Pop's lap and snuffled under the gnarled hand sitting loosely in his lap.

"Pop," Rush said, crouching down beside his chair.

The old man's eyes opened, softening when he saw Rush. "Boy," he said gruffly. "Merry Christmas. Hi, Riggs." He gave Riggs a rub on his head.

"Merry Christmas, Pop." Rush's shoulders eased almost imperceptibly.

"And who's this pretty thing?" Pop's bushy white eyebrows rose as he caught sight of Lily.

She stepped forward quickly to shake his hand. "Hi, Mr. Callahan. Lily Hart. It's so nice to meet you."

"Don't 'Mister' me," he said, shaking her hand warmly. "Call me Pop, the same as he does." His smile turned sly. "It's about time he brought a girl like you around."

"Pop," Rush started, his own cheeks flushing a bit.

Lily smiled, undaunted by a little family teasing. She was a Hart, after all. "I'm glad to be here."

Up close, she noticed other similarities between them. Both were large framed, although Pop's frame was much thinner, devoid now of the powerful muscles of his grandson. Both had the same square jaw, Pop's covered in white bristles and Rush's in black.

Rush reached into his coat pocket and set a small package in Pop's lap. "Brought you something."

Pop's gnarled fingers opened the paper until the top of a green bottle peeked through. His eyes lit up. "Bay rum," he said with a smile. He uncapped the cologne and inhaled deeply. "Joanie always liked it when I wore this out to dinner."

Rush nodded, his eyes crinkling at the corners. "I remember." He helped him cap the bottle. "Figured you might be due for a new one."

"How are the girls? Rachel still bossing everyone around?"

Rush's mouth curved slightly. "She tries. She's good. Sarah's good too. They're both good. They're on a ski trip, but they'll be here with me next week."

"I remember," Pop said, patting Rush's hand. He turned to Lily. "He did right by those girls, you know. Raised them up steady when he was just a boy himself." His eyes went a little wet at the corners. "His mom would've been proud of the man he is."

Rush's jaw clamped, but he gave Pop's hand a gentle squeeze.

"I'm glad you're here," Pop said, but his eyes were distant now, slipping into the past. "I'm taking Joanie out to dinner tonight. Can you give me a shave?"

Rush's throat worked, but he just nodded. "Yeah, Pop." He didn't look at Lily, but he answered her silent question. "Joanie's Gram. She's been gone almost ten years, but in Pop's mind, she's still right there," he said quietly.

Lily nodded, but the lump in her throat kept her silent. She doubted Rush would've wanted anything from her anyway. He was practically humming with tension, even as his hands were gentle when he tucked the blanket more securely around Pop's knees.

He pushed the wheelchair toward Pop's room, holding the door with Lily following. When he held the door for her, her fingers brushed his. He didn't pull away, but he didn't hold on either. The small space between them suddenly felt wider than the room itself.

She sat in one of the two chairs while Rush settled Pop by the window then grabbed a shaving kit from the bathroom. He set it on the nightstand and lathered the brush, the motions automatic while Pop seemed to drift in and out of awareness.

"Hold still, Pop," Rush murmured, gently guiding the razor across the white bristles. The sharp scent of antiseptic mixed with the clean scent of soap, but Lily didn't mind this time. It smelled of caring now. Like devotion.

While Rush worked, he talked about his sisters, giving Pop updates about their lives, patiently reminding him every time he asked who he was, who the girls were, who Riggs belonged to.

And he avoided Lily's eyes.

Rush finished the last careful stroke and wiped Pop's chin. "There," he said quietly. "A clean shave for Joanie."

Pop's eyes cleared for a moment. "You're a good man, Rush. Better than you think."

Rush's throat bobbed. "Learned from the best, Pop."

By the time the words were out, Pop's eyes were closed again, already drifting again in a world where Rush didn't exist.

Emotions welled up and clogged her throat.

When they got back into the Chevy a while later, Rush turned on the heater and blew on his hands while they waited for the cab to warm up. Lily sat angled toward him with her hands in her lap.

"Rush," she said. When he turned to look at her, she leaned in to press a warm kiss to his cheek.

His shoulders stiffened before he cleared his throat and reached for the ignition, eyes fixed straight ahead.

"Thank you for bringing me to meet him," she said anyway. "I can tell he thinks the world of you."

"He was—is—the best," Rush said simply.

The truck's engine grumbled, but eventually heat pushed through the vents, filling the cab with warmth.

"Here," she said, taking a wrapped box from her purse. "This is for you."

She set the tiny box in his palm. He looked at it for a beat before peeling the paper back with those rough, careful fingers of his.

A cowboy-boot ornament rested in his hand, tan with a little Texas outline stitched along the side.

"I saw it at the Christmas market," she said softly. "Thought it might remind you of home... wherever you land."

She tried to smile as she said it, even though the words tasted bittersweet.

A faint shadow crossed his face as he ran his thumb over the painted outline. "Thank you," he murmured. His hand came to rest on her knee, warm and solid.

Lily turned to look out the window, wondering why she still felt so cold.

ANNETTE'S big yellow Victorian glowed brighter than Rush's Christmas tree when they pulled up. Laughter and shrieking children spilled out of the house, along with the scent of garlic bread and the ever-present aroma of tomato sauce. Mmm— lasagna—it was always lasagna and Italian sausages with peppers and onions on hard rolls on Christmas. Lily's stomach growled at the familiar mix of basil and simmering tomatoes.

Rush stopped at the bottom of the porch steps, the bottle of wine and bouquet in one hand. He raked his other hand through his hair, scanning the line of cars jammed into the driveway and spilling over into the street. "I didn't expect so many people."

"It's just my family," she said lightly. "You've already met most of them."

True, there were a lot of cars parked outside. Sisters, spouses, kids, aunts, and cousins... the entire Hart crowd. After Canalside and the quiet in Pop's room, she understood Rush's hesitation.

Oh well. Too late now.

She looped her arm through his and tugged him straight into the noise. Small children and dogs tore through the hallway in a blur of sound and motion. Savvie zoomed past in her purple dress, only to be scooped up by Davis before she could collide with the banister. "Careful, kiddo," he said, giving Lily a quick grin before disappearing again with his daughter squirming under his arm.

Someone claimed every chair, every armrest, and even the floor. From the kitchen came the bang and crash of pans—and then her aunts came barreling out, Aunt Rosa armed with a wooden spatula, Aunt Giulia holding a fork with a meatball skewered on it, and Aunt Sophia with her glass of wine.

Lily sighed. Of course they would line up like generals in floral-print aprons.

"Lily!" Aunt Rosa swooped in first. Her sparkly sweater matched her eyes, which went straight to Rush. "And the sheriff. So nice of you to join us."

"Thank you for having me," Rush said somewhat stiffly. Lily gave his arm a reassuring, *you're doing great* pat. This was the easy part.

When there was a pause, Theo appeared in the doorway. "Sheriff," he said warmly, offering a hand. "Good to have you. Any friend of Lily's is welcome here."

"Indeed. Welcome, Sheriff." Aunt Sophia lifted her glass, giving him a slow once-over. "No uniform tonight?"

A faint flush crept up Rush's neck, but he merely smiled. "Not on duty tonight."

"Shame." Sophia shrugged. "Next time."

Before Lily could die of mortification, Annette stepped forward, calm and composed as always. "Thank you for joining us for Christmas, Sheriff." She offered her hand, which Rush took easily.

"Call me Rush, please. Here," he added, handing her the wine and flowers. "These are for you."

"Lovely. Thank you," Annette's voice was polite, although cool.

Lily's stomach tightened. He was holding his own, but the tension still buzzed around him. She wanted him to feel what she felt here—to see how warm and welcoming her family was—but the distance between them didn't give her much hope.

Two little blond heads pushed through the room, heading straight for Rush.

"He's my Ken," Savvie shouted, skidding to a stop and making a grab for Rush's hand. She glared at Tessa, who was hot on her heels.

"You got to play with him last time." Tessa stomped her foot then made a grab for Rush's other hand. "It's my turn."

They tugged back and forth, glaring at each other, with Rush caught between them.

To Lily's astonishment, a grin—the first one she'd seen all day—broke across his face. He let the girls pull him into the living room, where Annette's old dollhouse stood waiting. Within seconds, he was planted on the rug, patiently listening as the girls explained his duties as Ken.

In the kitchen, Lily poured herself a glass of red and sat

down on a stool at the island. The aunts were already back to bickering about the right amount of sugar in the sauce.

"Ya did good, Lily," Aunt Sophia said, tilting her glass to drain it. "This one looks like he knows what to do with a woman, unlike that other pansy ass you almost married."

Lily groaned. "Aunt Sophia, you can't say things like that."

"What?" The woman sniffed. "If we'd spoken up earlier, maybe you wouldn't have wasted your time with that pig." She peered into the living room at Rush, who seemed to have enlisted the help of Claire, Sammy, and Ben, Allie and Davis's older kids, to play with them. "He's good with kids too? He might be the one."

"He has younger sisters," Lily murmured, ignoring the pang in her chest. No, he wasn't sticking around, but if he was...

"Subtle as ever," Amber's bone-dry voice cut in. She lowered herself heavily into a chair with her hand pressed to her belly and winced. "What fresh hell is it that you can have pre-contractions before the main event?"

Theo was there instantly, tucking a pillow behind her back and murmuring something in her ear that made her smile reluctantly.

"Sit," he ordered gently, pressing a kiss to her temple. "I'll get you a plate."

That Theo. Lily sighed again. Both of her brothers-in-law made it hard to settle for anything less than the very best.

Evie slid in quietly then, setting down a plate of Christmas cookies. "Don't mind them," she said under her breath as she leaned toward Lily. "They're vultures, but I think they like him."

"That's what I'm afraid of," Lily murmured. As far as she was concerned, Rush was the very best... Too bad he wasn't sticking around.

She relaxed after that. If Rush could meet her mother's cool gaze without flinching, and the aunts' teasing, he'd survive the rest of her family. Rugged good looks, those broad shoulders and that quiet, contained authority—no wonder they couldn't stop staring. He was striking and probably used to women staring, especially while he was in uniform.

But it wasn't their approval she wanted most. It was her mother's.

By the time dessert was brought out—gelato, biscotti, and cake soaked in rum Lily had her eye on—everyone was relaxed and even merrier, if there was such a thing. Rush was patiently letting them all fire off questions. The aunts wanted to know how work was going. Sophia wanted the juicy bits, which he sidestepped. Did he like Northfield (of course), and Sammy wanted to know if he carried his gun and cuffs everywhere (yes —he raised a brow at Lily before answering).

At any rate, Lily wasn't expecting the curveball.

"It's a good thing our Lily's got you now," Aunt Giulia said, leaning over Lily to beam at Rush. "She's always been fragile. First her asthma, and then that horrible Tucker cheating on her after all those years. We worry about her, you know," she added with a nod. "She needs looking after."

Lily's fork clattered against her plate. "I—" She forced a small, tight smile. "I'm fine, Aunt Giulia, really."

Her cheeks warmed as the table went awkwardly silent. She wanted to insist she wasn't fragile, that she didn't need looking after—but the words caught in her throat at the worried looks on her family's faces.

Fragile.

Maybe once she had been. The girl who'd bent herself into whatever shape made other people comfortable. The girl who stayed because she wanted a future more than she wanted the truth.

But that wasn't who she wanted to be anymore.

From across the table, Rush caught her eye with a silent question, but she looked away quickly.

"She's tougher than she looks," Annette said in the silence, her cool gaze sweeping the table before settling on her. "I raised her, after all." She held her glass up in a silent toast, which Lily returned, surprised and touched.

The conversation picked back up, and Lily relaxed back into the warm hum of her family. They weren't perfect—who was?—but she knew they loved each other. Really, what more could you ask for?

A little later, Theo leaned around Amber's belly. "Grant says he's waiting to hear back from you on your start date for the new job."

Aunt Sophia perked up. "Job? Are you moving?"

"Yes, ma'am," Rush answered. "I'll be taking a job in Boston the second week of February."

Lily forced herself to keep smiling. That damn job hanging over their heads would not ruin her Christmas.

Still, for the rest of the evening, the thought pressed like a bruise.

A few weeks. That was what they had left.

Chapter Forty-One

THE NEW YEAR hadn't made Rush any less restless about Boston.

If anything, the anvil hanging over his head felt heavier. Three weeks left, and he wanted to spend every spare moment with Lily, not patrolling the goddamn back roads of Northfield.

Since Christmas Day at Annette's, when Boston had come up and Lily's face had gone white, he'd sensed her pulling away, and it killed him that he was the reason.

Needless to say, he was in a foul mood when Myrna's voice crackled over the radio.

"Unit One, we've got a speeder on Route 14. Reckless driving. Caller says they're swerving all over the road."

"Copy that," he muttered, turning the wheel hard and putting on his lights. Snow and salt crunched under the tires as he gunned it toward the village. Perfect. Just what he needed. Something to sink his teeth into.

The car ahead blew past a stop sign, tires fishtailing, and Rush swore viciously. Whoever was driving that car was going to get their ass handed to them.

Then his stomach dropped.

The car was Lily's.

For a split second, the lights and snow blurred, and he wasn't on Route 14 anymore. He was back at the canal, and the water was black and icy, rising around Caroline Whitmore's car, and her terrified eyes were locked with his. He could feel her slick hand slipping from his grip. Hear Chloe's screams. And then, as he swam away, the silence, failure in the marrow of his bones.

What if it were Lily this time? What if he lost her too?

"Son of a bitch!" he yelled, slamming his hand down on the horn.

She didn't even tap the brakes.

He rode her bumper until she finally jerked the car onto the shoulder in a spray of gravel. Rush yanked his truck behind her and was out in seconds, fury boiling over.

"What the fuck are you doing?" he barked, striding up to the driver's-side window. "You could've killed somebody driving like a—"

The door flung open, and Lily all but exploded out. Her eyes were wild, and she didn't have a jacket on. "Rush! Amber's having the babies right now!" she screamed.

For a second, the words didn't compute. Then he heard it— Amber's guttural cry from inside the car—and Rush's blood iced over.

He yanked open the passenger door and dropped to his knees. Amber was braced against the seat, her feet on the dash, sweat dripping down her temple despite the cold air. Lily had scrambled back into the driver's seat, gripping her sister's hand with both of hers. Her wide green eyes met his, and whatever she saw there made her pale.

"All right, Amber, you're okay," he said automatically, his voice steady even as his pulse skyrocketed. "We've got this—"

Then he saw it. The passenger seat of Lily's car was soaked in blood. Too much blood.

Not again. Not fucking again.

His breath locked in his chest. His hands went numb. The world narrowed until he was back at the canal, in the icy water, Caroline's hand slipping out of his—failure twisting his gut.

"Rush!"

Lily's voice cut through the fog. She grabbed his arm hard. "Stay with me. She needs you. *I* need you."

Her voice hit like a rope thrown to a drowning man. Rush dragged in a breath, shoved the canal back where it belonged. This wasn't then. This was now. Amber was here. Lily was here. And he wasn't going to lose either one of them.

His training surged, clear and automatic. He forced calm into his face. "I'm calling for some help, okay, Amber? Sit tight. You're doing great."

He sprinted back to his truck to get the first aid kit, already talking to Myrna. "Dispatch, this is Unit One. I need an ambulance on Route 14, mile marker twenty-two—woman in active labor with twins and heavy bleeding. Get them here fast."

By the time he returned, Lily had Theo on speakerphone. Amber half sobbed, half screamed, her whole body trembling.

"Sweetheart," Theo's steady voice came through the speaker. "I'm almost there," he said soothingly. "My love, can you breathe for me? Just like that, yes."

Amber tried a few *hee hee, who whos* before screaming again, a raw sound that rattled the windows of the car. "I can't! I can't wait! Ahhhhhhhh!"

"Rush," Theo barked. "Where the fuck are you?"

"Route 14, mile marker twenty-two," Rush said, snapping on gloves. "Get here fast."

"Oh my God," Amber sobbed. "I don't want to have my babies in a Subaru! I want my epidural!"

"Lily, get blankets from my trunk. And water, if you have any."

Lily sprinted around the car while Rush crouched beside Amber.

"Have you ever done this before?" Amber asked shakily.

"Yes," Rush lied. Technically, it was a horse, and he was only assisting Gage when he spent a weekend at his lodge on Autumn Ridge. But the principles were the same. Mostly.

Amber wailed. "Oh, thank God."

Rush looked her dead in the eye. "You're doing great."

Lily thrust the blankets at him. Her fingers brushed his, and just that touch was enough to steady him.

"All right, Amber," he said, crouching closer and lifting her bathrobe. "One push. That's it. You've got this."

Amber screamed, and that was when he saw it—dark hair crowning, slick with fluid. His heart hammered so hard he heard it in his ears, but his hands were steady as his training took over.

He braced his palm under Amber's thigh, ready to support the baby's head as it emerged. "That's it," he coached. He forced his voice to stay calm, even as adrenaline coursed through him. "Breathe. When the next contraction comes, you push again. Don't fight it."

Amber sobbed, panting and shaking. "I can't—"

"Yes, you can." His voice sharpened with authority. "You already are. You're doing this perfectly."

It seemed to steady Amber, and she nodded just as another contraction slammed through her.

She bore down with a primal cry, and then—suddenly—there he was, shoulders rotating with a slippery twist, and then the rest of the baby slid into his waiting hands—warm, wet, and impossibly real.

A baby. A tiny, eerily quiet, but very much alive baby pushed into the cold January air and into Rush's arms.

For a second, Rush's heart stopped.

"Blanket," he said hoarsely. Lily pressed one into his hands, and Rush wrapped the newborn gently then placed him in Amber's shaking hands. "It's a boy."

Amber sobbed, clutching her son to her chest. "Is he okay? Why isn't he crying?"

Rush leaned over the tiny bundle, who was blinking with very serious, very calm eyes. He pressed his finger to the tiny, steady pulse in the baby's chest. "He's perfect," he said huskily.

"Oh, thank God," Amber breathed. Then, a look of utter panic crossed her face. "I don't want to do that again."

"Jesus H. Christ," Rush muttered, wiping the cold sweat from his forehead with his shoulder. Neither did he.

"You're incredible," Lily murmured, pushing Amber's damp hair back. She cupped a hand under the baby's bottom to steady him on Amber's chest. "Oh my God, Am. Look at your son."

The awe in her voice made Rush look up. Lily's eyes were wet. Hell. His were too. He smiled crookedly at her, in awe of the power of the woman who had just given birth and the one looking at him like he hung the moon.

But the EMTs better get here soon because as incredible an experience as it had been, he didn't particularly want to do it again.

Fortunately, headlights flashed in the dusk as Theo's truck skidded to a stop behind them a second later. He leaped out of the cab, ran straight for the open car door, and dropped to his knees in front of his wife.

"Oh my God," he choked, staring at Amber, at the tiny bundle. "Is that—? Are you—?"

"It's your son," Rush said gruffly. "The other one's not here yet."

"But she's coming," Amber moaned. "Take the baby. I have to push."

Theo looked stunned. Then, a huge, dazed grin broke across his face. "You were always so impatient," he whispered to Amber, kissing her sweat-damp forehead.

When the ambulance pulled up alongside them a second later, Rush had never been so happy to see EMTs in his life. He sat back on his heels, his adrenaline ebbing. His hands shook as he stripped off his gloves.

Lily came up beside him, her breath clouding in the cold air. "You did it," she whispered. Tears streamed down her face.

He didn't answer. Couldn't. His throat was too tight. But he pulled her to his side and held on tighter.

For the first time in a year, he was proud. And that was enough.

Chapter Forty-Two

AMBER LOOKED DISGUSTINGLY gorgeous for someone who'd just given birth in the front seat of a Subaru. Hours later, she was still glowing, propped up in her hospital bed like a queen holding court while everyone circled around her bed to admire her and the precious babies.

And they were so gorgeous.

Lily couldn't stop staring. More than staring—she was head over heels in love. Something had shifted tectonically inside her watching them being born, and she was still reeling. Amber's strength awed her, Theo's devotion left her aching, and the babies—God, those perfect faces. Lily could have watched them breathe forever.

"Everyone, meet Theodore Clairmont, Jr.," Amber announced, angling the swaddled bundle in her right arm so the family could coo appropriately. "Though if anyone calls him that, they're cut off. Teddy only. And this"— she lifted the pink-hatted baby in her left arm with a tender smile —"is Mirabella. Mira for short."

"Mira and Teddy." Evie sighed dreamily. "I love them already."

Amber's gaze softened as she looked at Theo. "He picked them. Been holding out on me with the fancy names."

Theo stood beaming by her side, though still a little pale from the ordeal. He'd been frantic, half ready to carry Amber to the hospital himself, but true to form, Amber hadn't waited. The EMTs had taken over, and she'd pushed with everything she had. Their daughter had arrived screaming with fury at her early ignominious entrance, a fiery contrast to her calm, drowsy brother.

"You're going to have the best time with these two," Allie said, leaning over to adjust Teddy's hat. "Savvie and Tessa are dying to meet their cousins."

Amber's eyes fluttered closed, exhaustion seeping in now that the adrenaline had drained away. "I wasn't ready for this. I needed those extra weeks of pregnancy to psych myself up. Shame they didn't take me seriously and decided to show up three weeks early anyway."

"They're perfect," Annette said firmly. "And you'll manage just fine with all of us here to help." She bent to smooth Amber's hair back from her damp forehead. "But you have to take care of yourself and rest when you can."

Amber's mouth curved faintly, her eyes still closed. "Oh, like I'm sure you did when you had twins?"

The sisters laughed softly, but Lily's throat ached. She was too full—of pride, of love, of longing. Watching her family expand, her sister glow, those babies take their first breaths—it cracked her right open.

After a little more chatter, Annette left with Allie, and Evie shortly after. Lily couldn't bring herself to leave just yet. She'd patiently waited her turn to hold Mira, and she didn't want to put her down just yet. Mira was warm and impossibly tiny in her arms as she rocked her. She nuzzled her pretty head, and Mira's tiny fist curled tight around Lily's finger.

Lily couldn't let go. Her whole body ached with it—with wanting. With love so fierce it hollowed her out.

The door opened again, and Lily glanced up to see Theo's older brother, Grant Clairmont. Grant might have shared Theo's dark hair and broad shoulders, but where Theo was polished charm, his brother carried himself like a man who spent more time on the street than in an office, which made sense because he was a detective in Boston. His suit jacket hung open, tie loosened, the worn strap of his shoulder holster visible, along with a badge clipped to his belt.

"Grant!" Theo said warmly, stepping forward to pull him into a hug. "Glad you made it."

"Wouldn't miss it," Grant replied easily. His gaze swept the room, landing on Lily with a grin of recognition. "Lily, right? We met at the wedding."

"How could I forget the stampede when you caught the bouquet?" Lily said, smiling.

Grant shrugged, looking faintly abashed, though the curve of his mouth suggested he hadn't minded all that much.

Amber leaned back against her pillows, exhaustion etched onto her features now, along with radiance. "God, I love them. Makes me wish I hadn't waited." She shook her head, eyes dreamy. "You're going to love this, Lily. You won't believe how much."

Lily kissed Mira's downy head, inhaling that newborn sweetness until her chest hurt. "I can't wait for my turn."

"Then don't," Amber said simply, as if it were that easy.

Before Lily could respond, a knock rapped on the door.

Rush stood in the doorway, uniform still on, Stetson in hand. For a heartbeat, her world tilted. He looked every inch the sheriff—the way he held himself, the energy coming off him—but the weariness at the edges of his face, the sadness in his eyes, tethered her heart so tightly to his she could hardly breathe.

Theo was already striding toward him, gripping Rush's hand and pulling him in for one of those man hugs that involved back pounding, which Rush returned with a surprised smile. "Man, I can't thank you enough. You delivered my son."

Grant greeted him next. Lily caught the flicker of surprise on Rush's face. "Didn't expect to see you here."

"Didn't expect to be here before you left for Boston," Grant replied easily. "But my niece and nephew had other plans."

The words sliced through her. Somehow, she'd managed to forget. Pretend. But hearing it out loud made the floor shift beneath her for the second time that day. So she rocked and thought and nuzzled her niece.

After a few minutes, Grant left to check into his hotel, and Amber insisted she couldn't rest until she had a shower.

"I think I need your help," she groaned, holding onto the arm Theo held out to get off the bed. "Can you hold Teddy for a bit?"

Before Rush could object, Teddy was in his arms, tiny and impossibly fragile against all that muscle. He came to sit on the bed next to her rocker. It wasn't lost on Lily, the strange, temporary family tableau they made. Teddy in his arms, Mira in hers.

"They're so small," she whispered. She didn't dare look up, or the tears would fall.

"Yeah." His voice was rough. "First time I held Rachel and Sarah, I thought I'd crush them. My hands didn't fit around something so tiny. But then they grabbed on, and I knew I'd do anything—anything—to keep them safe," he finished huskily.

Lily risked a glance at him. His jaw was locked tightly, but he held Teddy in his strong arms so naturally that it was both beautiful and unbearable.

She rocked Mira gently, tracing the curve of her cheek with her fingertip. "Aren't they beautiful?"

"Yes." When she looked up, he wasn't watching the baby. He was watching her.

Her chest squeezed. "You did good today," she whispered. "Delivering them."

His mouth tugged at one corner. "Panicked for a minute there. But then—" He shifted Teddy and rubbed the back of his neck. "Had to face it."

Something unspooled inside her at the admission. At the proof he could fight his fears. Proof he could heal. Proof he could stay... if he wanted to.

"Grant said you're still planning on leaving?" she asked softly.

"Yeah. Couple more weeks." His gaze stayed fixed on Teddy. "House is in talks right now. It's a nice family. Just what you wanted for the next owners." He said it lightly, but his eyes were tired.

"Yeah," she murmured. "Just what I wanted."

"Hey," he said softly, like it was already decided. "Let's go home. I'll make dinner and—"

Her heart leaped before she could stop it. For one sweet, dangerous moment, she almost nodded. To go home with him and pet Riggs and sit in that beautiful kitchen overlooking the apple orchard while Rush cooked, and she pretended for a little while longer that this could last.

But she shifted Mira carefully in her arms, pressing her lips to her soft hair and breaking the spell. "Rush... I've had two dreams my whole life. Dancing and sharing that with others. And having a family of my own." Her voice cracked. "I've made the first one happen, and I'm not giving up on the other."

He froze, his eyes wary.

"I can't go home with you," she whispered. "I can't keep doing this with you if I want my dream to come true. It hurts too much."

"Lily..." He shook his head, pain in his eyes. "I want this too. You know I do. I just—I don't know how to stay."

"Don't be sorry," she said, even as tears spilled faster down her cheeks. "You never promised me forever. I just didn't realize how much it would hurt... and how much more it'll hurt if we drag it out until you leave next month." A tear fell onto Mira's cheek. Gently, she wiped it away. "Sorry," she murmured to them both.

"Don't ever apologize for crying," he said hoarsely. "It means you care."

"Damn," she laughed, or tried to. "This wasn't the plan. I thought I'd kiss you goodbye when you left, let you go, and that would've been the end. But today changed something for me."

She looked down at Mira's tiny sleeping face. "I want this. So damn much it hurts. And I can't have it if part of me is still hoping you'll change your mind."

Another tear slipped down and landed on her wrist. She brushed it away quickly, but Rush caught her hand, his thumb skimming over her pulse.

"It's true," she added with a watery laugh. "I'm already halfway to falling in love with you. Okay, more than half."

He opened his mouth, but she shook her head.

"Don't. Just let me get this out."

She took a deep breath and tried to steady herself. *I am a still lake. I am a still lake.* But the mantra crumbled under the weight of him, of this, of everything she wanted pressing against her chest. Her vision blurred, and the tears slipped through anyway.

"I am in love with you, Rush. And I need to walk away because loving you shouldn't mean losing the life I've dreamed of."

Rush went perfectly still, like someone had cut off his air. "Lily—"

"Let me finish," she stopped him quietly. "I know you never promised me anything, and I kept telling myself I could handle that. That I could just enjoy what this was and let it end when it had to."

A breath shuddered through her. "But today made it really clear I can't do that anymore. I want this too much. And wanting it doesn't make you wrong. It just makes me... done pretending I don't. So it's better if we end this now."

She smoothed a thumb gently over Mira's cheek, blinking back a blur of tears. "We can walk away before it hurts too much later."

"Shit." He sighed heavily. "I'm not ready to say goodbye."

Her chest splintered at his words. "I know. That's why we have to. Because you feel like the best thing I've ever had—and the one thing I can't keep."

He caught her gaze. She could see the war behind his eyes but no answer she could hold on to.

"This doesn't have to be the end," he said, voice strained with the emotions she saw in his eyes. "I'll be back to see Sarah and Rachel and Pop. We'll see each other. We'll—"

"Don't you see how that's worse?" Sadly, she shook her head. "That's me settling, and I swore I would never do that again."

"Lily—"

"It's the same as me running from the altar," she said softly. "Only this time, you're the one running. I ran... and came back. You won't."

She leaned into his shoulder, absorbing his warmth one last time, until he tilted her chin up. His kiss was slow, reverent, a goodbye and a damn-you-not-yet kiss in one. It stole her breath and made her ache to say *never mind. Let's go home together. I'll pretend this is all I need.*

And still, she kissed him back, drawing him in even as it tore her apart—because she knew it was the last time.

When he finally pulled away, his voice was sandpaper. "I hope your dreams come true, Lily. You deserve everything."

He set Teddy carefully in the clear hospital bassinet, settled his Stetson low on his head, and walked out. He didn't look back.

And then it was just her and Mira again. Rocking, silent tears sliding down her face, wishing love didn't feel so much like loss.

Dreams weren't supposed to break your heart. But as Mira's tiny breath warmed her chest, Lily knew hers just had.

Chapter Forty-Three

Grant slid a fresh bottle across the table. "You look like you need something stronger than this."

Rush lifted his head, squinting against the sickly green neon light buzzing in the window. The dive smelled like fryer grease and stale beer. The jukebox in the corner wheezed out Springsteen, and the floor was sticky with spilled beer under Rush's boots.

He'd been in a hundred joints just like this one between deployments—cheap beer, cheaper whiskey, and a hum of voices that didn't belong to him. He hadn't belonged there either.

"Thanks." He tipped the bottle to Grant in a mock salute. Old habits. "Been a long week."

Grant took the stool next to him, loosening his tie. He looked as bone-tired as Rush felt. "Hell yeah, it has. How's the first month treating you?"

Rush took a drink, letting the sour taste sit on his tongue. "Fine." He shrugged. "It's work."

"Generally, that's code for 'it sucks.' What's the gig this week?"

"Corporate security detail." Rush's voice was flat. He was flat. Jesus. He needed to get out of this place, but his townhouse was even worse. He'd rented a sterile, modern box across from the river. All white walls, granite counters, and not a damn thing that felt like him. Riggs hated it too. He paced around the tiny postage stamp-sized yard, looking pissed.

Rush shook his head. "Spent forty hours standing outside a penthouse, making sure no one with the wrong suit jacket got past the front desk. It's fine."

Grant leaned back in his chair, giving him a long once-over. "Funny. You don't look fine. You look about as happy here as a cat in a bath."

Rush snorted, low and humorless. "I'm here, aren't I?" He shoved the half-empty beer away and sat back, rubbing his neck.

At the far end of the bar, two women were already about two drinks past smart. Rush had clocked them when he walked in. It was hard not to. Young, laughing too loud, leaning into a couple of guys who were buying their drinks a little too quick. They couldn't be much older than Sarah, which put his hackles up immediately.

Every so often, they'd cut glances his way. He ignored them. The last thing he wanted was meaningless chatter with someone whose name he wouldn't remember. Not when a pair of wide green eyes still haunted him.

One of them slid off her stool, drink in hand, and swayed closer. She leaned against the bar and smiled wide. "You guys look like you could use some company tonight. My friend and I would love to join you."

Rush shook his head. "We're all set."

The woman's smile dipped, and Grant added smoothly. "Appreciate it, though. Hope you two enjoy your night."

She blinked uncertainly then shrugged and returned the smile before making her way back to her friend.

Grant eyed him. "Guess Boston really doesn't do it for you, huh?"

Rush ignored that. "How's life?"

Grant smiled faintly. "About the same. I'm working that triple homicide in Dorchester. Lots of late nights at my desk, and then that one phone call comes, and suddenly your adrenaline spikes and you're chasing suspects down alleys." He grinned. "That part makes up for the paperwork."

"Yeah." Rush grinned back. "That's the fun part."

"Come on, Rush, you've got a good gig. The money's solid, good benefits, and nobody's shooting at you. What more could you want?"

Rush stared into the amber bottle. What more could he want? He'd been asking himself that question since he'd packed up the last of his boxes and Riggs's bed into his truck and left Northfield behind.

Grant let the silence stretch before leaning in. "You could always go back. Theo said they still haven't found a replacement for you." His eyes cut toward the two women still sneaking looks and narrowed his eyes thoughtfully. "You could see if Lily's moved on from your big dumb ass, or if she looks as sorry as you right now."

Rush shot him a lethal look. "What the fuck does that mean?"

Grant shrugged. "I spend my days reading people. From what I saw in that hospital room, you two looked like you had unfinished business."

"We finished it," Rush said broodingly.

"If it's not Lily you're running from, it's the accident," Grant said calmly, despite Rush's scowl. "Don't shoot the messenger. It's one or the other to leave a good job like that.

Your family's there, Rush. People don't just up and walk away from things that don't matter."

Rush didn't answer, but Lily's face rose up in his mind—her green eyes soft in ways he couldn't understand, yet wanted anyway. The look on her face when she'd whispered *I want this. So damn much.*

"It's her, isn't it? Lily?"

Rush's grip tightened around the bottle. "It doesn't matter."

"The hell it doesn't. You'd sit through firefights steady as a rock, but one look from her and you didn't stand a chance." Grant shook his head. "Don't sit here pretending Boston's the answer when every part of you wants to be back there."

"Even if I did, it wouldn't change anything." Rush blew out a hard breath. "I can't give her what she wants."

And there it was—haunting him again. Don't feel too much. Don't want too much. Don't love too hard. That way, when it all went to hell, no one could say he'd failed them.

He hadn't been strong enough to keep his distance from her. He'd just been a coward.

Deep down, he knew the truth. He loved her. Not the easy kind of love that fit neatly into his life but the kind that got under his skin and stayed there, no matter how far he ran. Jesus, but he loved that woman. A month had gone by, and he still woke up with her in his head, still saw her face every time he closed his eyes.

He missed her laugh—the way it came from her whole body. The smell of her hair when she curled into him. The way her voice softened when she said his name, like it meant something worth keeping.

Loving Lily wasn't the weakness he'd told himself it was. It was the only thing that made him feel alive.

"You don't know what you can give her until you try. What

I do know is that sitting here in this city, wasting yourself on corporate gigs, isn't it."

"You speaking from experience?"

Grant's eyes turned serious. "I am," he said quietly. "I'm done here too. I'm moving back in the spring."

"You going to give up detective work? I hear there's a sheriff position available," Rush said, aware of a bristling he had no right to feel about a job he'd given up.

Grant shrugged. "I'd like to keep doing what I do now, but I might have to take that position." He raised his eyebrows. "Unless you want it back."

Rush stayed quiet, and Grant went on.

"I'm missing out on everything I thought about constantly when we were deployed," Grant said quietly. "My family's back in Northfield. I want to know my niece and nephews and actually be there for them. I missed years with Lieren when she was in high school. And Ford and Landon and Georgie—I don't know how much longer we'll have with her. I want to be there while we still do."

Rush knew that ache. He'd spent the last month circling the same thoughts. Family. Pop. Rachel and Sarah. Babies. Lily. The image of her holding Mira had lodged itself in his chest like shrapnel—sharp and impossible to ignore. He wanted that too.

Grant tipped his beer in a mock salute. "Looks like we're in the same boat."

Rush's jaw flexed, but this time he didn't deny it. He couldn't because Grant was right. "Ah, fuck."

"'Ah, fuck' is right."

Rush let out a long breath. For the first time in weeks, he let the truth settle. He was miserable. Not because of Boston but because of everything he'd left behind.

Lily in the hospital room, rocking Mira with tears on her cheeks. Chloe's wide blue eyes in her angel costume, singing again. The accident had nearly broken him, and for months, he'd let the guilt define him. Sitting here now, he finally admitted what he'd been too much of a coward to face—he hadn't failed that night. He'd saved Chloe. He'd done his job. It wasn't enough to bring Caroline back, but maybe it was enough to stop punishing himself.

And Lily... Christ, it hurt to think about her, and the future she'd painted so vividly he could almost touch it. For so long, he'd told himself he couldn't give her what she wanted—a family, a home to share, a love that didn't walk away. The truth was, he wanted it too. He wanted it with her.

He couldn't keep running away from his guilt. Or from her.

Grant checked his watch and tossed some cash on the table. "You've got a choice, Callahan. Stay miserable, or go home."

"Yeah," Rush said. This time it wasn't a deflection. It was an agreement.

On his way out, he caught the bartender's eye and jerked his chin toward the brunettes. "Might want to cut them off—and keep an eye on those two guys."

The bartender gave him a pound. "On it, big guy. Appreciate it."

Outside, the night air was sharp and cool, biting against his skin with the March chill still lingering. He pulled his phone from his pocket. His thumb hovered, heart pounding harder than it had in combat, but he knew what he had to do. What he wanted to do.

He hit Dial.

"Mrs. Whitmore? It's Rush Callahan." His voice was husky with emotion but steady. "About that dinner..."

When he hung up, he looked down the empty Boston street, the neon buzzing behind him. For the first time in months, he wasn't running.

He was going home.

Chapter Forty-Four

Lily pressed her palms together at her heart and bowed. "Namaste."

"Namaste," her class echoed, though when she opened her eyes, Connie had hers cracked open and was looking at her. After forty-five minutes of yoga, Lily was wary of the glint in her gaze.

Lily rolled up her mat, turned off the stereo, and chatted with students as they packed up. Outside, March still clung stubbornly to winter, but the first yellow daffodils were just poking their heads up through the ground outside her windows. She noticed things like that now. New beginnings.

It helped when endings felt so damn sad.

But she wasn't thinking about that. At least not much. She tried very hard not to think about how much she'd fallen in love with Rush. Yes, she could admit it now. There was no halfway about it. She had gone and fallen head over heels for Sheriff Sexy, and it hadn't ended well.

She'd spent the last month practicing yoga and meditation, dancing when it got too sad and she had to move her body or risk picking up the phone.

Yes, she missed Rush terribly, but she also worried about him. Wondered if he was still punishing himself, if he was sleeping, if he could drive by the water without shaking.

She really wanted that for him, even if they hadn't worked out together. He deserved peace.

Once the last student left, she flipped the sign on the door to Be Back Soon and turned back, not at all surprised to see Connie and Gertie waiting.

"Look, darlin', we can't take it anymore," Connie announced. "That handsome sheriff of yours is gone, and it's killing us to see you sitting home alone."

"You're too young and too pretty to be this sad." Gertie nodded solemnly. "I have another nephew who's single. Very steady. This one owns a hardware store."

"Forget the nephew," Connie cut in. "My cousin Jimmy just divorced his wife. He's on those dating sites all the time now, looking for love."

Lily stifled a shudder. "Thank you, but no. I'm not dating right now."

Both women raised their eyebrows.

"You know what they say about riding a horse," Connie said. "The best way to get over one is to get under another."

Gertie smacked her arm. "That's not how it goes."

Connie shrugged. "Same idea. All I'm saying is there are plenty of men in Northfield who'd line up for a nice girl like you. Georgie Clairmont told me last week that her grandson Grant's moving back home soon. He's a handsome fellow too."

"Law enforcement." Gertie nodded knowingly. "There's just something about a man in uniform."

"I know!" Connie beamed. "Why don't I call Georgie and set something up between you two when he gets back?"

"No—I—" Lily began, but Connie was already pulling out her phone.

She shoved her glasses down her nose and squinted. "I can never see the damn screen," she muttered. "They make these so tiny."

Gertie patted Lily's hand with grandmotherly concern. "We just want to see you happy, honey."

Lily tried again, firmer this time. "Thank you, but no. I'm perfectly capable of setting up my own dates—when I'm ready," she added quickly. "But thank you for thinking of me," she added when they looked taken aback.

Connie and Gertie exchanged a look that said plenty. "Well, if you're sure," Gertie said doubtfully. "Let us know when you're ready."

The door opened, and when Lily glanced up, she did a double take. Tucker stood in the doorway.

"Hi, Lily," he said. He glanced at Gertie and Connie, who glared at him. "Can we talk?"

"When I said get back on the horse, I didn't mean this one," Connie murmured on her way out.

"He's more of an ass," Gertie sniffed, closing the door after them.

"What's up, Tucker?" Lily asked when they were alone, bracing herself. Thankful for small mercies, she'd avoided running into him or Madison over the last month. Looked like her luck had just run out.

Although as she studied him, he didn't look cocky or smug. In fact, he seemed kind of... small. Not in stature. He was still a linebacker, but for the first time in years, he didn't seem all puffed up with that excess pride she'd once mistaken for confidence.

He walked toward her slowly, tugging at his tie like it was strangling him. "I'll get right to it." He cleared his throat and met her eyes. "I owe you an apology, Lily. For all of it. For Madison. For not being the man you deserved."

He stepped closer and took her hands in his. She was so surprised she let him. "I ended it with her," he said, misery on his face. "I don't even know why I ever—God, I panicked. The wedding was coming, I could feel you pulling away, and instead of talking to you, I did the stupidest thing of my life. I'm sorry. I am so damn sorry I hurt you."

He raked a hand down his face. "For what it's worth, Madison never meant for anyone to see that photo. She tried to send it to me after you ran out, but she hit AirDrop instead of text. She didn't mean to humiliate you," he said quietly. "But she did, and I let it happen. I'm sorry, Lily."

Huh. She'd spent weeks imagining those words, and somewhere along the way, she'd stopped believing they'd ever come. The mystery of who sent the photo—finally solved. And yet it felt strangely hollow.

She drew in a slow, steady breath, her fingers brushing the rose quartz at her throat.

I am a still lake, she reminded herself. *Not the storm. Not anymore.*

The anger and humiliation that had once burned eased, not because she forgave him but because she didn't need to carry it anymore.

When she finally met his eyes again, calm settled over her—more peace than she'd felt in weeks. "Thank you," she said, because it felt right. "That means more than you know." Relief flashed across his face, and she realized she meant it. "What you did was shitty, about the shittiest thing you can do to someone."

Tucker flinched, but to his credit, he didn't look away.

"And I wasn't innocent either," she added, pulling her hands free. "I didn't cheat, but I wasn't honest. I knew you didn't want the same future, and I tried to pretend it didn't matter. I'm sorry for that."

"Yeah," he said, with a rueful smile. "Facing my mother

after you ran out was one of the worst moments of my life. I almost wished I'd run after you and just kept going because when I got back, it was hell. She really did want you to be her daughter-in-law."

"Yes, well," Lily murmured, not wanting to touch that sentiment. As far as she was concerned, she'd dodged a bullet having Angela Cawthorn as her mother-in-law. From Tucker's grin, he must have read that on her face. For a second, she glimpsed the boy she'd once loved—the high school quarterback with the reckless smile that had fascinated her.

They talked quietly after that, sifting through years of shared history like flipping through a worn photo album. First dates. Road trips. Inside jokes that had lost their shine.

Finally, when they'd exhausted all the small talk, he looked at her. "Lil, do you think we could ever find our way back to the way it was?"

Her heart trembled. Not at the man who betrayed her but at the boy who looked so damn lost.

"It won't work, Tucker," she said gently. "I'm not that girl anymore. Everyone already had us married with kids, and I got swept up in that dream too. But that was me clinging to who we used to be. I can't do that anymore."

Tucker's head dropped. "So it's really too late? There's nothing I can do to prove I've changed?"

Her throat ached with the truth, but she didn't look away. Tears welled, and she let them fall. "It's me, Tucker. I've changed. I need something different now."

She'd spent years believing that if she kept the peace—if she didn't ask for too much—she could hold on to love, but all it left her was loneliness. She wasn't making that mistake again.

He swallowed hard. "With him? The sheriff?"

A sad smile tugged at her lips. "No. That's not his dream either."

"You'll always be my first love, Lil. Even if I wasn't the right one."

She stood in the quiet studio after he left, waiting for the ache to hit the way it used to.

It didn't.

Maybe that was its own kind of goodbye.

SUNDAY DINNER at her mom's house was louder than usual that evening, the way it always seemed to be now. Every year, another baby—or two—joined the mix, stretching their hearts even wider.

Lily looked around, gratitude swelling in her chest. She didn't have her own dream yet, but her sisters' had come true, and that gave her hope. One day it would be her turn. Maybe Evie's too.

Annette's living room had turned into baby central—blankets draped over designer chairs, bottles lined up by the sink, a mountain of diaper boxes stacked on the rug. Teddy slept against Lily's chest, his tiny breaths soft and sweet, while across the room, Mira fussed in Amber's arms.

"He's the calmest baby, like his daddy," Amber said, adjusting Mira under her arm like a football. The baby latched then popped off with an indignant squeak, blinking up at her mother in protest. Amber kissed the soft fluff of dark hair on her daughter's head. "You, on the other hand, are bound to rule the world one day. Remember, good girls don't make history."

Theo leaned over her shoulder with a smitten grin for his wife and daughter. "She's already got me wrapped around her finger."

On the couch, Davis read a book to Tessa, who was snuggled up in his arms with her baby doll, while Savvie twirled in a sparkly dress in front of everyone. Allie tried and failed to snag her before she could bump into one of Annette's expensive vases, but Savvie darted away with a laugh.

Across the room, Sammy and Ben—Allie and Davis's boys—were building a Lego fortress on the coffee table. They were too cool for baby chaos but still young enough to make sound effects as the tower wobbled precariously.

"Let her," Annette said wryly. "She's going to do it anyway."

Allie finally gave up and came to sit near Lily. She glanced at Teddy's sleeping face then at her sister. "How are you doing, Lil? It's been a hell of a season for you."

Lily brushed her thumb over Teddy's satiny cheek, smiling when he let out a soft burp. "Such a boy," she teased then looked up to meet Allie's kind eyes. "I'm okay," she said. "Some days are harder than others, but then I hold these babies, or play with your kids, and it's easy to remember what I'm holding out for."

Allie reached over to squeeze her hand. "You've always been determined. If you want it, it's yours."

Lily looked at her in surprise. "You think I'm determined?"

"Of course I do," Allie said without hesitation. "Look at you—you opened a studio and built it from the ground up. You didn't let anyone's doubts stop you. That's determination, Lil."

Lily sat with that for a moment. She'd always thought of herself as the opposite of determined—someone who kept the peace and smoothed things over so no one would be disappointed. That was the lie she'd been living, but the truth was she was strong. Strong enough to walk away and strong enough to wait for the love she truly wanted.

"Thanks," she said quietly. "I appreciate that."

Evie sat cross-legged on the rug in front of the fire with her laptop open, listening. She met Lily's look and smiled at her. "You've always wanted more, Lil. Don't stop now."

She looked around at her family—messy, loud, imperfect—and felt the hollow ache of what she didn't have, but she no longer apologized for wanting more.

"Guess I'm greedy," she said with a crooked smile. "But I'd rather want too much than not enough."

For too long, she'd believed wanting more made her selfish or needy, but the truth was, wanting more just made her human, and she wasn't afraid of it anymore.

Someday.

Annette sat across from her, wineglass in hand, her eyes soft as she looked around at her family. "You girls know more than I ever did at your age. I'm proud of all of you."

Teddy stirred against her chest, sighing a baby sigh so sweet it broke her heart wide open. Lily pressed a kiss to his fuzz, blinking through tears.

She had her studio. She had her sisters and Annette. She had tenderness to spare. And a dream she wasn't giving up on, even if it made her ache tonight.

Her phone buzzed on the coffee table with an unknown number flashing on the screen. Her stomach dropped the way it always did when she saw that, reminding her of the moment a photo had changed the course of her life.

She shifted Teddy to one arm and fumbled with the phone with one hand. "Hello?"

A female voice. "Hi. Is this Lily?"

"Yes."

"Hi. This is Rachel. Rush's sister."

Lily's heart slammed so hard she almost dropped the phone. Panic crashed through her, making her dizzy.

"Is he okay?" she demanded sharply.

"Oh—yes! He's fine. Sorry," Rachel said quickly. "I didn't mean to scare you. He asked me to call."

Lily sagged back onto the couch, tears pricking hot behind her eyes.

Rachel went on gently. "Rush wanted you to know you could come pick up your box of Christmas decorations. He boxed them up for you. Is tomorrow too soon?"

Oh. Damn. The words hit harder than she expected. She almost told Rachel to donate the whole box. How could she possibly open it without her heart aching at the memories of spending Christmas with Rush at the farmhouse? She'd keep those close to her heart for as long as she could.

"Tomorrow's fine," Lily finally said. She cleared her throat, aware of her family watching her curiously. "I'll come by in the afternoon."

"Perfect," Rachel said, almost sounding cheerful. Lily tried not to wince. "I can leave the key for you under the doormat after my shift tonight."

"Oh," Lily managed. Her heart twisted. "Thank you."

"Of course, and Lily..." Rachel hesitated. "I wish we could've met. Maybe someday."

Lily pressed her lips together, staring at the baby sleeping against her heart. "Maybe," she whispered.

But inside, she knew she never wanted to—because meeting Rachel would mean thinking about Rush, and she couldn't.

Not when she still loved him this much.

Chapter Forty-Five

THE NEXT DAY, after her last class, Lily drove out to the farmhouse. She rolled the window down, letting the cool March breeze ruffle her hair. Spring was showing herself in Northfield more every day, teasing her with soft warmth in the afternoon and stealing it back at night.

She slowed as she drove past the canal, bare now without its holiday lights or skaters. The waterline sat low, a muddy ribbon where the ice had been. Soon the dams would open, the water would rush back, and boats and rowers would take the place of ice skaters. For now, it was quiet, suspended between seasons.

She turned onto Rush's long driveway. Her gaze caught on the wooden planter by the road.

The For Sale sign was gone.

A sharp ache pierced her. So it was really over. Rush had sold the house and moved on. And here she was, coming to collect the old box of Christmas decorations he'd left behind. Metaphorical, really, but she wasn't in the mood to appreciate it.

Maybe the new owners would put their tree in the corner by the fireplace, so the lights glowed through the windows. Next year, she promised herself, she'd have her own place. She'd drag home a big imperfect Christmas tree, string it with lights by herself, and make a new tradition.

The studio was thriving. It was time. Evie had sworn she'd be lonely without her in the guest room, and Lily would miss her too. Maybe she'd get a roommate. Better yet, maybe she'd get a dog. Did they let people adopt retired police dogs? She seemed to have a thing for Belgian Malinois now.

She gripped the wheel tighter, and suddenly the back of her neck tingled with awareness.

Her breath caught when she saw him.

Rush, leaning against the porch column. He didn't have a jacket on, just a navy flannel over a white T-shirt, and his baseball cap pulled low over his eyes.

Her heart kicked so hard it hurt. God, she'd missed him more than air.

She got out of the car slowly and walked to the porch, steadying herself.

I am a still lake.

"Hi." She swallowed hard around the lump in her throat. "I didn't know you'd be here." She looked past him. "Where's your car?" Details. They seemed easier than what she really wanted to say.

I love you.

I've missed you.

Please come home.

"Hi, Lily," he rumbled, the rough sound as dear as ever. "Rachel gave me a ride from the airport."

The words tumbled out of her before she could stop them. "Did you sell it?"

She couldn't see his eyes under the brim of his hat. Were they cool as stone or darker, like a storm threatening a soft spring evening? It seemed suddenly very important that she know.

"It's not for sale."

Confusion twisted through her. She barely felt her feet carry her up the steps.

"Come in," he said quietly, opening the door for her.

Inside, the house was stripped bare except for the box of Christmas things in the corner. Their tree was gone. Without furniture, her ballet flats echoed on the hardwood as she followed him into the kitchen.

"I'd offer to make you tea, but there's nothing here," he said.

Her hands twisted together. "Rush, why are you here?"

He turned then, leaning against the sink, and her breath caught at the expression on his face.

"Because I love you, Lily," he said simply.

"Oh." Her knees nearly buckled.

He took a deep breath. "I kept telling myself if I stayed away, I couldn't fail anyone again. That lie nearly cost me everything I want."

Her throat tightened, but she held his gaze.

"I had lunch with the Whitmores yesterday," he went on. "I needed to face it—to hear from them what I couldn't tell myself. That her daughter would've wanted me to live, not bury myself in guilt. I had to do that before I could come to you."

His beautiful face suddenly blurred in the wash of her tears. "Rush..."

"I want you to know I'm putting in the work," he said fiercely, stepping closer and taking her hands in his. "I'm trying to be the man you deserve, Lily. Because I don't just love you—I want to build a life with you."

He eased her closer. Outside, the sunset lit the orchard, the rows of bare apple branches glowing copper against the horizon.

"I want this house filled with your laughter. I want our kids running wild through that orchard, fishing in the pond, dragging in Christmas trees too damn big for the door."

She brushed away the tears as he pulled her tight into his chest, turning her so they faced the orchard. He wrapped his arms around her, his voice low in her ear. "And if you'll let me, Lily... I want to marry you under that apple tree."

She whirled, sobbing now, and pushed his hat back to see his eyes. Beautiful gray eyes, no longer shadowed with guilt or pain. They were pewter bright and full of love.

He dropped to one knee and pulled a small velvet box from his pocket. Inside gleamed a delicate gold ring, the square-cut diamond catching the last light.

"This was my mother's," he said, his voice gravely with emotion. "I want you to wear it. I want you to be my family. To build our family here, in this house. Lily Hart, I love you. Will you do me the honor of marrying me?"

For one dizzying heartbeat, she saw it all—what she'd once tried to have with Tucker, the safe but hollow life she'd clung to because she was afraid her real dream was out of reach. And Rush—the man who saw her clearly, who never made her feel foolish for wanting more. The man who, even at his most guarded, made her believe she was enough.

Her hand flew to her heart, tears streaming hot down her face. "I will," she whispered. "Oh, Rush—yes."

He stood up, scooping her into his arms, and kissed her through both their tears. When he spun her around the bare kitchen, she realized it didn't feel empty anymore.

It felt like home.

Epilogue

THE ORCHARD WAS in bloom again.

Lily paused at the sink and let herself soak in the view. The apple trees bent under the weight of fruit, and the blossoms drifted down like confetti in the soft September breeze. Golden hour was her favorite time of day, when the sun dipped low and painted their home in soft warmth. She felt the same grateful ache in her heart every time she saw it.

Just last year, they'd stood out there beneath the fiery maples and said their vows. It had been simple and perfect: a white dress, a fistful of wildflowers, and the man she'd once thought she could never have.

She could still see Rush waiting for her at the end of the orchard row, broad shouldered and impossibly handsome, his gray eyes locked on hers like she was the only person in the world.

There was not a single stargazer lily in sight. She'd made sure of it.

They'd eaten Texas barbecue, smoky brisket and cornbread passed down long tables under string lights, a nod to Rush's home state, and danced until the stars faded. Tessa and Savvie had fallen asleep on a quilt under an apple tree while their parents danced in the grass. Pop had given a toast that made everyone cry. Rachel and Sarah were folded into the Hart family as if they'd always belonged there.

She'd thought the way he looked at her during the ceremony would be the moment etched into her forever, but she'd been wrong.

It was later, after the dancing and the toasts and the teasing from their sisters, when the farmhouse was finally quiet and he carried her upstairs, that time stopped.

He closed their bedroom door with his foot, set her gently on the edge of the bed and just looked at her. Not like a man about to undress his wife but like a man trying to make sense of a dream he'd been handed with both hands.

"You sure you're real, angel?" he asked hoarsely, brushing a curl from her cheek, his thumb lingering.

"Touch me and find out," she whispered.

He did.

Slowly at first, reverently, sliding the straps of her dress down her arms, his mouth following every inch of bare skin he revealed.

"Been wanting you like this since the second you ran into my truck in that damn wedding dress," he murmured against her throat, easing her dress down until her breasts spilled free. Her breath hitched as he cupped them in both hands, brushing his thumbs over her nipples, making them stiffen and pout for his mouth.

"Look at you," he said gruffly. "My wife."

She curled her fingers into his shirt and tugged him closer, sliding her hands over the solid planes of his chest, down his waistband, feeling all that barely contained strength under her palms.

"Take these off. I want to see my husband."

His laugh rumbled against her palms, but he obeyed, working the buttons open one by one, unzipping and revealing himself to her inch by devastating inch. She drank him in: the hard muscle, the scar she'd kissed a hundred times, the deep V disappearing into a trail of dark hair between his legs.

Then he was over her, and she was already shaking. Rush lowered himself onto her, pinning her to the mattress with the weight of his body. His mouth trailed down her throat, across her collarbone, then lower. He took her nipple into his mouth, sucking deep and slow, holding her possessively as he pushed inside her. Lily buried her fingers in his hair and arched into him, her whole body answering his like it always had.

He took his time, worshipping her, loving her with a reverence that undid her. Her legs tightened around his waist, pulling him closer, and he let out a moan.

She didn't need him to say a single word—she already knew how he felt. He never missed a chance to tell her, to show her, his love every day.

Now, a year later, Lily curved her hand over the swell of her belly, wonder filling her. Her son shifted with a lazy roll, pressing against her hand, and she smiled through the tears pricking her eyes. Soon, there would be even more laughter and love. Another stocking on the mantel. Another heartbeat in this old farmhouse.

Behind her, the floor creaked, and strong arms slid around her waist. Rush buried his face in her neck. His scruff ticked her skin, and she melted back into him.

"What are you smiling about, Mrs. Callahan?" he murmured against her ear.

"Everything," she whispered, turning her face to him.

He pressed a hand over hers protectively, both of them cradling their son. "Guess he heard me," Rush said, his voice rough with wonder. He kissed her temple, his thumb stroking her ring. "Still can't believe you're mine."

She leaned into him, letting it all—the man she loved, the life they were building—flood her, fill every place that had once been only a dream, fill her up to bursting.

She wasn't waiting anymore. She'd chosen this. Her heart throbbed. Once again, she whispered the truth she'd known all along.

"I was always yours." She smiled through her tears. "Just as you've always been mine."

The End

If you enjoyed this book, I'd love it if you left a review. It helps other readers discover Northfield—and it means the world to me. Thank you so much for being here. 🤍

Don't miss Evie's story next in *Be Your Everything*.

When small-town librarian Evie Hart gets stuck overnight in an elevator with cocky architect Luke Holloway, sparks fly fast— and one reckless kiss turns into something much hotter. What begins as a clash of wills soon leads to a secret fling full of "lessons" Luke's all too eager to teach.

Sign up for my newsletter or follow me on Amazon to be the first to know when *Be Your Everything* is available!

～

Want more of Rush and Lily?

THERE's a bonus scene waiting for you! Swipe to the next page for EXCLUSIVE access to *"Santa, Baby,"* where Lily's pageant Santa bails, Rush steps in, and Christmas gets a whole lot hotter.

Welcome to Northfield -
Your next love story starts now

The Other Side of Forever - Allie & Davis
Maybe Someday With You - Amber & Theo
If You Were Mine - Lily & Rush
Be Your Everything - Evie & Luke

Bonus Scene

Craving more?

Rush and Lily's exclusive bonus scene, *"Santa, Baby,"* where Lily's pageant Santa bails, Rush steps in, and Christmas gets a whole lot hotter, is waiting for you!

Subscribe to my newsletter by tapping this link or scan the QR code below to get the **IF YOU WERE MINE** bonus scene sent straight to your inbox!

To keep up with my sales and new releases, follow me on Amazon for preorder and new release alerts.

Continue the Series...

Don't miss Evie's story next in *Be Your Everything*.

When small-town librarian Evie Hart gets stuck overnight in an elevator with cocky architect Luke Holloway, sparks fly fast—and one reckless kiss turns into something much hotter. What begins as a clash of wills soon leads to a secret fling full of "lessons" Luke's all too eager to teach.

Sign up for my newsletter or follow me on Amazon to be the first to know when *Be Your Everything* is available!

Acknowledgments

Writing this book was a wild, beautiful ride, and I couldn't have done it without some very special people.

To my husband, Tom, and our kids—thank you for loving me through the late-night writing sprints, the growing laundry piles I pretended not to see, and the general chaos that comes with living with a writer. You're my whole heart and my greatest cheerleaders. I love you more than words on a page.

To my friends, thank you for the pep talks, the coffee dates, the "tell me everything" texts, the brainstorming sessions, and the unwavering belief that I could pull this off... even on the days I wasn't so sure.

To my incredible early readers for *If You Were Mine*—Julie Days, Jessica Romito, Mari Luis, Jeanette Herald, and Amanda Knipfing, thank you for reading through my early drafts and offering critique. Your honesty, enthusiasm, and sharp eyes make every book stronger.

To my ARC readers—thank you for reading early, screaming with me, sending the kindest messages, and sharing these stories with the world. You help bring these books to life.

A special thanks to Michelle Rose Grosodonia-Maiola for the inspiration behind baby Mirabella's name.

And finally, to *you*, my readers. Thank you for picking up this story, falling in love with these characters, and coming back to Northfield with me again and again. Your support makes it possible for me to keep doing what I love most—writing romance that feels like coming home.

Until the next happily ever after... 💜
xx Norah

Connect with Norah

Northfield Bonus Materials

Want to read bonus scenes, listen to the playlists inspired by this series, and nab Northfield's most infamous recipes?

Subscribe to my newsletter for all the bonus content.

Join our Facebook reader group for bonus content, sneak peeks, sales, and book news.

Follow me on Amazon for preorder and new release alerts.

For book sales and news, follow me on BookBub.

Or tap the QR code to join my newsletter and get all the extras!

About the Author

Norah Pritchard has been reading romance novels since middle school when she found her mother's gold mine of mass-market paperbacks, and she hasn't looked back since.

She teaches in higher education by day, and by night, you can find her writing about swoony, sexy heroes and sassy, independent ladies who aren't afraid to ask for what they want. She lives in New York with her husband and three children.

Connect with her at norahpritchard.com.